Twelve Seconds to Live

Also by Douglas Reeman

A Prayer for the Ship
High Water
Send a Gunboat
Dive in the Sun
The Hostile Shore
The Last Raider
With Blood and Iron
H.M.S. 'Saracen'
The Deep Silence
Path of the Storm
The Pride and the Anguish
To Risks Unknown
The Greatest Enemy
Rendezvous – South Atlantic
Go in and Sink!
The Destroyers
Winged Escort
Surface with Daring
Strike from the Sea
A Ship Must Die
Torpedo Run
Badge of Glory
The First to Land
The Volunteers
The Iron Pirate
Against the Sea (non-fiction)
In Danger's Hour
The White Guns
Killing Ground
The Horizon
Sunset
A Dawn Like Thunder
Battlecruiser
Dust on the Sea
For Valour

Twelve Seconds to Live

Douglas Reeman

William Heinemann: London

First published in the United Kingdom in 2002 by William Heinemann

1 3 5 7 9 10 8 6 4 2

William Heinemann
The Random House Group Limited
20 Vauxhall Bridge Road, London, SW1V 2SA

Random House Australia (Pty) Limited
20 Alfred Street, Milsons Point,
Sydney, New South Wales 2061, Australia

Random House New Zealand Limited
18 Poland Road, Glenfield,
Auckland 10, New Zealand

Random House (Pty) Limited
Endulini, 5a Jubilee Road,
Parktown 2193, South Africa

Random House Group Limited Reg. No. 954009

www.randomhouse.co.uk

A CIP catalogue record for this book is available
from the British Library

Papers used by Random House are natural, recyclable products made from wood grown in sustainable forests. The manufacturing processes conform to the environmental regulations of the country of origin

Typeset by Palimpsest Book Production Limited,
Polmont, Stirlingshire
Printed and bound in Great Britain by
Clays Ltd, St Ives plc

ISBN 0 434 00874 5 (Hardback)
ISBN 0 434 01061 8 (Trade paperback)

For you, Kim,
The first rose,
With all my love

Contents

	Prologue	1
1.	Code of Conduct	6
2.	No Looking Back	18
3.	Survival	35
4.	Brought Together	51
5.	'During the Night . . .'	71
6.	Reaching Out	88
7.	Two of a Kind	105
8.	Narrow Seas	121
9.	The Catch of the Season	138
10.	Ghosts	153
11.	Face to Face	170
12.	The Quick and the Dead	185
13.	Under Orders	201
14.	A Matter of Time	218
15.	Yesterday's Heroes	231
16.	In All the Old Familiar Places	248
17.	Second Thoughts	264
18.	One Hand for the King	279
19.	A Hell of a Risk	295

They're all gone now, it's in the past
It doesn't fill my mind except on days like this
And sometimes in the lonely night.
I wonder why they went?
They must have gone for something
Mustn't they?
They can't have gone for nowt!

        Shaw Taylor, 'I Watched Him Go'

Prologue

Daylight had been slow to show itself, and even now everything seemed painted in varying shadows of grey. The sky was still heavily clouded from the overnight rain, the puddles black holes in the roadway.

And so still. Nothing to break the sense of desolation. Abandoned. And you never got used to it.

Only the car moved. A patch of colour at last, the shuttered headlights like slitted eyes, swinging very slowly this way and that as if feeling the way past looming buildings, nondescript in the grey glow, tall cranes or an occasional gantry, and some broken crates. A place of work. Like so many others.

The driver, a soldier, glanced sideways as a window squeaked down and the damp, bitter air filled the interior. It was very cold, and only September.

The passenger watched the slow-moving buildings and machinery. More clearly now, he saw the car's reflection pass one of the puddles, its camouflage and more obviously the wings, painted bright red, a familiar enough sight so near to the sea. To danger. With the window open the car's engine sounded incredibly loud, held in low gear, one of the driver's hands resting loosely on the gear lever, the other almost casually coaxing the wheel.

The passenger smiled, and felt his lips crack. Because of the cold? He knew otherwise. There was nothing casual about this work. *Not unless . . .*

The driver said softly, 'Here they are, sir.'

It never seemed to matter where it was, he thought. Like the anonymous groups of people they had passed on their final approach. It could have been any of those other places, any of those other times. Anxious, apathetic, impatient . . . it was none of those things.

He saw some figures near a gateway, authority marked by white belts and gaiters. The naval patrol. He felt his stomach tighten. The last contact . . . But that, again, was always the same.

A petty officer, very calm, peered into the car and saluted.

'Hundred yards, sir. I checked the marker meself.' Untroubled. But his eyes were saying, *rather you than me, mate.* Always the same.

He heard the other passenger shifting behind him. A rating to assist him, one he did not know. God knew what he was thinking. He felt his fist clench inside his pocket. *Always remember the name.*

'All set, Derek? Won't be long now. Should brighten up soon, by the look of it.'

The rating said nothing, surprised perhaps that the officer should use his first name.

His fist clenched again, and this time it remained rigid.

Somebody else could have done it. *Should have done it . . .*

He said only, 'Take cover, P.O., but have the tea ready!'

The petty officer grinned and saluted again, relieved. 'Something a bit stronger than that, sir!'

The car growled forward again. Nobody had said 'good luck'; nobody did any more. He stared at the road. Not after four years of war.

Only the car moved. And then, all at once, there it was. A ramshackle building with eyeless windows, a warehouse of some kind, one of hundreds which served this yard where supplies, weapons and all the materials of war came and went on the tides and in the wagons he had noticed in a railway siding near the main gates.

There was a bit of a breeze, too; the Met officer was right, for a change. And it *was* brighter. But he did not look at his watch. He got out of the car and stood beside it, the others watching him, men he did not know.

2

He glanced along the road, seeing the grey light moving down charred timbers, like black glass from the overnight rain: some recent hit-and-run air attack, although there were fewer of those now. But you could always smell it. Worse when it was in somebody's home, pathetic possessions scattered all around while you worked, your mind empty of everything but the job. *The beast*, they called it.

He rubbed his hands together, a dry sound, purposeful.

'You know what to do. Run out the line . . .' He faltered and stared at the marker, a green pennant of bunting lifting occasionally in the damp air. 'No heroics, Derek. Bolt for that shelter, just like they taught you.' He did not look at the driver. 'You can pull out. Thanks for the ride.'

Surprisingly, the soldier tugged off his glove and thrust out his hand.

'I'll be waitin', sir.'

It was almost the worst thing he could have done.

And just as quickly, he was alone, as if he had found his way here unaided. He touched his pockets, the little pouch he always carried, and lastly the stethoscope in his jacket. He had walked through a hospital once, and they had thought he was a doctor.

The hospital seemed to linger in his mind. On another occasion, probably months ago, he had cut his hand on a wire on his way to an incident, as the boffins termed them, and had gone to a nurse to have it bandaged. Your hands, your fingers, were the only instruments that really counted in this so private war of man versus machine. He could still remember her curt contempt when she had looked at him and his uniform. *Others are in far greater need*, or something. And that same nurse, after he had defused 'the beast' and she had realized what he had been doing. Tears, not shame but shock.

He turned slightly and looked back along the road. In less than an hour it would be a hive of activity, until the next time.

He felt his pockets again. He could smell the sea despite the charred timbers, and the smells of oil and machinery. It was never far away.

3

He measured the distance to the gantry he had noted earlier. The sailor named Derek should be safe enough.

He faced the building. The rest must not matter. There was nowhere to run.

He ducked past the green bunting and found himself looking down into a cellar. The sappers who had attended the incident, and had thoughtfully started to rig a tarpaulin canopy to keep out the rain, must have got the shock of their lives.

It was still impossible to estimate the skills and dedication of scientists and mechanics who could design a fuse so delicate and yet so strong. As in this case: the beast had dropped from its aircraft and smashed through at least one roof and a reinforced floor into the cellar. And it had not exploded. He could see the tell-tale parachute, sodden and torn, which had dragged after it like a great tail. Now there was only silence, although he knew it would take no more effort than a man tapping his watch to restart it to set the fuse alive.

It was a magnetic mine of the deadliest kind. Dropped into the sea, it could sink a cruiser or overloaded troopship with ease. He glanced at the dripping bricks. Or flatten sixteen streets . . .

He was standing beside it, one shoe filling with water. He should have been properly prepared. The voice in his mind repeated, *There was nobody else.*

He studied it without moving. About nine feet long, its nose was buried in broken boxes, its tail pointing at a jagged hole in the roof. He looked up. Beyond, the sky was clearer, almost blue.

He unfolded his stethoscope and hung his cap on a piece of woodwork. Then he crouched and waited for his breathing to steady, or to stop. He had his safety callipers in his hand. The mine was undamaged as far as he could tell; he would fix them to the fuse to stop it coming alive as he was working. Unless there was another trick, some new booby-trap they had not yet discovered.

Water pattered down from the sappers' canopy and he stared up once more at the patch of sky.

A breeze, then. He felt the metal again, cold and impersonal. But all he could hear was her voice.

It's best this way. We're finished.

4

He groped for the stethoscope but froze as something fell heavily from the floor above.

He stared at the mine, and he knew.

He had twelve seconds to live.

1

Code of Conduct

H.M.S. *Vernon*, the torpedo and experimental establishment and one of Portsmouth's many shore stations, was a navy within a navy. From the first days of creating and using this new and untrusted form of warfare, most of the work had been carried out here, in various hulks and even in an old ship of the line, which both mine and torpedo would soon turn into history.

Vernon was a new and well laid-out establishment, with its own dry dock and jetties, a fleet of small craft, and comfortable quarters by any naval standards. It even boasted its own squash and tennis courts, the envy of the peacetime navy. But that was then.

In the first months of war *Vernon* had seen and shared the worst of it, night after night of relentless bombing, hundreds of people killed or badly injured, thousands rendered homeless, and fires raging unchecked for days. The main dockyard had not escaped; a third of it was flattened, and one bomb had exploded in the very dock where Nelson's *Victory* lay. But the damage was minor, and when the smoke had finally thinned she seemed to shine through it like a symbol.

Many famous buildings were destroyed. The George Inn on the Point, where many great names had stayed before joining a ship or a fleet, where Nelson himself had paused when leaving for the last time in *Victory*. The cathedral, so isolated now, had escaped destruction by fire solely because of the courage of *Vernon*'s night watch, who had clambered onto St. Thomas's roof at immense personal risk to extinguish the incendiaries.

With the ever increasing demands of war *Vernon*, like other establishments, had been forced to spread her resources in order to increase the training and satisfy the need for more and more men. And women. These incarnations varied from a former holiday camp on the windy east coast, once used by car workers from the Midlands, to Roedean, the exclusive girls' boarding school near Brighton. Determination and creativity worked wonders; fresh paint and the White Ensign did the rest.

But here in *Vernon* it was another ordered, disciplined day. Classes being marched from one instruction to another. Some men grouped around stripped torpedoes, or sliced-open models of moored or magnetic mines. Squads in diving gear flopping down to the dock like ungainly frogs, urged on by torpedo gunners' mates who were never short of rough encouragement.

In the main office section which adjoined two heavily protected bunkers, one door stood apart from all the others.

It was marked, UNDERWATER WEAPONS – PASSIVE.

That alone had caused some blunt and lurid outbursts from trainee and instructor alike.

There was one marked difference about this day. A flag officer was making an inspection. More to the point, it was The Admiral, as far as *Vernon* was concerned.

Rear-Admiral 'Bumper' Fawcett was liable to appear at almost any time. At *Vernon*, or aboard a depot ship at some awkward moment to observe a diving exercise or demand explanations for any delay or incompetence. Fawcett had been retired from the service between the wars and living on a commander's half-pay; he had eagerly returned to the only life he cared about. Those who knew him either admired or hated him; there were no half-measures. It went for the man, too. A goer, they called him, a character: charming when he so intended, ruthless when he did not.

He had commanded a submarine in the Great War, one of the first ocean-going boats of around eight hundred tons. He had been lucky and successful until the ill-fated Dardanelles campaign and the eventual retreat from Gallipoli. Fawcett's command had attempted to penetrate the Turkish defences but had gone aground. Later, when he had managed to free himself and surface in safer waters, he had received a curt signal from his admiral. *Where were you?*

Just as curtly, Fawcett had responded, *Bumping along the bottom!*

The signal was never recorded. The nickname, however, had stuck.

But memories were long in the Royal Navy, and Fawcett's career had been cut short even as the clouds of war were becoming obvious.

The office was much like others in this administrative building. It faced Vernon Creek where smaller craft came and went daily, with a view beyond the little inlet to the heavier places of work, the machine shops and experimental sheds. Filing cases lined one side of the room, and there was a long rack hung with clips of signals above carefully labelled lockers. By the window was a large desk with trays of more signals, already sorted, and an updated duty board, so that the great man could see at a glance anything he needed to know.

On a clear day there was still a good view of the creek and the boats, but it had rained overnight and the window, like all the others, was almost encased in stacked and white-painted sandbags: this was Portsmouth, and the enemy was only an hour's flying time away. The deep crack in one wall had been repaired and painted over, but it was testimony enough.

A Wren third officer was sitting behind the desk, legs crossed, with a telephone to one ear, and another on the waiting switch. An unfinished cup of tea stood near her free hand, with a smudge of lipstick on the rim. She was tired, and had been here since dawn. She was used to it.

She glanced at her watch as the door opened and closed, the cold air swirling briefly around her ankles. Like herself, he must have been up and about early. Lieutenant-Commander David Masters tossed his cap onto a chair.

'Where is he, Sally?'

'Beehive, sir.'

Masters walked to the steampipes and held his hands over them. He had come straight from his quarters near the main gate without stopping for breakfast in the mess, although he had scrounged some coffee from one of the stewards. He could still taste the bitterness. No wonder they called it 'U-Boat oil'.

He tried to clear his mind, to prepare for whatever new scheme or suggestion Bumper Fawcett might have dreamed up.

His eyes automatically scanned the clipboards and the lists of names, those on duty, those ashore. He did not see the girl watching him, as if she was trying to understand, to recognize something.

Masters was twenty-nine years old, but had the authority and natural confidence of one much older. A keen, interesting face, with deep lines at the mouth, and a clenching of the jaw that told of that other man, the one which made the Wren officer frown as she answered the second call. The Beehive was a giant concrete bunker, which was separated from here by a long underground corridor. Brightly lit at every hour and built to withstand anything, it was the nerve centre for the most important and delicate tests and experiments.

Masters could remember Fawcett's first visit there. He had glanced around cheerfully at the staff and technicians, and said, 'Well, if the worst happens, you'll all be safe enough down here, what?'

But he had been quick to learn; he never seemed to make the same mistake twice. The Beehive was in fact reinforced to protect the rest of the base if any explosion occurred. Those inside would be obliterated.

Masters walked to the other desk, his own. There was a miniature mine on it as a paperweight, which had been presented to somebody or other in 1940. There was not a face he did not know, or remember. They came and went, promoted, decorated, killed in action, missing. *And I am still here.*

Perhaps today.

He straightened his back and immediately checked himself. He did not need to test either his feelings or his memory. It would always be there.

The Wren said, 'He's leaving the Ops Room, sir.'

Masters glanced at the mirror which hung by the steel helmets and the notices about gas attacks and *'careless talk costs lives'*. Someone had brought it back from a party aboard one of the sweepers.

9

In one corner there was a picture of a voluptuous, scantily clad girl, and the advertisement read, *Try one of mine.* The offer was unclear but a few suggestions had been scratched underneath.

He touched the pale, comma-shaped scar on his left cheek. It had been that close.

The door was opened by one of the lieutenants, and Rear-Admiral Bumper Fawcett, his cap with its double embellishment of gold oak leaves tilted at the familiar angle, embraced the room.

'Ah, Masters, glad to find *you* up an' about at least, what?'

He did not shake hands; he never did unless with some senior officer, when it was unavoidable. Masters had become used to these irregular and unorthodox visits. Resentment was pointless: it was just Fawcett's way.

He had in fact been shaving at five-thirty when the blare of Reveille had shattered the silence and sent the gulls screaming up from the parade ground and the roof of *Vernon*'s little church. Across the harbour and the barracks bugles had sounded, and from hundreds of tannoys in ships of all classes and sizes quartermasters had added their own chorus to the squeal of boatswains' calls.

Wakey wakey, rise and shine! And the response of as many curses.

But the most remarkable thing about Fawcett was his appearance. Until a day ago he had been at the naval base in Portland; this morning he must have been driven straight down the Portsmouth Road either from his quarters in London or the Admiralty bunker itself. There was not a crease in his impeccable doeskin uniform, and his shoes shone as if they had just been polished, and as he laid his cap on the desk and flashed the Wren a smile his hair looked as if it had been recently trimmed; it always did. Not a tall man, and not prone to quick gestures, yet he gave the immediate impression of energy. Now in his fifties, he had an alert, mobile face dominated by clear blue eyes, as if the younger Fawcett were still looking out.

The door closed behind the harassed lieutenant and Fawcett said, 'Your people are on their toes, I'm pleased to see. Too much over-confidence in some of the places I've been lately.' Then, 'Any tea going, Sally?'

He rarely got a name wrong, and never with women. She picked up another telephone and nodded. 'Sir.'

10

Masters had noticed the admiral's tan, and felt another unreasonable touch of envy. Fawcett had been sent to Sicily; *the first thrust in the right direction*, he had called it.

It had once seemed unattainable. After the months, the years, of setbacks and disasters, Dunkirk, the constant bombings and the inability to hit back, the Atlantic and the U-Boats scattering and savaging desperately needed convoys, and even the gallant Eighth Army retreating to the very gates of Cairo. And now everything had changed. The Eighth Army, the Desert Rats as they were known to everyone who could read a newspaper or watch a newsreel, had turned at some unheard of place called El Alamein. Not only had they withstood the full might of the German Afrika Korps, under its equally formidable general Rommel, but they had broken the enemy and sent them into full retreat. Now the only Germans in North Africa were dead or prisoners of war. The invasion of Sicily had been the first step back into Europe. A combined force of British, American and Canadian troops, supported by every available warship, had carried out the landings. It had been decided that July was the most favourable month in the Mediterranean, especially for men in landing craft attacking in deadly earnest for the first time. The weather had turned out to be the worst for that time of year anyone could remember, but in three weeks they had done it. Masters looked over at the admiral. He was leafing through the top file of signals, his rectangle of bright medal ribbons shining in the harsh overhead lighting.

It would be Italy next. And soon. And this time the enemy would be ready. It would take every skill in the book to win.

And I shall still be here.

Fawcett said casually, 'I've been visiting the submariners too, y'know. First Sea Lord's idea. Wanted a frank report, for the P.M., actually.' He paused, one neat hand separating the signals, as if expecting an answer. 'We all laughed at the Italians when they started messing about with their two-man torpedoes and explosive motor boats, what? Until they sank the cruiser *York* a couple of years ago in Crete, and then penetrated Alexandria itself to fix mines to *Valiant* and *Queen Elizabeth*. A handful of determined men, and the whole fleet knocked sideways, just like that!'

11

There was a tap at the door and a small Wren entered with a tray of cups and saucers.

Masters saw the admiral's clear eyes move briefly to her. 'You were a submariner yourself. You can't turn your back on it. D'you imagine I don't understand how you feel about this work you're doing?' The hand came up in an unhurried signal. 'It has been my experience that courage and self-sacrifice are just as necessary, indeed vital, in the work of defence. As much, if not more, than the more heady individual acts.'

Another tap at the door, a leading signalman this time, with a pot of tea. Masters breathed out slowly. *What is the matter with me? Why today?*

Were a submariner. That was it. Always lurking, like a wound, like guilt. Perhaps they were right, and he was more suited here, or in some other office. Lucky, some might say.

Were a submariner. Only words, and casually spoken. Or were they?

The memory was as sharp as yesterday.

There is no other moment like it. Any submarine commander knows it.

His first command. Putting to sea without the dockyard people and the staff officers watching and making criticisms and suggestions. And later, after the commanding officer's final course, 'the perisher' as it was aptly termed, with the new boat and company. *Tornado*, a T-Class boat, had left harbour on a morning not unlike this, grey sky, the sea like heaving pewter, to most other craft just another submarine leaving port. Going to war.

But on that day nothing else had mattered. He knew Fawcett was talking to the leading signalman, bridging the gap. He always made a point of it.

He tried to push the memory away. But the moment remained. The first time . . .

A glance around the open bridge. Feeling the excitement, sharing it with the two lookouts.

Then, as if prompted, *'Clear the bridge!'* He could see the last lookout's face as he jumped down through the oval hatch. Their eyes had met, just for a second, but Masters remembered it. He had been only a boy.

Still clear, incisive. Lowering his face to the voicepipe, picturing the features and the minds of the men beneath his feet.

'Dive! Dive! Dive!' The scream of the klaxon.

Instant and vital, the craft and the man as one. Just once he had stared over the grey steel screen, had held his breath as the sea had boiled up over the stem and along the casing to surge around the four-inch gun as *Tornado* went into her dive.

And there it was. Like a flaw in a photograph, a brief gleam as it twisted in the glare before it vanished under the hull, and exploded.

He had heard nothing, nor had he remembered what had happened. Only the aftermath. The pain. The sympathy. The inquiry. He had never heard the announcement; there were enough of them in those days, anyway.

The Secretary of the Admiralty regrets to announce the loss of His Majesty's Submarine Tornado. *Next of kin have been informed.*

There were no survivors. They lay with the shattered hull, all fifty-eight of them, including the lookout with the excited grin.

He was coming out of it slowly. *Were a submariner.*

His first command. And his last.

He stared at the mirror again, imagining for a moment that Fawcett had asked him something and was expecting an answer. The admiral had not got up this early just to pass the time of day.

But it was not that. The leading signalman had gone, and the Wren Sally was covering the telephone with her fingers as she always did.

Fawcett was shaking his head. 'I distinctly *told* them!' It must have upset what he had been about to say.

She did not give in. 'Classified, sir.'

Fawcett snapped, *'Bloody hell!'* and almost snatched the receiver from her. 'I left instructions. Orders . . .' He broke off and stepped away from the desk. *'Where? When?'* He reached down, removing the telephone flex from around the teapot; he did it with great care. Then he said quietly, 'Took you long enough.'

Masters waited. He could sense Fawcett's uncertainty, irresolution. Like discovering a secret about somebody you thought you knew as well as he would ever let you.

'You're certain, then? Critchley?' He nodded once. 'Keep me posted.' He handed the telephone to the Wren officer without expression.

Masters turned. Critchley . . . Commander John Critchley. This same room. The smile. Persuasive, encouraging. His charm.

Fawcett walked to the window and stooped to peer out at the sky.

'Use the other office, will you, Sally?'

The door closed, and Fawcett turned to face him.

'You knew him, of course? A good officer. A leader, and an example, especially to all the green young types straight out of civvy street. He could charm anybody.'

It was as if Fawcett had read his thoughts.

'How did it happen, sir?'

'When I know *that* . . .' He looked up, angry and impatient. 'I was at the Admiralty. People listened, for once.' He walked across the room, but Masters knew he was unaware of the movement. It was like seeing a complete stranger. 'He was the man for the job. My choice.' He lowered his voice and said, almost offhandedly, 'A mine. Type Charlie, apparently. Army Bomb Disposal were involved. When I discover . . .' He broke off again and stared at the telephones. 'He must have been out of his bloody mind! Should never even have been there, for God's sake!' He paused by the other desk and patted his pockets. 'Don't have a cigarette on you, I suppose?' He glanced at the Wren's handbag hanging from the chair. 'I forgot, you're a pipe man. Now, a good cigar . . .'

Masters waited, watching him trying to come to terms with it. Like watching a hurricane, and trying to predict its course.

Fawcett said, 'At first I thought we'd never get along together. Not my style. Part-time sailor, R.N.V.R., plenty of money, he had no need to be in the service at all.' He stared at the neat lines of signals. 'Electronics, that was his business. I'll lay odds that half the equipment which ends up here began life in one of his factories.' He swung round and looked at him directly. 'Yet he was an *adventurer*, enjoyed taking risks. Used to race that bloody great Bentley of his, Monte Carlo, right? A fair yachtsman too, I believe.'

The pale blue eyes wandered, then settled on Masters again. The storm was passing.

14

'Taught *you* a lot, eh?'

'Everything, sir.' He had often thought about it, driving himself or being driven by something he could not contain. Because of *Tornado*, because of guilt, or a need for revenge. It was madness, and yet he had forced himself to do it. From an open bridge to the confined world of fuses and intricate mechanisms, theirs or ours; it all had to be studied, and learned by heart. There were rarely second chances.

In his heart, he had not expected to succeed. Perhaps he had even come to terms with it. Until that first incident, the mine which had fallen in Southampton Docks, and had been recognized as something quite new and different. His first 'beast'.

He said, 'He had the touch with people. Civilians especially, the ones who had to take it day after day, and nights as well in some places. That was his strength, and they loved him for it.'

Fawcett nodded. 'I agree. It's different for us in the Andrew. We obey orders, we do as we're told, we live, we die. It's what we are, what we do.' He gazed at the girl on the mirror. 'The civilians get another war entirely. Somehow they go off to work each day, worrying about the family, the bloody rations, not even knowing if the office or the factory will be standing when they arrive. More to the point, not knowing if their homes and families will still be there when they come back.' He pounded one fist into his palm without making a sound. 'Without that sort of strength, faith if you like, all our efforts would be a waste of time, and I mean that!'

Somewhere in another world, a telephone jangled noisily. Fawcett looked at the door, obviously restraining another impulse.

'The mine is a deadly weapon, and it is cheap to produce. It's effective because even the hint or the sighting of one can cause costly delays. The channels have to be swept, each fairway rechecked even if sweepers have carried out that thankless job only hours earlier. Mines, no matter what kind, don't just go away. They have to be tackled by individuals with the courage and the will to do it. When I was in Sicily I saw some of the defences Jerry had been preparing when he realized the Afrika Korps was on the run. The Italians were good at it. The Germans will be better, next time.'

Masters heard voices in the passageway, and could imagine the decision being reached.

Fawcett looked at the office clock. 'And I don't just mean Italy. The mine has no discrimination. It lies there. It kills and it maims, and cares nothing for the uniforms of those who laid it. If the final invasion – dare I speak the word after all we've seen – is to succeed, we must be ready to act *before* the first landing craft drops her ramp.'

What Critchley had been doing. Should have been doing. *My choice*, Fawcett had said. Was that only minutes ago? It was as if time had stopped.

Were a submariner . . .

On that same morning, the channel had already been swept. Ex-trawlers, and a lot of ex-fishermen too in the minesweeping service. And many of them had died.

It could have been one of their own, a solitary drifter, perhaps, from a local field. And he had seen it, for a split second.

He came back to the present as Fawcett said abruptly, 'He was married, of course. I suppose I'll have to say something.'

The admiral was almost himself again. He raised his voice slightly. 'Come in, and stop muttering!'

It was *Vernon*'s Chief Yeoman of Signals, a squat, solidly built man who over the years had grown immune to the ways of flag officers. As a boy signalman, he had stood on the bridge of Jellicoe's *Iron Duke* at the Battle of Jutland.

'Signal from *Tango Charlie*, sir.' He held out his pad. 'An' one on the scrambler from F.O.I.C.'

The blue eyes moved briskly along the lines of round, schoolboy handwriting, and he grunted, 'About time, too.'

The Wren officer was just outside the door, and Masters could hear the tramp, tramp, tramp of another class heading to its next instruction. *We obey orders, we do as we're told, we live, we die.* He saw, too, that the Wren's eyes were red, something he had never known before.

The admiral folded the signal and said quietly, 'I want you to take his place. The way back, remember?'

Masters straightened his back; always the reminder of being smashed into the conning tower. But there was no pain.

Faces stood out, the Wren openly crying now, the Chief Yeoman beaming, wanting to share it.

And the rear-admiral. Composed, and quite alone.

He scarcely heard his own reply but saw Fawcett give a brief smile.

'I shall make the necessary signal.' He lifted the gleaming cap and adjusted it to the expected rakish angle. 'Now, it's up to you.'

It was anything but just another day.

2

No Looking Back

The Dorset village of Chaldon St Mary, like countless towns and communities throughout the country which had been occupied by the armed services, would not be recognized by those who might have known it in peacetime.

On the fringe of Weymouth Bay, and more to the point as the Admiralty had noted from the outset, only five miles from the naval base and anti-submarine establishment at Portland Bill, the village had served a rural area of scattered but prosperous farms, and the road which had skirted it to head further west to Devon and Cornwall. It consisted of one street, a church, one pub, a school, and small houses which looked as if they had been here for ever. In those other times people had paused here, perhaps to fish or to sail. The more adventurous had pressed onto the West Country, leaving Chaldon St Mary in peace.

If you turned your back on the sea it might appear little changed, if you had known it before, amid the great sweeping beauty of the Dorset countryside, the hills, and even now the cattle dotted about in groups, or making their unhurried way to milking.

Only a trained eye would detect the massive posts mounted in every field, the only defence against troop-carrying gliders in those early days when invasion had seemed inevitable, or the gun emplacements beneath their camouflaged netting. Now the narrow lanes shook to the rumble of army trucks and armoured vehicles, and the snarl of despatch riders' motor cycles, scaring chickens and bringing shouts from servicemen on foot. The school was empty of children; all had been evacuated after the fall of France. The pub was busier than ever but always filled with uniforms, the older, local people a small minority. Only the fine church remained the same, with its well-kept memorial to the previous generation of plough boys and thatchers who had fallen at Passchendaele and Ypres. Now they had been joined by a neatly written list, more local names, and perhaps *El Alamein*.

But Chaldon St Mary had an inlet and faced the English Channel, and it was only sixty miles from the Cherbourg peninsula, German-occupied France, a few hours away by E-Boat or fast minelayer, much less by bomber or fighter.

As the old hands often remarked, 'They'll be back in bed with some French tart while we're still reloading!'

The inlet itself had experienced the biggest and ugliest change. It was wired off from the main road, with armed sentries at gates which were rarely left open. There was even a small regulating office for the master-at-arms, the Jaunty, and his staff, which had once been the school's bicycle shed. The school had become the wardroom, and the playground where local children had run and dreamed had been labelled *Quarterdeck*, where the White Ensign flew from its own mast. If you walked across the playground without saluting, you could expect no mercy.

The inlet was filled with various small craft, with what appeared to be a scrapyard at one end near the entrance, rusting hulls which had been cannibalized to refit others, a half burned-out landing vessel regularly used for experiments both above and below water, barbed wire running down and into the sea itself, where a long spit of stony sand was only visible at low water. There were deadly reminders, also, little boards with the skull and crossbones to warn of the minefield laid here at the outset, and a solitary cross, its identifying name long since washed away, where a sapper had put his boot in the wrong place at the wrong time.

It was a fine and surprisingly clear day, the Channel blue-grey in the distance but an almost smoky green in deeper waters and the approaches to the bay. There were plenty of people about, loading and unloading stores, being inspected or receiving orders for some new exercise, and two dogs were chasing one another along the waterside, local or unofficially owned

19

by some of the sailors; nobody questioned it. It was that sort of place.

A few turned to watch as a small, paint-spattered yardboat chugged past a trot of moored ex-fishing drifters awaiting refit or overhaul, and turned slowly towards the opposite shore.

The yardmaster, a civilian who had worked in and around the area for most of his life, eased the throttle, and watched the vessel moored across his course as it seemed to loom up and away from the disorder and scrap beyond.

He felt his teeth tighten around his unlit pipe and glanced at his companion. So many, and yet he never got used to them. Lieutenant Chris Foley, Royal Naval Volunteer Reserve, was on his feet, unaware of anything but the vessel ahead, a motor launch, one of the navy's Light Coastal Forces. Not a motor torpedo boat or gunboat, which made up the sharp edge of coastal forces, the Glory Boys as they were disdainfully or enviously called by those less active, but a hard-used maid of all work. And she was his own command, had been for almost two years. It was still hard to believe.

The yardboat turned again, slowing even more. Giving him time.

One hundred and ten feet long with a low, compact bridge and slightly raked mast, he knew every inch of her. She mounted a small three-pounder gun forward and twin Oerlikon twenty-millimetre guns aft, with a third amidships. The MTB and MGB types might betray a gentle amusement, comparing this with their nightly raids and clashes in the Channel or off the Hook of Holland, in the thick of it, but together they had seen and done it all. Escorting furtive coastal convoys in the dead of night along these same coastlines, chasing up stragglers and exchanging angry signals and threats with masters who had been at sea all their lives. Picking them up when their luck ran out, and bomb or mine had taken its toll. And burying them, if it came to that.

She was so near now that he could pick out the familiar scars and scrapes along her wooden hull, which even the new coats of dazzle paint could not completely disguise. Her number, ML366, freshly painted also, stood out like a private welcome.

20

Her three-shaft Hall-Scott petrol engines could still give twenty-two knots; she had managed twenty-five with the wind up her backside, as they said, and against all the rest she could have been a millionaire's personal yacht.

It was time. The yardmaster said, 'Done all we could. Only four days, remember?'

He shook his head; the lieutenant hadn't heard a word. Young and fresh-faced, he could smile more than some of them, and his men seemed to like him for it. And he had lasted longer than a lot of others he had met. Maybe that was it.

'No sign of rot, then?'

The yardmaster grinned. He *had* heard. 'Far as I could tell. Mahogany, though. Ripe as a pear if it gets the chance.'

They were alongside; two figures were waiting for him, and there was a fresh new ensign rippling from the gaff. He knew it, but it was still a surprise, even a shock. Harry Bryant, his Number One, had already left, promoted lieutenant and on his way to a course which would lead to his own command, a motor torpedo boat. It was what he had always wanted: he would be one of the Glory Boys after all.

They had been together for nine months. There were only twenty in ML366's small company, and there was no room for secrets. You knew a man's mind, his hopes, and too often his destiny. There were a few more sharing their cramped world now because of their new duties, *the job* as they called it. But without Harry Bryant it would not be the same. Even if it had to be, for all their sakes.

'Welcome aboard, sir.' It was Dougie Bass, the coxswain. A leading hand in fact, he ran the boat as if he had been born to it. In small craft you had to be competent in all kinds of tasks which extended far beyond the badge on a man's sleeve or his rings of authority. Bass had once been a waiter on the railway, the crack *Bournemouth Belle*, where among other things he had chosen to become an excellent cook. The signalman had been a fairground attendant, when he had worked at all, and had learned to shoot for prizes to pass the time. He was a good enough bunting-tosser; but put him behind their twin machine-guns and he could show where he truly belonged. Foley had recommended him for a decoration

21

after their last confrontation with the Luftwaffe. They were still waiting.

A gun boomed across the inlet, and they turned to look at the shore.

Bass studied his watch. 'It's over, then.'

There had been a ceremony of some kind; the establishment's captain had gone to it, some of the top brass as well. The press, too; they seemed to love anything like that.

Commander John Critchley had been a legend, the man who had never seemed too busy or too tired to listen. And a full commander; even now, after four years of war, it was still rare to meet up with an R.N.V.R. officer in a brass hat. *Really Not Very Reliable*, they had scoffed in those early days. It was different now: the amateurs had become the true professionals. The regulars who had not kept up or refused to change had become very thin on the ground.

Foley could recall the moment exactly. The morning after the farewell party for Harry Bryant. The hangover. Trying to discover what had happened, seeing the face and remembering the man. The legend . . .

And the date. He could remember tearing it off the calendar in 366's tiny hutchlike wardroom. September third. Four years exactly from the Sunday when war had been declared. Men had grown from boys in that time. An equal number had died. Commander John Critchley . . . He sighed and said, 'We'd better move ourselves, 'Swain. The new boss is coming today.'

He walked towards the bridge, past the storage space for the ground mines they sometimes carried. It was not the time to worry about a change of leadership. That was vague enough anyway, with more than a dozen departments working in countermeasures. It had been something new for them, or maybe Critchley had made it seem that way.

And if he thought about it, Foley knew he had been lucky. He had seen and done more than most, right from the beginning when as a young subbie, newly appointed from the Supplementary Reserve, he had found himself in charge of a motor launch and on his way to Dunkirk. His total experience had been evening or sometimes weekend training, learning the mysteries of pilotage and navigation on well-worn charts, squatting around tables at the local reserve

22

unit. Trying to read semaphore while somebody flagged signals from the church tower, or wondering what use it was discovering how to fix and unfix bayonets.

Dunkirk had changed all that. It was not fear he remembered, nor even the sense of helplessness and enormity. It was anger, and sometimes he could still feel it, even after all this time, when the actual scenes and events had become blurred, confused, like fragments of an old movie. The ceaseless attacks by enemy aircraft, while they had stared at the sky and prayed for the R.A.F. The unmoving queues of khaki on the beaches, if you could get near enough. Dying, broken ships everywhere; the navy had lost twenty-seven destroyers alone during the evacuation. The miracle, some had called it. But the little ships of Dunkirk were the true heroes. Pleasure launches like Foley's, which had probably never been out of sight of land before, tugs and fishing boats, and the proud blue and white hulls of the lifeboat service, old pros and yachtsmen in anything that could stay afloat. There had even been a paddle-steamer, one of the many which had taken families on trips to Southend and Brighton in those impossible days of peace. Foley paused at the hatch coaming above the ladder. Familiar smells: the galley, the ever-lingering stench of petrol. They had been together so long they did not need to be reminded of the brutal difference between this and other boats that were diesel-powered. Here you could brew up in seconds: the notice *No Smoking Abaft the Bridge* was only for visitors.

But, for a moment, the picture returned. The paddle-steamer, stopped and slewing round in the current, only one paddle thrashing at the water until it, too, fell motionless.

It had been attacked, raked by enemy aircraft; even as they had drawn near Foley had seen one of them through his borrowed binoculars, climbing so effortlessly, and sharply defined against a patch of blue sky.

The stricken paddle-steamer had to be taken in tow, and he felt the same frustration as on that day. Hazy memories of heaving-lines, and rigging some kind of tow-line. The launch was not powerful, and his small crew of sailors had been snatched from the training intake at Portsmouth. They were willing enough, but looking to their officer for a solution.

The worst part had been the listing steamer. They were near enough to read her name, *Worthing Queen*, and see her decks crammed with soldiers. There had not been an inch of space for a man to walk. Some stood in tight groups, huddled against deck houses and broken equipment; others lay together where they could, staring at the sky. Some might have been dead; there was blood near one of the paddle-boxes, and the scars of an earlier air attack. Some of them had been fully dressed, and were wearing their steel helmets and carrying weapons of some sort. Others were half-naked, perhaps dragged from the sea after some other disaster.

Only one figure had stood out. A soldier standing upright on the old-fashioned, varnished wheelhouse, a Bren gun held almost casually, it had seemed, a cigarette in the corner of his mouth. He had watched the little launch, might even have thrown up a wave or a salute.

Someone had yelled, 'The bastard's comin' back again, sir!'

Foley had walked to the boat's only armament, an old American stripped Lewis gun, probably a relic from the Western Front and the days of Biggles.

And all the while he had been conscious, deafened if that were possible, by the utter silence. Just the throb of the boat's engine and his own breathing. From the paddle-steamer with its helpless cargo of exhausted, beaten men, there was neither sound nor movement. And Foley had felt only anger.

He had heard the Bren first, sharp but brief; the magazine only held thirty rounds. Funny how that snippet of his peacetime training had remained; and the soldier had probably been hit anyway.

He had peered through the sight and felt the gun bucking wildly, the blurred arcs of the aircraft's propellors and the stab of machine-gun fire matched only by the insane scream of its engines.

A long, long time ago now, but it had stayed with him. The luck, and a moment of pride. Nobody knew if he had even marked the plane. Some of the German's fire had made a mess of the launch's foredeck, to within a yard of where he had been standing, but the plane had not returned for another attack. He had watched it, low on the water, fading from view, smaller and smaller until it was gone altogether. He recalled one of his men thumping him on the back and stammering an apology for forgetting himself. Another had been shaking his fists at the sky and weeping.

But the old paddle-steamer had made him remember it, and the exhausted, despairing men who had seen this as their last and only chance of getting back to England. After the retreat through unknown and sometimes hostile countryside, the waiting and the attacks and the diminishing hopes, his lonely gesture of defiance and fury on their behalf had done it. As if they had been given new life, every man had seemed to be on his feet, cheering and waving, clinging to one another, some shouting wildly across the water towards the launch. Even those unable to stand had attempted to join in. And others, who would never stand again, had somehow shared it. It was not something he would ever forget. Or want to.

He was about to lower himself down the vertical ladder when he heard Bass call, 'Boat comin' alongside, sir.' He sounded as if he was covering up a grin.

Foley turned and rested his palms on the handrails. He could even feel the faint tremble of machinery. One of the Chief's generators, but it felt like 366's own breathing. He shook himself. He had to be on top line today. They all must, with the new boss coming. And a regular officer, too, not like Critchley. Even he had somehow heard about the Dunkirk incident, had punched his arm and given his famous smile. Things might be different from now on . . .

The boat nudged alongside, Bass watching grimly until the rope fenders were in place.

The sub-lieutenant who climbed lightly aboard was almost what Foley had expected. He knew all that there was to know about 366's new Number One. Nineteen years old, three months' sea time in a clapped-out destroyer, a short course at H.M.S. *Hornet*, and now here. He looked even younger in his brand-new Number Fives, his reefer dragged off one shoulder by his respirator haversack.

He saluted. 'Come aboard to join, sir. Sorry I was held up – lot of traffic on the road.'

Foley tried to push his thoughts aside. Harry Bryant was gone. It was the way of the Andrew. *Never look back.*

He thrust out his hand. 'Glad to have you. I'll put you in the picture while you settle in.' The subbie's name was Tobias Allison. A bit of a mouthful, he thought. 'What do you like to be called? This is a small ship, so we'd better get it right from the start.'

Allison stared at him and then smiled. '"Toby" suits me, sir.'

Foley glanced over his shoulder. 'Have Number One's gear taken below, 'Swain!'

He could almost hear Dougie Bass saying, 'Old Chris'll soon get *him* sorted out!'

He smiled. It had been a long time. *Old Chris* . . . Foley was twenty-five.

He led the way down to the wardroom, which his own little cabin adjoined. Foley had served in two small craft before 366, and was accustomed to the lack of space; his cabin, like an enlarged cupboard, was a luxury compared with the others. He saw Allison's eyes moving everywhere, and wondered what he was thinking. An elderly destroyer on the East Coast run would seem like a cruiser by comparison.

'I'll show you around myself as soon as I can. I've got to hang about until I know what's happening. We have a new senior officer taking over today.' He smiled at the subbie's uncertainty. 'I *think*!'

It was strange for the boat to be so still, as if she were listening. The W/T office which was just through the door was silent, without the usual stammer of morse or the crackle of some garbled broadcast. And music, sometimes; it was vaguely unsettling to hear German voices.

But they had been given three days' leave, more to allow a quick overhaul than for anyone's personal benefit.

Foley came from Surrey. A long way there and back in wartime, but it was worth it, and his mother and father were always glad when it happened. Almost grateful, he sometimes thought.

Allison had removed his new cap; he had fair, unruly hair, and looked even younger without it.

He said, 'We heard about Commander Critchley often enough, especially at *Hornet*. When I got to Dorchester I was told about his death.' He hesitated and looked around at the small space they would share, perhaps understanding for the first time how his life had changed.

Foley said slowly, 'It was a bit of a shock to everybody. He made quite a mark in our sort of work – everywhere he went, really.'

He heard someone bringing Allison's cases down the ladder, whistling tunelessly. Another face: Titch Kelly, seaman gunner, a Scouse from Liverpool who had managed to get into more trouble than most in the three years he had served in the navy. He had somehow managed to find himself in the notorious Detention Barracks at Canterbury, and had survived. As a final chance or out of sheer desperation, somebody had accepted his request to join the new Special Service, risks or no risks. The drafting office had jumped at the idea, and Titch Kelly had not faced a defaulters' table since.

If he had not been away on that brief leave, Foley wondered if he might also have gone to the memorial service. There would have been some familiar faces, friends too, the ones you tried not to worry about in case it was their turn. Or yours.

But mostly it would be ceremonial. Showing respect. Not like the usual funeral: the burial march, the grim faces, the eventual firing party. The worst part was seeing the parents, if they were present. He thought suddenly of this last visit to his home in Surrey. How old they had looked. Like those others . . . Critchley had no parents, and in any case there would be nothing left to bury. There never was, with a beast.

He heard Bass's boots on the ladder. He did not even have to raise his voice.

'Some of 'em are returnin' now, sir. Look pretty smart too, like a bank 'oliday!'

You never knew with 366's killick coxswain if he was being serious or not. It was probably the best way to leave it.

Foley said, 'Go up and have a look,' the slightest hesitation, 'Number One.'

He felt for the keys in his jacket pocket, but realized that Allison was still standing by the narrow table, his fair hair shining only inches below the deckhead light. He looked serious, even solemn. Vulnerable.

He said, 'I won't let you down, sir. I wanted more than anything to be here, in a boat like this.' He paused. 'I'm ready.'

It was strangely moving, and Foley tried to smile. 'Shove off,

Toby, and watch your step. They're a good bunch, I'd not ask for better, but they have their difficult moments.'

Surprisingly, Allison grinned.

'*The new officer*, you mean, sir?' He picked up his cap and the light glinted on the label inside. Gieves, not one of the cheap tailors which had sprung up around every base and barracks as soon as the recruiting had started. 'I'm ready for that, too!'

The curtain fell across the door and Foley glanced into his own cabin. A bunk, chart drawers underneath, a steel cupboard that still rattled at sea despite all the Chief's efforts. Seagoing gear always within reach, oilskin and the faithful duffle coat, the cap with a badge so tarnished that it was almost green. And the scuffed seaboots, broken in at last and comfortable, but difficult to kick off in an emergency if you wore thick stockings. But it could be done: his others were on the bottom of the North Sea with the boat. *It could be done.*

He picked up the folding picture frame. His parents in one, his young sister in the other. A little girl such a short while ago. Not any more. It was all his mother had been able to talk about. She was in love, with an airman she had met at some local dance for a fund-raising charity to help the disabled. A flier, apparently. His mother had been upset, even outraged.

'A Pole! Not one of *our* boys, but a Pole!' It had sounded almost obscene.

He had spoken to his sister for only a few minutes before he had gone to the railway station. They usually got along very well, but this time he had been aware of the difference. It was all too common in families separated by war. His mother might have good reason to worry.

Foley had had some experience with women, but only once had he felt something which had truly disturbed and excited him. She had found someone else. That, too, happened often enough.

In love. Even his sister's voice had changed. Lovers, more likely.

He peered at his reflection in the little mirror. The same face, but visibly tired and strained. Because of the visit home, the long haul back here? He recalled Allison's quiet determination. *We were all like that.*

He pushed the thought away and returned to the adjoining compartment. He could almost see Harry Bryant slouched in his usual corner, with one of the terrible magazines he always seemed to find somewhere.

It hit him like a fist. That day when the news had broken about Critchley, after the farewell party. Bryant had been trying to close an overfilled suitcase, and had turned his head to stare at him. There had been no smile that time, no shared joke.

'Critchley? I always thought he was a shit! I never trusted him for a bloody minute!'

Foley left the wardroom and went to the ladder. Soon he would be too damned busy to have time to brood.

But Bryant's words refused to leave him.

'Almost there, sir.'

David Masters came out of his thoughts with a jerk, his mind tired, or merely dulled by the car swinging this way and that, hedgerows or slate walls almost touching the side.

'Thanks.' He saw her gloved hands on the wheel, the effortless way she manoeuvred around a parked farm wagon. It was a powerful vehicle which had been sent to collect him, a Wolseley, someone's pride and joy before the war, he had no doubt.

He had seen her watching him in the driving mirror, the same way as she had greeted him after the ceremony. Formal, even distant; she was used to this sort of mission.

It was cold: there was no heating in the car, and he could see little of her face above the woollen scarf and upturned collar.

He had found it difficult at first to become accustomed to women in uniform around every naval base and establishment. Now it was impossible to imagine being without them, in offices, or working with coding and signals departments, in Operations rooms or at the daily grind of cooking in shore-based galleys. Always there to cheer when an escort returned from some dicey convoy when, perhaps, a U-Boat had been accounted for. Or watching in silence at the other returns, with the flag-covered bodies laid out on the deck.

Masters moved his shoulders against the damp leather, recalling the ceremony. Many senior officers; even an admiral had come all the way from London. Bumper Fawcett had been there, but had made a point of keeping his distance apart from a brief, 'Good turnout, what?' and a searching gaze. No display of warmth which might be mistaken for favouritism. Without realizing it, he had come to know Bumper Fawcett's set of rules.

The car braked and he thought he heard the girl mutter something through her scarf.

It was another farm truck. A big man in boots and heavy coat, probably the farmer, was pointing with his walking stick and speaking with three others. It was something else which had taken a lot of getting used to: they wore British battledress, which was marked with coloured patches to distinguish them as Italian prisoners of war. Working on the land where they were most needed, replacing men who had been called up or volunteered for the armed forces, they might even have taken part in the battles in North Africa.

Things must be more promising if they were allowed to work in an area like this, so close to the sea. Did they accept it? Did they never think of escape? One of them was nodding and smiling at the old farmer, the others turned to stare at the car, and the girl behind the wheel.

Masters said, 'They look happy enough.'

She let in the clutch and swung past the truck. 'They get what they want around here, or so I'm told, sir.' Angry, bitter, or just impatient. 'Here it is, sir.'

He saw open gates and a curved drive, a stone house with shutters, larger than most of those he had seen on the way. It had the usual shabby wartime look, the drive lined with weeds, the ground blackened by oil from parked vehicles. There was a van here now, with *Royal Navy* painted on the side, into which some ratings were loading boxes, while a petty officer stood nearby with a list, smoking a cigarette.

The Wren said, 'Your gear arrived this morning, sir. The P.O. steward took care of everything.' She half turned as if to look at him, or the house. 'His name's Coker, by the way, sir. Long service, three badges.' The scarf had slipped; she had a nice mouth. But she did not smile at her own concise summing-up of the man who obviously ruled these commandeered quarters, where Critchley had lived for some of the time.

Masters felt the car door open. The working party stood in various poses of attention, the P.O. was saluting, the cigarette gone.

'Lieutenant-Commander Masters, sir?' The eyes moved briskly over him. 'All ready for you, sir.'

It was suddenly very quiet, apart from a wind through gaunt, leafless trees. The journey had taken less than ten minutes, but with the sea hidden by a rounded shoulder of hillside he could have been a hundred miles from it.

She was out of the car too, reaching for his case and respirator. Beneath her jaunty cap with its H.M.S. cap tally her hair was very dark, almost black.

The petty officer asked, 'Got enough petrol, my girl?'

She nodded without answering and looked at Masters.

Dark eyes, too. Off for a run ashore; somebody's girl, he thought.

It was getting worse. Amongst total strangers, like losing contact on the field telephone at the moment of confrontation with a mine . . .

He said, 'I didn't catch your name, in all the rush.'

'Lovatt, sir. Leading Wren.'

He heard the sailors shuffling their feet, wanting to finish their work and go.

'Going somewhere nice, I hope?'

She reached for the door handle. 'Dorchester, sir. Another passenger.' She looked past him. 'Petty Officer Coker is coming now.'

It still would not fall into place.

Then he heard himself say, 'Lovatt. I knew someone of that name . . .'

She was back in the car, the window wound down despite the keen wind.

'My brother, sir. He was in *Tornado*.' She let in the clutch, and the driveway was empty.

The strident jangle of the telephone was like the scream of Action Stations, and for what seemed an eternity Masters was pushing at the bed as if he was trapped by something. And yet the lights were still on, the room exactly as it had been before he had fallen on to his side and closed his eyes.

31

The table with the cigarette box, an ashtray with his filled pipe beside it, unlit, unsmoked. He could almost hear Bumper Fawcett's words. *I forgot. You're a pipe man.* The strange room, high-ceilinged, wallpaper faded and colourless in the harsh lights.

He picked up the telephone and realized for the first time that he was fully dressed. The petty officer named Coker had wanted to provide a meal. Instead . . . He glanced at the decanter and empty glass on the bedside locker.

He cleared his throat and peered at his watch. Who on earth would be calling now?

He said, 'Masters.' The line was dead. They probably thought he was too tired or too drunk to answer.

'*There you are!* Thought I'd get you in the end. Settle in, old chap?'

Masters rubbed his eyes. It was impossible. It was Bumper Fawcett, at this ungodly hour.

'You'll get it from Operations shortly, but I thought you'd like it from me, what?'

Masters straightened his back, waiting for the pain. There was none.

'Operation Avalanche is a fact of life! The invasion of Italy has begun! It's official!' There were sounds in the background, and another voice, a woman. Masters stared across the room, through the door to an adjoining one.

He had opened one of the tall, old-fashioned wardrobes, and been confronted by a complete uniform hanging there like a silent onlooker. He had not needed to see the three wavy rings on the sleeves, the decorations, and the oak-leaved cap neatly placed on the shelf above. There had been a smell of perfume too, although the house had been stripped of everything else, and he had wondered why Critchley's uniform had been left behind. Until today he had never met Critchley's wife, younger than he had expected, and accompanied by a Wren officer from the admiral's staff in London, no doubt to keep her company, comfort her if need be. Otherwise she would have been the only woman at the service. She was still quite alone.

A quick glance, a handshake, her fingers like ice, her face obscured by the hat and the veil. And she had lived here, in this

32

commandeered house, been here when they had told her what had happened. Perhaps on this same telephone.

'You still there? *Good.* Now listen. As soon as more reports of the landings come in, we'll have a meeting. Things will move fast – the Germans are not going to like their Italian allies if, or rather *when* they cave in under the attacks!'

Masters gazed at the window; there was a hint of grey around the blackout screen. He felt like death. Bumper must have the very top security rating if he could spill so much over the line.

There was a click. The admiral was no doubt already ringing someone else.

He put the receiver down slowly and considered it. Expected, and yet still a surprise. The campaign was spreading, and only two months after Sicily. *The way back.*

He thought of all the faces he had seen today, the hands he had shaken. Some he had known since the earliest days, when he had taken his first instruction, almost cold-bloodedly, it seemed now. Officers drawn to the risk or the danger by the obscure call from the Admiralty, for a secret mission with the Land Incident Section. Some volunteered because they were bored with their appointments, others because they were too young and untrained to know any better. There were a few who had nothing more to live for.

Was I one of those?

Magnetic mines, growing more sophisticated and treacherous with every passing month, ruled their lives. The training done, there was always the first incident, the beast.

A driving force, obsessive; Masters could feel it now, and wondered how he had survived, let alone found himself guiding others on the same dangerous course.

It had become personal. His mind, his ears, his fingers not only against the weapon but a human being, somewhere, who had designed and set the beast into motion. A living *thing*, an entity.

It was behind him now. It must be. For others, if not merely for himself.

There were faces he did not know, yet. Ones who asked, *The new boss, what's he like? A* man you could trust your life to? Or just another stranger? He touched the scar. No wonder the girl had been watching him in the driving mirror. Her eyes might have been saying, *Why him, and not you?*

He strode to the window and dragged the screen aside. It was still dark, but he could discern the curve of the hill and, he thought, the ragged line of trees.

And there were a lot of faces missing. Too many . . . Inexperienced, over-eager, careless. In most cases you could never know, unless by some last desperate call over the intercom. And even then . . .

He thought of Critchley again, the abandoned uniform. Like a reproach. He had scanned a brief report, the discovery of the mine, a petty officer's statement, how he had been surprised that such a senior officer had been sent to deal with the incident. The driver, who had described how he was told to take cover at the very beginning. Rear-Admiral Fawcett had pencilled in an aside to explain that Critchley had been at a meeting when he had been informed of the mine. An officer of the nearest Render Mines Safe group had been delayed in a car accident. Critchley must have acted on impulse. To *show them* . . . Masters could hear him saying it.

He leaned forward and felt the cold air through the glass. From this height he could see beyond the hill to a harder, darker line beyond. The sea.

He heard someone moving about downstairs. Coker, the P.O. steward. *Long service. Three badges.* As mixed a collection of people as you could discover anywhere, to be welded together, to use all their experience in protecting and saving others, part of the ultimate weapon for victory.

It's up to you.

He heard footsteps on the stairs, and the clink of crockery, and looked at the sea again.

Me, and a few thousand others.

He smiled, surprised that it came so easily, after so long.

He was back.

3

Survival

David Masters had been about to leave for Portland when the call
had come through. At dawn that day there had been an air raid
alert, common enough even when some of them proved to be false.
Masters had heard the staccato bark of gunfire while he had been
sitting on the edge of the bed in the room with its damp wallpaper.
Not close, and it had not lasted for long.

Captain Hubert Chavasse, who commanded the establishment
at Chaldon St Mary, had been wary about it.

'You were going to Portland anyway. Rear-Admiral Fawcett
will be on the phone before another hour passes, I've no doubt
about that, so perhaps you could let *me* know what's going on!'

Chavasse was a precise, if impatient, officer of the old school,
abrasive when he considered it necessary. The inlet was littered
with hoists and machinery, and surrounded by makeshift huts
for the ratings, further disfigured by hastily built air raid shel-
ters for these occasional hit-and-run attacks. But to him it was
a naval establishment, and in his eyes it would stand against
any other.

It had been a solitary plane, spotted flying in from the Channel,
low over the water, then climbing and turning above one of the
beaches near the road to Weymouth and the Bill. No bombs had
been dropped, and there had been no reports of mines being laid
in or around the bay.

By a twist of fate the aircraft had been caught out by one of the
army's local mobile batteries, which had been formed to deal with

similar individual attacks. The plane had been shot down. The army was dealing with it.

Until the telephone call. Portland had sent a mine disposal team; the admiral had thought it necessary.

Chavasse had said, 'Just take a look, Masters.' He rarely used first names. 'No chances, right? Can't afford to lose *you* at this stage!' His short, barking laugh had followed Masters out to the waiting car.

It had taken more than an hour to cover only a couple of miles; the road had been jammed with service vehicles which seemed to reach as far as the eye could see. Impatient military policemen, redcaps, on foot or motor cycles, were somehow managing to turn the traffic round on the narrow road and divert it through Dorchester.

An air attack now and half the transport in southern England would be wiped out, Masters thought.

He was not the only passenger. Paymaster Lieutenant-Commander Brayshaw was also going to Portland on a mission for Captain Chavasse. He was the captain's secretary, and probably knew more about the organization, the efficiency or weaknesses of the establishment, than anyone else. Quiet and easy to talk to, he was doubtless just what Chavasse needed. Masters suspected he had been sent along to make sure that things remained under control.

The car, the same big Wolseley, jerked to a halt, the tyres embedded in the roadside mud.

'Up there, sir. I can see the turn-off.'

It was even the same driver, cap tilted forward, hair black against her collar. Masters had heard that she had applied for a transfer to Plymouth, where she had originally been stationed, the day after his arrival. Five days ago. She was still here.

Another redcap appeared and waved them around the last bend in the road where a barrier had been erected, and while other cars and lorries headed away for the diversion, the Wolseley was suddenly alone. Brayshaw wound down a window and peered at the sky. It was completely clear and blue, no vapour trails to betray aircraft, only the distant line of barrage balloons towards Weymouth, like basking whales in the hard sunlight.

He shut the window and shivered. 'The old stable door policy,

I see.' Then, 'What do you expect to find when we get there, David?'

Masters had heard him asking questions in the makeshift wardroom. Not mere empty curiosity; he was genuinely interested. Perhaps the white cloth that separated the stripes of gold lace on his sleeve also separated him from the ones who went out to risk, and often to die.

Masters watched the road curving again beyond the windscreen, the way her gloved hands controlled the wheel; one who was used to driving. Strange if you thought about it. It took so long to train drivers when there were more essential trades to learn that they were always asking for people who had already learned to drive, in that other world before the war. The leading Wren was one of them. He smiled to himself. He was not.

He considered Brayshaw's question and waited for the face to form in his mind: Lieutenant Clive Sewell, who seemed too old for his rank, and must have scraped through all the objections to achieve it. A serious, intelligent face, thinning hair, and a careful, deceptively hesitant manner of going about his work. He looked like a schoolmaster, which in fact he had been before joining the navy and volunteering for the misleadingly named Land Incident Section almost as soon as he had passed out of *King Alfred* as another Wavy Navy officer.

They had met several times, had even completed part of the mine warfare training at Roedean together. A man you could trust with your life.

He replied, 'The plane might be a minelayer. A Junkers 188. Not used as such normally, but you never know. Clive Sewell will have a pretty good idea. Otherwise it would all have been tidied up by now.'

He saw the driver's hair catch on her collar as she turned slightly. Listening? Or keeping her distance? She had applied for a transfer back to Plymouth, a base where she would be too busy to remember. To blame.

Brayshaw straightened his back and exclaimed, 'Here they are!' He seemed genuinely excited, free, for an hour or so, from Admiralty Fleet Orders, signals on every subject, inspections and official functions, and Chavasse's daily routine eccentricities, of which apparently there were many.

Another group of khaki figures and two parked jeeps, and, further along, a field ambulance, the red crosses very stark in the sunshine. Like blood.

There were also blue uniforms. Something of a relief.

Brayshaw said, 'May not take too long, eh?' He saw Masters' hand move to the scar on his face. He knew quite a lot about Lieutenant-Commander David Masters: how he had turned his back on the sea and had thrown himself into the private, deadly world of mine disposal, becoming one of *Vernon*'s leading authorities before arriving in Dorset. Dedicated, and yet something more. A man who would be attractive to women, although he had heard nothing about that.

Masters said, 'Here comes somebody who'll know.' He had not heard Brayshaw; he had been recalling Fawcett's comment. The mine was cheap to produce: it caused costly delays. It would certainly play hell with the exercise at Portland which he had been invited to observe. The admiral would be livid.

He studied the figure by the roadside as the car rolled to a halt. Tall and square, with a strong, weathered face, he wore no oilskin or protective clothing over his reefer jacket, as if he were oblivious to the bitter air. Short grey hair beneath his cap, and medals from another war. He carried the single thin stripe of a warrant officer on his sleeve, a Gunner (T) from the Portland team. Another old sweat. What might have happened without them?

The man saluted, fingers very straight to his peak, as if on parade. Chavasse would have approved.

He said, 'Bird, sir. I got the message that you were comin'. Managed to keep the gawkers away.' Clipped, formal. Efficient. In the navy anybody named Bird was always called Dicky. Masters could not imagine anyone who would dare with this formidable gunner.

He climbed out of the car and glanced around. A stone wall, and another big field beyond. It could have been anywhere.

Bird said, 'I'll show you, sir.' He pushed open a gate and indicated some deep mud. 'Watch yer step, sir.'

Masters turned and looked back. The sea in the background, the car with one door hanging open. Brayshaw had gone round to sit beside the driver, perhaps to get a better view.

A few of the soldiers were tossing stones at a tree stump in some sort of contest. Eager to go, bored with it. Only the quietly throbbing ambulance was a reminder.

He was still surprised that he could walk and climb without becoming breathless, or checked by the pain in his back, like those first months after he had left hospital.

Bird watched him grimly. 'Over there, sir. Follow that line of bushes.'

Masters studied the side of the field and took out his binoculars. A slight adjustment, and the scene seemed to leap at him. He took another breath and looked again. The aircraft must have been partially under control when it had plunged out of the dawn sky. The field must have appeared safe, and a desperate, perhaps injured pilot did not have much choice; the hedge would slow if not halt his landing. It was clear enough now in broad daylight. The last barricade of hedgerow was piled up and over a thick stone wall, an old building or barn, its crumbling beams just visible. But the wall was solid, had likely been here for a century or more.

The aircraft had been torn apart, but had not caught fire. Only the tail section looked undamaged, the swastika holding the light as if still unvanquished.

Bird said quietly, 'Mr. Sewell's over there now, sir.' Masters felt his eyes. 'Knows you well, 'e tells me.'

Masters nodded, lowering the binoculars to allow his mind to settle.

'Does he have his rating with him?'

'Aye, sir. There's a deep ditch over there, by the far gate. He's in there, intercom in use. Should be safe enough if . . .' He did not continue.

'I'll crawl over and have a word with him.' He saw the gunner's sudden concern, could almost hear what his orders had been on the subject. He added, 'The intercom, that's all.'

The gunner almost smiled. 'I should 'ave said, sir. One of the Jerries is, or was, still alive in that lot. But Mr. Sewell thought it best to keep things as quiet as possible, until . . .'

Masters saw the pensive, schoolmaster's face in his mind again.

39

It was what he would think. And all this time they had been stuck in crawling traffic. He stood up and said, 'Stay here, Mr. Bird. If I duck out of sight, you hit the dirt, right?'

Bird studied him again, impassively. 'Be right 'ere, sir.'

Masters walked deeper into the field. There was a fold across it which he had not noticed in the binoculars. It was deeply scarred, with fragments of metal flung on either side to mark where the aircraft had struck and rebounded for the last and fatal impact.

Two, perhaps three times he dropped to his knees, ready to cover his head and ears with his arms, but there was only silence, and the light breeze in the bushes. He wondered what the admiral would say if he eventually turned up with his uniform covered in mud. He stopped it right there. If you could joke about it, you were over the edge.

He waited, and then out of nowhere he heard someone speak. 'Got it, sir. I've put it all down!'

The ditch was a good choice; he was on top of it without even seeing it, or the upturned face only feet away. He put a warning finger to his lips and then lowered himself down beside the rating, Sewell's assistant. *All those other times.* The assistant was dressed in seaman's rig, a torpedoman's badge on one sleeve. Masters knew he had been with Sewell for some time, and yet he looked more like a boy than a man. He was kneeling on an oilskin, his cap nearby on his tool pack, and he wore a headset with speaker attached, something Sewell must have invented for the job. The usual intercom lay nearby, humming softly.

Masters took out his binoculars.

'All quiet?'

'Yes, sir.' The eyes moved slowly across his uniform, the rank. 'We knew someone was coming, sir, but . . .' He lifted his head and peered again through the bushes.

Masters recognized the anxiety, the strain. Waiting was always the worst part. Almost.

He said, 'What's your name, by the way? I'm Masters – I know your lieutenant pretty well.'

He saw the young sailor's breathing steady as he nodded and answered, 'I know, sir. He told me about you.' He looked down and Masters saw the drawing pad he was holding against his knee.

He noticed the hands too, well shaped, almost delicate. 'My name's Downie, sir.'

One hand flew to his switch as a voice came out of the intercom. 'He's there with you, is he?' Sewell, sounding clear and untroubled. 'Tell him I can't hang about any more. The kraut has just died, poor chap. I'm going to have a go.' The smallest pause. 'So be ready, all right?'

Downie said quietly, 'There were three in the crew, sir. Two died in the crash. The other one was too smashed up to move. And Mr. Sewell said it was too risky.'

Masters took the pad. 'May I?' Downie was already worried. His own arrival would not have helped.

The sketch was clear and professional. 'This it?'

Downie nodded, his head still half-turned, watching or listening it was hard to tell.

Masters studied the drawing and the calculated measurements, and pictured the two of them discussing it on the intercom, Sewell with a dying German beside him. About two feet long, not unlike the ordinary incendiary bombs which were released in thousands across towns, docklands and factories, anywhere within the bombers' range. But thicker, and heavier.

He heard Downie say, 'He said he'd never seen anything like it before, sir.'

'Neither have I.' He knew Downie was staring at him, perhaps surprised by the confidence. But he was seeing the aircraft in his mind. A Junkers, a stretched version of the original JU 88, which had made its mark as a bomber and reconnaissance plane in several theatres of war. But usually with a crew of four. A new role, then?

He raised his head again and trained the binoculars towards the wreckage, and the stone wall beyond. One small bomb. To be dropped on its own? No others had been reported. Something would have been found by now. He thought of Captain Chavasse, with Bumper Fawcett breathing down his neck. They could all wait.

He said, 'You're a bit young for this kind of work, aren't you?'

Casual and easy. For both their sakes.

41

'I'll be twenty in November, sir.' The defiance made him seem even younger. 'I did quite a few jobs for my father before I joined up. Wiring, that sort of thing.'

The speaker crackled again. 'Ready, Gordon? I'm going to take another measurement.'

Masters lifted the binoculars once more. 'I'll bet your parents got a shock when you joined this section.'

Downie's pencil moved quickly on the pad, but he said without raising his voice, 'It was because of them I transferred, sir. They were both killed in the big raid on Coventry.'

'I'm sorry. I didn't know.'

The youth looked at him. 'It's all right, sir. This is important to me, that's all.' He touched his switch. 'Shall I tell him it's *you* here, sir?'

Masters shook his head. 'It's hard enough without someone looking at your efforts.' He saw another face, that of the man who had been his own rating assistant, in those early days of 'the job'. He had gone back to general service, to a battleship. *For a quieter life*, he said when they had shaken hands for the last time. He had been a torpedo gunner's mate when last he had heard. A regular, he might end up with warrant rank like the formidable Mr. Bird back there on the road. He felt his mouth quiver. *Dicky.*

The silence seemed to press down on him. Waiting. Doing nothing to help.

'Have you always wanted to do this kind of work?'

The same quick, almost shy glance. 'I hoped to be a vet, sir. I'm good with animals.'

Masters watched his hands, supple, but stronger than they looked. He could well imagine him with animals.

The voice again, calm and unemotional.

'I'm having a go now. The first screw, and the little crescent-shaped catch I described. Have you got it down?'

Downie looked at his pad. 'Got it, sir.' Then he said, almost in a whisper, 'Take care, will you?'

But Masters saw that he had switched off the speaker before he had spoken. He tried to imagine what it must be like working in a half-wrecked plane with three dead men for company.

He studied Downie's drawings again. He had noted that the

bomb, or whatever it was, had no markings on it, unlike the usual unclassified information stamped or painted on such weapons. Experimental? Untested?

He shifted his hip and briefly felt the old pain in his back. What fate had drawn so many strangers together? A boy who had wanted to be a vet, a schoolmaster, a lieutenant he had once known who had been a comic on the stage at Blackpool. And Critchley, the adventurer, Fawcett had called him. *And me.*

The speaker said, 'Coming out now. Hold your breath, Gordon, my lad.'

Masters felt his jaw clench, remembering it exactly. That first, purposeful contact.

He saw Downie close his eyes tightly, then open them as if someone had spoken to him, reminded him.

He said, 'Past the gate, sir. A sort of stone bridge.'

Masters nodded. The last resort, and the first lesson if you wanted to survive. You always marked your line of escape. Just in case. For Critchley there had been nowhere to run, and he had known it. Must have done.

The speaker murmured, 'It's *out*, by God!' They could hear his harsh intake of breath. 'Now write this down.'

Masters watched the pencil. It was quite steady. Poised.

The next voice was that of a total stranger. Disbelief, anger, and a stark acceptance which was even beyond fear.

'Get out! It's blown!'

Masters' mind clicked like the switch. The drawing was a good one, Sewell's instructions precise. The fuse had become active; there was no time to reach the other ditch.

He swung round, horrified, as he saw the youth standing fully upright and staring at the wrecked Junkers.

He seized him and pulled him down, sprawling across him, fighting him as he tried to free himself, their faces inches apart.

The detonation was like a thunderclap, and the sky filled with flying debris and great clods of sodden soil which seemed to kick the breath from his lungs. Smoke too, and the sound of flames; the aircraft had finally exploded.

But through it all he heard Downie's voice. So close to his face that he could feel his anguish, the wetness on his skin.

And his words. *'He was my friend!'* Torn out of him, like an epitaph. It was something he would never forget.

Captain Hubert Chavasse stood with his feet apart, hands in his jacket pockets, the protruding thumbs jutting forward like horns. The room was very bright, and slightly hazy with smoke although Masters could not recall seeing anyone pausing to light a cigarette. Outside the shuttered windows it was dark, and had been for some time; he could hardly believe that it was still the same day.

He glanced at the others, Brayshaw, the captain's secretary, making notes, clarifying an occasional problem if Chavasse threw him a question. Two lieutenants from Operations, a Wren second officer representing the signals department, another Wren, a petty officer, legs crossed, taking shorthand.

Chavasse stared around the room. 'Nothing left out, I think? Countermeasures Section informed from the outset. The boffins from *Vernon* will have been and gone by now. Not much left to sift through, I'd have thought.' He hurried on. 'Rear-Admiral Fawcett is fully in the picture, and we can expect him down here tomorrow. I sometimes wonder if he ever sleeps! So we must be up and about early. I'll not have anybody finding fault with *my* establishment.' He looked at the clock. 'So, if there's nothing further . . .'

One of the lieutenants asked something about the army being included in his report; Masters barely heard him.

He was remembering the blazing fuel, the fragments of the fuselage flung about like so much rubbish. Chavasse had been right. *Not much to sift through.* A sickening job at the best of times, when there was nothing at all after an explosion, an 'incident'. Rags and torn flesh, but the boffins from *Vernon* were hardened to it. They needed to be.

When he had given his own account he had been conscious of the utter silence. Only the Wren's pencil had moved as he related what he had seen and found at the field where a man he had known had been killed.

Perhaps, like so many, Lieutenant Clive Sewell, ex-schoolmaster, would have died for nothing. But the drawings and notes on his assistant's pad, coupled with any scrap of material evidence the

44

boffins might find in that blackened, grisly confusion might in the end save lives.

He had been aware of Chavasse's irritation when he had added, 'In my opinion, it was a new type of weapon, unknown to us until today. Strong enough to be dropped from an aircraft without exploding on impact, but small enough to be used against moving targets, ships or personnel.'

Chavasse had snapped, 'We can't jump to conclusions. We don't know anything for certain.' It had been an open rebuke.

Masters had said, 'But for Lieutenant Sewell's persistence, and the information he relayed to his assistant, that might be true, sir. But I believe we have discovered something important, perhaps vital.'

He had sat down, and had seen Brayshaw give him an almost imperceptible nod. Sympathy or support, he could not decide which.

Brayshaw had stayed with him all day. They had continued on their way to Portland, where the flag lieutenant had told them the proposed exercise had been postponed, if not cancelled, due to the incident, and that the admiral was either too angry or too busy to hold the meeting. He stared at the shuttered window nearest to him. He would have to go back to that house again. He could not recall if he had told the driver, or even if he had eaten anything. Every bone and muscle was aching, but he knew he would not rest or sleep. *We obey orders, we do as we're told, we live, we die.* Was it that simple?

Across the table, Lieutenant-Commander Philip Brayshaw carefully folded yet another batch of signals and tapped them into shape.

He had seen the strain on Masters' face as he had described the burned-out aircraft, and the explosion before that, and shared the emotion of Sewell's last words. But even that had been forced into the background by what he had seen for himself following the thunderclap of the explosion. Soldiers running with spades and extinguishers, the big warrant officer calling his own men but striding off without waiting for them. And the ambulance, suddenly coming to life and moving down the road very slowly, as if it had a will of its own. Brayshaw had still been sitting in the front passenger seat, the door wide open; he had long legs, and there was a better view of the field from the front of the Wolseley.

The Wren driver had not spoken, other than to answer a question he had asked. He did not know her very well, but had seen her often when she was driving some V.I.P. A very attractive girl, he thought, but withdrawn, even hostile if somebody tried to get too chummy. A good driver, too. He had heard somewhere that her father was a doctor, and he had been the one to insist that she learn to drive just before the war.

The explosion had come without warning. He could vaguely recall twigs being ripped from some of the bare trees as if caught in a strong gale and earth and mud spattering the car's roof, although he knew they were a mile or more from the fallen aircraft. And then the smoke, drifting over them and staining the sky, like something obscene.

He had felt the sudden grip on his wrist, her gloved hand bruising the skin. He had been torn between trying to çomfort her and finding out what had happened. All he could remember were her eyes, wide, but not afraid. Pleading, unable to get the words out of her mouth.

He had said something, he did not know what; there were never the right words anyway. Like those carefree faces in the mess you never got to know, but wished you had after they had bought it in some incident, or even during a practice run with an explosive device.

And then they had appeared by the sagging gate, although he knew that some time must have elapsed. Masters, the binoculars swinging around his neck, his uniform covered with mud . . . Brayshaw could see him now, as if it was still happening. Pausing, offering his hand to a young sailor as he lurched against the gatepost.

Masters had called to him, 'Stay put, Philip! It's all over, I'm afraid.' Then he had opened the rear door and said, 'Get in. You've had about enough for one day.'

The rating had stared at him, had opened his mouth to protest or refuse, but instead had climbed mutely across to the seat behind the driver. Some memory or instinct had made him stare at the leather and try to wipe away the mud with his sleeve.

46

The Wren had spoken for the first time. 'Don't worry about that. It's due for a clean, anyway.' She had tugged off her glove and reached round to touch his face. No words this time.

Brayshaw thought it was the bravest and the saddest thing he had seen for a very long time.

The warrant officer had arrived and more orders had been shouted.

He had heard Masters say, 'No, Mr. Bird, this one is riding with us to Portland. Tell the transport P.O., will you?'

It was hard to accept in this stale office which had once been a classroom. So calmly said; he could have been arranging a taxi for a run ashore.

By the time they reached the base at Portland everyone seemed to know what had happened. Some of the sailors had gathered as if to greet them, but there had been no sound except for the car's tyres on the cobbles.

The flag lieutenant had been waiting, harassed and concerned, a master-at-arms close by, his eyes on the young torpedoman called Downie.

Then Brayshaw had seen something else he would not forget. Masters had turned as Downie had climbed from the car and said quietly, 'I shall be leaving in an hour or so. I broke the rules today by attending an incident without back-up. I shall not hear the last of it.' No smile, no emotion, and yet Brayshaw had seen the youth, for that was all he appeared to be, look up for the first time. Dazed, puzzled, anxious. It was all there.

He said, 'Me, sir?'

Masters reached out and touched his arm.

'If you'd like that.'

Brayshaw had been unable to hear the reply. He doubted if anyone did.

But two hours later when they returned to the gates Downie had been waiting with his bag and hammock. He had climbed into the car, beside the driver this time, and they had driven along the coast road in silence.

Brayshaw noticed that Downie had not looked back.

The meeting was over, papers were being packed away, Chavasse was snapping his fingers for his steward. He rarely drank in front of subordinates. A careful man, Brayshaw had decided long ago.

Masters waited for him and said, 'You must be dog-tired, Philip. Not at all your scene, I'd have thought.'

He was smiling, so that he looked roughly his age again, the strain temporarily diminished. But it did not reach his eyes.

Brayshaw halted by the door.

'That was a fine thing you did for the lad. He'll never forget it.'

Masters looked past him into the waiting darkness. A very long day . . . He thought of what Brayshaw had said, and Downie's frantic cry. *He was my friend.*

He said, 'Sometimes it's not enough just to survive.'

Brayshaw was still gazing after him when the door closed.

The car was waiting by the 'quarterdeck' and she opened the door for him as he walked past the flagless mast.

For a moment he hesitated, feeling the tension, the barrier. The guilt.

He said, 'I was told you had asked for a transfer.'

She ran her glove along the top of the door.

'I changed my mind.' She turned away. 'Sir.'

'I'm glad.'

He was asleep before the car had reached the main road.

Leading Wren Lovatt watched the looming bushes and walls in the tiny, shielded headlights. Nothing had changed, despite what had happened. A man had died, and she had seen others behave in a way she had not seen before, or shared. She tried not to think of her brother. She was afraid to.

Something moved swiftly from left to right and she braked. A quick blink of eyes, most likely a fox, and it was gone.

She glanced in the driving mirror, but there was only darkness. He was still asleep, or pretending to be.

She thought suddenly of her last leave, how it had disturbed her. Petersfield, a small market town, had always been her home, until the war had changed everything. A friendly place where people went about their business without fuss, except on market days, which had created the bustle and excitement she and her brother Graham had loved as children.

On that last leave she had been unsettled by the way her parents had been unable to accept what had happened to their only son. His room was as he had left it, and there was an album of his photographs on the old coffee table.

Her father had lived in the area all his life; her mother had met him when she had been a nurse at the local hospital. They were respected, trusted and, in many cases, envied.

Her hands tightened on the wheel. Like the car, for instance. Even now, her father as a doctor was privileged to have a petrol allowance, which he would never abuse, of that she was certain.

It was as if Graham would still come home, when things settled again. In some way she understood it, or had tried to. He had been so full of life, always surrounded by friends, good at everything. Doing what he liked most, rowing – he had pulled an oar in the college eight at university – and dinghy sailing. He was into everything. Maybe that was it; she had always been a little in awe of her brother. *We all were.*

Her mother adored him; she could only recall one occasion when she had expressed any criticism.

Graham had left university to join the navy as soon as he could after the outbreak of war. He had been selected as a C.W. candidate, for wartime commission, but even there his impetuous gift of independence had made him volunteer instead for the submarine service. It had meant that his chance of a commission would be delayed, if not forfeited altogether.

Her mother had said, 'I can't understand you sometimes, Graham. So full of ideas and things you want to do! How can you bear to be sealed up in one of those things?'

Did she ever remember those words now?

She glanced in the mirror again, recalling her disbelief when she had been told about Commander Critchley's replacement. She should have requested a transfer right then back to Plymouth, to apply for Wrens' motor boat crew, which so many of the girls wanted. Speeding around with mail and stores among the ships and men who were daily fighting the war at sea, in Western Approaches and across the breadth of the Atlantic.

Her mother would never understand what it was like to be a part of it, the link which held them all together. Some remained alone, like the man behind her. A man she had been prepared to blame, even to hate, who was compelled by something far stronger than she could ever know. Yet still able to give a part of himself, as she had seen with the young sailor Downie. She had driven plenty of officers who would have gone about their affairs without giving it a passing thought.

She saw the familiar stone gates of the farm; the house was next.

At least the driving gave her a kind of independence. Some of the girls thought she was a bit stuck-up, even prudish. She had told herself that she was not touched by some of the escapades they recounted to shock her . . .

She said, 'We're here, sir.'

After today she knew she wanted to be a part of it. Like a challenge. She half smiled. Or a warning.

She felt his hand on her shoulder, as if she had spoken aloud, or he had read her thoughts.

'Don't get out. I've kept you up long enough.' The door opened and shut, and she saw him standing by the car. Such a short time, and yet she had noticed the respect others had for him. Even Brayshaw, who knew everybody, and whom the girls called 'Old Sweetie' out of earshot, had been unable to hide his emotion when the explosion had shaken the car, or his relief when Masters and Downie had appeared by the gate.

She recalled Critchley, his amusement, the way he had looked at her. Like the two Italians who had stared at her in the road.

Masters was studying the sky. There was more cloud now, but no moon for the bombers.

'I'll get another driver for tomorrow. Early start, it seems.'

He did not need to tell her, or to talk at all. He did not want to go into the house, with Coker fussing around all the time; she sensed that he wanted to be alone. She tried to think of her brother, the dream she had often had, the submarine lying in perpetual darkness. How could she have misunderstood? Being alone was the one thing he had feared.

'I'll be here, sir.'

She reversed carefully and edged out onto the road. Somehow she knew he had not moved.

She belonged.

4

Brought Together

Leading Seaman Dougie Bass, ML366's killick coxswain, eased
the spokes half a turn, this way and that, his glance dropping to
the faintly lit compass. West-by-south. For some, the compass
card might be difficult to read; to others, newcomers, it seemed
a glaring invitation to be attacked.

Like the even, steady motion, he was used to it. He half listened
to the sounds around and beneath him, his trained ear seeking
anything unusual.

His salt-encrusted lips smiled. In the early days some people
had asked him how he had become so accustomed to the changing
moods of a small, fast vessel. *After being a civvie?* He had never
bothered to explain. Now he did not need to. But anybody who
could serve soup when the old *Bournemouth Belle* was racing
across points at sixty miles an hour soon learned to keep his
balance. Or pouring a dry sherry for some first class passenger
when you were shooting through a tunnel, to the exact level and
without spilling a drop. He either got it right, or found himself on
the dole.

Now he could imagine being and doing nothing else. Even his
hands, resting almost loosely on the spokes, were as hard as any
true seaman's. And his hair, longer than regulation requirement,
was the mark of a veteran. Big ships were different. Here, in
Harry Tate's Navy as they called it, it was something else. But
if any outsider tossed an unfriendly remark, it would usually end
in a brawl.

Neither moon nor stars defined the line between sea and sky. They had been to Portsmouth, as part of the escort for two landing craft, something to do with forthcoming exercises. He was glad to be rid of them. He could not imagine what they must be like to steer and handle in any kind of a sea.

Dark, and yet he knew where every man was, or should be at this time. Gun crews fore and aft, Bob Chitty the signalman a few feet away on the starboard side of the low bridge, night glasses at the ready. If the boat moved too heavily into a sudden trough he might hear the faint clink of metal from the twin machine-guns, which Chitty would swap for his lamp and flags at the drop of a hat. Worked in a fairground at one time, on and off, as he had put it, when he had worked at all. But show him a blinking signal, or put him behind the two Brownings, and he was another man.

Like the Oerlikon gunner just abaft the bridge, his tuneless whistle drowned out by the muted growl of the motors: Titch Kelly, not much between the ears, and one who had been in trouble more times than that, until 366. But of course he was from Liverpool. In the navy it was always the same, as it was if you'd sprung from Birmingham, for some reason. Scouse or Brummie, and it would be, 'I'll be watching you, my lad!' He had even heard the Jaunty down at their makeshift base say something of the sort.

He heard someone clear his throat and smiled. Allison, the new Jimmy the One. The smile broadened to a grin. *Tobias.*

Seemed nice enough, but you never could tell so soon. Anyway, the lads would have their little jokes. The smile faded. Until it got out of hand. 'Killick' coxswain carried its own responsibility. And trust went both ways. There had been some talk of possible promotion, a petty officer's course. What would the old-timers on the *Bournemouth Belle* say if he turned up in fore-and-aft rig, gold badges and all?

He felt the same sense of uncertainty, but it went far deeper than that. Like being here in the Channel . . . He had started in Coastal Forces on the east coast, Grimsby, Lowestoft, Hull, places that smelled of fish. Small ports which had become a first line of defence, and attack. Harwich and Felixstowe combined were the main base of the convoy escorts, destroyers and sloops. He thought of the Number One who had just left them. And the Glory Boys. Right down as far as the Dover Strait, Hellfire Corner as the war correspondents liked to call it. They didn't have to sneak the convoys through, with the krauts just on the other side of a twenty-mile strip of water. The lads called it Shit Street. It suited.

He thought he heard voices from the chart space below and forward of his position. The skipper and the new boss, the two-and-a-half from *Vernon*, Masters. They seemed to be getting on well enough, so far. But then, they had both been through the mill.

He considered promotion again. Face it, he thought, you don't want to leave the boat. Not after all . . .

The sub-lieutenant moved up beside him, his duffle coat pale against the sky and sea. Brand-new, probably. Like him.

'The Needles are abeam, estimate about ten miles, 'Swain.'

Bass nodded, his eyes on the faintly lit compass. 'Who needs radar, eh, sir?' and for a moment he thought he had gone too far, then Allison said, 'She handles well.' He reached out to steady himself as the hull lifted and dipped again, spray drifting over the bridge like gentle rain.

Bass had seen him the previous day when they had left the inlet, wearing his second-best jacket, but the single wavy stripe was still like new, and the trousers also. He had heard the skipper say cheerfully, 'Grey flannel bags are my advice, Sub.'

Sub. Bass had noticed that, too. As if the skipper could not yet bring himself to forget Harry Bryant. A good first lieutenant unless you crossed him. Then, you thought a cliff had fallen on your head.

Anyway, they were heading back to base. Three hours, maybe more if there was other traffic around Weymouth. He licked his lips. Time for some 'ki'. The skipper would already have thought of that.

Steps on the short ladder, two darker shapes against the new paintwork.

'Some ki, 'Swain?'

Bass grinned.

'Jarvis, shift yerself! An' don't spill any of it!'

He wiped his face with his hand. No, he did not want to leave her . . . not yet in any case. That was what he always said.

Foley glanced at his passenger. 'Getting rather lively, sir.' And to Bass, 'Alter course a point to port, 'Swain. The currents hereabouts are a bit bothersome.'

Masters said, 'You know this area well. Good thing, on this kind of work.' He had learned quite a lot about 366's commanding officer, what he had achieved both before and after getting his own boat. He had survived the loss of his last; they had been shot up somewhere in the North Sea. His skipper and seven of the ratings had been killed. It had been bitterly cold, freezing, when the rest of them had baled out, their only support a small life raft. Another had died before a rescue launch had found them, eleven hours later.

Masters had asked him about it, why he had not received a decoration of some kind. Foley had just given a distant smile.

'Well, you know this regiment, sir. You don't get a gong just for staying alive.'

For an instant Masters had imagined it was aimed personally at him. But he knew, even after so short a time with this young officer, that Foley would be unable to tell you a lie to your face. He wore the blue and white ribbon of the Distinguished Service Cross, but, like the smile, it seemed as if it were shared with the boat, and the rest of his small company.

Foley heard the rattle of the cocoa fanny, and imagined his men throughout the hull reaching for their chipped and battered mugs.

Petty Officer Ian Shannon, the Chief in this vessel, knew more about the three-shaft Hall-Scott motors than anybody. Withdrawn and taciturn, in his thirties, he was the oldest man aboard. He had managed a small garage on the North Circular Road outside London, and had wanted to buy a small café-restaurant to adjoin it. The navy, the war, and separation had put paid to that, and he never spoke of it now. His wife had gone off with an American serviceman. It was only evident when the mail boat came alongside, and Shannon received nothing.

His second hand in the engine room was Stoker Petty Officer Maginnis, who had served in a light cruiser, but had changed to something livelier when the chance came his way. Larger than life, always ready with a tot of rum and some boozy song, he should have got on Shannon's nerves. Chalk and cheese . . . maybe what they both needed.

Foley was thinking of his conversation with Masters. A man who thought deeply about every aspect of the job, quick to ask a question if he needed something clarified. Interested, and interesting. It was hard to believe there were only four years between them.

Foley knew about the most recent incident, and the officer who had been killed. He even thought he might have met him at some time; the navy was like that. And the young seaman Masters had taken under his wing as his assistant was on board too, acting as messenger. In Motor Launch 366, everybody had at least two jobs.

Masters was saying, 'When we get in, I'd like to discuss the exercise with you.'

Foley turned swiftly as a lookout called, 'Light, starboard bow, sir! Low down!'

It was Signalman Chitty. It would be.

Foley pressed his mouth to the voicepipe. 'Chief, dead slow, watch your revs. There's something in the drink.' It was as if he had shouted, but he knew he had not even raised his voice.

He reached out and took Allison's arm. 'Pass the word, Toby. Nice and easy . . . Got it?' He felt him nod and released him.

It could be anything. *Never take chances.*

He pictured the chart they had been studying, well-worn where it was folded over the table; shelf was a better description. Frayed by countless calculations and fixes, stained at the edges with circles from mugs like the one he was still holding. Part of the boat. Of himself.

He glanced at the sky. In two hours it would be daylight. In three or less, they would be alongside.

Allison asked, 'What is it, d'you think?'

Foley held out his hand and felt somebody take the mug. 'A corpse, most likely.' He sensed that Masters had turned towards him. Surprised, perhaps, at the unnecessary brutality of his answer.

He moved to the opposite side of the bridge and stared down at the sea alongside, the bow wave, snaking away, but not even breaking. Black glass. He thought of all the other such lights he had seen. They didn't last for long; usually they didn't need to. Sometimes a couple clinging in a last embrace. But one had to die first. And occasionally they were in groups.

Allison said quietly, 'I had to pick up a man who'd been washed overboard in a gale. We lowered a whaler.' Nobody said anything and he fell silent again.

Masters said, 'What do you reckon, Chris?'

The casual use of his name caught Foley off balance. It was probably the timing: returning to base, the last hours when men became too relaxed, even careless. Thinking of tomorrow. Of somebody.

He answered, 'An airman, I expect, sir. One of theirs, one of ours – either way, trying to get home. I'll let Air-Sea Rescue know the score later on.'

He moved to the compass and peered at it, his eyes showing briefly in the feeble glow. It was routine. There was no point in losing time to stop and haul a corpse aboard. Unless . . .

Masters said, 'You're not happy about it?'

Foley shook his head. 'You never know.' He looked at the small, bobbing light. Suppose there was someone clinging to life by a thread, still able to hear, to feel the muted tremble of the boat's engines. Then being left, the bitter cold reaching for the kill.

I should never need reminding.

He said, 'Tell Harrison to stand by, starboard side forrard. I'll try and touch alongside.' He reached out as the anonymous figure made to scurry away. 'Tell him, boathook and net if need be. I'm not lowering a raft.'

Harrison would not need telling. A leading seaman and gunlayer on the quick-firing three-pounder, he was a first-class hand. He had pulled enough men from the sea in the months they had been together. Foley gripped a stanchion. *In this boat.*

'Chief? Be ready to stop, port and starboard outer. Dead slow until I give the word.' He heard Shannon's clipped acknowledgement, could picture him down there with his dials and levers and the pulsing heat of his three charges. And the knowledge that he would be the first to brew up if the worst happened. There was scarcely enough room to stand upright.

Another look at the sky. Maybe his eyes were sharper now after

56

the shaded chart-light below. He stared astern. Patches of grey, the dying wash. Hardly anything. He bit his lip. But visible.

'*Now*, Chief.'

The motion increased immediately, the hull swaying and rolling in a succession of troughs. He could see black shapes on the foredeck, shining faintly like seals in their oilskin coats. Then he saw the dinghy. It was right under the starboard bow, rising and falling, sliding away when the boathook tried to snare it. Someone was clinging to the low guardrail where the scrambling net was lashed for a full-scale rescue attempt. The little light was suddenly extinguished, and he thought he heard Bass give a sigh of relief.

It was not being callous. There was no point in hanging about, asking for it. And they trusted him.

But it seemed to be out of his hands. '*All stop!*'

The motion increased still further. Foley heard someone swear as a mug and spoon rattled across the deck covering, and a man slipped on the Oerlikon mounting abaft the bridge.

All the sounds of sea and movement seemed to crowd into and over the hull. Foley seized the screen, willing himself to concentrate, to respond to something which had reached far beyond mere instinct.

He felt the chill at his spine despite the layers of clothing, a sharpness, a premonition which something inside him had refused to ignore.

It was impossible to gauge the bearing or what distance it might be. But it was there. The *thrumm . . . thrumm . . . thrumm . . .* of those powerful, deep-throated engines he had learned to hate and fear on the east coat. E-Boats.

Dougie Bass had picked it up too. 'Jerry's about, sir!'

Foley gestured quickly and heard someone hurry forward to warn Leading Seaman Harrison.

In his mind, he could even see the old chart. *E-Boats.* From one of the Channel groups this time. Two of them, but one much stronger and steadier than the other. *A lame duck.* In a fight somewhere earlier, and now creeping back to base, Le Havre probably, or even as far as Cherbourg. Damaged or not, they could have ripped this boat to pieces with their heavier armament and superior speed.

They might still have seen or heard something. Enough to bring one or more to investigate.

Minutes passed, but it seemed like hours, and Foley knew that the danger was gone. This time.

The messenger returned. 'The chap's dead, sir. One of ours. Badly shot up.'

Foley felt the seaman watching him intently through the darkness. He could see the shape of his face now, and Bass's left hand moving the lifeless wheel. Waiting to move. To get the screws racing again.

Trying to get home. But for the dead airman, drifting alone in his little dinghy, they might all have died this morning. They were safe now.

'Tell Harrison to . . .' He looked at the compass, so faint in the growing light. *Cast him adrift, make a signal to Air-Sea Rescue. Nothing more we can do.*

But he said, 'Go forrard, Number One. Get the airman aboard. Somebody will be waiting for him.'

Masters watched him move closer to the voicepipes again. The dinghy was already spiralling abeam, caught in a surge of foam as the starboard motor roared into life.

He saw Foley lift his hand to his battered cap; there was a rising breeze now. But it looked, just for an instant, like a last salute.

Rear-Admiral Fawcett clapped one hand to his ear as another explosion crashed and re-echoed around the cliffs like a full-scale bombardment.

'God, aren't they *finished*?' He glared at the drifting smoke. 'I do believe the bloody marines get a kick out of doing that!'

Masters saw some khaki figures scampering down a steep crevasse in the cliff below them. They appeared to be skipping from ledge to ledge, weapons and tackle glinting occasionally in the misty sunlight.

Portland Bill. Nobody had ever really explained it. A great five-mile spur of rock and stone jutting due south into the Channel. Nothing grew on it, and it was linked to the mainland only by a narrow causeway and a road that overlooked Portland Harbour. In other times convicts from the local prison worked here, cutting the stone that eventually formed the pavements of London and many other cities. The Bill was the southernmost point of England. Masters smiled. Only their lordships would have dreamed up a place like this for a base and an anti-submarine establishment.

Fawcett was saying, 'I was a little hot under the collar hearing about your involvement when Sewell bought it. No heroics, remember? Can't afford any more unfortunate accidents.' The blue eyes steadied. 'But Captain Chavasse seemed fairly optimistic. He quite surprised me, in fact.'

Masters saw a motor launch, not unlike 366, moving away from the land, a two-flag signal whipping from her yard. The exercise was over. There were some senior American officers at Portland today. Everything had to go just right. He watched the ML until it had rounded a jagged pillar of rock, and thought of Foley and his company of volunteers. Men from all walks of life, garage manager, milkman, telegraph boy, clerk, even a railway restaurant car waiter. Now, they were the true professionals.

Fawcett made up his mind. 'Actually, the boffins are quite pleased with their findings, such as they were. The drawings were the decisive factor, I think. Sorry to lose Sewell, of course, but not in vain this time.'

Masters waited. It was like getting blood out of a stone. 'An anti-personnel device, sir?'

Fawcett's manner was characteristically evasive. 'You'll hear soon enough through Operations, but I'll tell you now. There have been a few setbacks on the Italian front, another new weapon.' He hurried on, as if afraid of saying too much. 'Our people have known about German experiments with rockets – they began just after France threw in the towel, if not sooner. There have also been reports from the Russian front, but, well, you never know.' He seemed to come to a decision. 'They used guided rockets against the bombarding squadron. H.M.S. *Warspite* was hit by one of them and had two near misses. The Old Lady was badly damaged, lot of casualties, boilers flooded – she only just managed to crawl out of range before another attack. She was taken in tow, but she'll never be the same again.'

It was rare for Bumper Fawcett to reveal such feeling.

But it was like that in the navy: good ships and bad ones,

and nobody could ever explain why. Happy ships, and those which brought nothing but trouble to captain and company alike, with the defaulters' table always fully occupied. *Warspite*, the veteran battleship which had been at Jutland, and had served with distinction ever since, was always a happy ship. Even if you had never laid eyes on her, you heard stories about her characters, and the admirals who had hoisted their flags over her. Admiral Cunningham, the C-in-C Mediterranean, and perhaps the most popular flag officer on the list, would feel it badly. She had been his flagship.

Fawcett added angrily, 'A rocket, fired from an aircraft and *guided* onto its target. Some American ships were hit, too. A cruiser was in a sinking condition when I last heard.' He gestured with his cap towards the distant buildings. 'I'll lay odds that's what our American allies are discussing right now, what?'

They both turned as if some signal had been given and walked back along the cliff path.

Fawcett said, 'In Sicily, the weather and some stupid mistakes were the problem. Salerno and beyond, we've got rockets to expect. In France, for instance, where we shall have tidal variations to contend with,' he shot him a glance, 'which they do not have in the Med, landing vessels will be in even greater danger if the bombarding squadrons can be held at a distance!'

The mood changed and he raised his hand to one of his aides, who was hurrying towards them.

'About bloody time! The gin pennant must be hoisted at last!'

Masters said, 'What about Intelligence? They must have been following it.'

They both stopped, and he saw the ML reappear far below them. He thought of the inlet, lost in the mist along the coast, as it had been the morning when Foley had brought his boat alongside the makeshift pier. Despite the hour there had suddenly been crowds of shadowy figures, coming to take 366's lines, or to watch in silence. One seaman had shaving soap on his face; another, a cook, had been carrying an empty coffee pot, which he had not appeared to notice. Signals must have called an ambulance; its crew went about their routine with detached efficiency.

Masters had seen the airman before he was taken ashore. A

pilot officer, young, early twenties, if that, with one of those ridiculous moustaches beloved by the R.A.F, the 'Brylcream Boys'. Pathetic but somehow moving, he had thought, with the moustache plastered across the face, the eyes fixed and staring as at the moment of death.

A telegram, a letter from his C.O., a few belongings to be sent home. It was all too common.

Masters contained his sudden anger. Being with Foley and his company, in a living, moving ship of war, no matter how small, he had been doing something. It was all that really mattered in the end.

Fawcett said, 'I'm in touch with D.N.I., naturally. Commander Critchley was too – right up his street, I'd have said. I'll chase them up anyway. About time they did something.' He waited as a lieutenant appeared around a sandbag barrier. 'There you are. I thought you'd never get here!'

Masters followed them in silence. *Critchley*. Dead or alive, he was never far away. The rest was all too vague: hold-ups in the Italian campaign, and the unforeseen air-to-surface guided rockets. Fawcett was right about one thing; any invasion in the future would be doomed without full covering fire from the sea.

No heroics, Bumper Fawcett had warned. He thought of the experiments he had watched at *Vernon*, and in deep bunkers which would trap those working on some new time-fuse or suspected booby-trap. Where there were risks men would take them, if they thought it worthwhile. Men like Sewell, and the others he had known over the months. And Critchley, who had perhaps become careless or over-confident. That was as fatal as the sapper's boot on the landmine still marked by its weatherworn cross.

Once more he thought of Foley. A man with instinct, that second sense born of experience and danger. Foley was good, unassumingly so. No conceit or bravado. A rare balance.

They walked through a side gate, and more salutes greeted them; they parted to allow the rear-admiral to pass unhindered. Masters hated this part of it. Too much to drink. False bonhomie. The post-mortem over the exercise they had watched might easily be lost in paperwork.

A lieutenant, vaguely familiar, stood his ground and said, 'Excuse me, sir.'

Fawcett frowned. 'Laker, isn't it? Operations?'

The lieutenant looked uncomfortable. 'Lawson, sir.'

Masters remembered him. He was one of the officers present when he had been describing the incident and Sewell's death, when Captain Chavasse had been so scathing. He had since changed his tune, according to Fawcett.

'Well, what is it?'

'Just had a signal, sir. I was told to inform you personally.' But he was looking at Masters.

A steward hurried past with a tray of glasses and Fawcett said, 'Get on with it, man!'

'Another bomb has been found, sir. Just outside Bridport. The sappers have sealed off the area.'

Masters recalled Sewell's voice on the intercom, the young sailor's supple fingers sketching the device, his private debt to his dead parents.

He said, 'Bridport. How far is that?'

The lieutenant looked relieved. It was already out of his hands.

'About twenty miles, sir. I've got a fast car and escort. I even brought your rating along.'

Masters looked at the rear-admiral. Any agitation or uncertainty was gone.

'You deal with it, but keep me informed all the way.' Fawcett turned to the lieutenant. 'Now, Mr. *Lawson*, let me see the signals, and be ready to connect me with D.N.I. the moment I tell you.'

He tapped Masters' arm. 'Remember what I told you. You're doing well. Keep it that way.'

Masters nodded. *No heroics.* 'I'll not be on my own, sir.'

Fawcett watched him leave, and walked purposefully through double doors which opened onto a throng of khaki and blue. He smiled as his cap was taken by a steward, and took a glass from another's tray as he passed.

One step at a time.

Lieutenant Chris Foley strode out of the Operations building and paused in the pale sunshine to regain his composure. The

Operations section looked harmless enough from the outside: it had originally been three small cottages which had been knocked into one, but inside it was like a madhouse. There was a flap on, and everyone seemed to speaking at once. Captain Chavasse was there; Foley had seen him holding a pair of headphones loosely to one ear, while speaking tersely into another handset at the same time.

When he had eventually found an officer who was senior and interested enough in his problem, he had received no satisfaction. ML366 was at twenty-four hours' operational stand-by. It was just one of those things. The word came from high up; that was all there was to it.

Except that he had granted his boat's small company local leave. Not that it presented any real problem; there was only one pub in the village, and no transport unless you hitched a lift to get to anywhere more exciting. Or the wet canteen right here at the base where the NAAFI supplied all the beer any Jack could wish for. Senior rates were to have been given overnight leave, if they had anywhere to go, and there was one, the boat's Chief, Petty Officer Shannon. If they were under orders to move it was important, and the proposed exercises had taken second place. If the Chief was nowhere to be found . . . He almost collided with the captain's secretary, Lieutenant-Commander Brayshaw, who was carrying an armful of files.

Brayshaw was always easy to talk to. And that was as far as it went, although he must have been tempted a few times when he heard what some of the more junior officers said and thought about his lord and master Chavasse.

Foley said, 'A flap on?'

'Something to do with another device, I understand. All very hush-hush at the moment.'

Foley smiled ruefully. 'Which means it's all over the south coast by now!'

'Anything I can do? I'm told that you're on operational stand-by. Rather short notice, I thought.'

Foley nodded. Brayshaw missed nothing.

He said, 'I've got my cox'n and a couple of hands rounding up the libertymen. It's the Chief I'm bothered about.'

63

Brayshaw pursed his lips. 'Overnight leave?' and raised an eyebrow. 'In *this* place?'

'I heard there's another pub somewhere. On the way to Lulworth, I think they said.' He clenched his fist. 'It might as well be Scapa Flow for all the chance I've got. I wanted to get him working on some new gear – I thought we'd have plenty of time at the rate things are moving here.'

Brayshaw smiled. 'You do pretty well, from what I hear.' He was serious again. 'I think I might help. If it's the pub I remember, I can take you there myself.' He paused. 'If you like, that is.'

They both turned and stared at the Humber staff car, its Royal Marine driver standing beside it, cleaning one of the windows.

Brayshaw said gravely, 'I have a couple of errands to run. Lulworth may well be on the route. Seven or eight miles, no problem. I'll leave word with my chief writer.'

He hurried away.

Foley stared towards the anchorage, more crowded than ever now. A flap on . . . Bass had told him some cars with red-painted wings and motor cycle escorts had been seen speeding away on the Weymouth road. Another device, as Brayshaw had described it, maybe like the one that had killed an officer from Portland, which Masters had been sent to investigate. Brayshaw had been there, too.

He thought of his new Number One, and wondered how long it would take for him to find true confidence. Allison was eager and intelligent, but he knew nothing yet of the total dependency required in a small warship. He could be thrown into command on their first operation. He heard Brayshaw returning and was glad of it.

The marine driver's eyes moved over his extra passenger, pausing briefly on the D.S.C. It was apparently enough.

The gates opened and Brayshaw spoke to the master-at-arms nearby. Through the open window Foley heard the distant wail of air raid sirens. The balloons would be up, the A.A. guns alerted. Hit-and-run raiders no longer had it all their own way, at least not in daylight; there was a new squadron of fighters a mile or two inland. He recalled the dead pilot officer, the fixed stare. He might have been one of them.

No use going over it again. He concentrated on his new orders, or what he knew of them. Two other MLs would be joining 366, coming round from Poole. The senior officer was Lieutenant-Commander Tony Brock, R.N.V.R. like himself, and said to be in line for a new flotilla all of his own. Foley had come up against Brock several times. Big, like his reputation, a man who had once skippered a luxury yacht for some rich Greek before the war. A man who had a way with women, if half of what was said of him was true. An old R.N.R. hand had once remarked on that aspect of Brock, 'Like a rat up a pump! Anything in a skirt!'

But he was brave enough. Perhaps too brave, if that were possible.

He recalled Harry Bryant's parting comment on Critchley. *I could be wrong about him, too.*

He tried to relax and watch the road across the marine's shoulder. *People look at you and they think it's easy. Because you don't appear to worry. Because that's how they see you.*

He recalled his last leave, and the others before that. His father had served in the trenches in the Great War and had been gassed, like so many, when all the rules had been thrown away. He wanted so much to do something to help the war effort, but even the Home Guard had reluctantly turned him down. A civil servant, he now worked for the Ministry of Food, perhaps essential, but not the war as he still saw and remembered it. And Claire, his young sister, and her 'sinister' Polish airman, as his mother would have it.

He had always lived near the Thames. It was beyond coincidence, but when he had learned to sail a dinghy it had been at one of the local boatyards above Teddington Lock. ML366 had been built by that same yard, like so many others which had quickly learned to adapt to a new purpose, or go under. Small though she was by naval standards, she must have seemed like a battleship in that quiet backwater of the river.

Foley saw the driver's eyes shift to his mirror, his brows tighten with irritation.

Brayshaw half turned. 'Damned fools, far too fast on this road!'

There were no marks of rank or authority on the Humber, not that it would have made much difference, Foley thought.

It was a three-ton lorry, with barely enough room to overtake as it roared past, dust and straw flying from the sides while its driver gunned the engine for an approaching hill. There were a few faces, khaki uniforms, patches of colour: Italian prisoners of war on their way somewhere. Whoever was in charge obviously did not care, or was past caring.

Foley jerked upright, his mind suddenly clear, ice-cold, like the air from Brayshaw's window.

He heard Brayshaw exclaim, '*Brake*, man!'

The marine was already doing just that, the big car swaying on the rutted road as if fighting back.

Foley had time to see the top of the other vehicle, nothing more, as it was hidden by the hill's sudden hump. He heard the crash, then another, and imagined that both vehicles had collided head-on.

They braked sharply on the crest, and Foley pulled himself out and on to the road. The marine muttered, 'Jesus, that poor bastard's bought it!'

The car must have been struck a glancing blow by the speeding lorry. It had swerved into one of the low stone walls and gone out of control; the impact of the second crash had smashed it sideways into a tree. One wheel was still moving and there was a stench of petrol. But no fire.

Foley found himself running, the others behind him. He vaguely heard the squeal of brakes somewhere, the lorry stopping at last. But all he could think of was the dead airman being carried ashore, and the Wren standing by the car, this car, holding her cap in her hands. And he had not forgotten it, how she had looked. *For all of them.*

'Let me!'

He dragged open the door. The car was half on its side, the tree forcing the other door inwards; the roof too was folded like wet cardboard. There was glass everywhere.

He heard the marine call, 'Switch it off, sir!'

Somehow he managed to reach out and lean across the girl's body to turn the ignition key. The immediate silence was almost worse.

Very carefully he put his arm around her shoulders, between her and the damaged door. There was glass in her hair and near her eyes; one leg was folded under her. She had been hurled aside by the final impact. It was like being someone else, like *watching* someone else. The jacket was half open and he felt inside. A faint heartbeat, or was it imagination? It was like that sometimes . . .

'I think she's alive!' He unbuttoned the rest of her jacket. His hand was wet; she was bleeding. Then he saw the sunlight coming through the door where it had been caved in by the collision. The panel had burst apart and the glass had splintered through it like long, jagged knives.

'Bandages, *anything*!' He heard distant voices, the men off the farm lorry. He wanted to kill them.

He straightened her leg and carefully pulled her skirt up over her knees. A lot of blood. He gripped her thigh, his fingers slipping on the blood-soaked skin, harder and harder, until a hand came over his shoulder, a bandage, a duster . . . he never knew. He felt a muscle contract and looked into her face. Her eyes were wide open, so still that for a moment he imagined it was too late, then she moved her head slightly, but her eyes never left him. Her hand came from somewhere, more glass falling around them, until she had found and gripped his. Understanding what had happened, and what he was doing.

She tightened her grasp. *'Please.'* He withdrew his hand from her thigh and covered the blood with the makeshift bandage. 'That's better!' She was trying to smile, but the pain was winning. 'My father's a doctor, you see?'

She must have seen Brayshaw for the first time, and tried again to cover herself.

Foley heard another vehicle pulling up. Voices, authority. It would be out of his hands soon. Too late . . .

He put his hand over hers and said, 'I'm Chris, by the way. You'll be all right now. I'll make sure of that!'

She nodded, but her eyes were so dark she could have been unconscious once more.

He said, 'We're going to move you. Very carefully.' He felt the marine's shoulder hard against his, knew the man had turned to look at him as he persisted, 'What's *your* name? I'd like to know. Very much.'

Brayshaw murmured, 'Ready now, Chris.'

Perhaps it was the use of his name which sparked something.

She tensed against the pain, but held on just long enough. 'Chris . . . I'm Margot.' Then she fainted.

It all took time. Police arrived, military, and one local constable on his bicycle. A breakdown crew came to drag away the smashed car, and an ambulance from an army hospital.

Foley stood in the road, the girl's cap in one hand.

Brayshaw signalled to his driver. 'I'll go with the ambulance. You'd better take the Old Man's car. You are on operational stand-by, remember?'

'I'll not forget. If you're there when she comes out of it, tell her . . .'

Brayshaw smiled.

'I'll tell her.'

The marine waited for Foley to settle into the seat beside him. He had not even noticed the blood on his uniform, the cuts on his hand.

'I expect you could do with a wet, sir?'

Foley looked at him. 'I'll buy one for you, too. Thanks.' He wanted to thump his arm, but his hand did not move. It was still gripping her skin, with her fingers in his.

The marine grinned to himself. Not so dusty after all. They could pick up the lieutenant's missing tiffy at the same time; even Pusser Chavasse couldn't moan about that.

It was late when Foley eventually arrived back at the inlet, the lengthening shadows hiding the scars and giving back some of its original memories. The wardroom was a village school again, the operations section only three small cottages huddled together facing the sea. You could even imagine bathing suits hanging out there to dry for another day.

They had found Petty Officer Shannon in the pub and he had downed his drink without comment or protest. The marine must have warned him in some way to say nothing about Foley's bloodstained uniform.

Brayshaw's chief writer had been waiting for them. Captain Chavasse had been told about the car's errand of mercy but not, he suspected, its other mission to the pub outside Lulworth.

ML366 was strangely quiet, considering that her full company was aboard. Pitching gently at her moorings, with just a hint of music coming from the crew's messdeck, and the occasional stammer of morse from the W/T office opposite their tiny wardroom.

Foley entered his cabin and examined the girl's cap, which he had brought with him, unwilling to leave it, or let it go, as if it were a kind of talisman. He held it to the light; one of her dark hairs was caught in the H.M.S. cap tally, and a small piece of glass. He held it between finger and thumb. Brayshaw had even found time to pass a message to his chief writer, who had written it meticulously on the back of an old Request Form.

She will be OK. Don't worry. Keep your head down.

Foley laid the cap on his bunk and looked down at the stains on his jacket. In the pub nobody had mentioned it. *Careless talk costs lives.*

He wondered what Brayshaw had left unsaid. Was she badly hurt? So much blood . . .

He opened his locker and took out a bottle of gin. He would have to watch it, be on top line tomorrow. He felt the deck quiver. The Chief was down there now with his machinery. They trusted him . . . *Our Skipper.*

Someone shouted, 'Pipe down! Remember the watchkeepers, can't you!'

But there were no watchkeepers, apart from a sentry on the bridge. A small company, brought together by something nobody ever bothered to explain.

He looked at the Wren's cap again. She had been afraid. But more of what he was doing to her, exposing her body, than for her safety. *My father's a doctor, you see?*

Where was it leading, anyway? He looked at the empty glass, but could not recall filling it, let alone drinking the neat gin.

In Coastal Forces, the 'little ships', each operation might be the last. They all knew that, or should by now.

He wondered what Allison was doing. Avoiding his skipper, most likely. Or worrying about tomorrow. Foley glanced at the bottle. *Like the rest of us.*

He thought of the wrecked car, and the girl holding her cap. This cap. *For all of them.*

A crooner's voice drifted aft from the messdeck. *'I'll see you again . . .'*

It was drowned out instantly by, 'Turn that bloody row off!' And there was laughter as well.

He picked up the cap, and after a slight hesitation put it into his drawer and locked it.

He wanted to smile, laugh at himself. But all he said was, 'Margot.'

5

'During the Night . . .'

Petty Officer Bert Coker lifted the reefer jacket from its hanger and eyed it critically in the filtered sunshine.

'Best I can do, sir.' He picked an invisible hair from one lapel. 'But you did give it a rough time, if I may say so.'

David Masters leaned one elbow on the desk and tried to remember the name of an officer he had spoken to earlier. It seemed impossible that things could have moved so fast since that moment when he had left Rear-Admiral Fawcett at Portland.

After the 'incident' he had returned here to learn of the unexpected operation which required the removal of Foley's ML and two others from the special countermeasures team. Temporarily, he had been assured, but the boats were needed elsewhere for their normal duties, the staff officer had explained: normal duties meant just about everything.

Like the incident, perhaps Bumper was keeping apart from it until he could issue further directions. Or apportion the blame.

He had thought several times of Foley and the dead airman. Fate or luck? Something had made him hesitate, and avoid acting too hastily. An ML was no match for a couple of E-Boats, even if one was damaged; Foley would know that better than most.

At Bridport he had found the army sappers, and a local render-mines-safe officer with his team who had answered the call from Plymouth. The device was in shallow water near an unused slipway, and had been discovered because its parachute had tangled around some old mooring piles. The lieutenant in charge of the Plymouth team had been impatient to act, clearly irritated by the presence of so many *'gawping squaddies'*.

It was so often something simple that brought disaster. Masters had never forgotten one particular house where a magnetic mine had been reported, again betrayed by the parachute caught around a chimney stack. Somewhere in south London, not all that far from Clapham Junction, the ever-busy and, in wartime, vital span of track and sidings. It had been his third 'beast'.

The area was completely cleared, dead. Only a wireless blaring somewhere, abandoned when police and wardens had sounded the alarm.

But there had been a small cellar, which nobody had remembered or found time to search. Used as an extra air raid shelter, someone recalled afterwards.

The critical moment . . . the safety callipers closing around the fuse. Holding his breath. Then the first pressure.

He had felt someone move behind him, and in a mirror above a dust-covered sideboard he had seen what looked like an apparition rising out of the very floor, not five feet from the suspended mine.

Old, ragged, wild-eyed, he too had been covered in dust and fallen plaster.

Masters had spoken loudly enough for his rating to hear him from the other side of the jammed doorway.

'Run for it! Warn the others!'

The apparition had spoken for the first time. 'I was in the Royal Engineers in the last dust-up, y'know. Worked on these things when I was on the Menin Road. Not so big, of course.'

The callipers had taken hold. He would never forget. The vagrant with the cultured voice, and the fuse which he had been too eager to make safe.

Like Bridport. There had been an old fishing drifter moored by the slipway, so dilapidated that even the naval shipwrights could find no use for her. When Masters had told him to have the drifter warped closer to the sodden parachute the lieutenant had almost forgotten himself.

'Take too long, sir. I've got divers who can go down right now and deal with it!'

He had seen the lieutenant's expression alter when he had said quietly, '*Do it*. I'm not here to argue with you.'

From the size of the parachute it was obvious that it was a small bomb of some kind, similar to the one Downie had sketched, and Sewell had dislodged from its rack in the Junkers before it had killed him. Not large enough to destroy a vessel of any size, too powerful to waste on an isolated target.

Something in his manner and tone had warned the lieutenant, or maybe they had already formed their own views on Commander Critchley's successor. A long warp had been rigged, and all the spectators ordered to retire from the moorings. Some of the men had been openly amused at the precautions. *A sledgehammer to crack a nut.*

The drifter was cast off, and from behind the nearest buildings more men took the strain on the line.

The youth, Downie, had exclaimed suddenly, 'Magnetic, sir!' No question of doubt. How it must have been with Sewell.

Masters had watched the old hull swinging on the warp, felt his hand on Downie's shoulder even as he was shouting, '*Down*, all of you!'

Even then a few faces had turned to stare, or humiliate the new boss. The explosion, muffled though it was by a few feet of water, was loud and violent. Gulls had risen screaming from the other vessels nearby, and when the spray had settled the drifter was awash, and two boats beyond the slipway punctured by flying fragments. Perhaps their first real evidence. The experts would know. *Might* know. And nobody had died for it.

He had left the lieutenant in charge until a recovery team arrived; a shamefaced officer, but one with a previously successful record. Masters had told him, 'Always look for the unlikely. That will be it!'

He had eventually arrived back at the base to hear about the change of orders. The first thing he had seen had been the wrecked Wolseley piled onto the back of an army pick-up truck inside the gates.

He had seen Captain Chavasse immediately. He had been almost affable.

'Seems my secretary took it upon himself to take charge of things.Wouldn't have thought it of him. A paybob after all, eh?'

The girl was in hospital. Out of danger, they said, but it seemed a near thing.

He stared at the telephone. The hospital, when he had finally got through, had been less than helpful. 'Your officer was dealing with it. I'm afraid that's all I'm permitted to say.'

Your officer was Brayshaw, and he had been sent to Portland with some additional information for Fawcett.

And now this. He glanced around the room, and through an open door at the rumpled bed where he had tried to sleep. Nothing had changed, except Critchley's spare uniform had disappeared.

His suitcase was on the bed, still open and, he guessed, perfectly packed. Coker was good at his job, and never seemed surprised or ruffled by anything.

Masters looked at the signal pad beside the telephone. Today he was going to London. Just like that . . . He contained the anger, realizing that it was because he was tired. He wanted to wait and hear if any useful information had been gleaned at Bridport, and why it had been considered necessary to take the three MLs away from his control at this very moment.

Coker was saying, 'I've got all the details here, sir. The car will take you to the station and the Rail Transport Office will be ready to look after you.' He was ticking the points off in his mind, his smooth, pink cheeks slightly puffed out in concentration. 'The R.T.O. will be expectin' you in London too, sir, no matter what time the train gets in. Hotel room, ration card, travel warrant, all taken care of. Might make a nice break, sir.' He gauged the moment. 'All the lads think you've earned it.'

He walked to a window and readjusted the limp curtains. He had served over twenty years in the navy, with only one year's break when he had been discharged, in 1938, before the Germans had marched into Poland. He had joined up during the depression, when the streets had still been full of men from the Great War, selling matches, wearing their medals in the hope of some sympathy, or simply begging. He was an orphan, raised by an uncle in the East End of London who had been more than eager to rid himself of the responsibility.

Chatham Barracks had been his first encounter with the peacetime navy. Overcrowded, noisy, and sometimes violent, it had been a harsh initiation. Coker had never been particularly strong, and had almost failed his medical examination. *Never make a seaman. But you can always apply to be a cook or a steward.* As if they were the bottom rung of the fleet's ladder.

Coker had never looked back. He could shrug off the messdeck jibes about nursing the officers, *the pigs down aft* as they were often dubbed, and discovered a new strength by watching and studying his charges in the wardroom, something denied him in Mile End and the Hackney Road.

He had met and served all kinds of officers. Good, arrogant, and downright useless. Others stood out, but not always the ones you might expect. When he had been promoted to leading steward, he had served in a battlecruiser where the captain had been a baronet. In a destroyer, the commanding officer had worn the Victoria Cross, a true hero in every sense, yet a man who never forgot your birthday or some other special date, when he would offer you a glass of his own Scotch.

He regarded Masters thoughtfully. Never seemed to sleep, never appeared to rest when he was up and about, not bothered about food either. Always at it. And yet he'd found time to ring the army hospital about the Wren who had been driving him since he had joined the base from *Vernon*. Coker gave a small smile. No wonder the hospital didn't want to chat. Most of the inmates were ATS girls who'd got themselves knocked up by the local Romeos in uniform.

He glanced around the room. A dump, he thought. It had been a vicarage in the old days when the farms had all depended on this one village, then a boarding house, but who would come here, he had often wondered. The war must have been a bloody godsend to the landlords, whoever they were. He nodded to himself. *But it'll do for me.* It was no use thinking about after the war; it would go on for ever at this rate. North Africa, the Atlantic, Sicily, now Italy. *After that it'll be across the Channel for the real push. And there'll always be the Japs at the end of it.*

He ran the place much as he wanted it. He could always get fresh eggs and good cuts of meat when he needed them; it was surprising how some duty-free tobacco, or NAAFI chocolate, 'nutty', could dodge around the ration book. Over twenty years in, and three badges on his sleeve. He would rate Chief Steward yet. With some cushy, shore-based admiral, maybe . . .

Coker had never married. It had been close, but she had made it a condition that he should work his ticket and leave the Andrew. After what it had done for him? The places he had been and seen? China and the Yangtze, the Med where all the blood and shit was flying right now, even down with the South American squadron in those far-distant days when the mess bills had bankrupted many a green subbie. Give it all away to be the ragged kid with his arse hanging out of his trousers? The drunks on a Saturday night, and their screaming women. He smiled. And the cops coming down on all of them, and enjoying it.

Masters asked suddenly, 'Commander Critchley's wife, did she reside here most of the time?'

Coker came out of his thoughts. One thing you learned as a senior steward was the importance of discretion.

'Hardly ever, sir. They had a fine house in London, Hampstead, a lovely place. I went there a couple of times, to help out. They had other houses too. A real gentleman, 'e was.'

Masters nodded. The place had lacked any woman's touch. Coker knew a lot more than he would admit. On guard, as he was now, when he had dropped an aitch, something he was usually careful to avoid. He would make a perfect gentleman's gentleman.

It hit him again. London. To have a meeting with an officer or officers from Intelligence. Because he had made waves about it? Or had Chavasse been upset by something he had said or done?

He stared through into the other room, almost expecting to see the uniform and oak-leaved cap still hanging, the constant reminder. *A real gentleman.*

But the smell of her perfume still lingered. He glanced at Coker's smooth features. He would know that, too.

Coker said, 'Car's arrived, sir,' and closed the suitcase carefully. 'Good driver. Fixed it meself.'

Masters thought of the wrecked car, the dried blood on the buckled door. Did she still blame him for her brother's death?

'If any letters come for me . . .' He picked up his cap. There

76

would not be any, except another bill from Gieves. Coker knew that as well.

'I'll see to it, sir.'

Ushering him out, the car door already open and waiting. He looked up at the windows. A vicarage . . . He should have noticed their shape. Now only the old church remained to remind the local people, and it no longer even warranted a full-time clergyman. One cycled over from Lulworth Cove for special functions, and another part-time padre, an ex-deepwater fisherman by all accounts, filled in the gaps. On Sundays the organ was played by one of the base telegraphists. The congregation usually numbered about a dozen.

Coker cleared his throat. 'It's not my place, sir . . .' He hesitated and knew the driver was cursing him, looking pointedly at his watch.

Masters smiled.

'Go on.'

Coker continued, 'An old ship of mine, a P.O. steward like meself, over at Harwich at the moment.' He made up his mind. 'He tells me that 'e served with your father when 'e was captain of *Senegal*. Always speaks proud of 'im when we get a chance to meet.'

Masters looked at the sky; it would rain again shortly. He had learned something of Coker's background and upbringing in the short while he had been here. They had one thing in common. They were both orphans.

He said, 'The young rating who helps me—'

'I heard, sir.' The aitch was back.

'He's at a loose end. Find him something to do while I'm away. He's good with anything electrical or mechanical.'

Coker smiled. To anybody else it would have looked like a wink.

'Say no more, sir!' He stood back as the car turned towards the road.

His friend the petty officer chef joined him by the fence. He wore a filthy apron over his white trousers, and a cigarette dangled from his lip.

'You an' your bleedin' officers, Bert! Come an' 'ave a bacon sandwich an' a wet!'

Coker glanced after the car, frowning, then decided against it.

'No wonder you stay holed up in your galley!'

The chef grinned. 'Roll on my twelve!'

Coker ignored it, used to him. He was thinking of the officer who had just left for the station. How long would Masters last, he wondered. He walked into the high-ceilinged entrance hall and looked at the silent telephone. It was so easy to see her standing by it, as she had been that morning.

Suddenly he was glad he had told Masters about his father and his ship, *Senegal*.

'Now, about that drink, Nobby!' and they both laughed.

The navy's way.

'Right then, settle down, everybody. This shouldn't take too long.' Lieutenant-Commander Tony Brock, D.S.C. and two Bars, R.N.V.R., looked around the wardroom table. 'And remember, we have two gentlemen of the press with us, so mind your manners.'

Foley lowered his notepad to glance over at the two in question. One, of whom he had vaguely heard, had swept-back fair hair and was wearing khaki battledress, with a bright red silk scarf around his throat to give the right effect. His companion, much older, looked uncomfortable, even nervous amongst the officers of the three MLs.

Brock was in his element, totally sure of himself, big and broad-shouldered, his ginger beard perfectly trimmed, his hair almost brushing the deckhead, eyes everywhere until they suddenly came to rest on someone or something. His boat was slightly larger than the others, Canadian-built and fitted with better ventilation, so that the rising cloud of cigarette and pipe smoke hardly intruded.

He said, 'You know the drill. We shall clear the coast around sixteen hundred, no earlier unless the brass kick up a fuss. Head sou'-east and make for Cape Barfleur and then Seine Bay. A minelaying run, but as we only carry nine each we're not going to start another war.' He laughed and showed his strong teeth, enjoying it. Watching the nervous journalist as he wrote something on his pad.

He flattened the chart on the table. 'The krauts have been running a lot of fast coastal convoys of late. Too many, or so their lordships would have it. But the R.A.F. have been knocking their railway system around, and they don't have much choice.'

Foley saw it in his mind; he had done it often enough, but not recently. He looked at the other commanding officer, Lieutenant Dick Claridge of ML401. His Number One was whispering something in his ear. Another new boy, like Allison. Could hardly sit still. Brock's first lieutenant was Royal Naval Reserve, ex-merchant service, with a lined, experienced face. Foley wondered what he thought of his skipper. Brock carried an extra lieutenant who was from Operations, *one of Captain Chavasse's trained spies* as he had cheerfully introduced him at the outset.

Brock turned quickly as an engine roared into life, and his eyes moved to Foley, who gave the slightest nod. It was 366, testing something.

A lot of people said Brock was too full of his own desire for publicity, or glamour, some called it. But he was as sharp as a tack and tolerated no slackness.

Brock said, 'Your man Shannon's on the job. Good show, Chris.'

He continued, 'We lay the mines as directed, and return to base. We shall have back-up from C/F of course. Three MGBs to make sure we don't get lost.' There were a few wry grins, and Dick Claridge's new subbie said, 'We'll show *them*!' That brought some real laughs.

The journalist with the red scarf leaned back on the bench seat and asked, 'Is there some other reason for an isolated operation like this? I'd have thought with all the activity in the Med they'd have greater call for Coastal Forces craft.' He smiled. 'Even MLs, in that theatre?'

Brock nodded. 'True. But the route along from Cherbourg to Dieppe has been getting away with it. Should go smoothly enough – you won't need your brown trousers, not yet anyway!'

They both grinned. Like adversaries, Foley thought.

He leaned over to Allison. 'All right?'

Allison rubbed his chin and stared at his own notes. 'I was thinking of our last run, sir. Those E-Boats could have been based around there.'

Foley thought of the dead airman . . . the girl on the pier . . . the smashed-up car.

He said, 'Check the Met report, will you, Toby? Don't want it too damned clear.' He saw his sudden uncertainty. 'We'll drop the bloody things and run for home.'

Allison seemed satisfied.

Foley stared over at the journalists again. He could see it in print already. *During the night, units of our light coastal forces, under the command of Lieutenant-Commander Tony Brock, carried out a daring raid against enemy shipping.*

Brock was saying, 'That wraps it up, I think. We shall slip and proceed as planned. Commanding officers' conference at fifteen hundred.' He looked at each face in turn. 'Nobody goes ashore, no matter what cockeyed reason he gives, right?' His eyes rested briefly on the lieutenant from Operations as he added drily, 'No careless talk that way, eh?'

It was breaking up, each man glad to get back to his own command. Lieutenant Claridge followed Foley to the ladder and said, 'I see you've lost your old Number One. Gone to better things.' He looked at his own replacement. 'We all have to start somewhere, I suppose.'

Foley thought he didn't sound very convinced.

He felt someone touch his sleeve. It was the other journalist.

'I'm told I'm to come with you – Mr. Foley, isn't it?'

Foley smiled at him: there was not much else he could do. The man looked either unwell or scared to death. Behind him he could hear Brock laughing and joking with the star journalist, with the red silk scarf. Once the visitors had gone Brock would be opening the bar. He had been heard to say, 'Well, you can't take it with you, can you?'

Foley said, 'Just Chris will do. I'll take you across now so you can look around the boat, speak to anyone you think will help. What's *your* name, by the way?'

'Mark Pleydell.' It came out like an apology. 'Can you show me the lavatory, before we begin?'

Foley guided him up the ladder, pausing only to wave to Brock. Brock did not respond, but he knew he had seen him.

'We call them heads, um, Mark. Might as well get it right when you're dealing with a bunch of hardened sailors. You've not done much with the navy, I take it?'

They were on deck, and the wind was cold and damp. Perhaps there would be some rain. It might help things along.

The other man said, 'No. The R.A.F., usually.'

Again it seemed apologetic, but it caused Foley to turn and stare at him. Mark Pleydell: the name and the voice he had heard on the B.B.C. programme *At the Front*, which his father always listened to. The sea, the air, the desert. The voice that brought it to living room and bar, to parents and friends, to lovers, all those who were left behind.

Pleydell had been on one of those massive air attacks, over Hamburg or some other heavily defended city. So calmly described, and recorded over a main target, a shipyard, as it had been happening. Hard to believe it was the same man; only the voice lingered. And now all he wanted to do was find the heads.

He said quietly, 'Use my cabin, such as it is, Mark. The heads are right next to it. If you need to know anything,' he tried to grin, 'and I'm not too busy, just ask away!'

Pleydell grasped the guardrail and allowed a seaman to steady his arm while he climbed over to the boat alongside.

'*You* I know about, Chris. Forgive me, but I asked for your boat on this trip.'

Allison found him in the wardroom.

'The Met report forecast is dry and clear in the Channel, sir.' He looked surprised when Foley grinned and said, 'Good. Then we're probably in for a Force Ten!'

He had seen Bass waiting by the bridge. He would speak to 366's small company and put them in the picture. By now, they counted on it. And they had more than earned it.

Allison said, 'Our journalist,' and looked uncomfortable. 'He's not quite what I anticipated.'

'I expect a lot of people say that about us, Toby.' He nodded to Bass. 'Muster the hands, 'Swain. Then get them all fed and ready for sea.'

He peered into his cabin and saw the locked drawer. She was going to be all right, might even be allowed to listen to the radio, if it was that kind of hospital. He heard the thud of shoes and seaboots on the sloping planking. The three MLs were filling the inlet, or almost, as 366 must have looked in that Teddington boatyard all that time ago. When his sister had still been in school uniform, and would never have dreamed of falling for a Polish airman.

Once they were at sea again there was never time to indulge in impossible hopes or solutions, if that was what they were. People rarely spoke of them. It was too dangerous.

He tried to shake it off. Unless you were Tony Brock, of course.

He heard Pleydell struggling with the pump in the heads. How did they manage in a Halifax bomber?

He heard someone laugh, and knew Bass was ready for him.

A girl named Margot, whose father was a doctor . . .

But all he could hear was, *During the night, units of our light coastal forces* . . .

He went on deck.

'Slow ahead, all engines!' The muffled clicks of telegraphs and repeaters seemed deafening in the open bridge, but he could still hear the sea surging along the hull, the occasional splash as a small offshore roller cruised beneath the raked stem.

'Revolutions, seven-zero, sir.'

Foley raised his binoculars again and felt the strap rub across his neck. On this kind of work you tended to flatten your collar even if you were freezing, avoiding anything that might conceal the sound of an approaching enemy. He watched the varying depths of darkness, and imagined the chart as he had last seen it. He would not get another chance.

In his mind he could see his small command as clearly as if it were broad daylight. Half the armament fully manned, the rest within reach of the men waiting to release the mines. Nine of them. One might catch a ship, and if not their efforts would still cause delays and cancellations. As they did to convoys on both sides of the Channel.

He felt Pleydell move beside him, and somehow knew he was shivering. Trying to keep out of everybody's way.

He said, 'Enemy coast on the starboard bow, Mark. Nothing much to see.'

Chitty the signalman murmured, ''Ere comes Number Two, sir.'

One of his hands rested against the machine-gun mounting at the rear of the bridge.

Foley said, 'Pass the word forrard.' Chitty had eyesight like a cat. Then he saw it, the frothing moustache of a bow wave as Claridge's ML surged out of the darkness. Tony Brock had already dropped his mines and had gone ahead to cover the rest of his little group.

Now it's our turn. He thought of Allison, down aft by the twin Oerlikons. He would learn more up here on the bridge, but you never put all your eggs in one basket. He shut it from his mind.

'Starboard ten.' He heard Bass's instant acknowledgment, imagined his eyes glinting in the faint compass light as he brought her round.

'Midships. Steady. Steer North forty-five East.'

Foley raised his watch and peered at the luminous dial. Eight o'clock. Right on time.

He heard a sharp clink from abaft the bridge, and imagined somebody getting a savage blast from Richmond, the leading hand in charge.

'Ready, sir!'

He said, 'Tell the Chief. We're starting the run.'

Bass eased the wheel as the deck lifted and pitched in the offshore current. He kept his eyes on the compass, and tuned his ears only to Foley and the voicepipes, but he could feel the nearness of land, smell it.

There were some faint explosions, but nobody spoke. *Crump. Crump. Crump.* There might have been flashes too, but Foley had been right about the Met report. There was low cloud everywhere. Perhaps Allison would remember his prediction.

He tensed as a column of water lifted like an awakened ghost, and vanished just as quickly.

The seaman with the handset said, '*One,* sir!'

'Very well.' It always made him jumpy, as if he expected the mine to explode against the hull, although if it did none of them would live to hear it. The depth was eight to ten fathoms hereabouts. A good channel for a fast convoy making the best use of the darkness.

He heard more explosions. Flak, the R.A.F. carrying out a

83

raid somewhere. He glanced over at Pleydell's slight form. He would know.

'*Seven*, sir!'

He heard Bass mutter, 'Get a bleedin' move on!'

Foley looked up as the belly of one cloud bank lit up with a dull flash, fire rather than explosion.

Pleydell said, 'One of them has bought it.' A different voice, perhaps a different person. As if he was there, seeing it, describing it for all those people.

Like my own father.

Foley could hear the engines now, labouring, at least one of them coughing and roaring. The clouds flickered with fire, and the sounds were already much louder.

Chitty said, 'Comin' down!' Later, on the messdeck, he would be sorry for them. But here and now you thought of number one, and your mates. And the boat.

'*Eight*, sir!' The seaman's eyes glowed as he peered at the sky, but his voice remained calm.

'Tell the Chief. Stand by!'

Foley swung round as the seaman called, 'Number Nine's jammed, sir! Richmond says that the release bracket 'as sheared!'

A live mine. And a new piece of equipment which had broken down, the very item on which Shannon had worked before putting to sea. It was hard to think. The noise seemed to be over and around them, defying all they knew.

Richmond was a good leading hand, one of Shannon's own mechanics; he was down there now. Waiting. They all were.

The sea suddenly opened up, everything standing out in the eye-searing glare of light and fire as the aircraft broke through the low cloud and began a shallow dive towards the sea. It was so bright that he could see the camouflage on the body and wings before the flames engulfed it, so as it hurtled overhead it looked like a giant crucifix, the sparks still trailing after it as it hit the water.

Pleydell said softly, 'Somebody was still trying to fly it.'

Foley found that he could ignore it, had already forgotten that men might have lived through the furnace.

A terrible death. Maybe the worst, if there was any choice.

But this time it was to *use*. A weapon.

The reflected glare was all but gone, and he knew that, temporarily at least, his night glasses would be useless.

But it had lasted long enough. The choice was his. There, right across the dying glow, was a convoy.

Maybe only three or four vessels. An hour later and they would have been right amongst the mines. He pounded his fist on the screen and allowed the sudden pain to steady him.

'Close up, action stations!' He waited, counting seconds, expecting the night to come alive again with star shell and tracer. Like that other time.

He called, 'Full ahead, all engines! Port fifteen, steer due north! Steady as you go, 'Swain!'

The sea seemed to boil past either beam, and where there had been faceless water Foley could measure their speed as the hull bounded across short, steep waves. Shannon and his mechanics must wonder what the hell was happening.

Someone shouted, 'Here we go!'

Foley watched the tracer, so deceptively slow, rising like livid balls of green fire before streaking down across its own reflection with the speed of light itself.

The enemy were as startled and blinded as they were. *You must believe that.* He cupped his hands. *'Open fire!'*

The sea was being torn apart by the tracer. He saw Chitty duck as metal whined above the bridge.

And there was a live mine still on board.

Chitty gasped, 'That was bloody close!'

Bass bared his teeth. 'Shouldn't 'ave joined then, should yer!'

Down aft, Sub-Lieutenant Allison was clinging to a stanchion with all his strength, and yet, as the hull reeled over in response to the full rudder, it felt as if he was going over the side. It was hard to think, to gauge distance as the twin Oerlikons suddenly came to bear on a target and hammered into life. Allison saw the gunfire reflected on the streaming side of another vessel, so that it appeared to be shooting back at them. A low, anonymous shape, smoke pouring from a funnel or perhaps a shell burst, and then all at once rearing up and above him. In the unbroken clatter of automatic fire he saw the heavy bow, even some crudely painted numbers, the stem rearing around as if it and not the ML was still turning. Allison felt bullets

85

hiss past him. In the flashes he saw a man lying by the after hatch, hit by gunfire or unable to stay on his feet, it was not possible to tell. He knew he was out in the open, barely able to hold on, and yet he was able to see and record everything. Faces appearing on the other vessel's side, staring, mouths open in silent anger or terror. Another burst of machine-gun fire swept through them, and Allison heard the wheelhouse glass shattering as the bullets searched out another target. The Oerlikons fell silent, and he thought he heard the gunner swearing, meaningless words, while he waited for new magazines to be slammed into place.

But above that, in the smoke and flickering fires, he could hear someone screaming. Like a woman or a trapped animal in terrified agony. It was neither.

'You all right, sir?' He felt someone gripping his arm, dragging him up the deck, which was already tilting in the opposite direction as the helm went over. Allison nearly choked, his mouth doused in salt water. It tasted of petrol.

It was suddenly important to remember the sailor's name. 'I'm sorry . . .'

The man shook his head and his face opened up in a huge grin. 'I dunno! Some mothers do 'ave 'em!' He was actually laughing, face and oilskin flashing in the renewed gunfire. It was almost worse than the scream.

Allison watched the nearest vessel beginning to burn fiercely. Perhaps they were carrying fuel or ammunition? But she was going fast, and he saw more splashes, men jumping or falling overboard as the Oerlikons found their target again. Another was firing from amidships: the Scouse who had served as much time in the detention barracks as at sea, until this boat.

One of the guns had jammed, and Allison found himself climbing up the mounting, his cap gone, one hand bloody as he shouted, 'I'll fix it!' Somehow he contained the desire to laugh. 'Cormack, isn't it?' He had remembered this one's name.

The seaman peered at him and wiped his face with his sleeve.

'Then you must be Dr. Livingstone?' They both clung to the guns as the deck heeled over once again. Cartridge cases rattled on the deck; somebody was using a fire extinguisher beside the life raft.

Another shouted, 'Hold on, Bill! Don't try to move, for God's sake! The skipper's turning – Old Chris'll get us back, you'll see!'

The roar of engines eased slightly and Allison saw another ML moving purposefully to intercept. Just for an instant he had thought it was something else. A split second, less. But he had imagined the clatter of an E-Boat's cannon shells. It was the senior officer's boat.

Perhaps it was getting lighter. But the clouds were still there. He peered around, his eyes stinging and raw. Of the small convoy there was no sign, just hazy fires, and thick banks of smoke, dark objects rising and dipping as the ML's wash swept through and over them. As if they were rising from the dead.

Brock's voice, metallic and hard in his loud-hailer, cut above everything else.

'Well done! Take station on me! We will return to base! Watch out for fighters!' He raised his hand and held it above his head as his boat increased speed again.

Allison saw that the other journalist was propped on something below Brock's bridge, his red scarf pulled up over his face. He turned away and retched. It was not the scarf. He had no face left.

The seaman watched him. *Poor little sod. But give him the benefit. He might be all right after this.*

Allison tried to say something, to make him understand. It had all happened so fast. No long-range weapons, no radar, no steel plating. *And I am not afraid.*

'Skipper wants you with him on the bridge, sir!' The man sounded strained, impatient. 'Chop-chop, that means, *sir!*'

Allison groped his way forward, trying to put things in order, to remember each separate moment.

Ships had probably been destroyed, men had been killed, and he had come through it. But the unknown voice seemed to rise above all else.

Old Chris'll get us back, you'll see!

He gripped the handrails of the bridge ladder and stared at the sea surging past on either beam. Black no longer. The night was almost over. He heard Foley's voice, then somebody else gave a quick, nervous laugh. *So be it, then.* He looked at the sea again.

He heard someone say sharply, 'Move that clutter, Len, Jimmy the One's comin' up!'

The real battle was over. He belonged.

6

Reaching Out

The army hospital was certainly off the beaten track. The driver of the naval mail van peered at the shabby building and said doubtfully, 'I 'ope you can wangle a lift back, sir.'

Foley climbed down and felt the gravel drive rise up to meet him. He could hardly remember ever being so tired. He waved to the driver and turned towards the main building; it had been a lodge for fishermen and nature lovers, someone had told him. There was the faint glint of a river just beyond a line of trees. He tried to concentrate. The Frome, that was it.

Maybe he should have waited until he was feeling himself again. He looked at the empty, bleak windows. She might have been moved, might not even want to see him . . .

A tall military policeman stepped out of a doorway and, after the slightest hesitation, threw up a salute.

'Sir?'

Foley explained, his mind still crowded with the busy hours since he had conned his command alongside that same pier again. They had been lucky. Both of the other MLs had taken casualties; Brock's had lost two men killed, not including the war correspondent. Brock had sounded more peeved than sorry. 'Wouldn't keep his bloody head down when I told him! He was a useful chap, too!'

They had ditched the last mine while still a few miles offshore, and Signalman Chitty had finished it off with one rifle shot. There had been an immediate session in Operations, when Captain

Chavasse had interrupted the debriefing repeatedly with pointed and impatient questions.

366's only casualty had been a seaman named Howard who had been knocked almost senseless when he had slipped and struck his skull on a winch bracket. Bass had commented, 'The last place 'e'd feel it!'

Allison was back there in charge, and pleased about it, or so it seemed. As if he had suddenly gained the equivalent of another year's experience, a long time in this service. Or had somehow found his place at last in their small, intimate world.

The redcap led the way through another building, his boots thudding noisily on the uncarpeted floors.

There were a few figures sitting in one of the rooms, wearing the familiar blue dressing gowns you found in most military and naval hospitals. Filling in the time . . . until when? Foley knew it was his own fault, but he had always hated hospitals, and would never forget his last stay in one. It was the same in this godforsaken place, he thought. Unfinished card games, a cribbage board abandoned on a table. A radio was playing some music, turned down until it was almost inaudible, presumably so it would not disturb other patients.

Some of them looked up and a voice called, 'Up the navy!'

Another added, 'Right up, you mean!'

There was not a whole man amongst them.

Foley paused and said, 'You've got it made here, haven't you?'

They all laughed, as he knew they would. He had been there. But it never helped.

Another door. *No visitors without passes. Out of bounds to unauthorised personnel.*

The redcap stopped. 'I'll fetch the sister in charge.'

Foley peeled off his raincoat. 'Any chance of a lift back to the coast when I leave?'

'Like askin' for gold dust, sir.' His eye fell on the medal ribbon. 'See what I can fix.'

Foley walked to a window. How long did it take for a building to start feeling and smelling like a hospital, he wondered. He plucked at his shirt, the same one he had been wearing when

89

366 made fast. The cuffs were soiled, and he knew he stank of high-octane.

It was better not to weigh the risks and set them against the possible gains. Like the blazing bomber crashing into the sea with the sound of thunder. Like their own solitary airman. It was stupid to measure the cost . . .

The sister had arrived. Very neat and clean, not a hair out of place around her little white cap.

'It was good of you to telephone first, Lieutenant. We don't have many visitors here.'

'How is she, Sister?'

She did not reply directly. 'It was a bad accident, I understand. She was very fortunate, I would say lucky, under the circumstances.'

Foley thought of the wrecked car, a wheel still spinning, the engine running, her face so pale and still. And the blood.

He said, 'I thought there would be a fire, you see.' He was not making sense. 'What we always fear the most.'

'Are you feeling quite well, Lieutenant? Can I fetch you a cup of something?'

Foley pinched the bridge of his nose between finger and thumb. Maybe she had said that she didn't want to see him. That made it all the more important.

'I would like to see Miss Lovatt, Sister.' The lie came easily. 'I am under orders at present.'

'This way, then. The doctor will be along on his rounds shortly. Then, I'm afraid . . .' She did not finish it. Foley remembered that about hospitals, too. They never needed to explain.

The room was small and completely square. It had no windows, and might have been part of an outbuilding, with a skylight in the middle of the ceiling. There were two beds facing one another, and the one nearest the door was empty, but in use.

The sister said, 'Your visitor is here. I can't say how long you can have.'

She was only in her twenties; perhaps the severity was her own form of defence.

Foley did not even hear the door close behind him. He had only seen her in uniform before and it was almost like meeting someone else, a total stranger. She was wearing a nightdress of some kind, with a blue dressing gown over her shoulders, and she lay half propped on a rank of pillows, with a newspaper opened across her knees. She adjusted the dressing gown to cover her bare arms and he saw a bandage on her wrist.

But she was smiling at him, pleased, but shyly, as if she was still unprepared.

He said, 'How is it?' and looked around. 'I wanted to bring something – I don't know – flowers maybe, to cheer you up.'

'Tell me.' She reached out with the bandaged arm. '*Tell* me, Chris,' and hesitated. 'There, I said it.'

He took her hand and turned it over very carefully. 'I was worried about you.'

She repeated, 'No, Chris, *tell* me. I've been thinking about you since the pile-up. You see, I knew you were on some operation, a sudden decision. Otherwise . . .'

He returned the pressure of her hand. Like that moment together in the wrecked Wolseley.

'Otherwise I would have stayed with you. All the time. No matter what.'

He felt her dark eyes watching him, her grip as firm as ever.

'It was bad, wasn't it?'

He shook his head. 'You're the one in hospital, Margot!' He sensed her flinch. Her name. 'It's just been a bit busy, that's all.' They looked at one another, and he said, 'Have you been up and about much?'

'They say I'm on the mend. In fact, they're talking of sick leave. I'm black and blue all over, but the gash in my . . .' Her free hand moved as if to touch her thigh but stopped against her hip, 'is healing well.' She waited for him to look at her again. 'All thanks to you.'

Another door opened, which he had not noticed before, and a girl in a similar blue dressing gown crossed the room and climbed into the other bed.

She glanced over and said, 'I'm Mary,' then she lay down and placed a damp cloth across her eyes.

Somewhere a bell was ringing urgently, and there were voices, authority.

Foley said, 'Are you going home when you get leave?' He saw her nod and hurried on, 'And afterwards, will you be returning to the base, or moving somewhere else?'

She had both her hands over his now and had leaned forward slightly, so that the gown had dropped completely from one shoulder. From below the armpit was the beginning of one huge, black bruise where she had been hurled sideways by the impact. She was gazing into his face, from which he knew he could no longer hide the strain.

'What is it? Please tell me.'

'I want to see you after this, Margot.' He was shivering, and yet his hands were quite steady in hers. Like being two people, one in control, the other wanting to touch her bare shoulder. Until she understood.

'I'd love to see you again, Chris. Do you think I could ever forget what you did?'

More voices, closer now.

He said, 'I meant to bring your cap with me.'

She stared at him, her mouth softening. 'So *you* have it? It must be the only part of my uniform that stayed in one piece!'

Foley stood up carefully and smoothed the edge of the bed. He saw the opened newspaper, the headlines screaming at him, a photograph of a battleship at anchor. *ITALIAN FLAGSHIP SURRENDERS UNDER THE GUNS OF THE ROYAL NAVY.*

The 'other war', which they discussed endlessly whenever time permitted. Ships and faces they knew or had known, subjects of argument and speculation. But the other war. The real war.

Not the war he had come to know and expect. Wooden hulls of the little ships: punctured, splintered, bloodstained. Men living in one another's pockets, sharing everything. You soon understood what really counted when you were less than twenty yards from the muzzles of the enemy's guns.

'I'll have to be leaving soon. It seems a bit frantic.'

She said quickly, 'Not yet. I so hoped you would come. Find the time—'

He took her hand again. 'You *knew* I'd come. But you know what they say about getting too close in wartime . . . I . . . I'm not sure . . . for your sake.'

She did not look away as he lifted the gown to cover her bare shoulder, his fingers brushing her skin. 'I want to protect you, Margot . . . and now it seems like the other way round.' He tried to smile. 'I must see you again. *Soon.* I'll call the hospital . . .'

'Ah, I see you're just leaving, Lieutenant!'

A white coat, a fixed, tired smile, a stethoscope, the sister close behind him. It was over.

Foley touched her hair and felt her press against his hand.

'Sorry to be such a mess,' he said.

The sister was moving a screen towards the bed. They would examine her, pull her about. The anger was irrational, but he could barely contain it.

She lifted her chin and regarded him steadily. 'If I'm moved from here I shall send word.' She moved as if to extend her hand again, but instead put it to her breast. 'Take good care of yourself, Chris. As you did of me.'

The doctor said, 'There, now—'

Foley was outside the door without knowing he had moved. Like saying goodbye at a railway station, too common a sight these days: so much longing, but never the right words. Until the train begins to move. Until it is too late.

He strode back through the room where the soldiers were sitting, waiting for something to happen. One was rolling a cigarette, expertly moistening the paper with his tongue. He had only one hand. Another, who appeared to have lost a leg and an arm, was slowly turning the pages of a tattered magazine. Someone should tell *them*, he thought. They're the real heroes in this war.

He caught sight of himself in a wall mirror as he was leaving and shook his head. It was a wonder he hadn't scared her to death. He ran his fingers through his tousled hair and jammed on his cap.

It was absurd. He hardly knew her. He had acted out of instinct and had shared her pain, her need.

The redcap was grinning at him, and there was a car of some sort waiting by the door.

But Chris Foley knew he had never been closer to anyone in his life.

*   *   *

93

'Try that chair over there, old chap. Take the weight off your feet. You deserve it after that little lot.'

David Masters smiled and loosened his jacket. His first meeting with the Naval Intelligence people and a few other privileged parties had been long and surprisingly demanding. Like being in the spotlight, more so because of the brightly illuminated screen of diagrams, statistics, and photographs.

The senior present had been a vice-admiral on the First Sea Lord's personal staff, a haughty-faced officer with hooded eyes and a petulant, unsmiling mouth. It was hard to believe, let alone remember, Masters had thought. The vice-admiral had been the commander in his first ship, an old training cruiser, when he had still been a midshipman. The commander, the Bloke, as he was always known, was second only to the captain, but in many ways had more contact and influence in any large ship, especially where the 'young gentlemen' were concerned. As far as he could recall, they had all liked him. Keen on team activities, boatwork and sailing, even sports ashore when time and opportunity allowed, he was always there. Ready to advise, and often to demonstrate.

Sitting in that underground room, one hand tapping occasionally on an unopened folder, it was impossible to see him as the same person.

Perhaps the navy was a little like the Church, the step from wardroom to flag rank much like country parson to a bishop's palace.

He looked at his host. Captain James Wykes of the D.N.I.'s department was thin, wiry, and never still. He was dressed in a pale grey suit which looked well-worn, if not actually shabby, but Masters guessed it had been both expensive and tailored to fit a then sturdier figure. His hair was the same colour as the suit, and there were deep shadows beneath his eyes.

Wykes exclaimed, 'Stuffy lot for the most part, but you mustn't mind them!' He lit a cigarette and fanned the smoke aside, turning his head away to control a spasm of coughing. Masters had noticed that he smoked a lot. Coughed a lot, too. It had roused the vice-admiral's irritation, and he had given the ashtray a significant glance.

But Wykes had looked after him from the beginning. Guiding

him, and fending off what he considered to be pointless or time-wasting interruptions, quick to jump to his feet and emphasize a point, or to snap his fingers at the screen operator to flash back to an earlier item of interest.

He thought of the others who had been there. A commander from H.M.S. *Vernon* he had once worked alongside; there had only been time for a handshake and a brief greeting. There were men in civilian clothes who arrived and departed together, but were not introduced, nor did they appear to speak to one another throughout the entire session.

And two officers of the Free French navy, somehow alien in their original pre-war uniforms. One held the same rank as his own, *Capitaine de Corvette,* the other was his superior, a full captain with a neat beard; you would have known him to be French had he been wearing a boiler suit. He had an interpreter sitting at his elbow, a woman in a dark suit or dress who occasionally leaned over to murmur something, or to jot a few notes on a pad.There had been other women present, but she had been the only one out of uniform. Whenever she had looked up she had shaded her eyes with one hand against the glare, and he had seen a brooch of some kind when she had moved, the only adornment against her shadowy outline. He had also noticed that the French officer appeared to be following the progress of the meeting without much need for an interpreter.

Wykes was saying, 'I expect a drink wouldn't come amiss, old chap? Sun's well over the yardarm, I'd say. What'll it be, Horse's Neck? Scotch, if you like?' He chuckled. 'R.H.I.P., you know!'

Masters took out his pipe and pouch. *Rank Hath Its Privileges.* The vice-admiral who had once been the training cruiser's 'Bloke' had probably said that too. But it was difficult to believe now.

Wykes was opening a cupboard and slopping drinks into a pair of finely cut tumblers. Masters looked at the clock. It was six in the evening but it could have been any time, any place. Impossible to imagine London's traffic still roaring somewhere high above this maze of rooms and offices. The main bunker of command, or was there always another one, even more influential? No wonder Bumper Fawcett made a point of appearing here.

Wykes studied him through the smoke while he filled and tamped down his pipe.

He said, 'Your people are having good results. But as the pace hots up, as it must and will as we draw nearer to invading, forcing that second front all the newspaper experts are demanding, the enemy's strategy and tactics will be preparing to meet it. From the start Germany was in the lead with pattern and then strategic bombing. Factories, docklands, road and railway systems a year or so back, and they nearly succeeded. The country was almost at a standstill, production at an all-time low, convoys unable to fight their way across the Pond to fill the gaps.'

Masters watched the smoke. 'A lot of men died trying to combat the enemy's skill where bombs and mines were concerned. Army Bomb Disposal lost so many officers in those first couple of years that it was looked on as a suicide job.' He shrugged. 'And now we're playing our part. I've seen some good chaps set off for that last beast. Not knowing it *was* their last.'

Wykes put down his tumbler. 'That lieutenant of yours from Portland, the one who worked on the crashed Junkers, he discovered a lot more than he realized, poor chap.' His eyes moved very quickly. 'And you, much to the fury of your rear-admiral, "Bumper", you call him? You stumbled on a second device in Bridport. The people at *Vernon* have discovered similarities. Smaller devices, mines if you like, which can be dropped at short notice, and timed to explode after a given period or be set off by magnetic fields of their own.'

'I would have expected that our section would have been told first, sir.' It came out more curtly than he had intended. 'We *are* on the sharp end of it.'

Wykes was unmoved. 'Exactly. Which is why I wanted you here, face to face. I'm not much of a one for classified phone calls, and all that cloak-and-dagger nonsense.' He reached over and refilled Masters' glass, smiling. 'While you get the chance, right?'

At that moment a telephone did ring, almost a gentle sound after the clamour of other offices Masters had passed.

Wykes picked it up. 'Right on time.' He replaced it. 'Air raid warning. Not to worry, I'll have one of my chaps take you to your hotel. What's it like, by the way? I've only dropped in

96

once myself,' and frowned as the telephone whimpered again. 'Excuse me.'

Masters tried to relight his pipe; it was not his usual tobacco. 'A bit of Pussers was all I could get, sir,' Coker had said.

He had in fact hardly noticed the hotel, except that it was near the Thames; he had seen the river when the car had dropped him there, to book in and show his credentials. The train had been late arriving, hardly surprising after its endless journey from Dorset, with stops on the line to allow a troop train to tear past, or while some unexplained delay was dealt with, and it had been packed with passengers, most of them in uniform of one kind or another. With London opening out to greet them he had seen vapour trails twisting like ghostly writing against a washed-out sky. Two or three fighters. Young men trying to kill one another. One had eventually fallen from the sky, its smoke like a dying brushstroke.

Someone had exclaimed angrily, 'That's one less of the sods!' He might easily have been wrong.

'As I was saying, old chap.' Wykes was back, legs crossed as he slumped in the opposite chair. His ankles looked as thin as a child's wrists. 'The Germans have had a lot of practice. In the Spanish civil war they had a team experimenting with landmines. Nobody *saw* or *heard* anything, of course. In Russia they've been using new ideas, with some success, but we only learned about that recently.' He turned down his mouth. 'From a neutral source, need I say?'

He glanced at the clock. 'I have to go. Must see the gallant *Capitaine de Vaisseau* Lalonde over the side. He's been very helpful in this matter.' He smiled briefly. 'But you know the French. They've never forgiven us Waterloo!' He dusted some ash from his tie and lapels and added gently, 'While I'm away, just think on this, old chap. A bit closer to home. Say, the Channel Islands, for instance? What if the answer to your device is right there for the asking?'

He gestured to the cupboard. 'Help yourself. I'll be ten minutes at the most.'

Masters stared at the door as it closed after him. A remarkable man, astute and clever. Dangerous if he wanted to be.

He tapped out his pipe in an upended shell case and tried to think back on all he had seen and heard.

This was a completely different world. At sea, or at *Vernon*'s various outflung sections, you always felt you were in the front line, the sharp end, as he had described it to Wykes only minutes ago. It was timeless here, too. But when the car had collected him at the terminus station he had been surprised by the crowds of jostling people. Every uniform and from every country, even those like the French captain Wykes had gone to see over the side, whose homelands were under occupation. It hardly seemed like a capital under siege. If a stick of bombs had been on its way down nobody would have heard it above the din of voices and traffic.

The Channel Islands? It seemed unlikely. He leaned forward in the worn leather chair. The only part of Britain occupied by the enemy, because there had been no way of defending them so close to the French mainland, and because of the death and suffering any such attempt would have caused. And the recriminations which would surely have followed.

He was still contemplating it when Wykes returned, rubbing his hands.

'Gone off as happy as a priest at a funeral!'

He sat down, his fingers latched together on his bony knees.

'Thought about it?'

'I'm still floundering.'

Wykes did not relax or smile. 'Your predecessor, Commander Critchley, was a man of importance and not a little influence even before he donned the King's uniform. I had dealings with him through this department. He was helpful with some enquiries which we were making about a certain Raymond de Courcy.' He paused, his eyes asking an unspoken question. He seemed satisfied and continued, 'Another powerful man, head of an electronics group in France. And at some time a partner of the late Commander Critchley.' He broke off in another fit of coughing. 'The war came. Raymond de Courcy found himself on the other side. A collaborator, they call them now, but often the only way to survive, I'm told.'

'But surely Commander Critchley didn't have any idea what was happening.'

'He wanted to avoid the issue, of course. We were the ones who

98

started to stir things up. *Then*, we were only poking sticks in the dark. Now we know.'

The overhead light flickered momentarily. Distant traffic or a bomb; it could have been an earthquake and nothing would change down here.

Masters said, 'Where do I come in?'

Wykes smiled gently. 'I've studied your record, both before and after the unfortunate loss of your command.' He held up one hand. 'It is a vital part of this job. Other lives depend on my being right or wrong, as much as if I had my own ship – more, in many ways. I was impressed by what you have achieved since that other time, and since your appointment to the countermeasures section down in Dorset. You've made a lot of progress.' He gave a slight shrug. 'Otherwise you and I would never have met!' It seemed to amuse him.

Masters tried to come to terms with it. 'When we really know what it is we're up against . . .'

The telephone buzzed twice and stopped.

'When we know that, old chap, the war will doubtless have been over for six months.'

Masters stood up. It really was another world. He thought of Foley, in his own command, the feel of it when he had been aboard, when they had been running for base but had stopped to pick up the dead flier. There was nothing else like it; it had been infectious, even though he had tried again and again to put it behind him, not to lose himself again. Otherwise, survival was meaningless.

Wykes was peering around and patting his pockets, for more cigarettes no doubt.

'You can scoot back to base, day after tomorrow.' He saw the sudden protest in Masters' eyes, and said evenly, 'Can't be helped, I'm afraid. The top brass must know what's happening, and be convinced. You'd think they were paying for the whole war themselves!' He tapped his sleeve, with what Masters sensed was a rare intimacy. 'In fact, I was having dinner at the Savoy a few nights back. The place was wall-to-wall with red tabs and gold lace up to the elbows. My guest remarked that it would be quite a catch for Jerry if he managed to drop a bomb right on the lot of them. I corrected the poor fellow. Told him it would more likely do a hell of a lot of good for all concerned!' He laughed and coughed again.

Then he said, 'Don't worry about your people. I shall see that you are kept informed until you get on that train for Dorset.' A glance at the clock. 'Now, to another meeting.'

He shook hands, and their eyes met. 'You'll hear from me soon. Until then . . .' He looked at the clock again. 'Cloak-and-dagger indeed!'

For several minutes Masters stood alone in the quiet room. Critchley . . . was he never to be allowed to melt away like all those other faces? He thought of the old house with its damp wallpaper, the wardrobe where the uniform had been hanging as a reminder. And what of de Courcy, the collaborator? Perhaps he would learn more when he was himself fully trusted. Investigated. He half smiled. Cloak-and-dagger . . .

'Your car's ready, sir.'

He felt the man watching him as he walked out, and into the glare of the white-painted corridor. He probably saw many come and go from here. Maybe it was better not to think too much about it. Petty Officer Coker had the right idea.

'Will you be requiring anything further, sir?'

The waiter was very small and molelike, his hands folded around a napkin like paws.

Masters looked across the dining room. Only a few tables were still occupied, and everyone was in uniform, even the only two women present.

He massaged his cheek, feeling the scar. The hotel was not large, but he imagined it had been expensive in happier times. He did not know London well, and had usually visited it only for official purposes. He grimaced. Like today. And tomorrow . . .

He could scarcely remember the meal, although the waiter had provided a bottle of wine to make it seem more of an event. It was no use pretending that rationing and shortages did not exist. Maybe it was different at the grander establishments. He thought of the enigmatic Captain Wykes. *Wall-to-wall with red tabs and gold lace up to the elbows.*

'A brandy, perhaps? Is that possible?'

The little man looked around and murmured conspiratorially, 'I think we can manage that, sir.'

Masters glanced down at his wrist on the table, the two and a half gold stripes. His whole life. Once he had wanted nothing else, only the future and the next horizon. He shook his head, cursing himself. He should not have had the wine, not on top of Wykes' Scotch. *R.H.I.P.*

Maybe a walk before turning in . . . He felt his jacket pocket. At least he would be able to smoke his pipe without ruffling everyone's feathers.

He remembered that he had seen a bellboy march past the restaurant with a sign on a cane, the sort they usually displayed when tracing a guest or visitor. All it had stated was *AIR RAID WARNING IN PROGRESS*. As far as he could tell, no one had taken any notice.

He heard a woman's voice, low but insistent. 'No, thank you. I can give it to him myself.'

Masters turned in his chair and saw her walking between the other tables, apparently towards him, the little waiter peering anxiously after her. She was wearing what looked like one of the old-style naval boat cloaks, a must for every young officer and hopeful in the peacetime programme of regattas, reviews, and at some of the more desirable ships' parties; the collar was turned up, and she had covered her head and shoulders with a shawl. As she moved beneath the lights he saw heavy droplets of rain on her clothing. He was also aware that the room had fallen silent, and faces were turning to stare.

He got to his feet but she shook her head. 'No, no! Please do not disturb yourself. I hoped I might catch you, you see . . .' A small bag appeared through the cloak and she snapped open the catch. 'We thought you would be looking for it.'

She took out the lighter he always used for his pipe. It had a flame longer than most, something to be avoided if you were holding a cigarette.

'Captain Wykes said you might be here.' As she spoke she unconsciously pushed the shawl from her hair, shading her eyes, exactly as he had seen her in the conference room.

He took the lighter from her hand and said, 'I hadn't even noticed. Thank you.' He felt stupid and clumsy, unable to think properly. 'It was very good of you . . . I'm sorry. We were not introduced.'

She said, 'I shall sit for a moment,' and sat easily on the next chair. 'But *only* a moment. You must be tired out after your full day here.' She waved the little waiter away as he approached.

The cloak had opened across her knees and Masters saw that she was no longer wearing black or dark blue, he had never determined which in the glare and shadows of the conference room, but a dress of dark green, cut low at the neck, beneath which she was wearing the same glittering brooch.

'You are staring, Commander Masters!' She softened it with a smile. 'Perhaps I should not have been so direct. I have been told it is a bad habit of mine.'

Masters heard the murmur of voices returning to the restaurant. Who would not stare at her? Beautiful, striking; she was both, but very relaxed, and in control. She knew Wykes, but of course she would. And Wykes had a reason for everything he said or did. He was far too busy with yet another meeting to care about a lighter being abandoned in his office.

He said, 'The brooch . . . I saw it earlier.'

She glanced down at it. 'Jasmine flower. Yes, I like it a lot.'

It gave him a chance to watch her. Her hair was uncovered completely, and in the lights it had the colour of rich chestnut, loose across her forehead, and captured at the nape of her neck, he guessed, by a ribbon or cord.

'Have you been out for the evening?'

She looked at him again, very directly. 'I am just going out, Commander!'

She glanced towards the entrance. There were voices, and Masters recognized the tall figure of Capitaine Lalonde, impressive in full uniform, speaking on a desk telephone, wagging one finger to emphasize something.

She said, 'It is best to be certain these days. Two seats for a cabaret are not easy to obtain.'

Masters looked at the long curtains which hid and disguised the shutters and blackout screens. He saw them shiver, and imagined he could hear the dull thump of anti-aircraft fire.

He said, 'Isn't it rather risky?'

She had turned towards him again, one hand resting on her small bag.

'You are not one to be afraid of taking risks, I think.'

It was not a casual remark. It was like a challenge, and at the same time, a barrier.

She raised her hand to readjust the shawl, and from the other room Masters heard someone laugh, and the telephone being slammed down. It was almost over. It had never begun.

He heard himself say, 'I hope we meet again. After all, you know who *I* am.'

She regarded him calmly, the brooch giving the only hint of her breathing, her composure.

She half turned, frowning, and Masters saw Capitaine Lalonde standing in the doorway, beckoning urgently.

'Come, Elaine! It is time!'

She deliberately reopened her bag and took out a small mirror, but did not use it. Used to having her own way. Or was it something else?

She had eyes like the sea, he thought. Blue, or smoky green. She snapped the bag shut and pulled the cloak across her body.

'Yes. I think we may.' She regarded him as if coming to a decision. 'I am Elaine.' She turned up the collar, the rain still sparkling like diamonds, as if to prove that they had spoken only for a few minutes. 'Elaine de Courcy.'

Masters watched her leave, imagined her getting into a car with the French captain. And later . . .

'Your cognac, sir.' The waiter had returned.

'Thanks.' *Just in time.*

He looked at the empty chair, seeing her there. Imagining her with someone else. How it would be.

Why was he making an idiot of himself, when he needed all his senses? Perhaps it was Wykes' way of involving him completely.

She had the same name as the collaborator. She wore no rings; in any case she was too young to be his wife. Daughter, then?

103

The glass was empty. He signalled to the waiter, but the little man shook his head and said sadly, 'I'm afraid that will have to suffice for tonight, sir. I'm so sorry . . .'

Masters touched his arm. 'I know, my friend. The war. I'll just have to wait until tomorrow!'

They both laughed, but this time no one turned to stare.

He picked up the lighter and thought of her hand, so close, holding it out to him.

And it mattered.

7

Two of a Kind

As soon as the train pulled into Dorchester station Masters sensed that something had changed. It had been a long, slow journey, one of those special trains that seemed to move only at night. The powers-that-be obviously thought it a good way to avoid feeding anyone.

At Poole he had hurried from the train while some troops were being offloaded and checked by their NCOs, and attempted to telephone the base. He had been unsuccessful, and most of the telephone kiosks had been occupied in any case.

The town was even busier. He was tired and uncomfortable and needed a shave and a clean shirt, if only to make himself feel normal again. There was an unfamiliar car and driver waiting; he had been expecting it, but somehow it still came as a surprise.

The driver, another Wren, was very different as well, with short blonde hair poking out from beneath her cap and a cheeky, pretty face which, he noticed, was quick to respond to the whistles that came her way.

But she saluted and took his suitcase, her eyes taking in every detail of his unshaven appearance.

Masters had stood in the train's corridor for the remainder of the journey after Poole, having given his reserved seat to a young A.T.S. subaltern who had been sitting on her luggage. She had looked worn out, and her brilliant smile of gratitude had been worth the apparent resentment of his seated companions.

'Has something happened while I've been away?' He watched

the Wren toss his case into the back of the car, half expecting it to fly open. He was no match for Petty Officer Coker's expertise.

She stared at him, wide-eyed, obviously pleased that she had found somebody who had not heard the news.

'It was on the wireless, sir! Our midget submarines have clobbered the battleship *Tirpitz*!' She flushed. 'Sorry, sir. I meant that they exploded their charges under her.' But the excitement was irrepressible. 'Right up there, in the Norwegian fjord where she was holed up!'

Masters recalled Bumper Fawcett's interest, perhaps even involvement, with the midget subs, X-Craft as they were officially known. And they had done it. But at what cost? He might even know some of those who had taken part. It was hard not to compare, or to remember. *Tirpitz* was Germany's last true battleship, probably the most powerful in the world. While she had been lying in her fjord, out of range of most air attacks and safe from surface damage behind her booms and nets, she was a constant menace. If she had broken out and reached the Atlantic no convoy would be safe; no escort could hope to survive her massive armament. And while she was 'holed up', by her very existence she had tied down capital ships and, more to the point, the many desperately needed destroyers and cruisers which were required to screen their heavier consorts.

Nobody needed reminding that her sister ship, *Bismarck*, had broken out of her lair just over two years ago, and had sunk the battlecruiser *Hood* with the loss of all but three of her company. She had also put the brand-new battleship *Prince of Wales* to flight; *her tail between her legs*, the German press had gleefully announced. *Bismarck* had been sunk before she had been able to reach an Atlantic coastal base, but it had taken the skill and courage of the pilot of an elderly Swordfish torpedo bomber and half the Home Fleet to achieve it.

Masters recalled what Fawcett had said about Italian frogmen and their explosive motor boats. Courage and determination could bring down a giant.

He got into the car, an old Humber this time, while the little blonde Wren held the door for him. She smiled broadly as two army warrant officers marched past and saluted, although there was no need at this crowded station.

One, a regimental sergeant-major with a moustache like a brush, said as he passed, 'That'll show 'em, sir! Well done!'

It was the uniform. *A part of it.* Something they all wanted to share.

He noticed that there were several dents in the car's doors and wings, which even the camouflage paint did not disguise. She slipped behind the wheel and he wondered idly how she managed to see over the long bonnet. The clutch went in with a jerk, and he felt the ache in his back which rarely troubled him any more.

'Sorry, sir!' She was watching him in the mirror and must have seen his expression, and slapped her fist on the horn as an armoured scout car pulled out of the yard in front of her. She murmured, *'Idiot!'*

The other driver put out his hand in a brief but obscene gesture.

Fortunately, as far as he remembered, it was only five or six miles to the coast.

He turned to watch a group of sailors spilling out of the station, looking around for their transport and loaded down with bags and hammocks. Joining a ship somewhere, and obviously all strangers to one another. But the same infectious excitement had already drawn them together. On the plans and maps at the Admiralty's command bunker the effect of the X-Craft attack on *Tirpitz* would already be measured in careful statistics. More escorts freed for the vital convoys to North Russia, and capital ships, spared from their endless vigil in case the great battleship should break out of Norway, to lend their support in theatres of war where they were truly needed. But to the ordinary seamen it was more personal. For the *Hood*, and all who had died with her.

Or, as the sergeant-major had remarked, *'That'll show 'em!'*

He saw the first hedgerows as the car turned onto the familiar road; it seemed impossible that he had been away for so short a time. Dry branches scraped along the side of the door and he winced, and felt his stubble catch on his collar. He knew from experience that things could change very quickly, and it was still less than a month since he had taken this appointment. He confronted it once more. Since he had replaced Critchley.

He had gone over the London visit again and again in his thoughts. He had not seen Wykes before he had left, but had received a scribbled note of thanks from him, ending with *Will be in touch.* Perhaps nothing would come of it. But he had thought of the woman called Elaine de Courcy more than he cared to admit. He had not see her, either. He tried to shrug it off. Nor had he seen her escort, Capitaine Lalonde.

But he could not forget how she had looked, her direct manner of speaking . . . testing him perhaps, for Wykes, or for reasons of her own?

He saw the farm gates and then the old house as it loomed above the ragged trees.

He said, 'I'll not be long. I need to change and make a couple of phone calls.'

The little Wren nodded.

'I'll be here, sir.'

Petty Officer Coker had the door open before he could climb the worn steps.

'Heard you were coming, sir. The R.T.O. called from Dorchester.' He took the case, glancing at the Wren by the car. 'Made it without killing anybody, did she?'

Masters walked into the hallway. It was as if the house had been waiting for him. So still.Waiting.

Coker was saying, 'I've got a bath running, and some coffee on the go. You'll feel as right as rain, sir.' He took Masters' jacket and studied it critically. 'A quick press, I think.' Then he beamed, 'What about *Tirpitz*, sir? One in the eye for Jerry!'

Masters walked into the other room and looked at the telephone on the desk. There was a long envelope which Coker must have propped beside it, with Philip Brayshaw's name and rank printed in one corner.

He loosened his tie and perched on the arm of the chair. He dared not lie down.

He heard Coker bustling along the landing, whistling to himself. Glad to have things to do again. Glad to be in charge.

The envelope contained one signal pad flimsy, written in Brayshaw's fine, almost copperplate hand.

A full report of the MLs' action was waiting for him, with details of damage, if any, and casualties. All three boats were once again ready for operational work with the countermeasures team. He had already heard about the war correspondent who had been killed aboard Lieutenant-Commander Brock's boat; there had been a long and solemn announcement after the B.B.C. news, just before he had met Elaine de Courcy in the hotel restaurant.

His mind lingered on the last item. A new officer was joining the Land Incident Team. Eventually he would replace Clive Sewell at Portland . . . Masters felt his head drop but roused himself with effort. *He was joining today.*

Coker was waiting for him when he emerged from the bathroom.

'That was quick, sir!'

Masters buttoned the clean shirt. In submarines you soon learned to wash and dress standing on a pocket handkerchief.

'In the past, did you ever have a young woman named de Courcy visit here?'

Coker fenced the question. 'Would that be a foreign lady, sir?' He shook his head. 'A few ladies did come here, from time to time. Commander Critchley's friends – guests, that is.' He was clearly uncomfortable.

Masters glanced at the wardrobe mirror, where the uniform had been hanging.

'You'd remember this one, all right.'

Coker was polishing the peak of Masters' cap with a duster. 'Of course, sir, it's not for me to say, or speak ill of the dead, but Commander Critchley had quite a way with the ladies. Nothing serious, of course, he an' 'is wife were like one person together.'

Masters took the cap, vaguely satisfied. Coker had dropped an aitch.

He swung round as a clock chimed somewhere in the house; he recalled seeing a tall grandfather clock when he had first arrived, but he had never heard it strike.

Coker grinned. 'That young seaman, Downie, he's been a tower of strength while you've been away, sir. He's made things work which I've *never* seen in use – he even repaired my old watch. He's a marvel with anything electrical or mechanical.'

Masters walked to the stairwell. No matter how big the war became, the small, personal touches remained. And they mattered.

He could still hear Downie's despairing cry. *He was my friend.*

He started down the stairs. 'Could you call that army hospital for me? Find out how our Wren Lovatt is getting on?'

Coker watched him pause to examine the old clock. He called, 'She's bin moved, sir. I called meself, yesterday.'

He heard the car roar into life as the front door closed behind Masters' shadow.

He thought of the talks he had had with the kid, Downie, while he had worked on some repair job or other. About the officer who had been killed. Not like hero worship, but the kind of deep friendship you rarely discovered outside service life. Some might sneer at it; others might be more suggestive. But Coker had stood at so many tables and listened to his various charges, his officers, that he had learned not to fall in with the easy smut.

And Masters, who seemed to have no life of his own beyond duty and authority, could still find time to care about the lonely ones like Downie. He smiled. He should think a little more about his own troubles.

He studied the telephone, which was linked to the one downstairs. Where he had last seen her. It must be the same woman; she had been enough to turn any bloke's head. He had thought so at the time . . .

He heard one of his messmen clattering about in the 'galley', as the P.O. chef called it, and looked at his own sleeve. *Get three gilt buttons on your sleeves, and a chief petty officer's badge, and you can say what you like. Until then, keep your thoughts to yourself.*

He heard the car roar out of the gate. Lieutenant-Commander Masters would have to watch his step. After that other telephone call, he had never seen Commander Critchley again.

The Officer-of-the-Day was in a bad mood. The whole thing had got off to a really foul beginning. It had started at Colours when the captain, of all people, had noticed that some ratings out of the rig of the day had been loitering near the quarterdeck, a couple of them not even bothering to salute when the ensign had broken out in the stiff breeze. You could never be too careful with Captain Hubert Chavasse, especially when you were the O.O.D. He stared out of a window, hating what he saw. A silted-up creek, half cluttered with wrecked or damaged vessels. An old school building and some bricked-up cottages, and yet Chavasse insisted on treating it as if it was Whale Island's gunnery school, or some other crack establishment. It took more than barbed wire and the White Ensign to perform miracles.

He saw Jowitt, the master-at-arms, watching him from his own little lobby. The Jaunty would be enjoying it, seeing an officer all screwed up at the start of his day.

He looked at the clock. Masters would not be back for an hour. The Operations officer was adamant. *We have to deal with it. There's a flap on.* There usually was in this damned place, he thought.

The master-at-arms was speaking with his subordinate, the regulating petty officer, the crusher, as his breed was known on the lower deck. He saw Jowitt nod, his heavy face giving nothing away. Then, unhurriedly, he marched down his little path and waited for the officer to open the door.

'Got 'im, sir. Comin' in now, at the double, I told 'im.'

'Right.' He looked at the ensign, to make sure it had not fouled the halliards in the breeze. He did not belong here; it was simply part of a divisional course he had been ordered to attend. A bad report from Chavasse could ruin everything.

He saw the tall sub-lieutenant standing where he had left him. Very new, very young, and if he was anything like a few of the others he had met here, very sure of himself.

'I've found a rating who can assist you. The transport's ready and waiting. You've got the location, I take it?'

Sub-Lieutenant Michael Lincoln, R.N.V.R., said, 'I've always worked with someone I've known for a while.' He glanced at the two straight stripes on the O.O.D.'s sleeve. 'It helps.'

'He's good at the work. Been doing it almost since he joined.' He was losing his way. 'That should be enough, surely?'

111

The Operations officer peered out at them. 'Still here? Better chop-chop, the beast is too close to the railway main line for comfort!'

The Jaunty barked, 'In there, my son!'

The newly arrived sub-lieutenant regarded the youthful seaman with the torpedo badge on his sleeve with more than a little doubt.

'You're ready for this, are you?'

Downie said, 'I'm experienced, sir. Eighteen months.'

The O.O.D. put in, 'A good record too, I'm told?'

'We did eleven major incidents together, sir. And others.'

Sub-Lieutenant Lincoln smiled. 'What are we waiting for?' He watched Downie pick up his pack. *Eleven major incidents.* He had known men killed dealing with the first one.

Lincoln had been well trained, prepared would be a better term, but had not expected to be given a job on his first day here. He had seen the O.O.D.'s expression, recognized it; it was still happening even now, when the navy was officered and manned by volunteers and hostilities-only personnel.

Another raw subbie, so give him hell.

He thought suddenly of his father, his amusement turning to anger when he had told him he had been accepted for the navy, leaving his work as trainee surveyor with his father's firm.

'They'll soon put you in your place. I know their sort, toffee-nosed lot, you'll see!'

His father was a builder, and their home was in south-east London. The war had meant a complete end to all non-essential building work; his father must have been staring ruin in the face. But he was a hard, self-made man, and when the bombing had started in earnest, especially in the docklands and East End, he had seen and seized his chance. Factories and even tiny workshops had to be kept moving, no matter what. War Damage Repairs became the key for the building industry, even those with little or no experience. And there was good money in it, too.

No wonder he had thought it stupid of his only son to imagine he could step out of line and become a naval officer. A pilot in the Fleet Air Arm at that!

Lincoln had failed in the first attempt. His eyesight was good, or so he had thought, but it seemed not good enough to fly. He had been ordered to take an appointment at the naval barracks in Chatham, where he had first entered the navy before going onto his officers' training course at *King Alfred*.

His father had been almost jubilant about it.

'Told you, didn't I? But you knew best!'

Then Lincoln had seen the blunt announcement in Admiralty Orders that volunteers were required for special and dangerous duty.

When he had been accepted for the Land Incident Section and sent to H.M.S. *Vernon* for training, he had told his father what he had done.

His father had always been one with the quick, often crushing response: Lincoln had seen his mother growing old because of it. Looking back now, he realized that on that occasion he had not uttered a single word.

There was a car waiting, and a camouflage-painted van warming up behind it. Lincoln had heard the cross-talk on whether he should be sent to the incident or not. There was a flap on . . . It seemed he was the only officer available at this time. He had heard Masters mentioned too, and remembered him from *Vernon*. Knew what he was talking about, and never pushed anyone to or beyond his limit. He had been there.

Downie was clambering into the car. Eleven major incidents. He didn't look old enough.

Lincoln said to the driver, 'You know the place?'

'Piece of cake, sir.'

The car set off, and Lincoln saw the master-at-arms turn away to deal with some sad-looking defaulters, obviously something that truly counted in his book.

He glanced at Downie's hands, resting on his knees, his pack held by its strap. They were completely relaxed. *Eleven major incidents* . . . Did he never consider . . . ? He stopped it right there. It was always the same. Looking for an excuse, or finding fault, like his father?

He said, 'Who do you work with on a normal routine?'

'I've been helping Lieutenant-Commander Masters, sir.' Defensive. Wary, too. 'My own lieutenant was killed.'

113

Lincoln bit his lip, unprepared for it. 'Bad show. I'm sorry.'

'It was worse than that, sir.'

Lincoln did not press it any further. Somehow it would be pointless. How did he know?

Instead he said, 'Can I ask how old you are? You seem pretty young for one so experienced.'

Downie turned and looked at him for the first time. 'I'll be twenty in November, sir.'

Lincoln grinned and thrust out his hand. 'Then wish me luck. I'll be twenty-one that month.'

The driver kept his eyes on the narrow lane, looking out for the next bend, but he had overheard most of it.

What a job. Must be tired of life, the bloody lot of them.

He did not understand that the first, important barrier between his two passengers had been broken.

It was fifteen miles to the reported location, but as on all those other occasions it seemed to take an eternity. The driver was a good one, and with a military policeman leading the way on his motor cycle, waving other vehicles to one side or off the road, the time should have passed in a flash.

Downie knew it would be different, and yet he was still shocked that he had been unable to adjust. He could have refused; Lieutenant-Commander Masters had said that he should be on light duties until . . . He stared at some small cottages as they passed. Or *unless*.

The sub-lieutenant, after their initial exchange, had lapsed into silence, leaning forward every so often to peer over the driver's shoulder.

Downie made another effort. 'I know the place, sir. About five miles from Corfe Castle, north of St. Alban's Head. The railway line from Poole is close to the sea.' He frowned unconsciously. 'Intentional or accidental, it could cause a lot of trouble.'

They passed a line of parked vehicles, mostly military, a couple of redcaps watching to make sure that nobody tried to get past. They waved to the M.P. on the motor cycle, and threw up salutes to the car.

Downie felt his stomach contract. He should have eaten some

114

breakfast. He had already heard about the flap, and had seen two other teams leave for incidents elsewhere along the coast. He should have refused . . .

The road was empty now; there were probably whole convoys of trucks and cars, drivers and passengers cursing to high heaven while they waited for the signal to move. Trains as well. A mine could bring everything to a standstill just by being there.

He pulled in his stomach muscles but the feeling would not go away. A tightness, almost like nausea. He should be used to it.

They were passing open fields now. A man with a dog watching from a sagging gateway. Like the one in that field where they had seen the crashed Junkers, and heard the injured airman gasping and whimpering as they had been digging in and arranging their equipment.

The driver was braking. 'Here it is, sir.'

Two more soldiers were in the road, another crouched on a bank of earth, a radio handset held loosely beneath his chin. He saw the vehicles and gave a thumbs-up to someone who remained invisible.

Downie knew that, too. The relief: somebody else had arrived to take over. He tried not to lick his dry lips. *Us.*

A corporal walked to the car and said, 'Two hundred yards, sir.' His arm was raised stiffly like a signpost. 'That clump of trees. There's an old shed of some kind, not used for years, I'd say.' He eyed the sub-lieutenant impassively. 'Not much cover, I'm afraid, sir.'

Lincoln climbed down and stamped his feet on the road.

'God, it's bloody cold!' He looked at the trees. 'You saw it, then?'

The corporal nodded. 'Reported it at once.' It sounded like *of course.* 'A big 'un. More than that, I couldn't say for sure. Parachute's caught in the trees. I've put a marker in position.'

Downie had picked up his pack and joined the others beside the car. He watched the driver, and heard the impatient mutter of the engine. Eager to go. He turned up the collar of his greatcoat and felt the same sense of shock; he did not even recall putting it on.

Lincoln looked over at him. 'All set?'

'Where's the railway, Corp?'

115

The soldier glanced at him, surprised. 'In direct line.' He pointed again. 'Couldn't be much closer.' He repeated, 'No cover there, either.'

The other soldier said, 'There's a pile of railway sleepers beside the track, sir. Pretty solid, although . . .'

Lincoln said, 'It's better than nothing.'

And then they were walking together, their breath floating beside them in the cold breeze.

Downie looked at the green bank of hillside. Somehow you always knew there was the sea beyond.

No houses this time. Not like all those others. Deserted, abandoned; small, personal things scattered or left where they had fallen. Like it must have been in his home town, Coventry, after the biggest raid.

He had never really known anywhere else in his life, not until he had joined up. In his mind he could always visualise that same street, as if it might still be there in some other world.

Even the school had been only two streets away. There had been a grocer's on the corner, and a pub on the opposite one. His father's shop had been next door to it. His father was a quiet man, gentle, but even he had shown annoyance when broken bottles and other unmentionable items were left abandoned in his shop doorway.

They handled any kind of wireless or radio repair work and, on rare occasions, the sale of a new set. Charging accumulators for the older radios, wiring, fitting electric fires, they never turned anybody away. People came to chat and pass the time of day, until the pub opened, and Downie, almost without knowing it, had become as expert as his father. He remembered his uncharacteristic anger when he had listed his various skills to the recruiting officer, and had seen him write down *shop assistant*.

Too shy, his mother said. *You must speak up for yourself in this world.* It had been much the same when he had joined up. The banter and the brutal humour of the lower deck.

Until his divisional officer had sent for him, and had told him about Coventry. Even their old dog Bertie had been killed. That was why he had wanted to be a vet . . . he remembered telling a grave-eyed Masters about it.

He recalled the pretty Leading Wren in the car, the one in which she had so nearly died. She had tried to console him, without words, just her hand against his face. Trying to share it.

Lincoln came to a halt. 'There's the railway at last.' He slapped his stomach. 'Out of condition. Too many pink gins!'

Downie glanced at him, knowing he was talking for the sake of it. Worried, nervous? Yet he gave off an air of confidence. Impatience, that was it. He heard his friend's voice, clear and sudden in his mind. *Confidence is a trap. It can kill you.*

He took a firmer grip of his pack and said, 'I can see the sleepers they told us about, sir. They look as if they could take a knock.'

'Good thinking. Run out the wire from there. You know what to do if . . .' He did not finish.

'Yes, sir. I know.'

They walked on in silence. Once, Lincoln turned to look back. Downie did not. They were quite alone.

He had only been home to Coventry once. The mass graves, places where he had grown up recognizable only by street signs, if they were still standing; like Portsmouth when he had transferred to H.M.S. *Vernon* to begin his training. He had felt it there, too, an army of dead spirits trying to rise through and above the ruins to take revenge.

The parachute was the first real marker. It usually was.

Downie felt something was wrong. Maybe his nerve had gone.

He heard Lincoln murmur, 'Not too sure about this one.' He was thinking aloud. 'Quite a steep slope, so the blast would make itself felt directly on the railway. There's nothing to stop it. Trains might have passed through after this one was dropped. The vibration could have set it off. Somebody should have made it clear before we came out.'

Downie waited. Lieutenant-Commander Masters had probably come along this same line. Poole was the next stop. He suddenly recalled the P.O. steward who had found him so many little jobs to do. *To keep you out of trouble, my lad.* How they had talked, about Coker's service life, and then about Masters' father who had been killed in a peacetime explosion at sea. A destroyer captain; one of Coker's pals had served under him.

Downie had found himself talking about the Junkers, how Masters had come out to the danger area, and had thrown himself

117

over him to protect him when the mine had exploded, filling the sky with debris and huge clods of earth.

Coker had commented thoughtfully, 'Never stops, that one. Something drives him all the time.'

He looked now at Lincoln. He had watched Sewell at work on so many occasions, had got to know and respect his different moods, had learned so much from them and from him. *Clive.* He was surprised he had not seen it earlier. Sub-Lieutenant Lincoln was nothing like Sewell or Masters. He was trying to prove something, perhaps for his own sake.

He stared at the trees, moving slightly in the breeze from the sea.

'Wind's getting up, sir.'

'Don't remind me!' He had spoken sharply, and added as if in apology, 'Must get closer. It's taking too long. All we need now . . .' He broke off to stare at the sky as a fighter plane, a Spitfire from the note of its high-pitched whistle, appeared over the hill, catching the sun and flashing like a dart before vanishing over the next ridge.

Lincoln grimaced. 'Doesn't know how lucky he is!'

Downie twisted the strap of his pack again. 'We can go together, sir.' For an instant he thought he had gone too far, that strain and memory had made him forget the rules, officer-like qualities, O.L.Q.s, Sewell had called them, and had made him laugh about it.

Lincoln said abruptly, 'It would save time, that's a point. One pair of eyes might miss something. You never know.'

Again, he was reasoning with himself.

They walked on, the trees reaching out as if to enfold them, the torn parachute whipping out in the wind.

The 'beast' was half-buried in earth, glinting dully, although much of the long, cylinder-like shape was coated with exhaust from the aircraft which had released it.

Downie watched as Lincoln got down on his knees beside it. The pile of sleepers was about thirty yards away. They might just as well be on the moon.

He opened the pack and laid it flat on the ground. His lips moved, as if he were speaking to himself, possibly checking each instrument, refreshing a memory, some past incident perhaps.

Downie had been this close to a mine at this stage only once before; Sewell had suffered an injured wrist earlier, when part of a roof had fallen on him. Together they had disarmed the mine. One very like this, about nine feet long. Magnetic. Like the small device they had dealt with at Bridport. Safe enough if . . . 'I think you should use the spare magnet, sir.'

Lincoln had the callipers in one hand, his other on the mine, holding his stethoscope in place. Kneeling, his head back as he took several deep breaths, he reminded Downie of an athlete about to spring forward into a race.

Downie saw his wrist straighten. Taking the strain. It was almost over. The keeping ring would hold until the fuse was withdrawn. Clive Sewell had done it several times. The worst part was . . .

It was like hearing someone scream. That had been months ago. This mine had been dropped only last night.

He said, 'There's paint, just by your knee, sir!'

Lincoln tried to turn and almost lost his balance.

'What the hell are you talking about? If you don't know how to behave—' He seemed to take control of himself. 'What paint, for Christ's sake?'

Downie lifted the second magnet from his pack. 'Another fuse, sir, I think.'

It was essential to move, he did not know why. He scraped his fingers across a painted sign on the side of the mine. His heart was pounding wildly, choking him, so that he could barely breathe. He felt a fingernail split, vaguely heard Lincoln snap something at him.

But his own voice was suddenly very steady. 'There's another fuse here, sir.' It made him want to smile, even laugh. *Sir*. O.L.Q.s. 'It's sealed with something.'

Lincoln put both palms on the mine and said thickly, 'A booby-trap, the cunning bastards!'

How long they stayed like that he never knew, with the wind shaking the bare branches overhead, and somewhere, in another world, Downie heard a blackbird singing.

Using both sets of callipers, they removed the booby-trap first, and then the main fuse. Very slowly, until it was free and away from its hidden slot. Otherwise, it would still have been waiting for the sappers to come and remove the mine to somewhere safe. Just one movement, an inch or less. That was all it would have taken.

Or if an all clear had been given and an express had thundered past: the effect would have been horrific.

Downie picked up the tools, something automatic, but the routine always helped.

Had it been dark they might never have seen the crude disguise on the second fuse.

It happened. You only heard about it afterwards.

He saw Lincoln on his knees, away from the mine, retching and vomiting into the wet grass.

Then he threw back his head and shouted, *'Now! I hope you're bloody satisfied!'*

Downie wanted to help, to do something. The soldiers would be coming; they would expect some sort of signal. He swallowed. Or an explosion.

When he spoke again Lincoln sounded very calm, as he had been when they met.

'Sorry about that.' He did not offer an explanation. Would Downie even believe he had been shouting at his father? 'I'd like it if we could work together. As a team.'

Downie reached out to help him to his feet. A near thing. Lincoln had momentarily cracked. It could happen again.

But the past could not come back.

He picked up his pack. 'I think we'll manage, sir!'

The sappers could handle the rest of it, and soon everything would start moving again.

And we are alive. It was enough. Until the next time.

8

Narrow Seas

Lieutenant Chris Foley wedged his body into a corner of the ML's open bridge and felt the sea mist clinging to his face and eyelashes. The cold was bitter and penetrating, and the towel wrapped around his neck was sodden; when he moved too quickly he felt droplets of water touch his skin like ice.

But for the mist it would be daylight, or as good as. He peered at the compass, something he tried not to do too often. Everyone was on edge; it was more fog than mist, and in the Channel you had to expect anything.

South seventy West. Somebody stamped his seaboot on the wet planking to restore the circulation, and Foley heard at least two voices simultaneously curse the unfortunate culprit into silence.

Fog was an enemy, fog was a friend. Fog was fog.

ML366 could have been completely alone, sealed off from the whole world. He listened to the steady murmur of the engines, pictured the hull lifting and pitching in the offshore current. Heading back to base, another thankless task completed.

They were not alone. The same two motor launches were ahead and to seaward. Between them was their ponderous charge, a tank landing craft which was being escorted to the inlet, probably to end up as another wreck after further experiments and exercises had been carried out.

There were also two minesweepers, sturdy wooden vessels, listed as non-magnetic sweepers. It was just as well, he had thought, as the cumbersome LCT had broken down twice with engine failure, and the sweepers had been able to offer a tow until repairs were carried out.

They had made their rendezvous off the Isle of Wight where the relieved escort, which had included three powerfully armed motor gunboats, had headed gratefully up the Solent and into Portsmouth. They had earned it. The LCT had been met and escorted out of Sheerness, down and around the North Foreland and into the Dover Strait itself. A lot of sailors feared it; all of them hated it. With the enemy and the notorious Channel guns just a few miles away, and aircraft and E-Boats at any time to contend with, the Narrow Seas had claimed too many victims to be taken for granted.

Foley wiped the lenses of his binoculars with a piece of tissue, but that too was damp and useless. He pictured the chart in his mind. The Needles, like gaunt sentinels in the mist, were well astern now, the Channel opening out for the next leg, south-west to Durlston Head. He felt his lips crack into a smile. It would be Dorset again, the right county at least.

In the North Sea it had always been busy and dangerous, but he had never felt so restricted, hemmed in, as in the narrow seas of the Channel. There had been fast runs across to the Dutch coast, and sometimes further north to rendezvous with vessels trying to escape from Denmark, refugees, people who had been in the wrong place at the wrong time. Frightened, desperate; he often wondered what had happened to some of them. What might have happened in England if the worst had come about.

'Listen.'

Nobody answered. It was the dull, tuneless clang of a bell. A wreck buoy. There were too many to count any more. *Clang, clang, clang.* As if some withered hand was still tugging a rope.

Dougie Bass murmured, 'Starboard bow, sir.'

It passed slowly down the starboard side, a faint dab of green against the enclosing mist. In daylight you could see them marking every channel. Ships which had gone down, torpedoed or bombed, or rammed by accident in the tight-ranked convoys hurrying through the night without lights, and relying for the most part on the merchantman's own style of matchbox navigation.

The coastline was also marked by forlorn mastheads and sometimes the rusting upperworks of ships which had tried to beach

122

themselves and so avoid blocking the vital swept channels. On the east coast it was the same, but there at least you felt you had the chance to hit back, to pursue and cut off the escaping attackers before they could reach their bases.

Foley stared abeam. Here, they had only spitting distance to run.

He wondered how Tony Brock was controlling his temper, up there ahead of their slow-moving little group. He had had plenty to say when the orders were delivered. There was no glamour or excitement this time; it wasn't even worth having one of his well-known war correspondents along for the ride.

'Think I've got nothing better to do, do they? I'll crack a few heads when I find out whose bean-brained idea this was!'

The other boat was Dick Claridge's 401, somewhere on the port bow of the group. A good skipper, and well liked, still remembering his men who had been killed on the last venture across the Channel.

A shadow loomed up beside him. It was Allison.

'You said to relieve you, sir.' Even in the poor light his oilskin shone like black glass. As if it had been pouring with rain, or they had been speeding through this same offshore current.

'Just for a minute, Toby. I want to check the chart again.'

It was strange, but he no longer questioned it. Allison was new, but he was capable. More to the point, he cared. Even the longer serving hands had accepted the change. In a small company like this there would always be the hardened piss-takers. He smiled to himself. Even for *Old Chris*.

It took him a few seconds to recover his bearings once he was below. Even the smells were different, the galley shut and empty, without the everlasting aromas of cocoa, grease and tinned sausages. The W/T office lit by an orange glow, the operator's shoulders hunched over the panel, headphones glinting faintly as he turned to watch him pass. Bush was a good hand, and they were losing him soon. Going on a course for advancement, which he richly deserved. Like some of the others before him, Foley had almost had to threaten him to make him accept the chance of promotion.

He switched on a light by the wardroom table and peered at the

123

chart. It was sometimes safer to keep it here, and avoid spilling light into the bridge in a sudden emergency.

He checked his notes again, and the date. It was October, and he had circled it with care.

He had received a letter from Margot Lovatt. At first he had thought it was bad news, or that somebody was writing to warn him off.

It was neither. She had asked someone to write for her. Her wrist, she had been told, was still too badly sprained to put to the test. Perhaps it was the girl in the other bed, who had covered her eyes and pretended not to hear what they had been saying, before the doctor had cut short Foley's visit.

You will know by now that I have been moved to a different hospital. I sent word through my quarters officer. I didn't want you to think . . . She had told the writer to cross out the next piece. *I am feeling a lot better, but quite bruised. I have been worried about you. I think you know why. When you can get the time, I'd so like to see you again.*

She had scribbled her name beneath it, injury or not.

Foley leaned both palms on the table, feeling the engines' beat, the ceaseless quiver of the hull, like extensions to his own mind and body.

He closed his eyes tightly. After all this time, was it getting to him? They always said there was a limit. *What is mine?*

He glanced at the other cabin, where her cap was locked in a drawer.

How could it be? And if it was not this boat, it would be another.

He straightened up and strode towards the ladder.

The telegraphist named Bush called after him, 'All quiet, sir!' But it went unheard.

He saw Allison swing towards him as he climbed into the bridge.

'Tell the hands to stand to, Number One.' He waited until he had spoken to the boatswain's mate and then said, 'When I leave you in charge, that means *in command*, for as long as it takes, d'you hear me?'

He grasped his oilskin and urged him to the side. 'See that glow down there in the trough? The fog's clearing! We'll be stark naked in minutes!'

Allison answered quietly, 'I'm sorry, sir, I thought . . .'

He stared down as Foley grasped his arm. 'No, Toby. I'm the one to be sorry. Try and forget what I said.' He moved to the forepart of the bridge and watched the compass glow. Fainter now, and he could see the slender barrel of the three-pounder pointing like a finger, the remainder of the forecastle still cut off in darkness. As if it had been shot away.

Allison had moved and was speaking with the boatswain's mate, whispering. Foley wiped his face with his hands. *Probably thinks his skipper's going round the bend.*

'Closed up, sir.'

Foley raised his glasses again. The fog seemed paler, but showed no sign of moving. Like that time in the North Sea, the sea suddenly clear, hard and bright like metal. The clatter of cannon fire. Men falling, dying. Wood splinters and blood.

He heard himself say, 'Another wreck buoy coming up any minute.' Nobody spoke.

He thought of her letter, dictated to someone to make him know and understand. Perhaps she had seen what he had so carefully overlooked. That the boat, his little command, was his life. All he had. It would be only right to tell her, before it damaged her in some way.

'Wreck buoy, green four-five, sir.' That was Signalman Chitty, in his other role with the machine-guns.

Bass eased the spokes and said, 'The old *Latchmere*. Was mined a year back, and then sank in a few fathoms. Full of scrap iron, she was.' He cleared his throat. 'Still is. They'll never bother to shift the old girl now!'

Foley let the glasses drop to his chest. What he said was true. Like folklore; Bass had not even been in the Channel when it had happened. The wreck had become a feature, something on which you could obtain a running fix at low water if you had gone off course. Ships large or lucky enough to be fitted with radar could use the wreck's rusty upperworks and rely on their instruments. You never questioned it.

He reached out and gripped the voicepipes to steady himself as the hull dipped into another trough. Like an ice-cold hand on the skin. The breath of someone invisible, right beside you.

You never questioned it.

'All engines *stop!*' It seemed to take an eternity before the sound and vibration died away. It probably took three seconds.

Foley pushed across the bridge, wiping his face again, as if to clear his vision. There was nothing. It must be worse than he had imagined. *Nothing.* And all the while Tony Brock was forging ahead with the others. Oblivious. He would be merciless.

Not even a dismal bell this time. Too well known. Too permanent.

Allison was pressed beside him. Wanting to know, but perhaps still smarting from the unfair outburst.

Foley said, 'The channel widens here. The last chance for a surprise attack. If the shore radar gets a fix, it will only show a faint blip. The old *Latchmere.*' He hurried on, afraid to stop, but unable to convince himself. 'I was doing a mine-laying run on the other side, a year or so ago. Watching for a kraut convoy, thinking we were to seaward of it. Like Dick Claridge is doing right now. I think there's one of them waiting to cut across our stern.' He gripped his glasses until his fingers throbbed. The sea was clearer now, hardly a swell to ruffle the surface. Another blurred patch of green: the wreck buoy. Nothing.

Chitty said, 'Oil on the surface, sir.' Calm, matter-of-fact.

Another commented, 'From the wreck, mate.'

Bass snapped, 'She was coal-fired, *mate!*'

Foley took two strides and saw the three-pounder gun crew peering up at him. He made a chopping motion with his fist, and saw the gunlayer swing back to his sights.

The air was even colder on his skin. At any moment the fog would begin to move, if not lift.

'*Stand by!*' He did not even think of Shannon down there with his engines and dials. He would be ready. He had to be.

He could see the whole of the forecastle now, the guardrails laid flat to allow the gun full movement.

Still no sign of the other vessels. Brock or one of the others must soon realize that Tailend Charlie had vanished astern.

Allison thought the same. 'One of them's pulling back, sir.'

Foley stiffened. 'No, Toby. *Listen.*'

Bass cleared his throat, and swore as Chitty tugged the cocking lever of his twin Brownings. It seemed loud enough to rouse the old freighter's crew.

First it was no more than a frothing sound, then with an ever-mounting roar of power the other vessel's engines shattered the stillness.

The bow wave, mounting even as they watched, was a great moustache of spray against the sea and fog, a sharp-edged wave rolling across the water as the hull heeled over in response.

Allison had heard it only twice before, when he had been serving as a midshipman in an old destroyer, and the last time, when they had stopped in this boat to pick up the dead airman.

The enemy had already increased speed, the three big Daimler-Benz engines joining as one, drowning out all thought as the E-Boat smashed through the sea.

Any second now, and the guns would open fire. At this range . . . Foley slammed his fist on the voicepipes. 'Full ahead! Port fifteen!' He jabbed at the button by his hip. 'Follow him round!'

It was impossible. A madness. But the E-Boat had not seen them. So intent on a kill, her commander had overlooked the possibility of an extra escort. Foley tried to empty his mind of everything else, but the thought persisted. Why should an experienced E-Boat commander wait on the mere offchance of catching this or any other small group of ships?

The gunfire had started. Green and scarlet tracer lifting and ripping down, interwoven and deadly. The heavier bark of the enemy's cannon, the staccato rattle of lighter weapons, while the fog lifted and writhed in a wild panorama of battle. Here and there a hull would show itself in exploding shellfire, or a patch of sea open up as a fast-moving bow wave fanned out to reveal the speed and fury of the attack.

'*Open fire!*'

The three-pounder responded immediately, the shells tracking and following the E-Boat's rising wash. Hits, damage, impossible to tell. Brock's ML was heading through the scattered formation, loud-hailer blaring, signal lamp flashing, men frantically reloading magazines and ammunition belts, ready for another attack.

127

Brock's boat was slowing down, the sea lifting and surging over the bows.

'Close shave, Chris! Good thing you were on the ball! Cheeky bastard, eh?' Suddenly formal again. 'Keep closed up! Report damage and casualties, if any! Dick's taken a few bricks, by the look of it!' The wash mounted again; Brock was on the move.

'If not us, then what was that E-Boat doing there?'

He did not realize he had spoken aloud. Allison said, 'Waiting for something bigger, sir? The LCT would avoid a torpedo, even at minimum setting.' He faltered. 'I think.'

Foley touched his arm and felt him jump. 'Or something smaller. Maybe you've got something.'

The E-Boat did not return, and at first light three Spitfires droned over the little convoy for the final approach to the inlet. One of the motor minesweepers had been raked by cannon fire, but nobody had been touched. Dick Claridge's ML401 eventually worked alongside the pier, with four canvas-covered bodies laid out on her deck.

Brock wasted no time when he came aboard.

'Good thing you had your wits about you, Chris. But mostly just luck, I suspect!' He was grinning, so that some of the sailors turned to watch, to share it. *Like old comrades.* But Brock left nothing in doubt. 'Otherwise, old son, even your famous luck wouldn't save you!'

After Brock had departed to make his report Foley walked slowly through the boat, greeted with nods and smiles and the usual thumbs-up from someone he had known longer than most. The Chief, Ian Shannon, came up to shake his hand, regardless of the oil which bonded them together.

Luck, but how could it last? Had he not stopped, the E-Boat would have raked them when it had passed astern at full speed. With the German's heavier armament and some forty-two knots to back it up, these decks would have been a bloody shambles.

He thought of the letter again. *I was afraid.* Something he had always managed to control, which any ship's company should be able to take for granted in their skipper.

Afraid, then. Perhaps because he had found something which was outside this perilous, overcrowded existence.

Bass called, 'The Boss is comin' aboard by the look of it, sir!' He waited, gauging the moment exactly. 'We're all in one piece. I'll bet Jerry wondered wot th' 'ell 'ad caught 'im with 'is pants down!'

He hurried away to make certain that the gangway was manned for visitors.

It was as well that he did not look back, Foley thought. Luck was never enough.

She lay very still on the bed, listening to the wind sighing around the old house, rattling the window of her room. Outside it would be pitch dark, the road deserted. She could faintly hear voices, even at this hour: the waiting room, where a few patients would still be sitting and exchanging conversation about their ailments, or managing to remain apart in their thoughts. She had been born in this house, had grown up with it.

There was only a table light switched on beside the bed. The familiar picture over the empty fireplace had been slightly tipped at an angle when she had arrived. She moved the sheet across her body. She had been here for five days. It was still hard to accept.

A door banged and she heard someone leaving, coughing as he or she departed. When he was finished in his surgery her father would come and see her. Even that was strange. *How's my girl coming along?* As he might to any patient, but not to a daughter. Maybe that was his strength.

She moved to one elbow and looked around the room; it seemed so small, not as she remembered it when she was back with the navy. Three weeks' leave . . . She felt guilty whenever she found herself counting the days before she would be going back to duty.

She glanced at the little drawer in the bedside table. His letter was inside, and she wondered why she had not told her parents about it. It had been delivered by a sailor on a motor cycle, according to one of the nurses. She had wanted to meet and talk to him, to try and discover . . .

She had read the letter several times. His concern for her health, the treatment she was getting. How long it might take. How she was missed. Nothing about himself at all. Maybe that said everything.

She thought of the moment she had been preparing to leave the second hospital, one of those which had only been partly taken over by the armed services. Unable to dress in the uniform a Wren had brought for her, she had held herself upright against a chair and stared at herself in a long wall mirror. She was lucky to be alive. Black and blue, dirty yellow where the bruises were beginning to fade. Her father had remarked on it when he had examined her that first time, when she had lain here listening to the car pulling away from the house.

'Plenty of rest, my girl. I wish we could do so much more for you. But at least I'm in charge, and can make sure nothing goes wrong.'

Her mother had been there, the nurse again. Calm and contained while her daughter had been lying naked. All the lights had been on then, revealing the bruises, the livid scar where she had felt the glass gouging into her thigh and groin. The pain, and the terrible fear that she would lose consciousness, and die without fighting back.

'He was just in time, inexperienced or not.' Her father had sounded almost detached.

She thought of the letter. The things he had not written, the things she had seen on his face when he had come to visit her. To find her. *Inexperienced.* It angered her more than she would have believed possible.

She touched her body; there was only a loose dressing now to protect the scar. Her inability to recall the crash, the sequence of events which had followed, was almost the worst part. She knew that piece of road very well, but could remember nothing of the impact, only a sensation of falling, losing consciousness. Then the awareness that she was unable to move, of pain, and a terrible sense of danger. And silence. Then the hands, his hands, firm, insistent, holding her, opening her clothing, pausing on her breast; he might even have been talking to her, willing her to hold on. She had imagined that his hands were warm, until she had realized the warmth was her own blood. Mostly she remembered the strength of his grip, hard into her groin, the sense of shock which had persisted even then. Of her arrival at the hospital she recalled little but vague shapes and looming faces, pain and the inability to move. She touched the dressing. The skin was smooth, shaved, and she had felt nothing. *A necessary precaution*, her father had said. Was that all it meant?

She heard the buzzer sound; the next patient was being summoned. She lowered her legs over the side of the bed and carefully

130

put on her dressing gown. Soreness, like the bruises, remained, but the real pain was gone. She caught her expression in the mirror. Almost . . .

Across the landing was her brother's old room. That had been the most brutal reminder of how things had changed in this house since Graham's death in the submarine *Tornado*. As if time had stopped, but could somehow be restarted at any given moment. She had gone into look for something and had been shocked to see it exactly as he must have left it, as he would find it if he suddenly walked through the door. The photographs of his cricket team, and another of him with his two best friends at college. Graham had loved listening to jazz, and his gramophone and its piles of records were all arranged as before. She had found herself touching the record sleeves; his old favourites, Louis Armstrong, Bessie Smith, and the top one, Fats Waller's 'Ain't Misbehavin'', had all been carefully dusted. Even his dressing gown was hanging on the door.

The room at least was still alive.

A door banged, and she heard Mrs. Warren, Lucy, calling out something to the departing patient.

Lucy had been here as long as she could remember. Receptionist, assistant, housekeeper and friend, she knew everybody, and newcomers often consulted her before making an appointment. Her husband – she only ever referred to him as 'Mr. Warren' – was retired, but was seen about with his helmet and gas mask in his role as air raid warden.

She walked to the fireplace and straightened the offending picture. Lucy at least had been aware of her uncertainty, the lingering shock of the accident, the close encounter with death. She could make a joke out of almost anything without offence; she was just being Lucy.

She had helped Margot to bathe and wash her hair, and had almost laughed out loud when she stood naked in the bath, confused and embarrassed.

'If Mr. Warren could just see you, Miss Margot! Like one of his pin-ups out of *Men Only*, you are!'

Her spare uniform was lying carefully folded on a couch. That was the next battle. It was not the thought of going back; it was the idea of remaining here, in her own home, for three long weeks. It

131

was so unfair to her parents, to Lucy, to the few other people she had seen since arriving, that she wanted to weep.

An aftermath of shock, maybe. But Graham's memory was alive here. And she did not belong.

She left her room and walked barefoot down the stairs. The practice had overflowed into most of the lower floor. Even the dining room was laid out for the first aid instruction her mother gave a local women's group.

Her father was in his study, his glory-hole, he called it. Littered, untidy, and lined with books, some so old that they were almost falling apart, but she knew from experience that he could put a finger on anything he wanted. How she had always liked to see him, relaxed, if he could ever be, reading, or smoking a pipe, which he rarely did anywhere else.

He looked up as she walked into the glory-hole. 'I think you should put some proper clothes on, my girl. It's a little draughty at this time of the year. Coal rationing, you see.' He chuckled. 'But you wouldn't know about that in the Royal Navy!'

She settled herself into one of the few chairs not littered with papers or medical journals.

She said, 'I'd like you to meet him, Daddy. I think you'd get along well.'

He put an unused pipe cleaner into his book to mark the page and said, 'I'd like to meet him, very much, of course I would. He was there at the right moment. We all owe him that.'

She touched her thigh and moved slightly to ease the tightness of the scar. Her father said suddenly, 'Goes deeper than that, does it?' He smiled. 'I know how you must feel, but gratitude is no true basis for something permanent, you know. Take it from me.'

The door opened slightly, and Lucy said, 'You're missing your programme, Doctor. Mrs. Hillier kept me chatting longer than usual . . . never knows when enough is enough, that one!' Just for an instant her eyes shifted to the girl in the dressing gown. 'I'll bring some tea in a minute.'

Margot looked away. Even Lucy understood. It was hopeless.

The radio crackled into life, a calm, unhurried voice. 'It was my first real introduction to the work of the Royal Navy's Light Coastal Forces.'

Her father muttered something and made to switch it off. 'Well, thanks to Mrs. Hillier, I've missed it!' He glanced across as Margot exclaimed, 'No, Daddy, leave it on. Please!'

'. . . I shall never forget it. The courage and determination of those same men, boys, some of them, left me moved beyond words. I saw men die; one was well known in this profession. I watched ships burn. I was afraid. What kind of men can confront these hazards, sometimes night after night in the seas around our coasts? There were faces which would not have been out of place at Jutland, or at Trafalgar. And one in particular, who for me symbolized the strength, and the modesty, which must surely lead to victory. The captain of this particular "little ship", still in his twenties, but with a record of gallantry which was already known to me, remained with me long after I was safely ashore. When we first met I asked how I should address him. "Chris will do," he said. I shall never forget.'

The B.B.C. announcer's smooth voice cut in. 'That was Mark Pleydell, in the latest episode of *At the Front*. Next week he will be visiting . . .' The set went dead.

She stood beside the other chair, her hands on her father's shoulders. She had not even felt herself move.

'Now do you understand?'

The war correspondent named Mark Pleydell had been there with him, had seen what Chris endured or expected every time he went to sea.

And in my way I shall share it. Gratitude does not come into it.

She felt her father lift her hand to his mouth and kiss it, something he had never done before.

He repeated, 'I'd like to meet him very much, of course I would.'

Another door slammed, upstairs this time.

As if Graham was back, and 'Ain't Misbehavin'' would soon be shattering the stillness.

The moment was past.

The messenger held the door only half open, and said, 'The O.O.D.'s respects, sir, and your transport will be here shortly.' His eyes flitted around the small room. 'Ten minutes at the most.'

David Masters stepped back from the tiny window that over-looked the Operations Room in the main part of the building, in time

133

to see the seaman's expression. No doubt wondering why a place so important should be crammed into such a dump. The window had only just been installed, and there was still brick dust on the pile of folders beneath it. It enabled him to look directly at the operational plot, as well as the big chart that displayed all the latest incidents, according to their importance or otherwise; in some areas there did not seem room for any more of the brightly coloured markers. It also allowed the staff to work without the feeling that somebody was always watching them.

The messenger jerked his head. 'There's a Lieutenant Foley who says he has an appointment—'

'Yes. I'm expecting him. Thanks.' He noticed the heavy drops of rain or sleet on the seaman's cap and watchcoat. He had not looked out of doors since he had arrived, and that must have been earlier than he had realized. He had heard *Colours* being sounded on the bugle, and then after the appropriate interval, *Carry On*, the little base and establishment returning to work as usual.

But it was not as usual, not this time. He had sensed it as soon as he had entered his cramped office, and the Operations Room in particular.

There, the day was marked by long periods of boredom, waiting for something to happen or some signal demanding action. And interludes of strain, dealing with an incident, or several, trying not to reveal involvement or distress when an operation went wrong, and someone paid for it with his life.

This morning he had felt an almost buoyant atmosphere, not unlike his return from London when the news of *Tirpitz* had broken.

He glanced at his greatcoat, which was lying over a chair. Brand-new, delivered from Gieves yesterday.

Like a stranger's, he thought. Something he had not owned since he had been promoted. A raincoat or comfortable duffle had seemed more useful, more appropriate. Or had he been deluding himself again? Trying to close the door on that other life, and where his old greatcoat now lay.

But Coker had been pleased. 'Quite right too, if I may say so, sir!' He had peered suspiciously at the grey light. 'Looks like being the right day for it, an' all!'

134

And there had been the phone call from Bumper Fawcett. Did he never sleep? Not alone, certainly. He had heard a woman's voice in the background.

'I'm coming straight down! Not having a bunch of chair-polishers getting the jump on *my* department! Remember, top security all round, it'll be like a bloody hornets' nest before you know it, what?'

Masters rubbed his chin, surprised that it was smooth. He must have shaved in two minutes. His case was on the floor near the greatcoat. Coker had insisted, 'You might have to hang about, sir. Don't want those *Osprey* people showing us up, do we?'

He heard voices, then a tap at the door.

Foley, too, was dappled with sleet, and had obviously walked up from his motor launch without bothering to put on anything heavier than his working uniform.

Masters smiled. 'Sorry to drag you up here, but I'm about to leave for the Bill and I wanted to see you first.' He saw the momentary uncertainty, the shadows beneath the lieutenant's eyes. 'Everything all right at your end?'

Foley nodded. 'A bit of a filter-pump failure, but we'll have it fixed before the end of the forenoon watch.'

Masters looked at the new greatcoat and its bright gilt buttons.

There it was again. Like Coker. Something personal, possessive. Foley had said *we*. Some skippers would have been content with *they*.

He said, 'It's all *Most Secret*, but in a place like this it will be hard to keep it that way.' He touched a signal folder on the littered desk. 'Your initiative two days ago brought results. I intend that in the backwash of things your part does not go unnoticed – unrewarded, if you like.'

'I don't understand, sir. It was only a feeling . . .'

Masters tapped the folder. 'Hear me out. A feeling, fate, luck, call it what you will. But you acted as you thought fit, when nobody was in close company to offer advice or orders to the contrary.' He had walked to the little window without knowing it. One of the duty officers was actually laughing at something, and others were drinking tea as if they did not have a care in the world. 'A Royal Air Force Sunderland of Coastal Command was returning from patrol

135

on that same morning when you caught the E-Boat napping, coming in from the Western Approaches, probably thinking of nothing but getting back to base and a warm bed.' Without realizing it he had raised both hands, like an arrowhead. 'They were flying low, very low, and trying to avoid the worst of that fog, remember?'

Foley said, 'Worst I've known down-Channel for some time.'

'And suddenly there it was, right beneath them. Not even the fog tried to hide it.' His hands came together. 'A submarine.' He saw Foley's surprise. 'A *midget* submarine, experimental or one of their latest secret weapons, there was no way of knowing.' He walked back acoss the room, his hand brushing Foley's shoulder as he passed. 'Fortunately, for us, that is, the Sunderland had already been involved in a fruitless attack, a U-Boat sighting report, and had dropped all its depth charges. Otherwise the midget sub would be just another cross on a chart.'

Foley leaned forward, his mind suddenly clear. There was always talk of Germany building midget submarines. One had been taken overland to the Mediterranean, allegedly for use against the Russians in the Black Sea. It had seemed unlikely, but it had been sunk anyway by American fighter-bombers before it even left harbour. Others were reported under construction in Germany, and in occupied France. After the success of the X-Craft against *Tirpitz*, even the Führer's well-known animosity towards his own navy might be tempered.

Masters said, 'That midget submarine is now safe and sound at Portland. Which is why I'm going to H.M.S. *Osprey* at this ungodly hour.' He watched Foley, the emotions crossing his face. 'You have an excellent record, in command and beforehand. Promotion, a half-stripe, is the next step, and you've more than earned it.'

'We were all in it, sir.'

Masters rubbed his chin again. So that was it. Not afraid of promotion, but the fear of losing his command and all she had become. Foley was the sort of person who would never accept that it was mainly because of his own work and influence that ML366 seemed different from all the rest.

'Think about it, anyway. But you know the drill – the choice is not always yours in the end.'

He turned as another tap came on the door, and without waiting for an acknowledgement it opened very slightly, and Brayshaw peered in at them.

'Come in, Philip.' He sensed that Foley was as relieved at the interruption as he was. But it was necessary . . .

'Heard you were leaving for Portland, David. Just wanted to say I'm only sorry I couldn't come with you. Heard some of it, guessed the rest. Besides which, the Old Man has some extra work for me to deal with.' He almost winked, but not quite. 'You may have forgotten with all this happening at once, but Trafalgar Day draws near, and the Old Man has no intention of allowing it to pass unnoticed. Standards, you know!'

'You'll have your hands full enough, I'd have thought. Rear-Admiral Fawcett is on his way, and there'll be plenty of the top brass to keep you on your toes.'

Brayshaw said, 'I think your car has arrived.' He turned his cap around in his bony hands. 'By the way, your driver, Leading Wren Lovatt – heard a buzz about her yesterday.'

Foley said, 'She's all right, isn't she?'

'Must be, Chris. I heard from her quarters officer. She's asked to return to duty.' He looked at Masters. 'To her old job, if that's possible.'

Brayshaw had been there when the accident had happened, had made sure that the girl was delivered safely to the hospital. And the expression on Foley's open face told the rest of the story.

It should not interfere. The top secret signals between Portland and the Admiralty must have burned the wires red-hot. But it was not merely another gallant and exciting episode. It was right here in this scruffy office, in the front line again. *The midget submarine was equipped for laying mines.* There had not even been a rumour about that.

But this was now. Personal.

He said, 'I think I can manage that. If not, I'm sure the Captain's secretary will pull the necessary strings!'

Afterwards, no matter what lay in store, he knew it had been worth it.

9

The Catch of the Season

Portland seemed bleak and unwelcoming after a comparatively fast drive along the coast road. Mist had moved in from Weymouth Bay, and the Bill itself was partially hidden. It gave David Masters an uneasy feeling to be returning here so soon after his previous visit, although he had somehow expected it, and prepared himself. Everything was dripping from the early sleet, and he guessed it would freeze before the end of the day.

There were delays at the gates, passes to be checked, vehicles examined, and he noticed that even incoming working parties were being mustered and counted before station cards were returned.

H.M.S. *Osprey*, the main anti-submarine establishment and training school, was accustomed to distinguished visitors and the events which had drawn them, in wartime even more so. In the constant battle against U-Boats every kind of experiment was conducted, and the men who would eventually carry that knowledge to sea began here. Masters remembered his first experience as a sub-lieutenant, when he had opted for the submarine service: like a series of war games with models and complicated diagrams, to get the feel of things.

An officer checked his identity and that of the Royal Marine driver, even though Masters knew his arrival was already logged and expected.

The commander of the establishment was waiting to greet him. 'Security? It's a bit of a laugh at this stage,' he said.

On their way to the main building the commander described

138

the arrival of the captured midget submarine at Portland, and although Masters could sympathize with him and his immediate responsibility he could barely hide a smile.

Portland had had its share of the war. Bombing, the comings and goings of hard-worked escorts, minesweepers and rescue craft, shocked and injured survivors being landed, too often outnumbered by the dead. The triumphant Sunderland flying boat, being short of fuel, had been forced to return to its base, its vigil taken over by a low-flying Anson. Motor gunboats had eventually arrived, but the final task of securing the then motionless midget submarine was given to the minesweeper *Quicksilver*. Signals must have flashed back and forth, and by the time the sweeper had reached the base with her tow half the population had turned out to greet her, according to the commander.

The minesweeper *Quicksilver* was a converted deep-sea trawler, and her R.N.R. skipper an ex-fisherman of the old school. 'He must have used every flag in his locker,' the commander had added. 'Don't know how he found the space!' The skipper's signal had proclaimed *THE CATCH OF THE SEASON*.

Security had closed down immediately; furious signals had come from all directions, finally from the admiral himself. It was said that the trawler's skipper was unrepentant, for reasons all of his own.

There were two submarines in the harbour lying moored together, dark against the stonework, only their ensigns making splashes of colour.

The commander had seen Masters' expression. 'Takes you back, does it? I can understand that. It's never easy to change things.'

Sooner or later everybody seemed to know about it. And it always seemed to come back at times like this.

The commander said, 'I've got to report to the Captain. I think he's getting nervous about all the visitors.' He glanced at his watch. 'The conference will be in the first dog watch – anyone who arrives later will have to wait in line.' He grimaced. 'The mess bills will be sky-high!'

A midshipman was waiting to take Masters to 'the Vault', as it was known. He followed him through a heavy gate, and then to another gate, where an officer was waiting to check his identity once more. It was very polite and very formal. Masters thought of the triumphant *Quicksilver* and her return to Portland and could understand Bumper Fawcett's concern about security and the stable-door policy.

'I shall be outside, sir, if you need me.'

The midshipman was new, pink, and nervous. *Were we ever like that?*

The door swung open for him, and he lifted his foot automatically to step over the old iron coaming. It was exactly as he had remembered it, a great cavern of a place, concrete and high-roofed, vaulted to withstand the weight of the buildings above. And cold. Bitter cold.

Powerful lights shone down directly onto the central area, and there were piles of chairs, still folded, for the expected visitors.

The midget submarine stood beneath one cluster of lights, supported by improvised trestles. He knew something of the work done by Germany on these first small battle units, as they were listed. He stood motionless, oblivious to a group of figures who were standing beneath another cluster of lights; if anything, it was surprise that gripped him. It was so small, smaller than he would have thought capable of operating in open sea with any chance of success, or survival. Like two torpedoes, one clamped on top of the other, less than thirty feet long overall. The upper part, which in a true torpedo would have been the warhead, was a cockpit and the controls. The main and after part contained the power unit. He stooped to examine the lower section, where the real torpedo would be until the moment of release. Without effort he could recall the order and tension in the control room, as he had known and shared it, cherished, even in the face of danger. *You were a submariner*, until the end. He could not compare this, or imagine what it must be like for one man, alone and at the mercy of tide and wind, handling such a weapon.

Where the actual torpedo would be hung there had been a container, now elsewhere being examined in readiness for the conference.

He was close now, his hand touching the curved steel, as he might make the first contact with a beast. By standing on the lower trestle he was able to peer into the small cockpit. It was not just simple, it was almost crude: minimum controls, and as far as

140

he could see no compass at all. The one-man crew, once installed in his narrow seat, was sealed in by a perspex-glass dome not unlike a dish cover. It was lying now on a bench, and he could see a notch in the perspex which was the aiming point when a torpedo was ready to be fired. The fore-sight was a plain iron spike at the forepart of the craft itself. Masters tried to imagine the countless problems and hazards the crewman or 'pilot' would have to overcome. He would have to operate in clear visibility and reasonably calm conditions if he was to get near enough to a potential target to have any hope of success. That would make his chances of being detected all the more likely. From the marks on the side of the carrier-torpedo, it seemed that the pilot's head would be only a foot or so above the waterline.

'Quite something, isn't it?'

Masters turned and saw a tall figure dressed in white coat and rubber boots watching him. He had thick hair, quite grey, even white beneath the glaring lights.

'David Masters, isn't it? We were expecting you.' He held out his hand, but realized he was still wearing rubber gloves and withdrew it. 'Come over here.'

The little group by the other bench parted to let them through. They all wore white coats, and were comparing notes; one was putting a camera back into its case.

'I've made sure the other items were set aside.'

Masters glanced at the small collection of numbered objects, and the dead man on the table. Naked, pallid, pathetic. One fist was tightly clenched, the other open and flat as if feeling for something. His eyes were closed, but in the hard lighting there was a faint gleam, as if he were still watching, listening.

'Already dead when the Sunderland spotted him, we're pretty certain of that.'

When Masters turned back the tall, grey-haired figure was being transformed, helped into his uniform jacket, that of a full captain, with scarlet cloth between the gold lace. As a surgeon it was not possible to rise much higher.

From his own experience, Masters had always thought naval doctors looked more like medical students in uniform. Not this one.

The surgeon captain was saying, 'Exhaustion, strain, hardly

141

surprising cooped up in that thing. Then breathing problems, oxygen failure – never knew what hit him.'

Masters looked at the objects on the table. A compass, one which would fasten to the pilot's wrist. A compact torch. A notebook and a folded chart; map would be a better description.

He said, 'How could they give anyone such a task? A small motor, no means of submerging as far as I can see, and a compass worn like a wristwatch, probably made totally inaccurate by all the gear in the cockpit.' He turned over a canvas folder and saw a photograph of a young woman holding a child, smiling and waving at the camera. 'What would make anyone volunteer for this?'

The surgeon said evenly, 'You're the last person who should be asking that, I'd have thought.' He smiled, and the mood was gone. 'You don't remember me, but I was at Haslar Hospital when you were brought in. You were a volunteer, as I recall.'

Masters walked back to the submarine. In X-Craft like those which had laid their charges under *Tirpitz*, there was a four-man crew. Even the earlier Italian 'chariots' had carried two.

He said, 'A special kind of courage.'

'You make him sound like a hero.'

Masters looked back at the other table, where the corpse was now covered by a sheet. Listening . . .

They walked out of the glare and into the shadows, Masters glancing back in time to see one of the surgeon captain's assistants kicking off a rubber boot and steadying himself with one hand resting on the sheet.

It was not even a true submarine; it might even be the only one of its kind so far. And had it been carrying a torpedo as intended, he might have heard nothing about it.

But mines had been discovered. A new type of mechanism or charge, that made all the difference. He was involved; there was no escape. In his heart, he knew there never was.

Outside the door the young midshipman was still on guard, Masters' new greatcoat carefully folded over one arm.

They would probably hold a Trafalgar Night dinner here in *Osprey*, although not on the grand but moving scale of pre-war times. As junior officers they had joked about it, the martial music from the Royal Marine orchestra, the feasting and the toasts, and a stirring speech from some senior officer to round it off. *The Immortal Memory*. And in its strange way, it had meant something. What would the little admiral think of this new navy? Guns that could fire twenty miles, torpedoes that listened, and honed onto a vessel's engine noise. And the mines, contact, magnetic, and now what? Perhaps Captain Chavasse was right to hang onto a glorious past, and leave the other war to the daring and the desperate.

'Shall I see you at the conference, sir?' But the surgeon captain had gone.

Osprey's commander met him in the main lobby. 'Saw it, did you?' He did not wait for a reply. 'Rear-Admiral Fawcett's office called. He's arriving within the hour. Wants to see *you* immediately. Sounds full of it!'

'Is he staying here, sir?'

'Funny thing actually, no. He's arranged to be billeted at a house in town. Owned by a friend of his, apparently. I was quite relieved. I'll have enough top brass on my plate as it is!' He beckoned to a petty officer and hurried away.

Masters was escorted to one of the cabins used for officers undergoing training. A chief steward commented that it was not what he might have expected, but his tone implied that he was lucky to get it, under the circumstances.

Two beds were made up, two others uncovered, the bare springs vaguely hostile. Alone again, Masters sat down and thought about the dead man in the Vault. Not old, not young. Not powerfully built, one of the Master Race. It had been an ordinary, unremarkable face.

He touched his cheek and felt the scar. A hero, for all that.

He was awakened in the chair by the same C.P.O. with a cup of tea, and the information that the conference was timed to begin in ten minutes.

Masters realized that he had not eaten anything since he had arrived, nor had anything to drink. Which was probably just as well, he thought.

Things were finally moving. It might even be constructive.

But as he straightened his tie and adjusted his jacket he found himself thinking of the unknown German sailor, and the photograph he had been carrying when he had died.

143

It was better, safer, not to see your enemy as something human, and ordinary. They were too often like yourself.

Chris Foley sat on the bunk in his tiny cabin and waited for his companion to finish his drink. Even with the door closed and the wardroom, such as it was, between them and the forward section of the hull, the din from the messdeck was overwhelming. It would soon be over, the jokes and the recollections, the moans and the yarns about old runs ashore, never anything bad.

Telegraphist Colin Bush was leaving ML366. Tomorrow his name might not even be mentioned. It was safer, or so sailors believed.

Foley saw his companion look up. Lieutenant Dick Claridge was the same age as himself, but was strained and on edge and appeared years older. Twenty-five, and there were grey hairs at his temple where his cap had left an impression. He was thinking of his own command, ML401, lying alongside; during rare breaks in the noise they could hear the squeak of fenders between the two hulls and the thuds of hammers, men working to repair the shot holes and other damage left by the E-Boat's parting fusillade.

Claridge said, 'I lost four good men. What with the others in the sickbay, it's like losing half your crew.' He watched Foley pouring another gin. 'Lucky we're standing down, Chris. Tony Brock would be somewhat pissed off if we were unable to put to sea if so required!'

Foley smiled. Brock was tough and unbending, and had never been known to turn and run, even against odds. But nobody really liked him. Maybe that was how he preferred it.

He wondered how much everyone knew about the midget submarine, or if Claridge resented not being told. *Not that I know much.* He thought of Masters, in Portland right now, in the midst of some complicated conference. Hating it, a man of action but, unlike Brock, one you could go to if you were at odds with something. And he had not been afraid to share secret information. Trust was the bonus.

Someone rapped on the door and called something. There was, if possible, even more noise.

Claridge said, 'It's breaking up.'

144

Foley looked round for his cap but decided against it. 'Time to do our bit!'

Claridge smiled for the first time and raised his glass, slopping some of the gin over his tie. '*Yours*, I think!' But he stood up anyway.

They were all making their way aft towards the main ladder. Bush was the only one properly dressed, already a stranger amidst the scruffy, seagoing gear and thick sweaters. There was a heavy smell of rum from carefully and illegally hoarded tots, no doubt kept for this very occasion.

Bush paused outside the W/T office and thumped the bulkhead.

'So long, you old taskmaster!' The others cheered, and one almost dropped Bush's suitcase.

Titch Kelly shouted, 'I told you you'd get promoted! All that sniffin' around the officers paid off, didn't it, you bugger!'

Bush seized his shoulder. 'And what'll you do without me to watch over you, you scouse git? It'll be back to the bloody glasshouse, you'll see!'

They grappled and almost fell. It made it all the more moving, Foley thought.

Leading Seaman Dougie Bass barked, 'Attention on the lower deck there!' He threw up a mock salute. 'Ready for inspection, *sir*!'

In the sudden silence Foley could imagine what the departing telegraphist would be thinking, remembering. There were no words needed. Bush had already had a drink with him before the messdeck farewell. A good hand, one of the longest serving in this boat. His replacement was arriving some time today. They said.

He held out his hand. 'You're doing the right thing, Sparks. Good luck. It wasn't all bad, was it?'

Bush grinned. 'Thanks, sir.' It was all he could muster.

Foley stood back in the wardroom and watched the bustling throng; they were making heavy going up the ladder, where either the Crusher or one of his regulating staff would be waiting to see Bush safely to his transport.

He rejoined Claridge and solemnly poured another drink.

'He'll be missed. It was bad enough when my Number One left.' He shook his head as more shouts and laughter drifted down from the upper deck. 'But his successor has done well. *Is* doing well, by the sound of it!'

Allison appeared at the door, his cap in his hand, his hair looking as if it had been combed with a rake.

But he was grinning. 'Glad I missed *that*, sir!' He nodded to Claridge. 'Telephone call at the ship's office. Lieutenant-Commander Brayshaw caught me as I came aboard.'

'Did he say who?'

Allison shook his head. 'Not a word.'

Claridge stood up as if to leave but Foley said, 'Finish the gin. I feel like opening another!' In fact he did not. His head was pounding like a drum, and the brutal sadness of Bush's farewell had touched him in a way he would have thought unlikely, something he could not afford to show.

For Claridge it would be worse. Four men killed, two wounded. They might be ordered to sea tomorrow, where a wrong move or some hesitant newcomer could bring chaos or disaster.

He arrived at the ship's office slightly calmer, his head clear again. It was cold and still misty; probably far worse over the Bill, he thought.

Brayshaw was not in the office. A leading writer pointed to a telephone on the desk.

'Might have been disconnected, sir. Lot of traffic today.' He collected an empty mug. 'I'll leave you alone, sir.'

Foley picked up the telephone.

'Lieutenant Foley here.'

It was quite silent, so that other noises seemed to intrude. Typewriters, and the monotonous clatter of a teleprinter. Somebody on another telephone. And then her voice, so clear that she could have been here beside him.

'Chris, it's me, Margot.'

'Where are you? Are you all right? I heard . . .'

She laughed, or it could have been a sob. 'Don't talk. I've run out of time. I could hardly get through.' She broke off, as if somebody had come in and was listening. When she spoke again he could hear her breathing, her lips touching the mouthpiece. 'I'm being allowed back. Tomorrow, or maybe the next day. It's all fixed.' Again the hesitation. 'You are pleased, Chris?'

He said, 'I can't wait to see you.' He tried again. 'I can't wait!'

Someone banged open the door, apologized and slammed it shut.

Foley heard neither. He said, 'Are you recovered enough? They told me . . .'

She interrupted him. 'I shall call you as soon as I can.'

There was a scraping noise on the line. He said quickly, 'I love you.'

But the line was dead.

Paymaster Lieutenant-Commander Brayshaw entered the office and said, 'Not too late, then?' He smiled gravely. 'I'm glad. *Very.*'

Foley stared around the office, unable to believe what he had just said. What would she think?

Brayshaw was saying, 'I spoke to her for a few minutes while I sent someone to find you. She sounded fine.'

He thought of the day in that same car, when they had been waiting for Masters, and after the explosion when he had appeared, helping the young rating at the gate. He had thought then, a girl who would be easy to love, but probably a stranger to it herself. And after the crash, when he had watched them together. He had felt it then.

'Light duties for a while, of course. But she told me she wants to drive again.' He remembered her husky laughter on the telephone. *I don't think they'll trust me with an old Austin Seven after this, sir!*

'It might be too soon for her, sir.'

Brayshaw looked at the telephone as it rang again, from another extension this time.

'She thinks not, Chris. And remember Trafalgar Day, will you?'

'I'm sorry, sir?'

Brayshaw had his hand over the mouthpiece and was smiling broadly.

'It's her birthday, you see.'

Masters folded his arms and pressed his spine against the iron-hard chair. There were about thirty people present in the Vault, only a few of whom he recognized. He glanced over to the midget submarine where Rear-Admiral Bumper Fawcett was sitting, with an aide who was endeavouring to make notes in the hard overhead

147

lighting. Seated on his other side was Sally, the Wren third officer who had often worked in the office at *Vernon*.

They had all met in the lobby and Fawcett had said casually, 'Of course, you know Second Officer Kemp, don't you? I was forgetting.' He had turned away to snap something at his driver and Masters had said, 'Congratulations on your promotion, Sally. You're on his staff too, I see.'

There had been no time left, but Bumper had insisted they have a drink before joining the conference. It could hardly begin without him.

To proclaim a victory. A conquest. He had seen Fawcett's hand on her shoulder while he was looking at some paper she was holding for him. The hand had moved to her hip, and she had not protested or stepped away.

Masters said, 'I'm not sure I should comment on . . .'

She had retorted, 'Then don't – it's none of your business, *sir*!' She had reached out unconsciously and touched his arm. 'But thanks.' She had let it drop to her side again. 'Can we leave it now?'

He had always thought he knew Sally quite well. Obviously, he had been mistaken. It also explained why Fawcett was not sleeping at *Osprey* tonight.

Somebody coughed and that started a chain of coughs, like a protest.

He had touched one of the fat radiators when he arrived. It had felt like ice.

Osprey's Staff Engineer Officer was delivering his conclusions on the midget submarine. The electric power unit could offer five knots and no more, so that point-blank range would be required for any certainty of a hit when using the single torpedo.

The imposing surgeon captain had already covered the other risks taken by any one-man crew, exhaustion, lack of sleep, loss of direction, failure to find the target, oxygen supply breakdown.

He had seen several faces turn towards the other bench, but it was empty now save for a rolled white sheet and the wrist compass.

A mines expert spoke next, but he could add little to what was already known. The midget had been fitted with a container for carrying mines; the mechanism had already been sent to H.M.S.

Vernon for the boffins to pit their skills against their opposite numbers in Germany. He had disclosed one piece of intelligence. The mines were of a new type, small and therefore easy to distribute. More to the point, a fuse had been removed from the container, which was apparently fitted with a photo-electric cell. Masters had been aware of the eyes directed towards him. Another new fuse? One which might be sensitive to light, or even the passing of a shadow?

'Then there's no time to be lost, is there?' Masters had not seen him arrive, but there was no mistaking the crisp tones of Captain James Wykes. He leaned forward but stopped, imagining for a moment that the light and shadows were playing tricks, like the first time he had seen her, in London.

She was standing by one of the concrete pillars, dressed in dark clothing, only her face pale in the glare. Her hands were invisible and he realized she was holding them beneath her armpits, and was shivering.

She was looking at him, had perhaps already seen him before the first speaker had taken up his position by the trestles.

With Wykes, or was she still in company with the French officer?

He beckoned, and saw her shake her head.

There had been a break; somebody was asking the speaker to repeat some figures for his notes. Masters stood up and crossed to the pillar.

'You must be freezing. Come and sit over there. At least this will keep you a little warmer.' He unbuttoned the greatcoat. 'You can christen it for me.'

She seemed about to protest, then let her hands fall as he draped the heavy coat over her shoulders. He sensed a sudden resistance when he touched her elbow and guided her towards the chair beside his own.

'I had no idea you would be here.'

She might have shrugged. 'I did not know myself, until the very last minute.' She glanced at the bright gold lace by her chin. 'Don't you feel the cold, Commander Masters?'

He smiled. 'Only when I'm being put in my place.'

She looked at him directly, as he remembered. 'It was good of you. I thought they could afford some heat for the occasion!'

149

The lights came on even more brightly, revealing the worn stone and damp brickwork; people were on their feet, peering at their notes and one another. A few were gathering around the midget submarine which had somehow dominated throughout the conference.

She said, 'I saw you speaking to that girl, the Wren officer, before I came into this ice-box!'

'She used to work with me sometimes. Very reliable, too.'

She smiled faintly. 'I know that look. I recognized it. I believe the young lady in question had rather deeper feelings than that for you?'

'Ah, here you are!' It was Wykes, this time in uniform, and in the ruthless lighting even more crumpled than when they had last met. The four gold stripes on his jacket were almost brown with age, and a floppy handkerchief flowing from his breast pocket added to the impression of a retired actor recalled to play an old and necessary role. He smiled and touched the greatcoat. 'Suits you, Elaine! I'm glad he's taking care of you.'

A lieutenant hurried past but paused to murmur something. Wykes turned and gave a mock bow.

'Good to see you, Keith! I thought we might get a speech out of you too, eh?'

Keith. It was Bumper Fawcett, a grin on his face, and certainly no resentment at such casual informality. Masters also noticed that they made a point of not shaking hands.

Fawcett said, 'James and I go back a long way.' He beamed and touched the gleaming lace on his own sleeve. 'But I made it – that's the difference!' He looked at his watch. 'Must be off. I've some other business to deal with.'

He slapped Wykes' arm. 'We must meet, discuss things, what?' He nodded to the others. 'Business first!' He strode away.

Wykes opened his cigarette case. 'I saw the "business" just now.' He shook his head. 'He never changes.'

Then he, too, hurried away.

Masters said, 'Are you really going up to London again tonight?'

She was looking past him, so that he was at liberty to study the chestnut hair, the high cheekbones. Beneath his coat she was wearing what appeared to be dark blue battledress, almost a uniform without markings.

150

'I expect so. It all depends . . .' She did not finish.

A voice called, 'Drinks will be served in the wardroom, gentlemen.' A pause. 'And ladies, of course.'

Someone shouted back, 'Quite right, too!'

'I've got a driver somewhere. If I could drop you . . .' He glanced up as a few flakes of cracked paintwork drifted through the glare like falling snow.

People were leaving now, some obviously relieved that the conference was over. The conclusions would be drawn later; others would make the decisions.

She had her hands up to the collar of his greatcoat, ready to slip out of it, to break the contact.

He said, 'You'd be quite safe, with me, I mean.'

She nodded slowly. 'I would make sure of it, Commander Masters,' and looked past him. A lieutenant had appeared from nowhere.

'A call for you, sir. In the commander's office . . . sorry to interrupt, miss.'

Masters said, 'Please excuse me, Elaine.' He did not see her surprise, or her sudden concern. 'Don't go, please.'

Wykes joined her. 'Getting along all right, Elaine? He's a good chap, uses his brains.' He touched the greatcoat. 'Not his rank.'

'He was just called away.'

'I know. Bad news, I'm afraid. One of his team died – just now, as a matter of fact.'

She thought of the falling paint flakes. The look on his face. As if someone had shouted, and he had been the only one in the place able to hear it.

Wykes said calmly, 'You'll be working together, up to a point. If you can't do it this is the best, maybe the only, time to say so.'

They walked in silence together, and when they reached the main building it seemed almost tropical in comparison. But she did not remove the greatcoat; if anything, she held it closer across her breast, and the brooch that glittered there whenever it caught the light.

She saw *Osprey*'s commander standing by an open fireplace, gazing up at a huge painting of Nelson's *Victory* breaking the French line at Trafalgar, although he did not appear to be seeing it.

The office door was open and she saw Masters by a desk, one hand gripping its edge.

She recalled how protective he had been; she had been surprised by her own reaction. She was not unaware of glances, or the casual touch of hands. Like the young Wren officer she had seen in the lobby, and later sitting beside the rear-admiral nicknamed 'Bumper'. She could cope. Had coped, until her guard had dropped. And yet, just now, she had felt something like a challenge.

She saw him put down the telephone, with great care. As if it mattered. He turned and stared at her, but, like *Osprey*'s commander, she knew he did not see her.

She said, 'I may have to go soon.' She ran one hand up and over the gold lace. 'You'll be wanting this.'

She walked across the carpet, her eyes never leaving his.

He said, 'A sub-lieutenant, one of the trainees. John Mannering . . . His father once served with mine, can you imagine?'

She did not speak or move. Someone had closed the door behind her. They were alone.

'Another incident, just now. A magnetic mine. Old hat, I suppose somebody said, after all we've discovered lately!'

She felt the sudden bitterness, anger, despair.

She said quietly, 'You knew, didn't you? I saw it in your face, your eyes.'

'There was nobody else available. How many times have I heard that? And the bad thing is, it's usually true. There aren't enough, like that poor devil in the midget sub, who are brave or skilled enough to do it.'

He moved as if to turn away, shut her out. She said, 'No, tell me. Hold me, if it helps.'

He put his hands on her shoulders, her hair against his face.

'He was only twenty. And he trusted me. Now he's dead.' She felt his body shake. 'It was his first beast.'

Afterwards, she thought it had sounded like an epitaph. For the young sub-lieutenant, and perhaps for the unknown German who had died alone.

10

Ghosts

Masters was to meet Elaine de Courcy sooner than he had expected or dared to hope. The parents of the sub-lieutenant who had been killed had requested that a service be held at the base, so that his friends and some of those he had served with could be present. John Mannering had not been in the service long enough to have many of either, but Captain Chavasse had been sympathetic, even eager to oblige, and with what outsiders might regard as unseemly haste it was arranged.

A firing party of gunnery ratings, drilled and vetted by a senior lieutenant who had, as one three-badged able seaman remarked, 'buried more poor Jacks than any undertaker', and a naval chaplain made an impressive display. Even the weather had eased. A lingering mist on the Channel hid the division between sea and sky, but there was sunshine too, and a light breeze to ruffle the sailors' collars and lift the White Ensign.

They met outside the wardroom building and shook hands formally, like strangers. She said, 'I had no time to tell you I was coming. Captain Wykes is here, too.' She smiled quickly and he realized that he was still gripping her hand.

He released it. 'Sorry. It's been a bit of a rush down here.'

Surely Wykes had not come this far for a memorial service for someone he had never even met. He was too busy, and their lordships would not be amused. The girl turned away slightly to watch the naval guard stamping into position and picking up their dressing, a gunner's mate breaking the silence with hoarse barks of command.

Surely it was no coincidence that she had come with Wykes; he had almost expected to see the French *capitaine* here as well.

Close to, in the fresh light, she was even more striking. She wore a dark fur coat, one hand holding the collar closed against her throat, but unlike the other women he had already seen her hair was covered with a silk scarf, not any sort of hat. On her, it seemed right.

He was still troubled, unnerved even, by his reactions that night, when he had been told about the subbie's death. He had tried to remember every part of it, her warmth, her body when he had held her. He wanted to smile, to mock himself and his clumsiness. But it would not come.

She faced him again, her hand shading her eyes from the watery sunshine.

'I had a quick look at the little church when we arrived. They care for it very well.'

Masters watched the gunnery officer making a final inspection of the firing party.

It was like sharing a secret. So she knew the church . . . Maybe she did not care. He found that he was going over it again. When she had been called away; a car had arrived to take her back to London. Just like that.

She had put the greatcoat over his arm and had been thanking him, at the same time waving to the driver and Wykes by the door. He said, 'We shall meet again soon.' And she had turned her face, a lock of hair falling across her cheek as he had kissed it. A second, no longer. And she was gone.

He had not imagined it. After she had gone he had held the collar of his greatcoat to his face. The same perfume still lingered in his quarters, something he knew he would never forget.

She was not a girl; she was perhaps the same age as himself. Intelligent, confident, someone used to men being interested, persistent if the chance offered itself. *I know that look. I recognized it*, she had said of Sally. The Frenchman, perhaps? Others?

Chavasse, with his secretary Brayshaw at his elbow, had reappeared, his eyes directed briefly at a bugler and then at the chaplain. He was ready.

The others took their places, including a Wren officer, the one

154

who had been with Critchley's widow on that other occasion. He had seen an officer of his own rank looking at him, giving a discreet wave, his successor at H.M.S. *Vernon*.

And the bereaved parents, the subbie's mother in tears, her husband grim-faced, watching the firing party critically, comparing them, perhaps, with something from his past.

They had already spoken; Masters could still feel it like a slap in the face.

'Well, I suppose you couldn't be expected to be everywhere, to know what's happening all the time!' Which was exactly what he *had* meant, and who could blame him?

The chaplain had opened his book, his surplice billowing around him in the breeze. They should have asked the padre from Lulworth, the fisherman. He, at least, would have understood.

The coffin was in position, a new flag folded over it, and Masters had seen the hearse parked near the main gates, ready to take the young officer back to his home town.

There would not be much to put in the ground. There rarely was.

Caps removed, heads uncovered, the bugler moistening his mouthpiece with his tongue. Only the firing party stood fast, the gunnery officer's face like stone. Masters could imagine what he was thinking. As a sub-lieutenant he had once been involved with an admiral's funeral. Peacetime: sword and cocked hat on the coffin, guard and band. Everything.

But all that really stuck in his mind was the senior gunnery officer who had been in charge of the ceremonial.

And during the period of Resting on the Arms Reversed, an expression of deep melancholy will be worn by all officers present . . . until Carry On is sounded.

She said suddenly, 'Hold my arm, please. I'm no good at this kind of thing.'

He slipped his hand into the sleeve of her fur coat, and gently gripped her wrist above the glove.

After all the preparation the service seemed to last only a few minutes. The chaplain did not once look at his prayer book; he knew it by heart, Masters thought. He felt her shiver, although her skin felt warm in his grasp. Remembering someone, or something?

'The days of man are but as grass: for he flourisheth as a flower of the field. For as soon as the wind goeth over it, it is gone: and the place thereof shall know it no more.'

Masters saw the dead subbie's mother lean forward as if to touch the draped coffin, her husband reaching out to restrain her.

Then the bark of commands.

'Firing party, *load*!' The metallic, precise clatter of rifle bolts.

'Pre-*sent*!' The rifles angled towards the misty sky, the ratings' caps all in line, chinstays down.

'Fire!'

He held her wrist more tightly as the crash echoed across the inlet in a single blast. Some gulls rose, flapping angrily from the water, and beyond the main gates Masters saw an old man stop on the road and remove his battered hat while he faced the sea.

'Re-*load*!'

'Fire!'

Someone was sobbing uncontrollably, and Masters heard Wykes break into a fit of coughing.

'Order *arms*!' The rifles came down together. Chavasse would be pleased; H.M.S. *Excellent*, the gunnery school, could have performed no better.

'Thank you.' She seemed very calm, but the blue-green eyes were misty. Like the sea. She repeated, 'Thank you.' She was trying to smile. 'David.'

It was almost over. The coffin had gone, the firing party were having their rifles inspected, bolts worked smartly in and out to make certain that not even an empty blank cartridge should escape the lieutenant's notice.

People began to move towards the wardroom building where the mess stewards would be waiting. All part of the drill, as Coker would put it. Chavasse was talking to Brayshaw, pointing at something, probably telling him to make sure the flag which had draped the coffin did not go astray. It was otherwise unused, and would be needed for the Trafalgar display.

A passing lieutenant said to his friend, 'I hope mine's as quick as that when the time comes!'

'Can't wait, can you?' They both laughed.

Masters said, 'Don't mind them. They care enough to be here.'

156

'I know that,' she said.

He saw Wykes disentangling himself from another group of officers and heading towards them.

She said, 'You don't have to take your hand away, you know.' She twisted her wrist, but that was all. 'Unless you feel that you must?'

Wykes returned the salute and cleared his throat noisily. 'Smoke from those blanks. Still, went pretty well, I thought?'

Masters smiled. There was something very reassuring about Wykes; he could have been commenting on a regatta or a cricket match.

Wykes raised a hand to someone, but came directly to the point uppermost in his active mind.

'I have some fresh information for you. We shall have to stay overnight at your quarters, I'm afraid – don't want to make things look too obvious, do we?' He did not wait for an answer; he never seemed to. 'We shall be undisturbed that way, eh?'

The girl said, 'You could have mentioned it earlier.'

Masters felt her hand slipping away from his. Her surprise was genuine; it must have taken her completely aback. *The perfume.*

Wykes was saying, 'You have a good staff there, as I recall. Nothing fancy, but something decent to drink, I hope?'

Then he sighed. 'We'd better show our faces inside, I suppose. I hate this part of it.'

They followed him towards the queue by the wardroom entrance.

She said, 'I'm very sorry.' She was calm again. In control. 'He does things like this. He's in another world sometimes.' Then, as if to change the subject, 'There's a pretty girl, one of your admirers, obviously!'

Masters saw a dark-haired Wren who had been talking with a Royal Marine driver, apparently discussing his car.

He exclaimed, 'Don't salute, not today!' and saw the uncertainty vanish, her face open in a smile as he took her gloved hand in his.

He said, 'This is Leading Wren Margot Lovatt.' And then, 'Light duties, remember? You shouldn't be here, really, and you know it.' They stood looking at one another, then she said, 'I wanted to come back. Needed to.'

The burly Royal Marine said, 'I'm keepin' an eye on 'er, sir!'

'Do that, will you?'

She murmured, 'Thank you for saying that.'

He released her hands and saluted her.

'Come on, I need a drink.'

He realized he had taken Elaine's arm, that she had not resisted.

'The girl who was in the car crash? I heard about it. She was lucky, very lucky to all accounts . . . That was a nice thing you did just now. Obviously she thinks the world of you.' She was watching his face, his eyes.

'Her brother was serving under me in *Tornado*. When she went down.'

'But she stayed with you, all the same.' She braced herself as Wykes and another captain came towards them.

She knew what she had just witnessed. What it had cost him, and the Wren, in their different ways.

She was moved by it, and disturbed; it had affected her more than she would have believed possible. And vulnerable, which must never happen again.

She took a drink from a passing steward and swallowed some without tasting it. She knew Wykes was observing her even as he was sharing a joke with the other captain. If she could not go through with it, he would drop her like a hot brick.

She turned and looked at Masters.

'Your little Wren had the right idea!'

A telephone jangled outside and a steward hurried through the throng, his eyes everywhere, searching for someone. She saw Masters tense, like that night at Portland, then relax with something like physical effort as the steward found the officer he was seeking. *And I will not see you suffer because of me.*

Somewhere a bugle blared. *'Hands to dinner!'* Some wag would always call, *'And officers to lunch!'*

Masters touched her arm and felt her hesitate, like that barrier when they had first met. It was never far away.

'We're almost the last to leave.' He felt her move her arm, the tension gone.

She glanced around the room, where children had once danced and drilled to an out-of-tune piano.

Now, only the ghosts remained.

The small van with *Royal Navy* painted on the side stopped at the top of a steep slope and stood rattling tinnily while Sub-Lieutenant Michael Lincoln and his assistant climbed out. The driver said, 'I'll try and chase up your transport when I get back to base, sir.'

Lincoln shaded his eyes and stared down the slope, which appeared to lead directly to the sea. The Channel had many faces, he thought. This morning it was flat calm, hardly a ripple, the horizon touched with a faint silver thread. There was a three-ton Bedford lorry parked by a pile of crates, where a gap had been opened in the rusting barbed wire barrier, and some Royal Marines in their camouflaged denims were sitting or standing around them. One was throwing a piece of driftwood for a rough-haired terrier to fetch and recover with unending energy.

An officer was standing apart from his marines and looked up when he saw Lincoln. He made a point of peering at his watch. The car which was to have brought them to this desolate-looking beach had broken down minutes after leaving the inlet. Lincoln felt a growing resentment. It was not an emergency, anyway.

'Got all we need?' It was something to say. Downie never needed to be reminded.

Most of the Royal Marines had turned to watch, and someone gave an ironic cheer. Their captain waited for Lincoln to reach him, and snapped, 'You took your time! If we have to wait for the next low water we'll lose a whole day!'

Lincoln attempted to tell him about the breakdown but knew he was wasting his time. It was a bad beginning.

'Let's get started!' The captain gestured to a launch which was being fended away from scattered rocks by some of his men. 'Muster the others, Corporal!'

They climbed into the launch and Lincoln hoped that it, too, would break down. It did not.

He looked around at the others. The marines were from one of the units based at Portland, highly professional, and employed mostly on demolition or clearing away wreckage after an exercise or training programme.

He shaded his eyes again and peered ahead past the bowman. At first you might think it was an isolated spur of rock. At low water you could see all that was left of the old freighter *Latchmere*. She had hit a stray mine along this coast and her master had tried to beach her where she would cause the least harm to other shipping: a hazard or an aid to navigation, it depended on the circumstances. Today the remains of the old *Latchmere* were to be destroyed.

The captain of marines was also studying the approaching wreck. Like many of her kind, most of the freighter's superstructure and cabin space was right aft. She had been carrying scrap iron when the mine had found her, and her cargo had broken open the hull and scattered where it would never be salvaged. He consulted his watch again. Just what he might have expected: a sub-lieutenant in battledress, working dress, as the navy chose to term it, with a wavy stripe on each shoulder so new that he must have been commissioned only months ago. So what was he doing with the special countermeasures section? And the rating . . . what were they thinking, for God's sake? He looked like a schoolboy, reaching out to fondle the dog which had somehow slipped into the launch.

The wreck was closer now, looming over them, another for-gotten victim of the narrow seas. Rust had overwhelmed most of the paintwork, and the bridge rails were badly buckled, the wheelhouse windows blasted away by that first explosion. There was other damage too, holes punched by cannon shells when a fighter bomber had used the old *Latchmere* for target practice. A pathetic sight, for anyone with imagination. The captain of marines had none. Newly promoted himself, he was proud of his unit, but saw it and its efficiency as a stepping-stone to something even better. Above all, he loathed amateurs.

Lincoln was aware of the hostility. It made him angry, but he was used to it. He looked over at his assistant. What did the snotty little captain know? Downie had dealt with eleven serious incidents, 'of major capacity' as it was described in his report. *Twelve, if you count the one he stopped me from screwing up.* He found himself smiling. *I'm getting just like my dad.*

He tried to concentrate on the job in hand. He had got all he could from Operations, and had even managed to speak with the first lieutenant of ML366, which had been confronted by an E-Boat right here only days ago. It was hard to imagine now. Lifeless, barely undulating water, the Channel empty of everything but two armed trawlers on their way to Poole or the Dover Strait. He saw the green wreck buoy, soon to be replaced by one with a beacon, which neither lookout nor radar could confuse with a lurking enemy.

The captain of marines was moving up the boat towards him. *Here we go.* He had heard most of the old jibes, including the R.N.V.R. *Really Not Very Reliable.* They had mostly died out now, or, like the young subbie who had been killed on his first 'incident', just died altogether.

'Now you know what you've got to do, right?'

They both swung round as Downie said, 'Check the bridge for any equipment not part of the wreck, sir.' He lifted his arm so that the dog jumped to snap playfully at his oilskin. 'The E-Boat was reported as an S80 type, so she only drew a fathom at the most.' He fell silent as one of the listening marines gave a chuckle.

Lincoln said, 'Nothing bigger would dare to come in so near.'

They looked at one another like conspirators.

It was not lost on the captain. 'Well, we can't hang about. The new wreck buoy will be here this afternoon. I've got more important things to do.'

A Royal Marine corporal murmured half to himself, 'I'll bet 'is mother just *loves* 'im!'

Lincoln turned away. He was not alone. He thought of the memorial service he had watched at the base; he had never seen a firing party in action before. He had met Masters there too, but only briefly. Of today he had said, 'No heroics. Just have a look around for anything strange or unexpected. We'll not get another chance, not with the old *Latchmere*, in any case.'

And he had seen the young woman Masters had been with. Tall, wearing a fur coat, like someone out of a film. He smiled again. *My sort of film, anyway.*

Downie was gripping the gunwale, staring up at the wreck. Even the boat's fenders would have a rough time on the jagged plates. It was probably a waste of time; he had sensed that most of the others thought as much, Lincoln too. Otherwise why would they have sent only him? Downie still did not know if he would ever understand him, or know him like Clive. Not afraid to stand up for himself. *Or me.* But he had a chip a mile wide on his shoulder.

They were level with the tilting wheelhouse now, the shattered ports and scuttles like blind eyes. On a bracket by the bridge door was a hanging basket, now rusty and bent like everything else. But it had once held flowers or potted plants, like the ones his mother had always cherished in their little garden behind the shop. He felt the dog rubbing against him; it only made it worse. *After all this time.*

'Stand by, forrard!'

He saw two large and ungainly rubber floats hooked on to the derelict superstructure, and some marines in frogman suits waving and jeering. They were met with cheerful insults, equally crude.

He would never understand the Royals, either. Soldiers one minute, sailors the next. They even called their quarters, a bunch of gaunt-looking Nissen huts, their 'barracks'. He had also noticed that despite their warlike, camouflaged denims, each man had a Globe and Laurel badge on his beret polished so brightly you could have seen it ten miles away.

The boat grated alongside, and grapnels brought them as close as possible. Downie peered over the deck. Trapped water moving this way and that, some carpet rolled tightly behind a stanchion. Perhaps someone had been cleaning the bridge, ready for reaching port, when the mine had blasted the ship apart . . .

One of the NCOs was shouting something, then their captain called, 'Look, let's not make a meal of it!' The wristwatch again. 'Not much time for my men to plant the charges. No point in dithering, is there?'

Lincoln said, 'I'll be as fast as I can, *sir*. Have you got the torch, Gordon?' He saw Downie nod, and two of the marines nudging each other.

It was a dangerous descent. Outside the wreck the sea had seemed calm, almost lifeless; once below the bridge deck it seemed powerful, heavy enough to take away your balance. Slippery and treacherous, with jagged glass and buckled plating adding to the risk of injury.

Somehow Downie had got ahead of Lincoln, although he did not recall seeing him pause or hesitate. He looked up through a broken skylight, the solitary funnel above it like a tusk against the sky. Even the sounds were different here, booming water trapped in the lower hull, or what was left of it. Hissing, rustling sounds, as if creatures still lurked here. He swung the torch, dipping the beam slightly beneath the water. Some broken cups in one corner, charts still folded in their rack, although he knew they would fall apart at the slightest touch. Water had lapped over his boot and his foot felt like ice. He peered up again at the skylight. The paintwork was stained but still intact, one part of the wreck which remained above water even when the tide was at its highest. He screwed up his eyes, trying to remember the correct naval term. He had heard the ML's young captain use it when he had been aboard that night and they had fished the dead flier out of the drink. His mother had warned him about doing that to his eyes. *Make you look old before you know it.* And he would be twenty next month. And Sub-Lieutenant Lincoln would be . . . He gripped a voicepipe and stared. Lincoln was crouched at the upper end of the sloping deck, gazing into the water, searching for something. His eyes were fixed, vacant. Like that moment near the railway. The extra fuse. The booby-trap. He had been unable to move or speak.

Downie heard more voices, but they did not seem to matter. His arm had become numb, and the torch had swung almost into the water.

He must have screwed up his eyes again without realizing it. When he looked again, he saw the brightly coloured cylinder bolted to the old varnished woodwork, the size of a small fire extinguisher. And a wire, also carefully stapled into place, leading perhaps to the skylight, perhaps the remaining funnel.

'Sir!'

Lincoln seemed to come alive, his eyes staring, questioning. But still he did not move.

Downie shouted again. 'Sir!' He gestured towards the cylinder. 'Stay where you are! I can get it!'

Two things happened at once. A piece of wood splashed into the slopping water, and the terrier followed it, mouth already open to retrieve the prize. Downie was already halfway into the water. It was surging around his body, running through his clothing, exploring his limbs, numbing all sensation. The explosion was almost incidental, uninvolved. The flash so vivid that it was white, colourless, and he knew he had been deafened by the blast. There was blood on the surface, all about him, and hands reaching out to seize his coat and drag him to safety.

But all he could see was the dead dog, still clinging to the piece of driftwood. Then there was nothing.

The Angel Inn was and always had been Chaldon St Mary's only pub. It occupied the same street as most of the other major buildings but managed to remain apart, as the centre of local affairs. It had a garden which was lined with trees, beyond which the Channel was just visible. Social events were limited to space and timing. The Rotary Club's Christmas dinner had always been considered special, the farmers gathered there for their N.F.U. meetings, and there was sometimes a wedding to celebrate, or the aftermath of a funeral. Almost anything which affected the village and the neighbouring farms had been decided here at the Angel. The war had changed everything. Children or entire families being evacuated, land commandeered by the armed services, troops billeted in homes left unattended; the locals soon found themselves a small minority. Many resented it. Some, like Ben Turner, the Angel's landlord, accepted it as a blessing.

The two main bars were packed every night. Sailors and marines from the local establishment which had once been the old school, airmen and WAAFs from the barrage balloon sites, and gunners from the surrounding anti-aircraft batteries. Ben Turner had been forced to employ three extra barmaids to cope with the demand, and a pianist as well, and the pub was usually so noisy with songs and laughter that locals tried to gauge their visits accordingly.

There was one small, additional bar named the Snug, where the ceiling was so low you could touch it with your hand. There was the usual dartboard, surrounded by a protective motor tyre, and the notices about blackout regulations, air raid instructions, and being careful with glasses. Servicemen often found it difficult to believe that it was harder to obtain new tankards and glassware than to replenish the cellar. There was a war on . . . The Snug was quieter than the other bars, the predominant theme being cricket. The landlord had been a well-known cricketer, at one time captain of the local team. He had gone onto play for the county and had been on the final selection for the England team to play New Zealand, when the war had changed that as well.

A cricket bat, in a glass case and autographed by some of England's greatest players, held pride of place near an open hearth with pictures of the King and Queen on either side.

At night, until the landlord had to use a megaphone to bellow, 'Time, gentlemen, please!' there was no privacy even here, and to attempt to be alone with a girl was just asking for trouble.

Ben Turner was leaning with both elbows on the bar, preparing for yet another battle with his friend the butcher. Rations, availability, delivery and so forth. It was a little past noon, although he made sure that the clock was always slightly fast, just in case closing time became too difficult. And it was quiet. A farmer was sitting by the log fire, his dog sprawled out asleep by his boots. The local postman was in one corner, sipping his ale, and apparently sorting his mail bag. Turner knew him of old. He was actually reading the postcards from God alone knew where, before he delivered them. The gossip king of the village. Postcards told him where such and such a serviceman might be, just as he would always know which wife or girlfriend was having it off with a sapper or some sailor from the inlet.

The butcher murmured, 'Heads up, Ben!'

The door opened and closed; the dog raised one eye and shut it again.

Ben Turner was about to say that at quiet times like this, in the middle of the day, there was no point in opening the Snug for only two clients. The place had to be lit and heated; in wartime you had to consider these things.

It was a young naval lieutenant with an even younger Wren. The butcher nudged him, but he had remembered anyway. The girl had sometimes stopped outside the Angel in the big Wolseley staff car, either to visit the post office or to call at the garage for something. She was the one who had nearly been killed in the accident. As pretty as a picture; it was hard to believe it was the same girl. And the lieutenant, smiling but uncertain, looking round for reassurance. Turner saw the medal ribbon on his jacket. Maybe he was the one who had gone to help her? He noticed that the postman was looking up, interested. He would know.

'Go into the Snug, will you? I'll put a match to the fire.'

Foley smiled at him and took the girl's arm. Gently: he had seen her frown with pain as her shoulder bag had swung against her body when they had been climbing over the gate from the cliff path.

She said, 'I feel *wicked*, Chris. Slipping away from everything and everybody. I couldn't believe it when you answered the phone just now.'

He waited for her to sit by the fireplace, watched her looking all around, the pleasure in her dark eyes.

The Snug bar opened, like two cupboard doors, Ben Turner's head and shoulders filling the space.

'What'll it be, sir?' He glanced at the Wren. 'A gin an' orange for the lady?'

Foley sat by the small table, hardly daring to move. He could hear music from somewhere, and the sounds of crockery being stacked in a rack. The fire was alight and crackling, but he had not seen anyone come in and put a match to the kindling.

He looked at the low ceiling, browned over the years by pipe and cigarette smoke. Here and there someone had written in the stain with a beery finger. Some of the messages had been wiped clean, and Foley could imagine why.

He said, 'I've waited for this moment, Margot. Now it's here, I can't think where to begin. You see—'

The shadow loomed over them and two glasses appeared on the table.

'Mild an' bitter, an' one gin an' orange for the lady.' He waved a big fist. 'Take your time.' He shuffled away and Foley somehow knew he was unused to waiting on table.

He reached out for the tankard, but instead covered her hand with his own.

'Sorry, Margot. I'm not doing very well, am I?'

She looked at the hand on hers and said softly, 'I'm not pulling away. I've thought about you a lot. Too much, I expect.'

'A toast, then?'

She took her glass. 'I've not had a gin since a chum of mine got promoted.'

166

He smiled. 'To you, Margot. That day when it happened, I'll never forget how I felt. How I wanted you to live, *needed* you.'

She twisted her hand to grip his. 'To *us*, then.'

A clock chimed somewhere. Another world.

'I had to see you. It's important, you see.' There was water running now, near the window, probably a hose swilling down the outside toilets. He heard another voice. The *heads*.

He found that he was very calm, as if all his fears were unfounded.

'I've got a little present for you.' Her hand moved, as if to protest, but he continued, 'Tomorrow.'

She was watching him, his eyes, his face, his mouth. 'Tomorrow?'

'Trafalgar Day, the twenty-first of October. Something else important happened on that date.'

She laughed, relieved, surprised, it was hard to tell.

'Somebody's been getting at you, Chris! Anyway, it was a lovely thing to do, but why not wait until . . .' She put the gin aside and grasped his hand in both of hers. 'Because *tomorrow* you'll be somewhere else?'

He released her hand, and said, 'You might not even like it.'

'Show me.' She watched him reaching into his jacket, a lock of hair falling across his forehead, glad that he could not see her face. She was back in her father's 'glory-hole', hearing the war correspondent's voice on the radio, but seeing this man out there, risking his life, leading his men, afraid only of showing fear. The same man who had blurted out *I love you* on that terrible line, when they had been cut off. Troubled now that he was making a fool of himself.

He had opened the little package on the table. He said, 'I saw it there, and I thought, it will look just right.'

It was a small velvet case. She could feel his eyes upon her, perhaps remembering too. How he had held her, touched her, and through all the pain and fear she had imagined, believed that it was life or death, *with him*.

It was silver, a fouled anchor encased in the framework of a heart, with a slender chain attached.

It had been his last resort, the jewellery shop in a side street of

Weymouth. The proprietor had been unhelpful to begin with, and had been about to produce something else.

The pendant had been sold in that same shop, shortly after the outbreak of war. A Norwegian ship had been detained by the Contraband Control guardship, and one of her officers had found his way to the shop. He had sold it, because he had no further use for it, or because Norway was about to be invaded. The proprietor recalled seeing the Norwegian pause outside the shop, as if he had regretted his decision.

She said, 'It's lovely,' and unconsciously touched her tie and the crisp white shirt. 'I shall wear it here, where I can feel it all the time . . . just as I felt you when you came to help me.'

The landlord was peering through the twin doors.

'Mister *Foley*, is it, sir? Thought you might be. Seeing as you're the only naval folk here today, for a change!' He laughed but it made him look strangely sad. 'Someone by the name of Claridge.'

Foley stood up, one hand still holding hers, afraid to let go. He had not even heard the telephone.

She watched him, somehow knowing he had been half-expecting it. Dreading it.

She held the little pendant and suddenly wanted him to see it on her. Put it around her neck. She clenched her hand. *Not now. Not now.* And tomorrow was the twenty-first of October. She wiped her cheek with her knuckles. And she would be twenty-one. There were voices; the telephone had been replaced. She stood up and faced him.

'Is it to be here? Now?' She did not even resist as he wrapped his arms around her.

He replied, 'Yes.' His mouth was against her hair. 'You know, "a bit of a flap".'

'I love the pendant, Chris. No, *don't let go*. You're not hurting me!'

They both stood still, then she said, 'For my birthday tomorrow.' She tilted her face. 'Kiss me!'

Ben Turner watched them leave the Snug together, the lieutenant holding the girl's arm, some money in his free hand.

Turner shook his head. 'On the house, sir. Call in again some time, eh?' He knew that his friend the butcher and the postman were both staring at him, but he did not care.

Music was blaring out of the other bar, and Turner swung round angrily. The new potman was making too free with himself for his own good.

'Stow it, will you!'

But the young Wren called back, 'No, leave it, *please!*'

Foley opened the street door and felt the cold air on his lips where she had kissed him. It would be far colder across the Channel.

The music followed them into the street.

Foley had heard it before, in 366's W/T office.

He felt her holding his arm very tightly.

Ain't misbehavin' . . . Savin' my love for you.

11

Face to Face

The Operations Officer unzipped his worn tobacco pouch and proceeded to fill one of his pipes with thrusts of his strong fingers. He was the senior officer of the team and therefore smoked when he chose and not to suit others. And, as everyone kept remarking, it was going to be a long night.

He struck a match and glanced at the big wall chart through the smoke. He did not see the Wren who was standing on a small ladder as she moved a coloured marker wrinkle her nose with disapproval.

He had been across to the mess to get some extra pusser's tobacco, and had waited just long enough to hear the Captain's special dinner getting under way. Chavasse had even managed to obtain some Royal Marine musicians for the occasion. You had to hand it to him when it came to flying the flag.

Another marker had been removed: the local flotilla had put to sea. He had heard them earlier after the briefing, the backchat and casual observations from some of the young officers. They would be on their way right now. Over in the mess they would be too pissed to stand before the action even started. If it ever did. He cocked his head as a teleprinter clattered into life. Trafalgar Night. What would Our Nel have made of all of this?

The outer door opened and Masters pushed his way around the heavy blackout curtain.

'All quiet, Tom?' His eyes passed over the chart and the plot. Then he smiled as the Operations Officer handed him his pouch.

'As a grave, David.' They held the same rank, and had briefly served together in that same old training cruiser as midshipmen. A million years ago.

Masters lit his pipe. Seeing the neatly filed signals, the diagrams and the coloured markers, brought it all back. Just two nights ago Captain Wykes had relayed the build-up of information about German minelaying and the latest details of their midget submarines. No glossing over, but Wykes in his terse, impatient fashion had brought it into the room. Perhaps the intelligence departments of the three services had too much to contend with, or did not allow for any overlap of information, but Wykes had left no doubt as to his thoughts. *I went straight to the top. Bloody man, couldn't see his arse for his elbow.*

Masters had looked over at the girl who had been sitting in one of the well-worn sofas. Coker had lit a fire, and she had kicked off her shoes, holding her stockinged feet to the warmth. She had smiled. She was used to Wykes.

The Germans had been moving equipment and supplies across France and out to the Channel Islands. Now some of it was just across the Channel in Seine Bay, where the local flotilla had already carried out fast forays of minelaying. Where some of them would be in a few hours' time.

Foley, at least, would be with his small company. Doing something, instead of . . . He returned the pouch. It was getting to him again.

He opened the incident book, and faces fitted themselves to names and ranks. Like a private navy, stationed in strategic areas, ready for the first hint of a magnetic mine or some new kind of beast.

Everything was in hand, just in case. There was even a unit at Lyme Regis where some fishermen had caught a suspicious object in their nets. No chances. No heroics, as he had said to the new sub-lieutenant, Michael Lincoln. Lincoln was over in the mess too; at least he had been spared any emergency call-out. Probably hating it.

Even when he had told Lincoln that the remains of a homing device had been found aboard the wreck of the *Latchmere*, he had sensed little reaction. The evidence had already been dispatched to *Vernon*. It might explain why the E-Boat had been there, might even connect the discovery with the midget submarine at Portland.

Chavasse had been openly delighted. 'Don't you see? A feather in our caps for a change! I shall put this whatsisname Lincoln up for a decoration, a Mention if that's all they can manage!'

Masters had told Lincoln about that, too. He turned his head as a burst of laughter and shouting penetrated the outer door. Chavasse had been too busy to take it any further. He obviously still was.

Lincoln had saved his rating's life, dragging him to safety. He was over in the sickbay now, bruised and recovering from shock and concussion.

When you worked so closely with one another it became something special. If not, another partner should be found without delay.

Masters had mentioned that Downie had more than proved his worth, and his courage, but that he had confessed he had always wanted to be a vet. It was obvious Lincoln knew nothing about it, nor any other aspect of Downie's character. He merely said, 'He should go on leave after this, sir.'

But Downie had nowhere to go. They had shared very little except danger.

He thought about Wykes again. He had said the Germans were using Russian prisoners of war as slaves in the Channel Islands. They were building the massive defences on the islands, part of Hitler's ambitious 'West Wall' against invasion. Starved, beaten, and driven without mercy by their guards, the Russians often dropped dead at their work; their bodies were usually tipped into the new concrete of the defences. Wykes had remarked, 'Some have been used for testing anti-personnel mines as well.'

Again he had glanced over at Elaine de Courcy. Her own father, willingly or otherwise, must have had a hand in it. *Collaborator*. So where did she fit in?

He had said, 'Do the Russians know about it?'

Wykes had groped for another cigarette. 'We and the Russians are fighting the same enemy. That does not necessarily mean we're both on the same side!'

He had decided that he would never understand James Wykes.

172

She would be with Wykes now, halfway to London, where all the loose ends would finally tie up. And still he knew hardly anything about her. Her mother was English, and living in the Channel Islands. If her father was working under pressure for the Germans, her mother would be seen as a ready hostage. Wykes had told him that at least two attempts had been made on Raymond de Courcy's life. Terrorists or freedom fighters; as Wykes said, it depends on which side of the table you're standing.

One fact stood out. Elaine de Courcy was a link between her father and Commander John Critchley. At some stage, and Wykes had gone no further, Critchley had been prepared to help de Courcy change sides yet again, for old times' sake. But who now would ever know?

A telegraphist peered around a switchboard. 'Phone call for you, sir.' His eyes moved from Masters to the newly made window in the wall. 'I can put it through to your office.'

Masters hurried up the steps, his mind swinging between the latest operation and the discovery of the homing device aboard the wrecked freighter. It would probably be Bumper Fawcett, demanding to know the latest progress. If any. *Don't fall astern, Masters. I'm relying on you, what?*

He recognized her voice instantly. Calm, almost matter-of-fact.

He said, 'You're calling from London. Did you forget something? If so . . .'

She answered, 'I'm here. We both are. It was decided, you see.'

'*Here*, at the house?' It was not making sense. Coker would be in a real turmoil. Or would he?

'Didn't want to scare you when you got back. In any case, you told me I would be safe here.'

She was playing with him. Wykes was probably listening, enjoying it.

And at the same time, he knew he was not.

He wanted to stop it. Prevent it destroying something which could never work.

The room with the uniform hanging in it, the smell of her perfume, still clinging to the place where she and Critchley had been lovers.

'Are you there?' Again the hesitation he remembered. 'David?'

'Thanks for letting me know.'

The door opened an inch. 'Can you come, sir?'

It had saved him. He snatched up his cap, and saw his great-coat folded over a chair. The way she had held it around her throat . . .

Lovers. Why should he care? Why should it matter? It happened.

The Operations Room had filled with people in that short while. *Nothing else must get in the way.*

He saw the Operations Officer tapping out his pipe, the yeoman of signals speaking into a handset. It was time.

Masters unbuttoned the top of his jacket and looked at the plot.

But it did matter. There was no going back. No choice at all.

The Wrennery, as it was nicknamed, stood a hundred yards or so from the church and the gates which guarded the naval establishment, one of the larger houses in the village, whose occupants had moved away soon after the outbreak of war. During the day it was pleasant enough for the girls who were quartered there, but at night, especially for those who were watchkeeping in Operations or the Signals department, it was prudent to await an escort from the main gates to avoid unwanted attention, and not only from passing servicemen. There was a bathhouse and shower room beneath the building which had once been a garage, and all the hot water was provided by a massive boiler. A young Wren had screamed the place down one night when she had seen the boiler man peering at her when she had been in the middle of a shower. An old man, but not *too* old, apparently, as someone had pointed out.

Leading Wren Margot Lovatt sat on a cushion, her back against the wall in the room she shared with three of the Wren contingent. She wore warm pyjamas, and there was always a heavy sweater and duffle coat close by in case the air raid alarm sounded. Like schoolgirls having an unlawful party in the dormitory after lights out, she thought. Everybody seemed to have known it was her twenty-first birthday. There had been cake supplied from the main galley, complete with coloured icing and a full array of candles. Other, smaller cakes too, for handing round, *enough to empty a ration book*, she could imagine Lucy saying.

Julie, another driver, with hair so blonde it looked white in the light of a solitary lamp, had given her some silk stockings. She had a boyfriend who was on the Atlantic run, which occasionally took him as far as the United States, where you could get such luxuries. She had touched herself suggestively and giggled.

'Mind you, he wants paying for them!'

And Antonia, known by everyone, even her officers, as Toni, who had presented her with a picture she had painted herself. She had been an art student until she had joined the Wrens, and had been regarded as a bit posh by some of the girls because her father was a knight. She took it all in good spirits, and could match any one when it came to humour. Like her painting, for instance. It depicted a squad of Wrens on a parade ground, although only their caps revealed their service. All were naked to the waist, bare-breasted and smiling coyly.

A massive gunner's mate confronted them, his face suffused with embarrassment and rage, while nearby a childlike subbie was hiding his eyes from the outthrust bosoms. The gunner's mate was yelling, 'Are you deaf, girls? I distinctly ordered a *kit* inspection!'

It would have a place of honour, except perhaps when Second Officer Tucker was on her rounds. A formidable woman, she had been a teacher at one of the better schools. As Julie had said of her, 'She would have been really at home with a swastika on her sleeve!'

There had been wine, too: Lesley worked in the supply office. She had said, 'It'll not be missed, tonight of all nights!'

Margot thought of the card and letter from her parents. Her mother had included a golden 'key of the door'; she had probably forgotten she had originally got it for Graham for his twenty-first birthday. Her father had sensibly sent money. Neither had ever commented on her returning to duty ahead of time. Like shutting a door; like Graham's room. A full stop.

Julie was saying, 'Let's have another look at it, Margot.'

She opened her pyjama jacket and turned slightly so that the little pendant might catch the light.

The girl from Supply, Lesley, said, 'It's lovely. He's got good taste, that's for sure.'

Julie reached out and unfastened the next button, and the next. 'Don't fuss, just for once!'

Margot sat still as the other girl pulled the jacket down over her bare shoulders. She repeated, 'Don't *fuss*, girl! Just imagine this is a lovely ball gown, and that the orchestra has just struck up!'

Nobody spoke, and the room, the whole house, was suddenly silent.

Toni, whose father was a knight, said, 'I'll do a sketch of you, if you like. Surprise him.'

Margot touched the pendant and her breast. 'When all the bruises have gone.' She wanted to stop, cover herself, but they were her friends. They needed each other. Sometimes more than they would admit.

A truck rattled past the house, and there was singing, lusty but strangely sad.

> Bless all the sergeants and W.O. ones
> Bless all the corporals and their fucking sons,
> For we're saying good-bye to them all . . .

Lesley said, 'The redcaps'll catch that little lot down the road!' But Margot heard none of it.

Today she had been there, but not in time to see him. Not soon enough to hear him speak.

Only the vibrant snarl of those engines, the flurries of pumps and the acrid smell of high-octane. *No Smoking Abaft the Bridge.*

She had imagined the sailors, some of his seamen, in their long white sweaters, chinstays down, a touch of smartness for leaving harbour, if you did not look too closely.

Loosening the mooring lines, singling up, a quick grin here and there, a shouted word to some particular chum in another boat.

They accepted it. They could even joke about it.

She had a glass in her hand and heard Julie say, ''Bout the last of it, I'm afraid. Bloody lucky I'm not driving tonight!'

Toni had wriggled onto her knees and had produced her familiar sketch pad.

'I'm going to do a rough right now. I can *see* it!'

Margot wanted to protest. Perhaps she had had too much to

176

drink? A motor cycle roared along the pitch-dark road. Probably a despatch rider with orders from H.Q. or Portland. But for those few seconds it sounded like the sudden surge of speed, the lithe grey hulls heading into danger.

She allowed the pyjama jacket to fall from her body and said, 'Then do it like this, Toni.' She wanted to say something to cover her true feelings, to joke about the picture of the gunner's mate. She knew that if she did, she would break completely.

Instead she held the pendant again and pressed it into her skin.

'I'm here, Chris.'

So that he would know.

Chris Foley leaned over the chart, his elbows pressed on the table while he concentrated on the pencilled calculations and fixes, feeling the pressure this way and that while 366 rolled on a regular, unhurried swell. Silent routine, with everything but essential machinery switched off, so that inboard noises seemed all the more intrusive. Boots scraping on the open bridge above, the occasional clink of metal as a gun moved restlessly on its mounting. Somebody coughing, then stifling it as if that might betray them.

He tried again, the brass dividers moving over the well-worn chart, tracing distances and soundings, the uneven line of the coast . . . *The enemy.*

Nothing new, not that far from their last minelaying mission. To hear them discussing it at the conference you would think it was too familiar even to question. The old hands knew it was dangerous, even fatal, to allow it to become familiar. The young ones soon learned. Or else . . .

You always felt vulnerable without power, without movement, but at times like this listening and hearing were more important.

The chart light seemed almost blinding in this small, screened space. He rubbed his eyes with his knuckles and took another look at his notes; he might not get another chance before the job was done. Or all hell broke loose.

He recalled Tony Brock's indignation at the conference. 'Why us? The R.A.F. could sort this lot out with a couple of raids! Waste of effort, I call it.' Brock was always able to work up a fury without effort. He was up there now at the head of the flotilla, still fuming. This time he was not the senior officer in charge, and taking orders from somebody else, a straight-laced regular, had been too much. Foley felt his lips crack into a grin. Brock's men called him 'Bash On Regardless' behind his back. It suited him.

He adjusted the towel around his neck. It was time to move. *Listen and wait.* The operation was to be carried out by vessels designed and built for the work, coastal minelayers, which carried fifty or so mines. The professionals. They were described as fast, but the best they could manage was fifteen knots, *after* they had unloaded their deadly cargo.

Foley massaged his eyes and tried again. The Operations Officer had said that reliable intelligence had located German midget submarines experimenting or training in the Seine Bay, either at Le Havre or close by at Trouville. They would need supplies, and because of the destruction of vital railway links those would have to come by sea, and at night.

Foley stood away from the table and straightened his back. *Maybe tonight.* He recalled what Masters had told him about the midget submarine which had been towed into Portland. It had been a secret, then. He moved out of the chart space and waited for his vision to clear. It was not a secret any more.

He glanced back at the chart space. Three coastal minelayers, a total of six motor launches and three motor gunboats as escort.

As Brock had said, 'In and out like a parson in a knocking shop!'

And then he thought of the village pub, how they had clung to one another, oblivious of the watching eyes, uncaring.

So much he had wanted to say. So much. Holding and kissing her. Afraid of hurting her, but barely able to let her go.

You will take care, Chris? For me? And that was only yesterday.

He thrust his way up the steps and into the open bridge. It was very cold. All the layers of clothing were not enough; the cold came from inside. *Keyed up.* She had told him how she had heard the correspondent on the radio, 'Talking about you, Chris! I was so moved, so proud!' Her eyes had been shining then, her cheeks wet. Yesterday.

He held onto a flag locker as if to get the feel of the boat, his command. The men at their guns, straining their eyes into the night, their ears for that hated sound of E-Boat engines. *See them first, and you've a fair chance.* The voice of experience.

Allison was in the forepart of the bridge. He lowered his binoculars momentarily as he turned to acknowledge him. More confident with every day, but still wary of his skipper after that brief flare-up. Signalman Chitty, muffled up to the eyes, one arm hooked around his machine-guns. Titch Kelly at his Oerlikon. The rest was lost in darkness.

Foley moved up beside the coxswain.

'Not much longer, I think.'

Dougie Bass, his legs straddled on his grating, hands gripping the motionless wheel, glanced at him. 'No mines on board this time anyway, sir. This'll do me!'

Foley beckoned to Allison. Was it that easy? Bass always had the knack of making it seem that way.

'Go aft, Number One. Check with the Oerlikons and the depth charges. Minimum settings, remember?'

'I've checked them, sir.' He added hastily, 'I'll do it again.'

Foley returned to the forepart of the bridge. If there were any midget subs about, a depth charge or two would put paid to them.

He considered it. There was no need to ride Allison. He was keen, and he was learning. Then why . . .

'Flak, starboard beam, sir!'

Pinpricks of light, too far away even to hear the explosions of anti-aircraft fire. A raid, perhaps. Or a straggler trying to get home. There was a lot of cloud, and the distant shell bursts were soon hidden.

Foley ducked below the screen and peered at his watch. Midnight. Trafalgar Day was over. He pictured the chart again. The minelayers should be unloading their 'eggs'. And she would still be awake. Would be wearing the pendant . . .

Allison was back. 'All checked, sir.'

'Warn the Chief, Toby. Stand by.'

He heard Allison speaking to the engine room, and could imagine the reaction. *What's up with Old Chris, then? Losing his bottle?*

He thought of all the other motor launches. He knew all the skippers, at least by sight. Survivors. He wondered if the telegraphist named Bush was regretting leaving 366 in spite of a likely promotion. Glad to be out of it, no matter how it had felt at the time. But when he was taken unawares, by the news on the radio maybe, *During the night, our light coastal forces were in action*, it would all come back. He remembered Masters' face when he had been talking about the midget submarine and its dead German crewman. It never really left you.

And there was Dick Claridge, following somewhere directly astern, no doubt cursing the folly of his superiors for sending his boat to sea without giving him time to break in the new hands. A good skipper, none better, but always on edge. He had got married six months ago, to a girl he had known since she had been at school. It was something you had to consider, whether it was fair to any woman to have to put up with the separation and the constant worry. It was not like having a shore job, or serving in some remote area. Any day, or night like this one, it might happen. And she would get a telegram, *the* telegram, which nobody ever mentioned.

Suppose Margot and I . . .

He heard the extra lookout-cum-boatswain's mate mutter something, and Titch Kelly's sharp retort. 'For God's sake, take it off yer back!'

Foley tried to loosen his muscles. The remark could have been directed at him.

The explosion was sudden, and because of the stillness all the more menacing. Not close, but he felt the vibration against the lower hull, a nudge more than anything else.

Foley waited, counting seconds. No flak, no gunfire. Maybe one of the minelayers had set off one of her own eggs? It was not unknown.

Or maybe an E-Boat had been out there, playing the listening game as well, until a target had crossed its sights. In which case . . . He said aloud, 'Well, 'Swain?'

Bass said, 'Torpedo, I'd 'ave said, sir. But nothin' like I've 'eard before.'

Foley did not move. One torpedo. The enemy coast was ten miles away, the minelayers less than two off the starboard quarter.

180

'Tell the Chief, *now!*' He had not even raised his voice. As if he had been told what to do. Obeying orders, except that nothing had happened.

He heard Allison speaking on the intercom and wanted to tell him to be silent.

It must have been a mine. The whole bay would be a hornets' nest within half an hour.

Allison called, 'W/T, sir. *Mayday from Galaxy. Torpedoed.*'

Foley nodded, trying to hold the fragments together. No wonder there had been no signals from the senior officer. *Galaxy* was his code name.

There had been no warning, no time. The minelayer was probably sinking, some of her people injured or killed by the blast. Why no second explosion?

Allison was standing close beside him, his night glasses moving slowly across the quarter.

As if he had been doing it all his life. Foley said, '*One* tin-fish, Toby. Because that's all those midgets can carry.'

Bass exclaimed, 'The leader's started up, sir!'

Brock was wasting no time, or chance. A twist of fate had changed things. He was in command.

Foley gripped the screen as the engines coughed and roared into life. They were moving again. Alive, and not sitting ducks.

'Warn all guns, Toby. Be prepared for small units at close range.'

He saw Allison's face light up, his eyes shining like two pinpoints of fire, the bridge fittings and machine-guns suddenly standing out against the darkness beyond. Then came the second explosion, the sound rolling across the sea like the crash of tropical thunder. The whole bridge shook, while faces peered into the dying explosion like strangers, caricatures. Then, abruptly, it was dark again, but Foley heard the tell-tale splashes of fragments falling into the water, some clearly visible from the bridge, like leaping spirits from the ship which had been ripped apart. She had not had time to drop all her mines after all.

'Starboard twenty! Meet her! Steady!' Like listening to another stranger, unemotional, cold. Almost indifferent.

Just as they had rehearsed, had carried out so many times.

Revolutions for twenty knots, until they knew what was happening. Keep station on the senior officer. Hold the formation, no matter what.

Spray dashed over the screen, like pellets against his skin. The deck bounced across the ragged wake from Brock's boat, Bass bending his legs slightly to withstand the motion, his teeth bared against the spray as if he was grinning. Allison was clambering into the bridge but stopped dead, his head thrown back to listen, staring around as if he expected to see it.

Foley heard it, too. An abbreviated whistle, rising suddenly to a high-pitched whine: a shell passing overhead.

'Get down! Down, all of you!'

But there was no explosion, no scream and rattle of shell splinters, not the bloody suddenness of a direct hit.

Chitty covered his face with his sleeve and gasped, 'Star-shell! All we need!'

Foley tried to shield his eyes against the glare. It was often described as turning night into day, but that was only half of it. It was like being pinned down, defenceless and stark naked in an unwavering, glacier brightness. The whole of the upper deck was laid bare, wide open; men who had been faceless shadows were, in an instant, larger than life itself. Foley saw two other MLs, still altering course to take station astern, their bow waves lifting and creaming away from the raked stems, one training her forward gun although there was nothing in sight, and the gunners were too blinded to see it if there was.

There was a patch of foam, caught momentarily in the light. Large, obscene bubbles too. All that remained of the minelayer.

Foley swung away and looked for the leader, Brock's ML436. Making plenty of wash, turning slightly to starboard, ready to form a screen for the remaining minelayers. The hull was casting a perfect reflection on the heaving water; even the dazzle-paint was clearly visible. *Night into day.*

Allison was clinging to the side of the bridge, staring down, barely able to find the words.

'Port beam!' He jabbed the air with his hand, his face working with disbelief.

182

Foley almost knocked him from the grating as he flung himself across the bridge.

It was so close that he could see every detail. Low in the water, its small curved dome showing no more than a foot or so above the surface. It was barely moving, but in the relentless glare which had stripped the flotilla of secrecy and protection he saw the face and eyes of the midget submarine's crewman. Exactly as Masters had described it. As if the face beneath the perspex dome was staring up, straight at him. In seconds 366's wash would hide everything. In his racing thoughts he sensed that the flare was already beginning to fade. When darkness came . . .

He cupped his hands. *'Chitty!'* He saw the signalman glance up at him, but he was already swinging and depressing his twin machine-guns towards the water. *'Open fire!'*

The three-pounder was training round from the forecastle, but the target was too close for it to bear.

Foley winced as the twin Brownings rattled into life, the bullets cutting a path of leaping spray across the churned water, the tracer making certain of Chitty's aim. Only seconds, but it seemed endless. The sparks and the foam churning around and over the little dome, the crewman's eyes flashing in the unbroken burst, his mouth wide like a black hole, a last scream, perhaps, as the torpedo-shaped hull exploded and went out of control. Another star-shell burst, well away to starboard, fired from a vessel closer inshore. Firing blind, not that it mattered. The Germans were prepared, and eager to prove something.

Foley saw the leader's boat altering course again. 'Keep station, 'Swain!' He watched the compass. Coming round, north by west. Breaking off the operation.

The mines had been laid. Tomorrow or the next day, the enemy would come out and try to sweep them. He should be used to it by now; they all should. But this was different. A minelayer had been sunk, by one man. The target might just as easily have been a troopship or landing craft, packed with soldiers heading for an allocated beach, like Sicily and Italy.

By one man.

'Leader's alterin' course again, sir!'

Foley dragged his thoughts into order again, but could still see the staring face of the trapped crewman.

The R/T repeater crackled into life.

'Leader to Dogfish!' Brock sounded hoarse, angry even now. 'Bandits to the nor'-west, *closing*! Tally-ho!' The speaker fell silent.

Foley licked his lips. 'Hard a-port!' He almost lost his balance as the helm went over. 'Meet her! Steady! Steer North forty-five West!' He did not hear Bass's acknowledgment as the triple screws added their chorus to the din.

The flare was already dying, but Foley saw the bow waves of the nearest MLs crisp and white against the dark water. Where were the three promised motor gunboats? Their extra firepower would be needed, perhaps vital.

'Stand by, all guns!'

Allison said, 'I'll lay aft, sir!' He stopped as Foley grasped his arm.

'No. Stay here, Number One. I need you with me, all right?'

The flare had died, but he had seen the surprise on Allison's youthful face. Experience, instinct; why had he told him to stay, breaking the rules?

Allison leaned towards him as if to speak, but stared ahead instead as vivid trails of tracer lifted from the leader's boat and ripped away across the water. Brock was in the van; he had made the first sighting.

Foley wedged himself against the flag locker again, his binoculars grasped against his chest.

The guns were moving, as if independent of the hands on their controls. Each man knew what to do, what to expect. *Fire as you bear.* They must have given the same order at Trafalgar.

He thought of Claridge's boat: some of his men had never been in action before, not with the same boat and company. He recalled being shown a photograph of the girl he had married.

'Here it comes, lads!'

Foley watched the bands of tracer lifting, it seemed from the sea itself, crossing and intertwining before tearing down onto an invisible target.

The enemy had opened fire.

12

The Quick and the Dead

Sub-Lieutenant Tobias Allison gripped one of the handrails below the bridge screen and felt his arm take the weight of his body as the boat heeled over again. It was hard to keep a sense of direction, the helm going this way and that, zigzagging and yet holding a mean course and bearing with the frothing wake of the next ahead. The tracer criss-crossed from every angle, the sharp rattle of cannon and machine-gun fire closing from all sides, as if 366 was the sole target.

Crouched around and below the bridge, Allison could occasionally see other figures, unmoving, clinging to their weapons, or waiting to reload them if they 'ran dry'.

No wisecracks this time, the only voice that of the skipper, and indistinct rejoinders from the coxswain.

Allison swayed over once more, his shoulder against the dripping bridge, feeling the mounting power and thrust of the engines. In deadly earnest. He found it hard to accept that he was still unafraid. He was part of it, no longer an awkward responsibility. He looked over at Foley, one arm thrust out to steady himself. He must have stood like that a thousand times, he thought.

For Allison it seemed this part of his life had already been decided, as if he had had no hand in it. He had entered the navy straight from school and been sent to the boys' training establishment, H.M.S. *Ganges* at Shotley. It overlooked Harwich harbour, and Felixstowe, the main Coastal Forces base on the east coast. Every day, while he had been learning to master the mysteries of bends-and-hitches, splicing or parade ground training, he had seen the little ships entering or leaving harbour, MTBs and motor gunboats, and others which could be twinned with ML366. Eventually he and his class had been allowed out on the water, boat-pulling in the big twelve-oared cutters. Hard work, but it took him closer to the dazzle-painted escorts, and the 'little ships'.

The seamanship instructor, a grizzled old petty officer, had remarked, 'Don't get mixed up with them lot! Won't last long if you do!'

Neither, it seemed, did many of the escorts.

After Allison had been granted a commission at the officers' training establishment, *King Alfred*, he had been appointed to a destroyer, one of those hard-worked escorts based at, of all places, Harwich. Air and E-Boat attacks, they had had their share of both. The destroyer was an old ship, one of the V and W class which had been built for the Kaiser's war. A happy ship, everyone said, with a tough and experienced company. Three days after Allison had begun training for Coastal Forces he had heard that the old destroyer had gone down in the North Sea, torpedoed by an E-Boat. *Won't last long if you do!*

He dragged himself round as another, deeper explosion boomed out of the darkness, followed instantly by a vivid mushroom of fire.

Somebody said, 'Got one of the buggers!'

Allison tried to moisten his lips, swallow, but his mouth was dried out. He saw the tracer swooping down across the port bow, the immediate *crack-crack-crack* of the three-pounder. It was not going to rip overhead. He wanted to call out, to move, but he could do neither. More shots now, cutting low down over the churning water, no tracer this time. He looked for the skipper, but he was almost shrouded by smoke from the three-pounder as it funnelled over and into the bridge.

He heard him call, 'Depth charge!' Then, *'Steady!'* Like somebody calming a startled horse.

Allison gasped aloud as the deck jumped under his seaboots. A shell had smashed into the hull and exploded. He gritted his teeth and made himself consider it like a spectator, picturing the deck beneath him, hearing sounds he now knew were steel splinters tearing through the boat.

His eyes pricked with acrid smoke and he forced himself to stare at the cloud which was spiralling from the companion ladder, dark and solid against the grey paint.

He turned to alert the skipper and gazed at him with shocked disbelief as Foley gripped the voicepipes and beckoned to him urgently.

'Deal with the fire, Number One! If it reaches the fuel . . .' He doubled over and a seaman caught him around the waist.

Bass said harshly, ''Ear what 'e said, sir? We'll all fry if that lot brews up!'

It was then that Allison saw the E-Boat, spray bursting over its stem like something solid, the stabbing flash of cannon fire reflected against the armoured cupola bridge. Fifty yards at most, but she seemed to be right alongside.

He was unable to move until he felt Foley's hand on his arm, and then around his wrist, like a band of wet metal.

'Do it! You told me you could!' The grip slackened. 'Get me *up*, somebody!'

Allison shook his head. 'Look after him, 'Swain!' He lurched away. 'You two, come with me! Cover your faces!'

He was running, half falling as another explosion rocked the hull, and for a second he imagined that the fuel had blown. A column of water fell across the deck, choking and blinding him. His reeling mind told him that a depth charge had exploded. He could almost hear Foley's voice. *At minimum setting.* It must have burst right alongside the E-Boat. He heard the screech of engines, violent bangs, as if the racing screws had been blown from their brackets and were hacking through the E-Boat's hull. All firing had ceased, except that which seemed a great distance away. He sensed that their own speed was reduced, the deck swaying drunkenly in the sudden backwash.

Above it all someone was screaming. High-pitched, inhuman, making thought impossible. Then it stopped, as if somebody had slammed a door on it.

A hand was holding his arm, and for another hazy moment

Allison imagined he had not moved from the bridge, that Foley was still gripping him, willing him to move, to act.

But it was the signalman, Bob Chitty, squinting through the smoke, an extinguisher in his free hand.

'All set, sir? Ready if you are!'

Together they groped down the ladder, past the W/T office and the wardroom. Allison stared at the telegraphist, the rating who had relieved Bush, crouched over his switchboard, one hand to his ear as if he was listening to some important signal. Water was spurting through the side where cannon shells had found their mark, and the spreading puddle of blood around the telegraphist's feet told the brutal truth. Allison muttered, 'I don't even know his name!'

Chitty merely glanced at him. 'The fire's in the galley. Let's 'ave a go at that first!' He retched, biting back the coughing fit. *If you gave into it, you were bloody done for.*

He called over his shoulder, 'Ready, Smithy?' He heard the other figure switch on his extinguisher, caught the pungent smell. Chitty wiped his face. The galley would be bloody useless after this. He almost laughed aloud. As if it mattered. At any second now another kraut would come charging out of the smoke, all guns blazing, and then . . . He could scarcely breathe, but the fire was retreating almost as he watched, a few spurting flames still flickering from a cupboard full of pusser's jam and marmalade. He thought of the coxswain, Dougie Bass; he fancied himself a chef from time to time. He wouldn't be too happy about this pot-mess.

The laugh nearly overwhelmed him again. He'd seen a few others crack up like that. He studied the young subbie, fanning his face with his cap, his fair hair plastered to a forehead blackened with smoke. *Tobias.* He relented slightly. *Not a bad bloke, for an officer, that is. Green as grass. Maybe not so green any more.*

'Okay, sir?'

Allison sucked in several deep breaths. The leaks would be dealt with by the pumps. There was no more fire. It was impossible to believe that the whole space had been a mass of flames, until you looked at the burned and blistered paintwork, the charred clothing hanging outside the messdeck. And through that bulkhead, the fuel was unharmed. *Not that we'd have known much about it.*

'I must go up. Can you cope down here?' Then he grinned and

reached out as if to grip his hand. 'What a stupid question! I'll send someone to relieve you.'

Chitty crunched into the blackened galley. He had expected to die. To be killed, not for the first time. He had seen the E-Boat surging towards him when his twin Brownings had jammed. He had also seen the skipper stagger, lose his balance; he had felt it as if it was his own pain. He had seen a few go like that.

It was strange to think about it. He had started work, earning a few bob, as a lookout for a street bookmaker in London. He was always quick on his feet whenever the police arrived or some rival bookie tried to break up the pitch; the betting slips had been safe in his keeping. He had graduated to being a bookie's tick-tack man at the local dog racing stadium, where he had become adept at using his hands to signal the odds and the chances in a sign language not unlike semaphore. Then working the fairgrounds, chatting up the girls, having a snog on the Ghost Train when a chance was offered, always just this side of the law. He smiled to himself. Even learned to shoot with a .22 on the fairground circuit.

He heard the engines increase their revs. On the move again. His companion, Smithy, who was raking through some burned-out boxes, said, 'Close thing, Bob.'

Chitty held out his hand and studied it gravely. The green young subbie had shaken it. This hand. What was he? Nineteen years old? He peered at the low deckhead. Right now, he could find himself in command.

'You shouldn't 'ave joined . . .'

The man called Smithy grinned, some of the strain draining away as he replied promptly, '. . . if you can't take a joke!'

Allison had to stop halfway up the companion ladder while he pressed his cheek against the handrail, to steady himself, and accept what he had just done. The rail was like ice, and like the breeze that greeted him it helped to drive away the memory of the flames, and the smoke which had seared his lungs. And the dead telegraphist, hunched intently over his instruments as if waiting for some last signal.

As his breathing eased he could hear Chitty and the one called Smithy laughing and coughing alternately while they raked the charred remains of their messdeck. A cramped space where men ate their meals, wrote letters, slept, or just sat and waited for the shrill of action stations. It was not much, but it was all they had.

He gripped the rail and hauled himself bodily into the bridge. At school, Allison had never had much interest in sport or team games, but he had always enjoyed acting in amateur dramatics, be they Shakespeare or something lighter. He had even tried his hand at producing some of them: quick changes of dress or make-up, scenery or fittings to be moved while the youthful audience whistled or stamped beyond the lowered curtain.

He breathed deeply, staring around the small bridge. It was like that now. Waiting for curtain-up, the players rearranged slightly, but not what he had been expecting. Dreading.

He saw Foley sitting on a locker, supported by Leading Seaman Nick Harrison, who next to the coxswain was the ML's key rating. Gunlayer on the three-pounder, Buffer of the upper deck when they were in harbour, he was a true seaman who could turn his mind and hands to almost anything. Allison looked quickly forward. The three-pounder was pointing over the port bow, a sprawled corpse nearby, jerking occasionally to the hull's movements as if still alive. The loading number: he must have been cut down in that last savage burst of cannon fire.

Allison stooped and said, 'All right, Skipper . . . sir?'

Foley raised his head and looked at him.

'Did you get it under control down there?'

Allison saw the torn jacket, the shoulder and side bare to the bitter wind and drifting spray, and the dressing which Harrison was trying to hold in position. And blood. Black against the grey paint, and the thin plating which could hardly deflect a spent bullet.

He said, 'Here, let me,' and felt Foley wince as he moved the heavy dressing. 'Sorry, sir. But I can do it. I took a first aid course at *King Alfred*.' He was speaking jerkily, afraid he might lose the impetus which had carried him this far. 'During the dog watches, usually. To get out of sporting events, you see . . .'

Harrison murmured, 'That looks good.' He sounded relieved, and possibly surprised.

Foley gasped as they covered him with somebody's duffle coat, then stared around the bridge again, coming to terms with it.

190

'Wood splinter,' Harrison said. 'Big as a baby's arm. An inch or so inboard and it would have done for 'im, sir.'

'I'll have another go when it's a bit lighter.' He broke off as Foley said, 'You're all surprises, Toby.' His teeth were very white against the dark backdrop of sea and cloud; he was grinning despite the pain, and the shock of being rendered helpless at the very moment the boat, his boat, needed him. 'I don't know what it is you've got, but don't ever lose it. Promise me that, will you?'

He tried to lift his arm but the pain stopped him. 'Take over.' He took another sharp breath. 'Number One. The E-Boats have pulled off, for the moment, but they might be back. The MGBs are here, *at last*.' He attempted to smile, but failed. 'One of ours is in trouble. Starboard bow. We're closing now. Get forrard and get ready to come alongside.' He shook his head suddenly. 'I can manage up here.' His hand came up again and reached Allison's wrist. 'And the fire really is under control?'

Allison made himself stand, feeling the heavier motion, the reduced speed, and saw the other motor launch for the first time. Drifting and out of control, smoke hanging over and around the hull, pale against the black water.

'The fire's out, sir.' Somehow he knew it was important for the skipper to be reassured. The rest, whatever it entailed, had to wait. He trembled. The stage must be reset for the next episode.

The hold on his wrist tightened. 'Good lad, Toby. I'll not forget.'

Bass looked down from his wheel. 'I'll take her in, sir.' He might have chuckled. 'Done it a few times.'

Leading Seaman Harrison said, 'I'll come forrard with you, sir.'

Allison nodded. He must have learned a lot since *Ganges*, he thought vaguely. Harrison's tone, for instance. The unspoken warning.

Somebody called, 'Watch yer step, sir!'

It was slippery, treacherous on the unsteady forecastle deck. Plenty of spray, but still a lot of blood as well. Allison recalled the terrible scream, the sound cut off like a slammed door. Somehow he knew Harrison had silenced the dying man, perhaps to prevent a panic, or to lessen his misery. A cannon shell had smashed him down even as he had reloaded the gun and had blasted off both his hands, and he had been badly wounded in several places by the same jagged splinters which had pockmarked the forepart of the bridge and chart space. Allison retched, but controlled it. One of the severed hands was caught around a mooring cleat, whitened by the constant spray, like a torn, discarded glove.

He tried to shut it from his mind, his brain, and made himself stare at the other motor launch. He could just make out the number on her shining hull, ML417, one of the extra boats which had been called in for the minelaying escort.

So unlike his time aboard the old destroyer, in the convoys, those long lines of hard-worked, rusty merchantmen. The flash of an explosion in the night as a torpedo had found its target, and then a ship falling slowly out of line, dying as you watched. And the commodore's signal. *Close up.* You must not stop. Fill in the gap, until the next one caught it.

This was different. People you knew, if only by sight, or responding to a wave or some witty signal when the senior officer chose not to be looking. He recalled the charred messdeck, the few possessions scattered amongst the debris.

He said, 'Stand by with the fenders!' and watched the other boat moving down on him, or so it appeared. But Bass was gauging it, and the skipper would be holding on. Making sure. Like hearing him speak. *Good lad. I'll not forget.*

He could smell the damage now, burned wood, and the lurking danger of leaking fuel. A heaving line snaked out of the night and a hand caught it neatly, as if it was broad daylight, and in harbour.

'Take her head rope!' Allison winced as the two hulls jerked together and the rope fenders took the full shock. He wondered what it must be like in the engine room, the Chief and his small team sealed in with the pounding machinery, the din which would drown out the sound of an approaching shell, until it was too late.

He heard the tough leading seaman say, 'Lieutenant Baldwin's the C.O., sir.'

Some of the injured men were being dragged across the treacherous gap between the two boats. Others lay where they had fallen. A sub-lieutenant, he guessed the Number One, was urging the last few to jump to safety.

192

Harrison murmured, '*Was* the C.O., anyway.'

He turned as Foley called down from the bridge. His voice seemed stronger. Unchanged.

'Cast off, Number One! She's going down!'

Allison stared at the other boat. If there was anyone else, it was too late.

'Let go! Fend off, forrard!'

A shadow moved up beside him. Without looking he knew it was the subbie, his opposite number.

He said, 'Lost seven chaps.' Someone cried out behind them. 'Skipper bought it in the first attack.' He let out a long sigh. 'So long, old girl.'

Allison watched the other hull turning on her side, bubbles bursting around the motionless screws and through the shell holes along the bilges.

The subbie turned away as somebody took his arm to guide him aft. But he hesitated, and then seemed to shrug.

'Maybe I'll do it for you some day, eh?'

The engines were growling again, and the next boat astern was taking up station even as the abandoned motor launch lifted her stern and dived out of sight.

Brock's boat came creaming past, rounding up the depleted flotilla. The loud-hailer was mercifully silent.

The E-Boats had gone. Allison felt something like weariness sweeping over him and had to shake himself. It was not the time to step back and be thankful. It never was.

He said, 'Clear up here, Hookey. Get more hands from aft if need be. Must get the three-pounder on top line again, right?'

It had come out sharper than intended, but Harrison replied, 'Right, sir!' He was satisfied although he would never say as much. *That's more like it. No room for passengers in this boat.*

He glanced at the corpse of the man he had known for several months. A lifetime. His knuckles still ached from the punch he had thrown to silence his screams; he had been finished anyway. He peered at the splinter holes and jagged scars. *Only two sorts of matelot in this man's navy. The quick, and the dead.*

He thought about the motor launch he had watched go down. He had had a good friend aboard her. He had not been one of the survivors he had seen dragged over the side. When it happened, it was the best way to go. With your mates. And with your boat. He thought of the other Jimmy the One, his quiet *so long, old girl*. It had broken through his defences, and that had surprised him.

A group of figures were scrambling towards him, the 'extra hands'. There was a lot to do before daylight found them again.

'Come on, you idle sods! Move yerselves!'

Leading Seaman Nick Harrison, the Buffer, was back.

Petty Officer Ian Shannon, the Chief, wedged himself in one corner of the bridge, an oilskin covering his familiar overalls to protect him from the keen air which must be a testing contrast to the heat of his engines.

'I've been right through the boat, sir.' He hesitated, looking over the screen at the sea, as if he loathed it. 'It's not a dockyard job, as far as I can estimate, but it'll keep us in harbour for a week or two.'

Foley held the enamel mug to his mouth and swallowed the last of the thick, clinging cocoa, 'ki', which Shannon had organized in the engine room. With the galley in ruins, it was all they had. A good tot of rum would help, but they were not out of danger yet.

He considered what the Chief had told him, and could picture the damage for himself. And the human cost. Scott, the new telegraphist, killed by shell splinters on his first trip in 366. He had only spoken to him a couple of times and could hardly recall his face. Hutton, seaman gunner, who had lost both hands in the attack, a likeable youngster who had been in their small company for six months or more. And another seaman named Miles who had been cruelly scarred across the face by wood fragments which might have blinded him.

Foley touched his side. It felt raw, and when he moved, it hurt like hell. A close thing. But he had been lucky and he knew it.

Shannon said, 'I'll be getting back then, sir.' Like so many of his calling he felt out of place on the bridge, away from his engines, which even now he was listening to, sifting each sound and vibration.

'You did well, Chief.'

Shannon smiled. 'We all did, I reckon, sir.'

194

Foley heard him retreating from the sea and sky. Did he ever think of the garage he had once managed, and the wife who had left him for somebody else? The only man aboard who never received any letters when the mail boat came alongside.

Another of the men they had taken from the sinking ML had died. That made eight, including her skipper. Almost half her complement.

He reached over and wiped the salt from the glass screen. It was still dark, but at this time in the morning watch you seemed to get a kind of second sight, the sea and full-bellied clouds acting like a warning. More ships were lost returning to base than on operations. Tired and spent, thinking of getting back to a warm bed, perhaps. Or maybe a letter from home. Allison always seemed to receive a lot of mail. It was hardly surprising. He could hear him now, speaking to some shadowy figure by the midships gun mounting. After this night nobody would try to take the mickey out of him again.

Dougie Bass returned to the wheel and took over from the helmsman who had relieved him for a well-earned break. Bass had been on the wheel almost continuously since they had quit their little base with its church and solitary pub.

What was she doing now? Asleep? Or had someone got news of the operation which had misfired? As if the enemy had known, and been waiting for them.

One minelayer sunk, and it was unlikely that anybody would have survived, and ML417 shot to pieces. Against that, they might have put paid to an E-Boat with the depth charge ruse. *Might, if, maybe.* It was hardly anything to crow about.

A voice seemed to ask, *And what about you?*

Foley eased himself to his feet, and sensed that Bass had taken his eyes from the compass to watch him. And there was Harrison, the tough leading hand, one of the hard men, who had been so concerned that he had been unable to accept that his skipper had been brought down. A wood splinter, *big as a baby's arm*, which might have ended everything.

And the other ML's Number One, older and probably far more experienced than Allison, who had seemed suddenly lost, crushed by what had happened to his boat, and to his skipper.

Was that how it would be?

'*Aircraft*, sir!'

Foley swung round and felt the dressing pulling at his torn skin. He cupped his hands to his ears, turning slightly to find and gauge the sound.

'Ahead, sir! Moving left to right!'

That was Chitty, at his station again. He missed nothing.

Foley said, 'Stand to! Warn the engine room!'

Allison was here, dragging out his binoculars, his jaw still working on a scrap of food from somewhere.

Foley watched his faint silhouette against the clouds. A youth who had dodged extra sport and studied first aid as an excuse; he could well imagine it. The same youth who might just as quickly have been thrown into command of this boat.

Cocking levers clicked into place, and a figure lurched aft with a new magazine for an Oerlikon.

Foley licked his lips and felt the cold air probing through his torn jacket and sweater, and against his skin. Then he heard it. One aircraft, perhaps searching for some clue which would bring the whole pack down on them at first light. Louder now; he could imagine the pilot, alone in his cockpit. A different sort of war.

At any moment he might drop a flare and . . . night into day again. He felt his teeth snagging together. Shivering, but not from the cold.

Bass muttered, 'Come on then, let's be 'avin' you!'

'There, sir! Starboard bow!'

Foley saw the small flares falling slowly towards the sea, touching the troughs and serried waves with colour.

Green, green, then red over green. The recognition challenge. Foley took a long, ragged breath. Probably one of Coastal Command. Looking for them.

There was a prick of light; the signalman must have been poised with his finger on the trigger, and then a solitary white flare exploded like a bright star before fading and drifting down again with the wind.

Tony Brock had replied to the signal.

There was still a long way to go.

Foley said, 'Go aft, Toby.' He was thinking of the young seaman who might have lost his sight for good. 'Find Miles for me, will you? Tell him we're going home.'

Afterwards, he wondered how he had managed to get it out.

A near thing.

The same Operations Officer yawned hugely and scratched his side.

'That about does it, David. Quite enough, too, for one bloody night, I'd say!'

David Masters studied the plot, and the scribbled comments and times on the wall chart. Outside it was very dark, or so it seemed away from these glaring lights. And yet he had heard Reveille sound over the tannoy system, what felt like hours ago.

It was a physical effort to think, but he went over it again. The two minelayers were on their way to Plymouth; a fresh escort should already be in company. The motor launches would enter harbour at ten o'clock. Handling parties would be mustered, ambulances standing by. It was a familiar scenario, and yet . . . He rubbed his chin, his hand rasping over the stubble; he could not remember when he had last had a good night's sleep.

He looked at the incident log. There had been three all told. Two magnetic mines had been reported, one in Swanage, about twenty miles away, and the other on the outskirts of Poole harbour. An unidentified sighting had been made off Durlston Head, and minesweepers were waiting until daylight.

It was all in hand; there was nothing more he could do. So why should he feel such a sense of frustration? He should be used to it. The teams were experienced. They were all volunteers. It would make no difference if he was able to be present with every one of them.

A telegraphist poked his head around the screen.

'Call for you, sir. In your office?'

'Who is it?'

The man grinned, despite the hours he had been on watch, the strain of listening to the reports. Ships vanishing. Men dying. Symbols on a chart.

'Rear-Admiral Fawcett, sir.'

The Operations Officer almost choked on his cup of tea.

'At this hour? Does he never sleep?'

The yeoman of signals muttered, 'Not on his own anyway, lucky bugger!'

It had been a long night, so the Ops Officer chose to ignore the remark.

Masters climbed the steps into his office and shut the door. He could smell the stale pipe smoke, evidence of his last brief visit.

Bumper Fawcett came straight to the point.

'I shall be with you at noon, or thereabouts. I've been following the situation, and I'm unhappy about it.' A pause, and Masters could hear his quick breathing. His anger. 'Are you there?'

'Yes, sir.'

'Well, I want a full investigation, and tell Brock I shall expect a report from him, not in some bloody document, *what*?'

Masters rubbed his aching eyes. 'I shall arrange it, sir.'

'Too bloody much of this cloak-and-dagger nonsense! Find out what's wrong, then stamp on it, that's always been my scheme of things!'

The line went dead.

Masters glanced around the office, hating it, and thinking suddenly of his last commanding officer, before he had been given *Tornado*. After a patrol, no matter how wearing and dangerous, his skipper had always appeared on the bridge shaved and smartly turned out for entering harbour. 'Not vanity, David. It's my way of saying thanks to our lads. Showing them that it matters.'

He peered at his watch and strode down to the Operations Room again.

'Can I have a car? Now?'

The Operations Officer nodded and gestured to a messenger. 'For the Big Chief?'

'For me.' He heard a car starting up, and reached for the blackout curtain. 'If anything . . .'

'I know. I'll call you right away.'

Masters waited for his eyes to accept the darkness and headed for the main gates. Groups of sailors were marching between the huts, and there was activity around the sick quarters: there would be wounded to attend to. Hope to offer, where there might be none. ML366 had been in action; Chris Foley had not been reported injured. But information was limited, censored.

The driver was a marine, the one he had seen talking with the Wren, Foley's girl.

The car moved off through the gates, where two ambulances were already waiting to enter.

'Bad luck, eh, sir?'

Masters touched the scar on his cheek. There were no secrets here.

He said, 'I'll be as fast as I can.'

The driver nodded. The officer had told him politely to shut up.

It only took a few minutes, but it seemed an hour. When he got out of the car he could see the house already framed against the sky, the line of trees beyond, and was suddenly angry with himself. What was he trying to prove? Every day men were being killed, by accident or by booby-trap, or by some device not even fully understood. He had met every one of them and sometimes had watched them go, on what had proved to be their last mission.

He groped for the door but it had opened. He stared at her, taken completely aback, and unable to conceal it.

'Elaine! I had no idea . . .'

She touched his arm. 'Come in and shut the door. I'll put on some lights.'

For a moment they stood looking at one another, then she said quietly, 'I knew you were coming. I don't know why.' She waved towards the stairs. 'I have a fresh shirt for you. Coker showed me.' She faced him again, the same defiance in her voice. 'I called the base. They told me you'd just left.'

Masters took her hands. 'What a way to begin the day. You look lovely.'

She was fully dressed, in the uniform-style tunic and trousers he remembered. Her hair was tied back to the nape of her neck, and inside the tunic she was wearing the diamond brooch.

'You look done in, David. You never give yourself a chance.' She tried to pull her hands away. 'Have a shower. I made sure that it's working.'

He released her hands.

'What about Captain Wykes?'

She shrugged. 'He left earlier. A phone call. I could have gone, too.'

'But you stayed.'

She walked to a table and moved a telephone book, perhaps without knowing it.

'I wanted to stay.' She looked at him directly. 'I'm coming with you.'

A door banged open and shut and Petty Officer Coker hurried into the light, hastily buttoning his jacket and staring at both of them.

'I – I'm sorry, sir, I was in the galley. I only just heard that you were back.'

Masters started to climb the stairs. 'It's all right, I'm being taken care of.'

'I'll make some tea.' He looked at the girl, tall in her sombre clothing. A real woman any man would kill for.

Or die for.

The lights dimmed suddenly, and then returned to their full strength. She had one hand to her throat.

'Was that a bomb?'

Coker shook his head. 'No, miss. That was a mine. A big 'un, I'd say.'

She looked up the stairs. 'He might be in the shower.'

Coker said, 'But he'll know, miss. You can bank on it.'

At that moment the telephone started to ring.

13

Under Orders

Sub-Lieutenant Michael Lincoln pushed open the door of the Ready Room, and after a slight hesitation entered and shut it behind him. It was empty, as he had hoped it would be. The room was not unlike the ones at local fighter stations, where pilots lounged about, hiding their doubts and anxieties while they waited for the order to scramble. Battered and roughly used armchairs, racks of magazines and newspapers, and a few tables where you could write a letter if you felt like it. A place of lively conversation or edgy silence.

Lincoln glanced at the newspapers, but they were yesterday's. A working party would arrive soon to clean up the place, empty the ashtrays, and prepare it for another emergency.

Outside it was cold but bright, the sky an empty, washed-out blue. How quickly the weather seemed to change along the Dorset coast, he thought. Fresh and clear, but the puddles of overnight rain were still evident. Normally he enjoyed his breakfast, the best meal of the day, even if it was spam and powdered eggs. That had not been the case today. The wardroom had been heavy with gloom, some doubtless the aftermath of too much gin and Trafalgar Night, but mostly, he suspected, because of the reported casualties.

For Lincoln it was made more unsettling by the occasional touch on the shoulder, a murmured, 'Good show, old chap!' Few of them knew him by name as yet. He should have gone straight to Masters, Captain Chavasse if necessary, to bang it on the head there and then. But he had not. As far as the wardroom was aware, and anyone else who was interested, Lincoln was up for an award of some kind. A gong, or perhaps a Mention, but it was something, especially for a comparative newcomer in their midst.

The worst part had been when he had visited Downie in the sickbay. He had been pleased about the recommendation, because, as he had put it, he felt a part of it.

He should have told him immediately. That the explosion had wiped the truth from Downie's memory was no excuse. It made Lincoln sweat to recall that he had said nothing.

He touched one of the chairs, remembering the lieutenant he had seen sitting there. 'Dicer' Lewis. In his twenties, but sporting a jaunty beard already tinged with grey, he had looked much older. Lincoln was uncertain of the nickname. Good with the liar dice? Or had he been one to take chances? He had only spoken to him once.

Like most people Lincoln had heard, and felt, the explosion; Swanage was only about twenty miles away in a direct line. And it had been a big mine, they said. Dicer Lewis had been on the job for two years, a true veteran, with many successful missions to his credit. A few failures too, but he had survived. This mine had been half-buried in mud after all the rain, the worst sort of obstacle, when the beast had to be dug, scooped out of its lair before it could be made safe.

A miscalculation, or maybe he had been too tired to prepare for something new, a trap he had never seen before. Two years might have made him over-confident.

Like those early days of bomb disposal Lincoln had heard and read about, when young army officers died at an ever-increasing rate, some said to match a subaltern's life span on the Western Front in the Great War.

He ran his fingers through his hair. He could picture it exactly, as it had been. Downie's torch, his voice quite steady, calm even, as he had called out what he had found and what he intended to do about it.

And I did nothing. I couldn't move or think.

He had thought of Downie again just now. He had seen a dog sitting by the road to the gates, Dicer Lewis's dog. Waiting. Not understanding.

Downie was fond of animals, but it had taken Masters to tell Lincoln what he should have learned for himself. Should have seen it that day on the beach, and later in the boat when they had been going out to the *Latchmere*. He had been making friends with that stray dog then, the one which had jumped or fallen into the trapped water where Downie had seen the device.

In the sickbay Downie had asked about that same dog. He remembered nothing else.

All Lincoln could find to say was, 'It saved your life.'

Downie had reached out impulsively, smiling, in a manner he had not seen before.

'*You* did that, sir!'

Lincoln had taken his hand, knowing in some confused way that it was important.

He sat carefully in the chair and looked around the room. Downie was back to duty again. They would be working together like the other times, as if nothing had happened.

One thing was stark and plain. He would be living a lie. He thought of his father when he had asked him once if they could have a dog of their own. His father had scoffed at the idea. A guard dog to protect his precious builder's yard was his only concern.

He was on his feet without realizing what he had done. He had written to his mother, told her about it. The lie was complete.

A seaman peered in at him, a broom and bucket balanced in one hand.

'Your assistant is 'ere, sir. Rarin' to go, too!'

He was still chuckling and shaking his head as Lincoln strode past him.

It were better cloudy and wet again, he thought. The flotilla would be coming back shortly, what was left of it. Sunshine and clear skies seemed an insult.

Downie was waiting by the covered way which joined the offices to the wardroom, dressed in his Number Threes, his collar newly washed and pressed, as he had been taught, no doubt, by some old three-badgeman. He looked fresh and showed no sign of strain, and if anything younger than ever.

And tanned, despite the nearness of winter. For something to say, Lincoln had remarked on it when he had made his visit to the sickbay. Downie had been sitting beside the bed, wearing some outsized pyjamas loaned him by the staff. The jacket had been partly open and Lincoln had noticed how brown his skin was.

Downie had said, 'There's a place up the coast – we used to go there sometimes when we weren't on call. It was good.'

Lincoln knew he was referring to the lieutenant who had been killed defusing a device aboard a crashed Junkers; the boffins were still delving into it, but the only real information so far was Downie's sketches. Not officer and rating, but *we*.

'Sorry to hear about Mister Lewis, sir.'

'You knew him?' They fell into step and walked towards the water.

'I met him, sir.'

Not quite the same thing. Lincoln glanced at the ambulances, a pile of stretchers partly covered by blankets.

Downie said, 'We had one once which had fallen into mud.'

Lincoln said nothing, not wanting to interrupt. *We.*

Downie was frowning, one hand held up to shade his eyes. 'We used a tackle, and borrowed a hose from some firemen. We did it in the end.'

Lincoln ignored the warnings, and said, 'When we're on the job I think we should drop the saluting and the *sirs*. What about it?'

Downie nodded slowly, his eyes grave. 'O.L.Q.s, sir?'

'Yes, that sort of thing.' He was losing it. Downie would probably laugh at him behind his back. Or worse.

Downie was looking at him, uncertain or troubled, it was not easy to tell.

Then he said, 'I'd like that, sir.'

Lincoln smiled. 'So be it, then.'

Someone called out, and the leading motor launch appeared around the headland, moving slowly, her ensign very bright against the shark-blue water. Downie watched the second boat appear, then darted a glance at his officer.

It could never be the same, and he did not want it to be. But he needed someone. He heard the snap of commands behind him. *And he needs me.*

One of the ambulances began to edge forward, the red crosses on its canvas sides gleaming like blood.

Downie looked round and saw that the place had filled with people, civilian workers from the makeshift yard, sailors and marines, some Wrens standing at the head of the jetty, leaning over to watch the slow-moving column of boats.

Only the dog lay as before. Watching the gates, and the road beyond.

As ML366 sighed against her rope fenders and the mooring lines fore and aft took the strain, her engines shuddered into silence.

Chris Foley climbed up on to the starboard grating and gazed at the upturned faces along and beyond the jetty, the only movement being the handling parties of seamen who had caught the heaving lines and made fast each of the returning motor launches.

'All secure fore and aft, sir!' Allison hardly raised his voice, but it seemed loud in the oppressive stillness.

Foley touched his cap with his fingers. 'Stretcher cases first.' He should be used to it. The aftermath. The clearing up. He recalled one commanding officer who had told some of his less experienced hands not to collapse at the first sight of men killed in a sea fight. *Think of them as meat.* He had bought it himself soon afterwards. Had he had time to remember those words?

They were already climbing aboard, stretcher bearers, sickberth attendants, and a pink-faced surgeon lieutenant carrying a small leather bag.

The walking wounded went first, the stretcher cases apparently preferring to go ashore on their own feet. Pride, dignity? Or perhaps the sight of the canvas-covered bodies gave them new strength.

A shadow fell across the bridge and Foley saw the other ML's first lieutenant waiting by the ladder.

He should be used to it . . . Foley had been a survivor himself, when his own skipper had been killed. He knew what the subbie was thinking, Allison too, when he had seen him fall.

They shook hands. Like friends meeting on a street, and parting.

'Good luck.'

'Thank you, sir.' He looked briefly at the others. Bass and Chitty, Allison and Titch Kelly. What he was leaving. What he had lost.

Allison, unwilling to interrupt, said quietly, 'Visitors, sir.'

Some of the spectators were parting to allow a group through, and Foley saw Captain Chavasse's gold-leaved cap, Masters beside him, and behind them the captain's secretary, Brayshaw, and the establishment's first lieutenant. He turned to finish what he had been saying, but the subbie had already disappeared.

He said, 'Now, the post-mortem!' and clapped his hand to his side as he stepped down from the grating.

'All right, sir?'

Foley forced a grin. 'I've felt better!'

'I'll fetch the doc.'

'*No*. Not now, Toby.' He moved to the rear of the bridge to watch the rest of the rescued sailors being seen over the side. There were a few grins here and there, a thumbs-up to somebody. Some tears as well. The aftermath . . . He saw one of the stretchers being loaded into an ambulance. It was Miles, the young seaman, his bandaged eyes turned towards the boat, one hand partly raised. *We're going home.* To what?

Chavasse was pointing with his walking stick, jabbing the air to emphasize something. Foley noticed that Masters was looking at 366, as if, over the jetty and bobbing heads, the stretchers and the carefully hidden coffins, he was trying to reach him in some way.

It was Chitty who spoke first. ''Ere, sir. Take my glasses.'

Foley took the heavy signals binoculars and raised them above the screen. The pointed stem, the three-pounder with its chips and scrapes from the enemy's cannon fire, where a man had been cut down, the stains and the splintered planking, all dropped out of focus as he trained the glasses on the figures at the end of the jetty wall.

Three Wrens standing side by side, the one in the centre lifting her hand to remove her cap, as if she was afraid he might not recognize her.

Foley took off his cap, and gritted his teeth as the dressing dragged at his torn side like hot wires. Then very slowly he waved the cap from side to side, until the pain made him lower it. He could sense Allison and Bass waiting to come to his aid, but nothing could stop him now. He saw her fumbling with her shirt front, pulling her tie to one side, then holding something bright where he could see it.

He thrust the binoculars out to Chitty: they seemed to have become suddenly heavier, and misty.

'Thanks.'

Chitty managed to summon one of his cheeky grins.

'My pleasure, sir.'

Someone else was saying, '*Told* you he'd get us back to base, didn't I?'

But something was wrong. Foley tried to clear his mind, to grasp what had happened. He was sitting down, his eyes watering in the hard sunshine while somebody was trying to support his head and shoulders.

Allison was down with him, his face only inches away. A boy no longer.

'It's all right, Skipper. She's safe with me.'

What did he mean? This boat, which had brought them home one more time? Or the dark-eyed girl who wore his pendant, so that he should know?

He said, 'Get me below, Toby. Give me a few minutes . . .'

'Take it easy, Skipper. I can deal with the visitors.' He thought of the Wren's cap he had accidentally seen in Foley's locker. 'I'll see that she doesn't worry.'

But Foley had lost consciousness.

Allison stood up again. 'Find that bloody doctor, somebody.' He did not recognize his own voice. 'Then man the side for our visitors. I'm just in the mood for it!'

When he looked over the screen again the coffins and the ambulances had gone.

Half to himself, he murmured, 'Welcome home.'

Foley opened his eyes and for a moment he believed that his mind had cracked. The sounds and familar movements, even the smells, were gone. It was like floating in space: everything white, blurred.

He moved his arm, and his hand brushed against his skin. He was naked, but when he tried to raise himself on his elbows he felt as if every ounce of strength had been drained out of him.

Sedated, or drugged without his knowledge, he had no idea. The pain in his side was still there, but, like this place, blurred.

He made another attempt. Lying on a bed, and when he turned his head very slightly he saw his torn and bloodstained seagoing gear folded in an enamel tray, his wallet and watch lying slightly apart. He swallowed hard. As if he was laid out, already dead.

Somewhere, in another world, he heard the faint trill of a boat-swain's call, then the disjointed sentences of some announcement. A door banged, and he recognized the sound of marching feet. It was coming back . . .

He had passed out on the bridge. Just now, last week? He peered at the watch, but it was well out of reach.

Then the smell. The smell of hospitals, like the last time, when he had gone to see Margot.

Her name seemed to drag his reeling mind to life again. Seeing her through the signalman's binoculars. The little pendant glinting in the sunshine, the other two girls shielding her from any attention or unwanted stares. Then there was a stretcher, one of those left by the walking wounded. Going down the brow; faces peering over him, a few hands reaching out to touch him, a voice calling out, 'Easy does it, Chris!'

He felt the dressing on his side. There had been a doctor, hard, cold fingers. Then later, more pain, something probing his flesh like a claw.

He could see the ceiling overhead, steeply sloped, like a church hall or an old-fashioned school room. He fell back on the pillow. It was the room used as officers' ward in the sick quarters; he had visited wounded and sick friends here several times. Four iron beds, equally spaced, the legs touching a painted white line, as if on parade.

Suddenly there was somebody beside the bed, a round, almost babylike face looking down at him.

'There now, all awake, are we?'

Petty Officer Sickberth Attendant Titmuss was known by his colleagues as 'Sister' Titmuss, sometimes even to his face. He seemed to enjoy it.

But always, Sister Titmuss was very much in charge, and his deceptively soft hands were like steel when it was necessary.

He was shaking a thermometer and smiling gently. 'Feel a little brighter now, do we?' He popped the thermometer beneath Foley's tongue without waiting for an answer. 'I forgot, you're the one who's not keen on the medical profession, am I right?'

It took an age. Titmuss examined the thermometer closely. 'More like it, I'd say.'

'How long have I . . .' He broke off; his throat was like a kiln.

'A few hours. They brought you from your boat. The P.M.O. was here – he dealt with you.' He puckered his lips. 'A real old vulture, that one, but a fair pro at his job.' He was shaking the thermometer. 'A few wood splinters were still in the wound. Had to put you out for a few minutes. If you ask me, you were very lucky. Another inch?' He shrugged. '*Nasty.*'

'I have to get up. I can't just walk away from it. You must understand.'

Titmuss gave him the gentle smile again. 'My! Quite the Captain Bligh today, aren't we?'

He walked around the room, his shoes clicking on the polished linoleum. 'It's all been taken care of. Staff officers, brass-hats by the score, even the admiral was here.' He hovered by the table. 'And you missed it!'

He was leaning over the bed once more, frowning now. Foley could smell talcum powder.

'Didn't do a bad job, if I say it myself.' He relented slightly. 'I shaved you while you were less troublesome.'

Foley tried again. 'One of my seamen was brought here – his eyes were damaged. I'm not sure if . . .'

The plump SBA regarded him sadly. 'He was sent straight to the Royal at Plymouth. They're better equipped, you see.' He readjusted the sheet. 'It was not good, I fear.'

Foley felt his fists clench, remembering the bandaged eyes turning towards the boat as he was being carried to an ambulance. One of their small, intimate world. The family, as the old Jacks still called it, no matter how much they cursed it at other times.

He said, 'I'd like a drink. Can you manage it?'

Titmuss pretended to be shocked.

'What are you asking me to *do*?' Again he relented. 'Besides, there's a young lady waiting to see you. What would she think?'

'Waiting? All this time?'

Titmuss minced towards the door, which Foley had just seen for the first time.

'Thinks you're worth waiting for, if I'm any judge!'

Foley turned onto one side. He felt weak, and stupid that he could not remember anything clearly. And how was Allison managing on his own, C.O. and Number One together?

He rubbed his face; it was a good shave. He had probably sworn at Sister Titmuss, unconscious or not.

And suddenly she was there, an arm reaching behind her to close the door again.

Then she was beside him, although he had not seen her move.

She said, 'It's all right, Chris. You're here and you're *safe* – it's all I care about!' Her dark eyes were very bright, but there were no tears. Her hand was on his shoulder, warm against his skin, then she moved it to his throat and the side of his face, not once taking her eyes from his.

She said softly, 'I wanted to be there when you came back. I'd heard about the engagement, I knew you were in it. I prayed you would be safe.'

He wanted to help her, console her, but all he could say was, 'I didn't want you to see me like this, Margot.'

The use of her name seemed to break her reserve. She put her face on his shoulder and whispered, 'That was how I felt when you came to see *me* in hospital. I was such a mess, and I wanted to look like a film star!' She was laughing and sobbing, her hair brushing his face as she pulled the sheet away from his fingers and kissed his naked skin. 'How long will it be, Chris?'

'Not long, I hope. The boat's a bit of a mess, and we lost two of the lads. Another one was blinded.'

She touched his mouth with her fingers as if to stop him remembering it.

'I know. The funny SBA told me about him. I'm sorry, so sorry . . . but my concern is you. I'm terribly in love with you, did you know that?'

Her jacket was unfastened, and she held his hand inside until he could feel the locket through her shirt.

'I love you too, Margot. I've never known anything like this before.'

She gripped his hand more tightly and moved it around her breast. He tried to speak, but she shook her head and pressed his hand more deliberately against her.

She said, 'I have to go soon. "Tommy" Tucker gave me some free time to be with you, but she only gives in occasionally and becomes human. Almost!' She was laughing, but there were tears now. 'I'll be here tomorrow morning.'

He reached out for her, but she was standing away from the bed, her tunic buttoned again.

She was backing towards the door, watching him.

She blew him a kiss and said, 'I love you. I want you.'

The pain was returning, and he was determined she should not see it.

When he looked again, the door had closed. Like the climax to a dream.

'All done then, are we?' Sister Titmuss had materialized in her place by the bed, automatically shaking his thermometer.

Foley realized for the first time that the room was almost dark, and he heard someone putting up blackout shutters in the next room. It *was* a dream.

Titmuss said, 'I can see the visit is working already. A very lovely girl, if I may say so, makes one quite envious!'

He went out, beaming all over his face.

Foley lay still, listening to his heart, remembering hers beating against his hand.

There were so many things he wanted to say. He could think of only one word. *Together.*

Rear-Admiral Bumper Fawcett was quietly and unhurriedly working himself into a temper, only his hands and his eyes moving to emphasize a point, or to quell any opposition before it was offered.

David Masters had seen him perform like this several times, at *Vernon*, and before that when he had been out there matching his wits against a beast or some other explosive device. Times when he had believed every incident might be the last. Now he was expected to send others to deal with the same challenges, without fear or favour, but he had never forgotten what it was like. Confronting it for the first time, trying to remain calm, and sound calm, while you described each detail over the intercom to your rating. Your last contact.

Fawcett had not stopped since his arrival. He had visited each of the motor launches, spoken to their commanding officers and senior rates, and even darted quick questions at the most junior hands aboard. 'Where were you when it happened? What was the range, the bearing, *what*?' Or, 'Well, dammit, you *should* know!'

Masters glanced at the others, Lieutenant-Commander Brayshaw keeping notes, occasionally checking a signal flimsy or a file. Captain Chavasse, looking strained and resentful; it was, after all, his own office which Fawcett now dominated. Tony Brock, arms folded, grim-faced, still smouldering from that first confrontation when he had said, 'If you want my considered opinion, sir?' And Fawcett's curt, '*If* I do, I shall ask for it!'

Fawcett's aide, a sharp-featured lieutenant, was also making notes. He must be tougher than he looked if he had to put up with Fawcett, Masters thought. Second Officer Sally Kemp was sitting beside the only other woman present, Elaine de Courcy, but they had not spoken to one another.

The senior Operations Officer, red-eyed and struggling not to yawn, and a lieutenant-commander from Portland completed the gathering.

Masters watched Elaine, who had been with him since he had returned to his quarters that morning. It must be all of nine hours ago. She showed no sign of fatigue, and her hair shone beneath Chavasse's hard lighting. Her legs were crossed, one foot tapping occasionally, unmoved by the uniforms around her. *And I thought she was just an interpreter.*

He knew hardly anything about her. Nor would he, probably.

She had spoken only briefly of her background, about her mother, who was still living in the Channel Islands with her husband, Raymond de Courcy. She was worried about her mother's health and the danger she might be in. She had gone no further.

212

Fawcett raised his voice. 'Only three months ago, when everyone said it was a pipe dream, we invaded Sicily, and took it, despite the bad weather and the foul-ups along the way. Next it was Italy, Salerno, Anzio, names written in blood. We faced a more determined enemy and entirely new weapons, missiles fired from aircraft, more accurate bombing.' He looked at Masters. 'And mines.' His eyes moved on. 'And now we know that Germany is working on several new weapons, and training the personnel to use them.' His voice dropped a little. Masters waited. *Here it comes.* Fawcett's gaze hovered on Chavasse. 'And yet there are still people in this country, people who should have known better, who think this day-to-day existence will continue. Because it suits them, because they are comfortable, happy with *their war.*'

Masters saw Chavasse's fingers clench. Like many senior officers who had been on the beach between the wars, cast out from the only life he understood, the peacetime navy, Chavasse was grateful to be back. Unable to accept that his navy had changed.

Fawcett raised one hand and closed it very slowly.

'And yet in less than a year, maybe a few months, we shall embark on the greatest invasion of all time.' The arm shot out, one finger pointing. 'Over there, the coast of France, with all it can throw at us!'

His aide looked round at a window as if he expected to see something.

Masters could almost feel sorry for Chavasse. Routine, tradition, order and discipline. *Maybe I would have been the same.* But in a few months, a year at the most, the real test would begin.

Fawcett was coming to the end of his speech; Masters had seen his aide fold his arms deliberately, so that his wristwatch was displayed.

'We are making progress, but in my view not enough and too slowly. Secrecy and stealth are all-important, now more than ever before. I shall be seeing the First Sea Lord tomorrow morning, although he is fully aware of my opinion. It was reckless to send the minelayers in the first place. Like having the Royal Marines marching ahead of them at full blast!'

Masters saw Chavasse flinch. Was that a reference to the musicians he had recruited for his Trafalgar Night dinner?

Fawcett picked up his cap. 'I have to check a few points with the countermeasures section.' Again he looked at Masters. 'It will not take long.'

Chairs scraped, people stood up, Sally the Wren second officer was making for the door, doubtless to ensure that the rear-admiral's car was ready and waiting.

Masters turned towards Elaine de Courcy and their eyes met, as if by accident, like that moment in the house when she had been waiting for him. This morning.

They reached the office in silence, Fawcett walking briskly without any sign of weariness.

Someone had switched on the lights, and the wastepaper bin had been emptied. Otherwise it was exactly as he had left it.

Fawcett glanced around and then purposely closed the little window that looked down on the Operations room.

'What a dump. You should have something better than this!' He sat and put his cap beside him. 'Captain Chavasse runs a long ship, what?'

Masters opened the cupboard. 'Time for a drink, sir?'

Fawcett grunted. 'Always. A Horse's Neck if you can manage it. Not too much ginger ale.' He leaned back, sighing. 'But then, Chavasse might not be in command for ever.'

Masters mixed the drink. It sounded like a threat.

He said, 'You heard about Lieutenant Lewis, sir?'

Fawcett swivelled round and accepted the glass, eyeing it critically. He took a slow swallow, and then said, 'You're doing a good job here. I made the right choice.' He looked over the glass. 'Yes, I knew about Lewis, the Swanage mine. Bad luck – he had a good record.' He seemed to make up his mind. 'Don't get me wrong, but sometimes I think you allow yourself to become too involved. Lewis was doing his job; he volunteered; he might have been careless or become too confident. Now he's dead. Nothing we can do about it, except perhaps offer the teams more help and information when we can get it.'

Masters did not rise to it. 'D.N.I.'s department is still coming up with that, sir.'

Fawcett smiled. 'I saw you looking at the woman from James Wykes's little crew. De Courcy, right? Wykes is a cunning old

214

bugger, always was. But she is something, eh?' He put down the empty glass. 'I checked up on her, thought it prudent. She's got top security status, y'know? You don't get that just by lying on your back, believe me!'

Masters picked up the brandy bottle, surprised that he was so calm.

What did Bumper Fawcett know or suspect? One thing rang true. Elaine de Courcy would never have been permitted to sit in at the various meetings, especially here, unless she was highly regarded.

The telephone rang, very loudly it seemed. 'Thank you.' He replaced it and said, 'Your car is ready, sir.'

Fawcett stood up, his eyes lingering on the bottle.

'Just remember what I said. Don't get involved. Keep your distance.'

Masters followed him outside into the darkness where the car was waiting, the aide ready to open the door for his lord and master.

Fawcett paused, his back turned so that nobody else should hear.

'Your, er, unfortunate predecessor had the right idea, for this work in any case. Always ready with a word of praise, sympathy too if it was required. But it went no further, and no deeper than that, what?'

A Wren stepped out of the shadows and said, 'I've been detailed to drive you when you're ready to leave, sir.'

In the faint glow of a police light Masters recognized her as the driver who had collected him when he had returned from the conference in London. When Elaine de Courcy had found him in the restaurant, and given him back his pipe lighter.

He said, 'Hold on for a minute or two. I'll go and find your other passenger.'

The Wren said, 'The lady has already left, sir. I saw her go. She seemed to be in a hurry.'

Masters climbed into the car, suddenly drained. What had happened, what had made her leave without telling him?

Perhaps Fawcett had been trying to warn him, prepare him.

Don't get involved. Keep your distance.

They stopped at the main gates where Jowitt, the master-at-arms, was still on duty, doubtless because of the rear-admiral's visit.

The Wren, whose hair was so blonde that it looked white in the gloom, called out, 'I'm on my way, Master!'

Jowitt peered into the car. 'Take it easy on them roads, my girl!'

Masters said, 'I saw you with Leading Wren Lovatt this morning.'

She gauged the first line of hedgerows, barely visible in the masked headlights.

'I know. I saw you too, sir.' She waited, seeming to consider it. 'She wanted to make certain.' She swung the wheel hard over, but did not appear to brake. 'About her friend.'

Masters said, 'He's going to be all right.' He thought of Fawcett again, and added deliberately, 'Tell her from me, will you?'

The girl nodded. 'She's my best friend. A real mate, sir.'

The house loomed out of the darkness, the headlights glinting across the windows as the car swung into the driveway.

Perhaps he would find out now what had made Elaine leave so suddenly. So that she would not compromise him? Or was it the other way round?

The Wren had wound down her window.

'She's been passed fit for duty, sir.' It sounded like a question.

He said, 'I'll be glad to see her at the wheel again. Will you tell her that, too?'

He groped his way to the door in the darkness, half expecting her to open it. Like this morning.

But it was Coker who greeted him.

'I 'eard the car, sir. Thought it was about time you got a stand-easy.'

Masters walked into the lamplight and looked around. Everything as it was, and yet so different.

He said, 'Is Miss de Courcy here?'

'Been an' gone, sir. There was another car waitin' for her when she came back. She only stopped for a few minutes. You might 'ave passed 'er on the road. She picked up a bag.' He hesitated. 'It was all packed an' ready.'

Masters walked to the adjoining room. Another car. A bag

216

packed and waiting. She must have known from the start, from this morning. All day, but she had said nothing.

He turned, off guard.

'What is it?'

Coker was holding a small package. 'She told me to give you this, sir.'

Masters took it to the table, beneath a standard lamp, and opened it with care, then stared at it as he held it in the palm of his hand. The brooch, the jasmine flower, diamonds blazing now in the light as he had last seen it on her breast. There was a note, too. A scrap of paper she had torn from somewhere in her haste to get away, to avoid seeing him.

Something she prized dearly. She had written, *Keep this for me. Until we meet again.*

The knowledge hit him like a fist. She had said nothing all day because she could not.

She was under orders.

14

A Matter of Time

The wind across the Bill of Portland was not strong, but it had an edge which seemed to pierce the thickest clothing. The sky was cloudless and very bright, and, to those who had ventured so far north, like the blue of the Arctic.

David Masters moved his shoulders inside his greatcoat and wished he had worn something more suitable. But senior officers were present, so that was that. He looked down at the sea, the strange contour of the Chesil Beach which pointed north-west towards Bridport. There were boats moving along the coast in line with the beach, and he could see figures hurrying along the water's edge, keeping pace. Another experiment, this time a different fuse, with a photo-electric cell which the experts believed to be a copy of the one detonated by the old fishing boat at Bridport. And perhaps the one which had killed Lieutenant Sewell, down there on the opposite side of the Bill, by the road he had used this morning.

He looked at his watch. It was almost noon. He thought of the girl who had driven him, Margot Lovatt; she had not said very much, perhaps because of the other passenger. Philip Brayshaw had come along with the excuse that he had some correspondence for Chavasse's opposite number, the captain of H.M.S. *Osprey*, the anti-submarine school and experimental base which was now just behind him. Brayshaw seemed to seize every opportunity to escape his more mundane duties for a touch of action.

Masters sensed that she had changed in some way. More confident and less reserved, perhaps more mature; a very different girl from the one who had told him about her brother upon his arrival from *Vernon*. Only two months ago? Less.

He had spoken to the P.M.O. about Foley. 'Could have been worse, much worse.' The great man had paused. 'What can you expect when they send young chaps out to fight in wooden boats? In this day and age!'

Foley was going to be all right. The girl had spoken to him only once.

'Thank you for your message, sir. My friend Julie told me. I felt a little better after that!'

He had seen her watching him a few times in the driving mirror. Had her blonde friend told her about Elaine de Courcy, how she had made such a hasty departure from the conference in Chavasse's office? It might make an interesting topic of conversation at the Wrennery, or even here, for that matter.

He came out of his thoughts as a whistle shrilled, and somebody yelled an order. Whatever it was, it bounced around these forbidding rocks and boulders like several different voices. Such a strange place . . . you could imagine a stagecoach clattering through, with Sioux warriors firing off arrows and looted Winchester rifles while they pranced up there against the sky.

There was a sharp bang, nothing more, not even a puff of smoke.

Masters heard one bearded commander growl, 'Waste of bloody time! Another dud!'

He watched the huddle of uniforms around the admiral who had come from Plymouth to observe. In other groups he recognized several members of the countermeasures section, some new to the work, others who had been on the job for months.

He was reminded suddenly of Fawcett's comment when he had mentioned Dicer Lewis. *Now he's dead. Nothing we can do about it.* Was that all it meant to him?

He caught sight of Sub-Lieutenant Lincoln on the outskirts of the largest group. His assistant, Downie, was with him, as if they did not belong to the main body of the gathering.

He turned as he heard Brayshaw's voice, or rather his laugh. Like Fawcett's aide displaying his watch, it was his way of sending a signal.

219

Brayshaw said cheerfully, 'Of course, David – you know Captain Wykes, don't you?'

Wykes thrust out a bony hand before Masters could salute.

'Good to see you again.' He nodded towards the beach and the dispersing onlookers. 'I've seen better fireworks at the last night of the Proms!'

They walked along the path while Brayshaw found something to interest him amongst the scattered rocks.

'I gather you are keen to see me?'

Masters said, 'I was worried about Elaine. But I expect you know what happened yesterday after Rear-Admiral Fawcett's inspection, the "post-mortem", as it were.'

Wykes glanced sideways at him. 'Bumper was in fiery spirits when he called me. Likes things to go his way.' He quickened his pace. 'I can't tell you a thing. But you know the drill as well as anybody. It was rather sudden, not a lot to go on, but I had to act on it chop-chop, just in case.'

'Dangerous?'

Wykes smiled. 'I didn't hear that, old chap.'

Masters felt the conversation slipping away from him. 'But she's a civilian.'

Wykes stopped in his tracks and looked at him. 'So were a lot of people before the war.' He gestured towards a column of sailors who were making their way back towards the harbour. 'Them, for instance. But not everybody wears a uniform.'

Masters faced him. 'Some time ago you mentioned the Channel Islands, how they might be connected with the supply of the new German explosives. Her father is or was involved. Responsible, even?'

'Putting two and two together does not necessarily make four.' Wykes looked back at the main group; the admiral's brightly oak-leaved cap was moving. It was over. For the moment. Wykes patted his pocket, ready for that first cigarette. Then he said, 'You have a quick mind, old chap. And a good memory. I can use both.' He reached out and touched his arm, like the day they had met. 'And you care. I'll keep you posted, when I can.' A shutter seemed to drop and he turned to throw up a salute to the admiral as he strode past. 'Good morning, Sir Richard. It's all coming along, I see?'

The admiral was looking at Masters, but answered, 'Still alive, are you, James? You must divulge the secret some time!' He nodded to Masters. 'Your people are doing fine work – tell them so from me, will you?'

Wykes watched the procession move on, and sighed.

'God has spoken.'

Brayshaw had caught up with them. He glanced from one to the other and said hopefully, 'Time for a glass before we leave?'

Masters stared at the sea, and measured the time and distance, recalling Fawcett's warning. Or had he imagined that also?

He answered, 'Always.'

He turned up the collar of his greatcoat. But the scent of her perfume had gone.

The yardmaster and his chief shipwright stood on ML366's fore-deck and compared their notes. It was the last of the four boats he had visited, and his patience had worn thin.

'I've already told your senior officer what *I* think, so I don't need to go over it all again.' He glared at Allison's single wavy stripe as if to emphasize the point. 'I could lose a month's work in this boat alone, right, Ben?' His companion nodded. 'But I'm told I can have two weeks and no more. After that, the powers that be have other ideas for you. An' besides, we'll need the berth.'

Allison listened to the whine of drills and the thud of hammers. The yardmaster had got all of his men working at first light, or so it had felt. A handful of key ratings would remain aboard for some of the time; the rest were being given leave or billeted ashore. In small vessels it was always resented, like an intrusion. As Bass had remarked, 'You need to screw everything down, or else the dockyard maties will nick it!'

Allison gazed across the inlet. Hardly a dockyard. 'I think we need more time.'

The yardmaster snapped, 'Tell *them*!' He closed his battered notebook. 'Say hello when you see your skipper again. I hear he's eager to get out of the sick quarters.'

Allison followed him to the brow. 'You know my C.O. then?'

The man opened his book again but changed his mind. 'Chris Foley? Who doesn't?'

'I'll tell him. And thanks.' When he looked again, they had vanished. *Two weeks.* He stared along the deck, at the chips and scars on the side of the bridge, the blackened paintwork by the companion ladder. Each time he saw it he could feel the searing heat, the flames darting ahead of their extinguishers, the splintered planking. The dead telegraphist.

Their senior officer, Tony Brock, had already been aboard to see for himself.

'You've got to keep an eye on things, Sub. All the time. They'll curl up and have a bloody snooze if they think they can get away with it.'

Allison had asked about the order and timing of things, but Brock had answered, 'Tell them what *you* want. You're the first lieutenant around here, so just get on with it.'

Allison and Bass had seen him over the side. The killick coxswain had remarked, 'We'll manage, sir. That'll stop some people fartin' in church!'

He had meant Brock.

The idea of some home leave had almost vanished. It would have been nice to be greeted like a hero by his mother and father, and maybe a girl he had got to know over the months and his irregular periods of leave.

Better still, a girl like the one he had bumped into at the sick quarters when he had visited the skipper. The one who had been here to see them return to their temporary base. A *real* girl. She was driving the Boss's car again, so soon after the accident. Another Wolseley, not the Austin Seven she had joked about. Foley had told him about it. Shared it. He recalled the yardmaster's comment, a man who was not, he guessed, easily impressed. *Chris Foley? Who doesn't?*

The cap she had been wearing was still in Foley's locker. What would it be like, he wondered. Really like? He had become used to blushing at some of the crude descriptions and remarks deliberately uttered in his presence, to shock and embarrass him. He glanced along the scarred deck. Here, at least, they seemed to respect him. But what would *it* be like?

'Anyone in charge 'ere?'

Allison came out of his thoughts with a jerk, and stared at the

222

newcomer in the filthy boiler suit who was carrying what looked like a tool box.

'I am.'

The man was unimpressed. 'You'll do, then. I'm the base engineer.'

Allison looked round for Bass but he had disappeared. 'You want the Chief.' He led the way. 'I'll take you.'

You're the first lieutenant around here, so just get on with it.

When he returned to the deck he was surprised to find a Wren waiting by the brow.

She was holding an official envelope and a pad for signature, and he noticed that she had the crossed flags and letter 'C' of a coder on her sleeve. More to the point, she was very attractive.

'Are you in charge?' The slightest pause. 'Sir?'

He nodded. 'First lieutenant.'

She opened her pad. 'I'd have thought . . .' She stopped and held out the pad. Allison saw her looking at the damage and then remembered. She had been one of the Wrens with the skipper's girl, on the wall when they had come alongside. Two days ago. It did not seem possible.

He ran his eyes over the envelope. 'I'll be seeing my C.O. later today. I'll show him this. He likes to know what's happening.'

Two yard workers were pedalling along the jetty on their bicycles. Both gave loud whistles, and one yelled, 'Wot about it, darlin'?'

Allison was suddenly angry. 'I'll report you!' He shook his fist, but they were already out of sight amongst the litter of fittings and repair work.

She was watching him, surprised, but smiling.

'Wow! That showed them!'

Allison tried to recover his dignity. She was very pretty, her hair a little longer than regulation requirements, and she had an accent which his mother would describe as 'cultured'.

She said, 'It looks even worse in this light. It must have been terrible. Your captain was injured.' And seeing his confusion, she added gently, 'His girl is a friend of mine.'

Allison walked with her to, and then down, the brow before he knew what he was doing.

She paused, looking at him, her lips parted as if she were going to say something.

Allison said, 'I was wondering. If I can get ashore. Maybe you'd care to join me for a drink somewhere.' He clenched his fists with embarrassment. It was happening again, after all this time. Like a hot flush. He was actually blushing.

'There aren't too many places around here.'

It was all going wrong. She probably thought he should have known, or maybe that he was too young. And she was right.

She pulled an old bicycle from behind a pile of oil drums and carefully dusted down the saddle.

'But call the Wrennery when you get a spare moment. If I'm off watch, I might be able to meet you.'

She hitched up her skirt and hoisted her leg over the saddle.

Allison felt as if his face was on fire. Even the regulation stockings could not conceal that she had very nice legs.

'Who shall I say . . . ?'

'Ask for Toni. It's what they call me!'

He watched her pedal unhurriedly down the road towards the Operations section, her hair blowing rebelliously beneath her cap.

He groped his way up the brow again.

Her name was Toni. What they called her. He thought of her smile when he had yelled at the dockyard maties.

Wow!

Bass was aft, apparently arguing with one of the work force. It had started.

He suddenly grinned and strode towards them.

He was the first lieutenant.

Chris Foley thrust his arm into his jacket and reached behind for the other sleeve, gritting his teeth against the pain. Perhaps because of the clean shirt, it seemed easier this time. He glanced at his reflection in the wall mirror as if he were studying a subordinate, or a total stranger. Looking for flaws. After the usual shabby seagoing gear he even looked different, he thought. Allison had brought him his proper Number Fives when he had made a visit to tell him about the repair work, and any other news he had been able to gather.

He buttoned the jacket carefully, but it felt looser than before.

The going had been rough, but he had not thought that he might have lost weight.

He looked at the bed nearest the door, occupied by a casualty who had been brought in during the night, the skipper of one of the trawlers used for laying marker buoys. A boring but necessary job, hardly ever out of sight of land. It was impossible to be vigilant all the time. Sister Titmuss had told him a German aircraft had come out of the sunset, an accidental encounter, perhaps, with the pilot already thinking of getting back to his airfield in France.

The man's jacket hung on a chair by the bed, bearing the single interwoven stripe of an R.N.R. skipper. Foley could see his head on the pillow; the sparse hair was almost white. A man who should have quit the sea long before this, but one who had been ready when he was needed. Foley was not sure how many the trawler had carried, but air-sea rescue had picked up only three. The trawler had disappeared.

The door opened an inch and Sister Titmuss murmured, '*That's* more like it.' He, too, looked at the occupied bed and pursed his lips. 'P.M.O.'s on his way, so if you . . .'

'I know. I'm going out right now.'

The SBA followed him into the corridor, watching every step. 'Don't try to climb Everest, will you? Not just yet, anyway!'

Foley walked out into the sunlight. Hard and bright, the air very cold like that last day on the bridge. He could hear the din of drills and saws from the yard, but made himself turn away towards the main buildings. They had their work cut out to meet the deadline; there was no time to be wasted looking after their commanding officer. They knew how he felt. Sightseers, like passengers, were no use at all.

He had worried about Allison, but perhaps in its way it was the best thing which had happened in his short career. He was cheerful, confident, altered in some way Foley could not define.

He had reached the offices, and saw Brayshaw's chief writer observing him from the door marked *Captain's Secretary*.

'He's expecting you, sir.' He glanced quickly over Foley's uniform. 'You look well, sir. I'm glad.'

Brayshaw gripped his hand but refrained from shaking it.

'Still sore, is it?' He waved him to a chair. 'Good of you to trot over here!'

Foley leaned back, with care. He had noticed that the Wolseley was not parked in its usual place. Masters must be away somewhere, visiting the site of an incident, meeting new officers who had volunteered for special service, like all the others he had seen since bringing ML366 to this small, crowded place. Or perhaps over at Portland. Margot would be with him, driving again, when it had once seemed impossible.

Brayshaw said, 'I suppose you've been told by just about everybody that you are still *officially* standing down from active duty?' He nodded. 'Thought so, although your S.O. will soon be screaming about being short-handed.'

'But I thought Lieutenant Baldwin was the only death?'

Brayshaw looked away at something. 'True. But Lieutenant Claridge has been sent on leave, so his Number One's holding the fort.'

Foley found that he was gripping the arm of the chair, his body suddenly chilled. 'What's happened?'

'There was an air raid on Southampton the other night. Hit-and-run. Nothing new, I suppose.' He looked at him directly. 'Dick Claridge's home bought it. His wife was killed.'

'He was always worried about her. Because *she* worried about him every time he put to sea. He never said as much, but it was always there.'

Brayshaw frowned as a telephone began to ring on his desk. It stopped almost immediately, intercepted by the vigilant chief writer.

'Situations change, people don't. In war you take risks – some take risks all the time, as you know better than most. But it can't change how you feel, how you *care*, right?'

He paused, looking towards the window. 'Lieutenant-Commander Masters will be here at any second. He and I have to see the Old Man about one of the subbies. A Mention in Despatches has come through.' He nodded. 'There's the car now. We should be tied up for an hour.' The merest smile. 'I shall make certain of it!'

Foley stood up. 'Thank you, sir. I'll not forget.'

Brayshaw called after him, 'I shall expect an invitation . . .' He broke off and sighed; Foley had gone. 'You're right for each other. The bloody war can wait!'

Masters came in and walked briskly to one of the big, old-fashioned radiators, and held his hands over the hot pipes.

'Did you tell him, Philip?'

Brayshaw touched the gold lace on his sleeve. 'About him being given a half-stripe?' He shook his head. 'About losing his ML and being given another command? I told him about Dick Claridge instead.'

Masters looked at him as if he had misheard. Then he nodded very slowly.

'You did the right thing.' He glanced at the window as a car door slammed. 'I envy them.'

Brayshaw thought of the girl with the chestnut hair, the way they had looked together, been together, in a room filled with people.

But he said only, 'We'd better not keep the Old Man waiting, eh?'

He had heard a lot about envy during his naval service. It was the first time he had seen it for himself.

She sat quite still, with her back pressed against the driving seat, her hands clasped in her lap. People who passed the parked car, going about their normal duties, would glance at her and imagine she was relaxed, perhaps bored, waiting for her passenger.

In fact Margot Lovatt could not recall ever being so tense. Even the smallest decision seemed beyond her; she could barely stop herself from looking at the dashboard clock. *Again.*

She looked into the driving mirror and saw the driver from the car behind standing beside it, yawning as he waited for one of the staff officers. A Royal Marine, he had been friendly enough when she had been put on light duties after her return.

Her friend Julie, also a driver, had warned her about him. 'Fancies himself, I can tell you, love. Fancies you too, so watch it. Don't let him get the grabs on you.'

She moved the mirror slightly and looked at the building where most of the offices were situated. Where she had dropped Masters. Another conference about something or other. How he must hate

227

that sort of thing after being at sea. She could even confront that now. *At sea in submarines.*

Masters had been withdrawn, troubled. It was unlike him not to talk; in that respect he was so different from other officers she had driven. Julie had told her about the woman with the French name who had arrived here with him, and left alone. He had been surprised. Hurt. Julie was a little scatty sometimes, but she did not miss much.

She bit her lip. Chris would be coming out soon. She would have to decide, and quickly.

She was surprised at herself, that she could think about it at all. No wonder the others had thought her standoffish, a bit stuck-up, as Julie had put it. How could she have changed that much, even to consider it?

She thought of her parents, her home in Petersfield, her brother's sealed room. How could she feel like a stranger there? It had been her whole life.

And her father, respected, trusted, loved. All the problems he must have encountered and solved, a new challenge every time the waiting room door opened. But when she had told him about Chris, he had compared love with gratitude. As if he did not know the difference.

She unclasped her hands and touched the door by her leg. She could still hear it, feel the shock and the pain of impact. The blood, the sense of helplessness, and fear.

And then his hands, holding, soothing her; talking to her all the time although she could not recall what he had said. Nor, probably, did he. It was simply an instinct to hold onto her, sustain her.

She tugged off her gloves and examined her hands. She had been surprised that she had managed to remain so calm that day when the boats, Chris's boat, had returned. The silent onlookers, the scars and shot holes, the ambulances revving up by the jetty. Like undertakers' men.

How she had managed to wave to him so jauntily she did not understand. She had changed. Maybe they both had.

She had telephoned her father and told him that Chris had been injured.

228

Give him our best wishes. I'm sure he's getting the best treatment.

But her father had not suggested that Chris visit their home; he had somehow avoided it. Perhaps it had been then, when she had put down the telephone, that she had truly understood.

She saw the Royal Marine turn towards her and change his mind, then he saluted.

She wound down the window. 'I'm here, Chris!'

He stood beside the car, one hand on the door, his eyes never leaving hers. Then he removed his cap and ducked his head through the window.

'Chris! Somebody might see!'

'Behaviour unbecoming an officer and a gentleman.' He smiled for the first time. 'Kiss me.'

His face was cold, but his mouth was warm. He kissed her again, harder.

She said, 'Get into the car, Chris. I'm not made of iron!'

He got into the rear seat and closed the door. 'I had to see you. I'm being discharged from sick quarters, tomorrow, I think.' He saw her eyes in the mirror, felt her tense as he touched her arm between the seats, and then held it.

'Oh God, Margot, I've missed seeing you. Do we both have to end up in hospital before we can meet?'

A squad of sailors tramped past, carrying rolled-up boiler suits, on their way to the yard. A petty officer in charge yelled, 'Keep in step, Thomas! Gawd! A mother's gift to a war-starved nation!'

She said, 'I was going to ask you if you'd like to visit my home.'

He gripped her arm more tightly. 'I was going to show you the Thames, where 366 was built.'

She lowered her face so that he could not see her expression.

'But it's not what I want. Not after what happened.' She looked up again, her dark eyes very steady. 'I want to be with you. Just you. Is that so awful?'

He looked across the road and thought of the captain's secretary, Brayshaw. All the things he had said. And had made a point of not saying.

And Dick Claridge, back at what was left of his home, and the girl he had known since school. Now he had nothing, except for his command.

He reached up and touched her face.

'I want that, too. More than anything. Soon, before . . .'

She touched his lips and whispered, '*Soon.*'

A shadow fell across the window. It was one of the regulating petty officers, a Crusher from the main gates.

He touched his cap. 'I'm sorry to disturb you, sir.' He looked at the girl. 'But we've a big lorry comin' into the establishment, so could you edge up a bit?'

He was being very polite. And enjoying it, Foley thought.

He said, 'I'd better be off. I'll call you when I know what's happening.'

She pulled herself up onto the seat and put her arm around his neck.

She said, 'Now kiss me. *Properly.*'

There were a few whistles, and somebody gave a cheer.

She sat for several minutes, staring directly ahead through the windscreen, imagining she could feel his face, the warmth of his mouth against hers. As if she had no control. Like discovering herself. Someone quite new to her.

She twisted round to look for him, but he had gone. As if it had all been a hallucination.

She adjusted her cap and stared at herself in the mirror.

Her heart told her otherwise, and she knew it had already been decided. *For both of us.*

While there was still time.

15

Yesterday's Heroes

The dream had been hazy and disjointed but was now suddenly expanded into nightmarish proportions. Vague shapes were concentrated into one presence, then a mouth, all teeth, filling his mind like a screen. The sound was enough to waken the dead, laughing, jeering, threatening, high up like a vast, vaulted building. He was hitting out, trying to stifle the din, throwing himself from side to side as if to get away.

There was something else now, a pressure, a force, perhaps fighting back at him.

It was dying, the picture suddenly dim, while the pressure on his shoulder continued.

And there was another voice now. Even, but insistent.

'Come on, old chap. Wakey, wakey.'

Sub-Lieutenant Michael Lincoln opened his eyes wide and stared at the stooping figure by his bed. The silence was complete, and he knew that his blanket and pillow were undisturbed. Another twist of the dream. Only his breathing remained fast and uneven.

The small cabin he shared with another junior officer was in darkness, but for a reading lamp which was alight by the other bed. The occupant lay on his back, snoring gently, a magazine still open across his chest.

Lincoln vaguely recognized the officer who had roused him, then he was suddenly wide awake. The lieutenant was from Operations.

'What is it? I'm not on call.' He was not making sense.

'Sorry to do this to you, old chap. But they want a team right away. One has already gone out, and the other officer has reported sick.' He grinned. 'So it's you.'

Lincoln sat up slowly. He had had a few drinks in the mess before turning in; word of his Mention in Despatches had got around. He was not a heavy drinker and he was not on call. And he was going on leave tomorrow.

'When do they want me?' He was sitting on the side of the bed now, although he did not recall moving.

The lieutenant replied cheerfully, 'Right now. The army have sent transport.'

He watched Lincoln walk to the wash basin and sluice his face with cold water. He could not leave until he knew it was safe to go, certain that Lincoln would not flop back down on the bed.

'Where?' He was wide awake now.

'Poole again. The brown jobs aren't sure when it dropped, maybe last night, maybe earlier when those others were reported.'

Lincoln thought of the empty chair, and the dog. 'When Dicer bought it.'

'Yep.'

Somehow he got into his working rig and comfortable boots, patted all his pockets and glanced at the sleeping officer in the other bed.

'Lucky sod!'

It was cold outside, and very dark. Not even a star or a wandering searchlight beam to break it. And quiet; hard to compare it with the noisy, bustling place he knew during the day.

He examined his feelings. Nervous? Apprehensive? Not yet. It would probably all be over and done with by the time he got there. Poole was about twenty miles away, and army drivers were not known for hanging about.

'Your rating has been sent for, by the way.'

Downie's first incident since the explosion aboard the *Latchmere*. He thought suddenly of the leave he had been granted. *Going home.* In her letter his mother had been full of it. Somehow or other the news of his Mention had got into the local newspaper. She was so proud, she said. That made it even worse. How could he go through with it?

232

Suppose Downie's memory came back? That one fragment of time when he must have seen and realized what was happening.

He thought too of his father. It must have taken the bluster out of him, for a change.

The lieutenant said, 'I'll give you the details and you can get going.'

He would be off watch shortly, and in bed soon afterwards.

It was glaringly bright in the Operations lobby, and he saw Downie sitting on a locker, his satchel by his feet. He looked remarkably fresh and wide awake.

Lincoln had not shaved; he doubted if Downie ever did.

'All set?'

Downie nodded. 'It'll still be dark when we get there.' He looked at his watch. 'I think I know the place.'

Someone handed Lincoln his package. Orders, observations, conclusions. And a map.

The army transport was waiting, engine revving impatiently, a fifteen hundredweight Chevrolet truck, the Royal Engineers markings and scarlet wings faintly visible in the shaded police lights by the gates. They squeezed into the front seat and the Chevvy jerked into motion.

Downie remarked quietly, 'The lieutenant's dog has gone, sir.'

Lincoln watched the feeble headlights swinging over some bushes. He did not have the heart to tell Downie that he had heard Captain Chavasse had ordered that all stray dogs in the establishment were to be put down.

For some reason it had disturbed him, and he was surprised by it.

He said, 'Get this one over and we can get away on leave. Just what we need!'

Downie said nothing and Lincoln cursed himself for forgetting. Downie had nowhere to go and nobody to greet him, not even a dog any more.

It was a bumpy, uncomfortable ride, made worse by the sappers' loose gear clattering around in the back of the truck. The driver said nothing, which was probably just as well, Lincoln thought, with the road being so twisting and narrow as they headed inland to take a short cut, until they emerged near the sea again.

The journey took almost an hour, and when they reached the main road to Poole harbour the sky was only just beginning to lighten.

Eventually they found and were stopped by an army checkpoint. Then onto another road; they could have been in Africa for all Lincoln could tell.

The Chevvy came to a quivering halt by the now familiar barrier and parked military police vehicles.

A young Royal Engineers captain came towards them. 'So you got here, then? I had to be here earlier, and I wasn't even on duty!'

Lincoln realized that he was more on edge than he had been prepared to admit. He snapped, 'Neither was I, *sir*! Now, if you'll just fill in the details *we* can get on with the job!'

The captain peered past him into the truck as if he expected to see a whole squad of sailors. Then he looked at Downie. 'Bit young for this, aren't you?'

Lincoln said calmly, 'Eleven major incidents, Captain.'

An M.P., barely able to hide a smile, said, 'Two hundred yards up, sir. They're building a factory there. Engineering, and machine parts. Only half finished.' He pointed vaguely into the gloom. 'But it's right beside the main road, close to the railway as well. It's all cordoned off.' He glanced at the captain. 'My chaps are there to guide you.'

The truck lurched forward again, and the driver shook out a cigarette packet while he steered with his other hand. He grinned broadly. 'Fag, sir?' He obviously disliked the captain and was showing his appreciation.

'Thanks.'

The sapper gestured to Downie. 'What about you, chum?'

Downie shook his head. 'No, but thanks. Makes me cough. My father . . .' He broke off.

They came to the last barrier. Always the same, Lincoln thought. The civilian policeman, still unfamiliar in a steel helmet after four years of war. A handful of soldiers, nothing else. He had not done many jobs as yet, but Lincoln always had the same feeling, as if time had stopped. The youth beside him had seen and done it again and again. He should have been given a medal. He thought how it had almost slipped out, something about his father. There was nobody to be proud of *him*, and he had earned it.

They stood beside the truck. It was silent now, until the return trip. Lincoln shivered. Or not . . .

They started off along the road, their footsteps unusually loud. There was a cold breeze from the sea, and here and there he could see the distinct outlines of trees, and the first small houses. All empty? Where were their owners?

A bird of some kind rose squawking from some bushes and he exclaimed, 'God, that made me jump, Gordon!'

He felt Downie turn to look at him, his face pale against the bushes. Because he had inadvertantly called him by name? Or simply because he had remembered it? He saw some builders' carts and wheelbarrows and piles of new bricks. How his father would like to get his hands on those . . . Then he saw the frame of a building, perhaps an unfinished wing of the new factory.

They stumbled over ballast and broken bricks, and found their way between cement-mixers and still more bricks, like a wilderness. Hard to imagine it full of people, with traffic on the road, and the sea somewhere beyond. You could smell it. Tangy and strong, like the coast.

He stared up at the steel framework and saw the tell-tale marker fluttering in the breeze.

They had both slowed down, as if the sound of their approach might rouse the beast.

That must have given the locals a shock, he thought.

It would be light in about half an hour. He peered at his watch.

'We'll take a break, okay? Then we'll have a look-see.' So casual, so adult. What would his father have to say about that?

Downie said, 'If it's been here for more than two days, it might be a dud.' He was thinking aloud, perhaps remembering a particular incident. 'But one of their new fuses can last longer. We were told that some months back.'

Lincoln glanced at him. *Before I came.* Theirs must have been a very close and dangerous relationship. It happened. But it was wrong. Unnatural.

He tried to clear his mind. Nothing else mattered, *could* matter, until the job was done. Observation, conclusion. Method. No chances, no bullshit. A magnetic mine was indifferent. Merciless.

He was wandering again. Suppose he stopped? Not cracked up, or lost his nerve, but simply stopped? It was not just his life. He shook himself, as in the nightmare. He knew all that.

He turned his head as Downie walked to a half-finished wall that came almost to his chest.

'What is it?'

Downie returned. 'Sand, builder's sand. Tons of it, by the look of it.' Even in the dim light he could see him nodding, and the familiar, unconscious frown. 'I could see a bit of parachute, directly under the marker.' He paused, perhaps making up his mind. 'It's in there. Half-buried, that's my guess.'

Lincoln stood up and felt another shiver run through him. The breeze from the sea must be getting stronger, although he knew it was not.

He was taller than Downie, and was able to see the great bank of sand without effort. Planking and a work bench of some kind. He felt his stomach contract. And the darkcr outline of the mine, at a forty-five degree angle. He faced it. The fuse would be under the bank of sand, no matter which type of mine it was.

Digging would be out of the question. Unless it was a dud. How many had died thinking just that?

He looked at his watch again. The face was clear now; he could even see the cuff of his favourite sweater poking out from beneath his battledress.

He said, 'I'm going down to have a look.' He tried to pass it off as a casual remark. 'You run out the intercom wire, just to keep you out of mischief, eh?'

Downie did not move. 'I'll stay with you. It needs two.' He was looking at him, his eyes like shadows in his face. 'Besides, I've done it before.'

Lincoln wiped his forehead with the back of his hand. *Tell him! Order him to do as he's told!* But instead he heard the jeering laughter, saw the mouth, and the teeth.

He said, 'I might be wrong. I could make a mistake, you don't know.'

He thought Downie shrugged.

236

'I trust you.'

Lincoln loosened his belt and fingered the tools in his pockets. As he looked up again he saw the nearest rooftop for the first time.

In a matter of minutes he could be dead. They both might be dead. He thought of another subbie with whom he had trained. He had been killed on his first mission, a magnetic mine, maybe a twin of this one. They had not found a badge or a button. He had simply disintegrated.

There was no choice anyway.

He said flatly, 'Let's do it, then.'

Using any kind of spade or tool was out of the question. If anything metal came into the mine's magnetic field it would end right there and then.

Using their bare hands they began to dig and scoop the heavy, wet sand. The air was as cold as ever, but after a few minutes Lincoln imagined he was sweating. There was sand everywhere, in his hair, inside his sweater and underwear, between his teeth.

And all the time it was getting lighter, so that small items stood out, an undisturbed tray of enamel mugs, where some workmen had been interrupted by something. An old and tattered *Daily Mail* and an empty cigarette packet. He paused and rested on both hands, feeling his lungs pounding. He must be out of condition. The thought made him want to laugh out loud.

He saw Downie, almost on his back, one leg hidden by the great trunk of the mine, and wondered what his father had been like. He would have been proud of his son right now . . .

Once he paused, breathless, to peer at his watch. They had been burrowing like moles for almost an hour.

Downie had produced a small brush from his satchel and was busy clearing away the last of the sand.

Just one wrong move now. Lincoln dragged himself over and down into the trough and said, 'Let me.' He took the brush and used his fingers to feel the way around the final curve of metal. It was like ice.

He said softly, 'Got it.' Their eyes met over the angled mine. 'Hold your breath, Gordon!'

Again, it was like watching somebody else, or going through

the drill as they had under training. The spanner in his hand was warm from his pocket.

He blinked rapidly as the wind blew some sand into his eyes. *'Damn!'*

Downie reached across the mine, his arm inches from the fuse, and dabbed his eyes with his handkerchief. Lincoln noticed in those few seconds that his hand was bleeding badly, cut on something in the sand. He recalled what Masters had told him about Downie's skill, and his ability to remain calm as he had been sketching the details of a mine while his lieutenant had been on the other end of the intercom. Doing it . . .

Lincoln licked his lips and took the first pressure. He felt the sweat running down his spine. It felt like ice-water.

'Come on, for Christ's sake!' He had spoken aloud without realizing it.

Downie put his hand over his and said, 'Here we go, then.'

The keeping ring moved, only a fraction. Lincoln nodded, his head jerking like a puppet's. 'Again!'

He felt it move freely. The worst was over. They had done it. He had no need of the stethoscope; it was so quiet he would have heard it had it gone active. And there was nowhere to run.

The fuse came out of its sleeve without obstruction. But if anyone had attempted to move the whole mine to a more accessible place Lincoln had little doubt as to what would have happened.

They lurched out of the trough. Lincoln even managed to pat the cold metal as he hauled himself up and into full daylight.

He leaned over, and for an instant thought he was going to vomit. Like that last time.

But he felt calm, if slightly unsteady. Like a hangover, he thought vaguely.

'Call 'em up, Gordon. Tell them the show's over!'

As Downie turned towards the abandoned intercom Lincoln caught him by the arm. 'Better have that cut seen to. The sappers may have a decent first aid kit.' It was not at all what he had meant to say. He made another attempt. 'I was thinking. We're both being given leave.' Downie was staring at him as if reading his lips, his eyes filling his face.

Lincoln said roughly, 'You can come up to my happy homestead.

You'd be more than welcome.' He saw all the doubts and questions as if they had been shouted aloud. 'My mother will make a real fuss of you. And besides, it's your birthday next Tuesday, right?'

Downie swallowed and wiped his hand on his filthy uniform as if it needed brushing. 'How did you know that?'

'I think you mentioned it just after we first met.' It was a lie; he had glanced at Downie's pay book, which had been on a bedside locker at the sickbay.

'If you're sure I wouldn't be in the way, sir?'

Lincoln smiled. '*Mike*, remember?'

Downie picked up the intercom and pressed the button. It took him several seconds to speak.

Lincoln turned and looked at the beast. It was madness of a different sort. And he was glad.

Perhaps it was only then that he began to realize what he had done.

Chris Foley paused outside the hut marked *Yard Master*, his mind still grappling with the news which had changed everything. In the navy, especially the wartime navy, you never took anything or any day for granted.

He swung round with one foot on the wooden steps and stared along the littered yard, the jetty where she had been standing to see 366 come in, where the ambulances had been waiting like those other times. For only a few seconds there was a lull in the din of saws and hammers, drills and clattering machinery, as if out of respect. Or dismissal.

He still could not believe it. Promotion to the acting rank of lieutenant-commander was one thing. In the past it would not even have been a dream. All those months, all those miles, different faces and accents, mannerisms and loyalties. Something you had to expect. But ML366 had always been there, his own command. People had come and gone, transferred or sent on courses, promoted, and sometimes put ashore for good, wounded or killed in action.

He had held command for longer than most. *Survived.* Maybe he had always taken it too much for granted. And now he was losing her.

He could see the main gates from here, where he had kissed Margot in the car to the accompaniment of wolf whistles they had scarcely heard. Yesterday. Masters must have known; so must the captain's secretary, but it all had to go through the right channels. Promotion, court-martial, sudden death, the navy had a correct procedure for everything.

A man in a boiler suit strolled past and remarked, 'You can go straight in, Guv.' He walked away, whistling, without a care in the world.

But Foley was still staring along the jetty, hearing the voices, seeing the various expressions of the men he knew so well when he had told them. Not like any big warship, or even the destroyer Allison had known before moving to Coastal Forces. It was true what the old hands said; it was a family.

What could you say? *I hope the new C.O. treats you well. It's been nice knowing you, even the skates amongst you.* That had raised a few smiles. Then what? Just walk away from it?

He rapped on the door and pushed it open.

Lieutenant-Commander Tony Brock was standing by a window and close to an old-fashioned stove. It was rare to see him in proper uniform; usually he appeared either in seagoing rig or a favourite fleece-lined R.A.F. flying jacket. And leather wellingtons which were so worn and stained it was hard to think of them ever being new.

Today he wore his best uniform, the wavy gold lace on his sleeves not even tarnished, the ribbons on his breast, the D.S.O., the D.S.C. and Bar, as fresh and clean as if they had just been stitched into position. He stood, square and upright, his eyes very calm, which was also unusual, Foley thought.

Brock said, 'Bit rough, was it? Decided I'd leave the stage to you just now. The formalities can wait.' He gestured to a chair. 'I thought it better if we met here. We'll not be disturbed. I hope.'

Foley sat in one of the chairs, careful to avoid rubbing his injured side, although he had not thought about it before. The yardmaster's office was remarkably clean and uncluttered, unlike his domain outside, with plans and printed lists of spare parts and accessories, and work schedules to match the noise of the men at work in the yard.

240

Brock was in his late thirties, old for Coastal Forces, and looked older. Even his neat beard and clipped hair did not disguise the strain.

'I'll come to the point, Chris. I know it's a bad moment, it always is. I've had a few times myself. But the war's moving on, and we have to keep up with it – it's what we do, what we are. I've been with Captain C/F this morning and he agrees, albeit reluctantly, that provided you don't officially object, you will be transferred to a new command.'

Foley thought of the neatly worded information. Without feeling. An experimental vessel, only just completed, a fast minelayer still in the builder's hands. At Falmouth, Cornwall. There was more, a whole lot more, but choice did not come into it.

Brock was watching him impassively. 'It is entirely voluntary, of course.' He smiled briefly. 'You know what they say about a volunteer in this regiment. It's a man who misunderstood the question in the first place!' He gave his short, barking laugh. 'I told CCF you're the one for the job. Experienced, smart and careful. Not one of those death-or-glory boys – I can manage without types like that!'

Foley said, 'I'm told that there are two of these experimental boats?'

'Right.' Again the grin. 'So much for bloody security, eh? But you're correct, just two, so far. Fairmile gunboat hulls, *four*-shaft motors, which will give you, wait for it, *thirty-six knots*, how about that?' He moved to the window and stared at the overlapping hulls and dipping cranes. 'I said at the time it was utter madness, or conceit, to send those coastal minelayers. Two slow, far too limited.' He punched one fist into his palm. 'Straight in, hit 'em, and out again, that's what we need!'

'It was such a surprise, you see . . .'

Brock waved him into silence. 'If you turn it down they'll let you keep your half-stripe, but I doubt if you'll command anything else, respect least of all! A lot of good blokes have gone west over the last four years, we've both seen them go, only too bloody often! If we don't owe anything to their lordships, and the people who *think* they're running this war, then we owe it to the ones we served alongside.' He winked. 'Good sales pitch, eh? Time for a noggin if we can find one!'

He walked to another door, then changed his mind and said, 'I know your thoughts pretty well. But let me put it this way. I've been through the reports so far, and I can assure you that ML366 will be laid up for some time.' He ticked off the points on his strong fingers. 'Shaft, starboard outer, is badly distorted, a replacement job and all that entails. Multiple hull damage from a whole year's operation without a proper refit.' He regarded him steadily. 'At best she'll be limited to inshore support and convoy work, something which would be wasted on someone of your experience. So take it while you can. I've no intention of becoming one of *yesterday's heroes* and used as a bloody door-mat when this lot's over and done with, and neither should you. You're good, so don't bloody well waste it!'

Almost what he had said to Allison just now. He had been surprised, shocked, his new confidence gone. He had simply stood there, framed against the burned paintwork where he had risked his life without question, had proved what he could do.

Quite subdued, he had said, 'I couldn't have done it without you.'

The door slammed open and the yardmaster marched into the office and threw some plans on his table. 'All done, then?' He smiled at Foley. 'Glad you made it. Time you had a break, in my opinion!'

Brock jammed on his cap and strode out into the sunshine. 'All right for some!'

Foley looked towards the jetty and the crowded moorings.

He had heard it said often enough about leaving one ship for another. No matter how close a relationship it had been, *never go back*. It is never the same. You might not even be remembered. The ranks soon closed.

They had to.

He said, 'Have they selected a new skipper yet?'

Brock casually returned a young sailor's salute.

'Oh, didn't I tell you? Dick Claridge is getting her. His own boat is in even worse shape. Experienced chap, keep him fully occupied during the refit, too.' He glanced at the vessels at their moorings, their ensigns bright in the hard sunlight. 'Tough about his wife, but there it is.'

He looked at his watch. 'The bar should be open by now.'

They headed towards the main building and Brock said, 'You will still be under my command, so to speak. I'll always be open to discussions. But one word of advice. Don't stick your neck out for anybody else.' Then he smiled, the mood passing. 'Door-mat, remember?'

Foley was thinking of Allison, and what might happen when Dick Claridge took command. They could be good for each other, and for the boat.

A new command. Moving on, like the war. But it was still hard to accept.

He would call Margot and tell her all about it.

That was the real difference. This time, he could share it.

Brock had stopped to speak with a nervous-looking midshipman, but caught up with Foley as they walked across the 'quarterdeck' and saluted in unison.

Brock said, 'Nice enough lad, son of the commodore at Harwich. But I told him he should get a decent tailor. He looks like something out of the scran-bag!'

They entered the wardroom and Brock tossed his cap at one of the stewards as he waved to various individuals who were already in the bar. Foley had known him for a long time, at a distance. The decorated hero, the tough commander who never backed down, 'Bash on Regardless'.

But afraid more than anything that one day he would be forgotten.

Captain James Wykes walked to a frail-looking safety rail and stared down into the shimmering green water. The lighting came from below and round the sides of what had once been a swimming pool, the main building having been a boarding school where many of the pupils were the sons of serving officers, or officials in the colonial service. Those boys were now evacuated, and some were doubtless already serving in uniform of one sort or another.

On the outskirts of Weymouth, it was suitably placed for Portland and even Plymouth, its change of role now accepted for the duration.

Swimming pools, especially in school, had a particular smell

243

which never seemed to change, regardless of time and use. Wykes could remember the endless instruction when he had been a cadet at Dartmouth, even now, after what felt like fifty years, when the call for *backward swimmers* had been sounded. Chlorine and wet bodies; those who could not swim and were frightened, those who would drown rather than admit it. Wykes had hated it, but he had managed, somehow, to get through.

There was a different sound also. An echo which had never left his mind, when someone had called out for help, or an instructor had pointedly humiliated another boy in front of his classmates.

He tested the rail with his hand and looked at the two frogmen paddling back and forth above the submerged lights. Like black seals. He patted his chest to restrain an early cough. More deadly than seals.

One of the frogmen had glided alongside the pool's main occupant. Even here, held in position by head and stern lines, the German midget submarine looked alive. Menacing, rocking this way and that as the first frogman clambered onto the small space behind the perspex observation dome.

The catch of the season, some wag had called it. Most people had forgotten all about it. The 'catch' on display in that gloomy vault, where he had first seen it, its dead crewman stretched out beside it, another exhibit for the experts to prod and examine with their usual relish.

The enemy were constructing a lot of them, more advanced even than this one. If they were allowed to run loose when the time came to invade occupied France, it could cause disaster. The reported sinking of the coastal minelayer was proof, if any was needed, what one determined man could achieve. Eventually, more direct action would have to be taken. That was not his concern.

This midget submarine, which had been captured after its pilot had lost consciousness, had been fitted for laying small mines. The boffins had stripped and reassembled the fittings and equipment again and again, until somebody high up had produced a full report. One torpedo, steered by a brave or reckless crewman, could destroy a big ship, filled with troops or vital stores. A few such craft, fitted with mines, could go even further; they would smash an invasion before it had started.

A simple idea, like the X-Craft which had crippled the mighty *Tirpitz* deep inside her boomed and guarded fjord. Or the Italian 'chariots' which mined the battleships in Alexandria, and had penetrated the anchorage at Gibraltar itself. Brave, lonely men, not unlike those who pitted their wits against the mines being dropped over here; hardly a week passed without hearing of a mine or unexploded bomb claiming another such hero.

He had often wondered in the past what made such men and women act as they did. Courage, a total disregard for personal risk, pride, or a need to take revenge? All or none of these? He thought suddenly of David Masters, what he knew of him, what he had seen of him. There was guilt, too. A debt to pay.

He had done that well enough.

There were voices on the stairway, coming up here, where proud parents had once stood and watched their offspring win events for the old school. Or being bullied as backward swimmers, he thought.

Like some of our own people. Agents dropped by plane, or put ashore from fishing boat or submarine, with a mission, or merely to contact a source of information. A tiny piece of the wider pattern. Wykes had met a few of them, but not many. There were others, better qualified, and hardened to that side of operations. Success was rare and priceless. Its cost did not bear thinking about. The torment and suffering of those who had been betrayed or captured, and the risk taken by every single agent was well known. He sighed and turned to greet his visitors. And yet there were those who readily volunteered.

They were an unlikely pair. The small, stooping man with thick spectacles who had difficulty standing or sitting still was called Beamish, and he was one of the top brains in the world of explosives and fuses, a leading boffin whom Wykes had met many times. Beamish would explain every device in detail, step by step, in the manner of a rather bored schoolmaster. It was a wonder he was still alive.

The other visitor, tall and powerfully built, and wearing the uniform of a *Capitaine de Vaisseau* in the Free French navy, was Michel Lalonde. An expert in matters relating to German bases and supply lines, especially in his own occupied country, he was a strong, aggressive character with, Wykes suspected, little love for his British ally.

He spoke and understood English perfectly. When he chose.

Wykes spread his hands. 'Well, gentlemen, it seems it is a time for action.'

They were both staring down into the pool, each viewing the midget submarine differently. No doubt the small, stooping Beamish saw it as another solved puzzle, no longer his responsibility. His straight-backed companion saw it as a means to an end.

Wykes said, 'It has been confirmed that the Germans are preparing to transport their supply of the new mines from the Channel Islands to the mainland. After that, it will be a much greater task to pinpoint their locations. They will be scattered. The exact timing of this operation is still unknown.'

Lalonde said bluntly, 'Our agents found the storage and assembly points months ago. They should have been bombed there and then.'

'The P.M. was unwilling to condone air attacks on the only part of Britain occupied by the enemy. It was considered bad for morale. The people there are suffering enough.'

Lalonde smiled humourlessly. 'He is less squeamish about bombing my country, which is also *suffering enough*!'

Wykes relaxed. This was the Lalonde he knew and, for some reason, respected.

'The mines are small, as you know, and in large numbers could compromise any invasion's main weapon, surprise. The Channel Islands were a good choice for the training and experimental stage as far as the enemy were concerned. Now they are ready to move on.'

He recalled the photographs which had been taken at great risk, and had arrived eventually on his desk. Ragged Russian prisoners of war, hands tied behind them, being driven across the experimental mines. As slaves they had no other value, and any islander showing sympathy or protest was severely punished.

The Channel Islands had been a sound choice for another reason. Commando raids or any attempt to land sabotage parties would be forestalled before they had begun. Only the few could have any hope of success.

He said, 'It will be soon, of that we are certain.'

Beamish removed his glasses and polished them briskly in a piece of tissue. Without them, his eyes looked tiny and ineffectual. He said abruptly, 'My department is satisfied, James. It is a good machine, and we have made it better!' He was not boasting. It was simply another statistic.

Lalonde stared at the green, flickering water. One of the frogmen was sitting on the craft's whaleback, his hood removed, smoking a cigarette.

As he turned to call something to his companion the little submarine rocked steeply. Even with the added weight of the explosives, it seemed too small and vulnerable for its hazardous work.

Lalonde returned his attention to Wykes.

'Have you heard anything? About Mademoiselle de Courcy?'

It was pointless to try and fob him off with the usual security sermon. Lalonde knew all about it. He had even been over there on a couple of secret missions, and had almost been captured after a woman recognized him and reported his presence to the military police.

A French woman, too! A friend of my mother's! The danger of capture and what would have followed seemed to take second place to such treachery.

Wykes said, 'I have received no further news. When I do, I shall call you.'

Lalonde shook his head. 'She should never have gone, never been sent.'

'I know. She volunteered. After that . . .' He shrugged. 'We were running out of alternatives.'

Lalonde strode to the safety-rail again, as if he could not restrain his agitation.

'And who will "volunteer" for this escapade, eh?'

Wykes took out his cigarette case and opened it deliberately.

'I think I know just the man.'

'Then I pity him.' He eyed him gravely. 'And you also!'

Wykes tapped a cigarette on the silver case. It helped. Gave him time.

'We cannot all be squeamish, *Capitaine*!'

247

16

In All the Old Familiar Places

David Masters walked unhurriedly along the jetty, giving himself
time to think, and taking care not to trip over any loose piece
of gear. It was evening, with a stiff, cold wind off the bay and
layers of dark cloud moving swiftly overhead. But there was a
full moon in the offing, so that the jetty and its moored charges
were occasionally lit up, like a stage set. A bomber's moon, they
called it, and even with fighter protection and anti-aircraft batteries
this was still a target worth risking. If the enemy knew or cared
enough about it, when there were so many bigger objectives.

There was always mention of security, and 'careless talk' in the
same breath. It had become more pointed recently when a local
woman whose husband was away in the army had been discovered
in bed with one of the Italian prisoners of war. To all intents and
purposes Italy was out of the war now, unless you were an Italian
unfortunate enough to be in the German-occupied area of the
country. The prisoners of war, who worked so willingly on the
farms and market gardens, had become part of the local scenery.
But all the same, there was the fear of careless talk.

He had spent most of the day near Weymouth, at the one-time
boarding school with Captain Wykes and some of his experts. He
paused and looked at the nearest motor launch, Foley's command
until today. How did he feel, he wondered. Something so familiar
and so personal. On the drive back from Weymouth Margot Lovatt
had been very quiet, even downcast. She knew about Foley's new
command, and what it might mean to them. It happened often

enough in wartime. Separation, and the fear of losing something only just discovered.

And there was Wykes and his new toy, the midget submarine. The chain-smoking captain had seemed surprised that he had known so much about the 'catch', even though he had had plenty of time to examine it, and check the details, on that first visit to *Osprey*. And later, when he had offered her a chair. And his coat.

Wykes had somehow reminded him of Bumper Fawcett. *Were a submariner.* And they had talked about the mines, the very real threat they posed, and what steps might be necessary.

And all the while the midget submarine had been lying there in the old school swimming bath, almost familiar.

He realized he was touching the scar on his cheek. It had all seemed unimportant when set against the news that Elaine was missing. As he had known in his heart. Feared.

Wykes had been unusually open and frank. He had told him a little of her background. Born in the Channel Islands; her mother was English, and her father, who had once had some business connection with the dead Critchley, a Channel Islander, although he had stronger inclinations towards France. She had come to England to complete her studies and to take up journalism, mostly connected with holidays and travel, for those who could afford it. Then the war, and the German occupation. She had been evacuated just before the first invaders landed, and her father had continued to work for the new masters.

Elaine de Courcy was fluent in French and German, and when her father's good friend John Critchley had introduced her to his naval connections she had found herself working, as a civilian, in the Admiralty Intelligence department.

Wykes had said, 'At no time was it even suggested that she should become an active agent!'

Masters was not sure he believed him. All that mattered was that she had gone, that night, after they had been here together.

She might be dead. He could not contemplate the alternatives.

'Evenin', sir!'

He turned and saw a tall figure, dark against the boat's pale hull. It was Bass, 366's coxswain. He could smell smoke, and guessed that Bass had a cigarette carefully secreted in the cupped palm of his hand, in the way of sailors.

'Work going well?'

Bass shuffled his feet. 'The usual, sir. You knows 'ow it is.' He added quickly, 'My rate came through, sir. I'm actin' petty officer as of today. 'E said he'd fix it. Course, that was before 'e knew about the promotion, an' 'is new command.' He flicked ash discreetly into the darkness. 'But 'e said 'e'd fix it. Never lets anyone down, does Mister Foley!'

'You'll miss him?'

Bass said without hesitation, 'I've stuck in for a transfer, sir. They was askin' for volunteers.' He grinned, his teeth very white in the darkness. 'As if they cares about that!'

There was the sound of marching feet; a patrol was approaching. *Security.* Bass straightened up and stood firmly at the foot of the brow.

Masters said, 'I'll put in a word.' He walked into a moving carpet of moonlight.

He had spoken to Rear-Admiral Fawcett on the telephone about it. Bumper had been evasive, not very forthcoming. Perhaps he already had someone else in mind for this appointment? Someone who could plan and delegate, and who could watch with detachment as men went off to be killed, because the enemy had schemed up another new trick.

'There'll be more centralisation, and soon too. D.T.M. at Admiralty has become top-level stuff nowadays, and the Director will be needing a new sidekick to speed things along. It would mean promotion, y'know, a brass-hat, not to be sneezed at, what?'

The Department of Torpedoes and Mines. Masters could imagine it. Still more remote, with the war at an even greater distance. At least you wouldn't see the people you were sending off to their last incidents.

He stood on a slipway, the weed slippery under his shoes. *Never walk to the end of a jetty*, his father had once said. Somehow, the superstition had remained with him.

Wykes had said, 'It will have to be planned to the last detail. No foul-ups, no chances.' He had gazed at him steadily. 'I don't have to explain the risk. I wouldn't know where to begin. But I

250

don't think there is any other way.' Unexpectedly, he had gripped
his arm. 'If anyone can do it, you can.'

And when had he said anything that made sense? When had he
agreed?

All he could remember was the French officer shaking his hand,
the one he had seen in the restaurant en route to a cabaret with
Elaine de Courcy. The boat cloak, and the same glittering brooch
which was now in Brayshaw's safe. When he had thought that she
and Lalonde had been lovers. And the small man with the bottle-top
glasses, bobbing and smiling; he, too, had shaken his hand . . .

He had glanced once more into the green water.

It was as if the little submarine had been waiting for him.

Masters ducked beneath a crane and turned back towards the
top of the yard. Another visit to Operations, and then back to his
quarters. He could not face the wardroom and the curious stares.
Ops would ring him if anything new turned up.

He saw the car parked in its usual place and went over to it.

'Don't get out.' He put his hand on the door and peered in at
her. 'I'll not be needing you again today.' He paused. 'By the
way, I'm seeing your quarters officer about getting a few days'
leave for you. You've been overdoing it since you came back.' He
gripped her wrist against the open window. 'Please, don't waste
it.' He noticed that she did not flinch; they had both come a long
way since that first day.

He could smell her perfume, very faintly. But he was thinking
of somebody else.

A siren had started up somewhere, and he turned away from the
car, towards the Operations section. It was suddenly bathed in eerie
light, until the next cloud bank. A bomber's moon.

He heard the car drive away and was suddenly glad of what he
had said.

Now, it seemed more important than ever.

Michael Lincoln shook his head and waved aside another drink. He
had already lost count, and he needed to be careful. Anyway, he
thought, it was strange to be offered a glass by someone you didn't
know, in the house where you had grown up and lived for most of
your life. The same house, and yet so changed. Packed from wall

251

to wall with people, drinking and eating the many snacks which were laid out on various tables. There was certainly no shortage of anything. Quite the reverse.

And his father; he seemed to have changed more than anything. Only a few months since that last leave, when they had parted with scarcely a word, but he seemed to have opened out, boisterous and very much in charge.

He was wearing a new suit, and his hair was well trimmed and slicked down over his shining forehead. And he was drinking gin, a lot of it. Lincoln had never seen him touch anything but mild and bitter before, unless it was Christmas or somebody's wedding.

In the few hours since he and Downie had arrived by taxi from the station it had not stopped. Some of the people he recognized; others seemed to be his father's friends or working acquaintances. It seemed he had become a somebody in the district, had even been elected to membership of the local council. His mother had managed to toss him fragments of information while she had been busily refilling plates and fetching fresh glasses.

'Your dad may stand for mayor one day, Michael. Just think of that! And he's so *proud* of you – just look at him, will you! Pleased as Punch.' She had winked at him. 'Won't do his chances any harm either, will it?'

He had not spoken to his father very much. Not alone. He had seemed surprised to see Downie, and when he had been taken aside by one of his minions had murmured, 'An ordinary sailor? What are you thinking of? Your fellow officers might not care for that!'

Lincoln could not remember how he had managed to remain so calm. Detached. His fellow officers were the ones his father had once referred to as 'stuck-up' and 'toffee-nosed bastards'. He had changed indeed.

He had already told them about Downie's parents in a letter to his mother. Maybe his father had forgotten, or was using the moment to put the boot in again. Just to remind him where he stood.

'He's my assistant, and he's been with me on every job, and many more before that. We have to take this leave together. He's got nowhere else to go.'

His father had grinned. 'That's okay, then. We don't want the neighbours giving us the old nudge-nudge, do we?'

252

His mother had been more tactful.

'The spare room's been made into another office for your dad. We can fix your young assistant with a camp bed, if that's all right.'

Lincoln had hugged her. She was getting so old, so frail, in stark contrast to his father, he had thought.

'He won't complain, Mum. And call him Gordon. We're not here as officer and rating, you know.' She had hurried away, smiling and shaking her head.

He saw his father pushing another man through the noisy throng and tensed. It was the editor of the local paper, the *South London Courier*. It was his father's idea. Pride? Or thinking of his own chances for mayor?

He should have expected it. He had been warned.

'You remember Frank Mason, don't you, Mike? He runs the *Courier*.'

'We've met a couple of times.' They shook hands. Mason's was like sandpaper.

'You've been making a name for yourself, Mike. I know we're not supposed to print anything until it's official, but I'd like to use the local angle for my paper. I get little enough to crow about!' He laughed, but Lincoln noticed that it did not reach his eyes.

Mason glanced around. 'You brought your helper with you, I hear?'

'He has nowhere else to go. He lived in Coventry.'

'Enough said. Too bad. I'd like to chat with him, all the same, if that's all right by you. *His officer*!'

Lincoln smiled, and wanted to hit him. 'I'll find him for you.'

He did not have to look far. Downie was in the kitchen, drying glasses while a woman he did not know washed them in the sink.

Downie listened with the characteristic frown and said, 'If you think I should.' He glanced at the woman and lowered his voice. 'I could slip away and get booked into the Union Jack club or somewhere. Don't want to be a nuisance.'

'I invited you. I want you to stay.' He touched his arm. 'And if you think you'd find a billet at this time of day you'd be in for a shock!'

Someone had started to bang out 'There'll Always be an England'

253

on the old piano, and there was a ready response from most of the guests; his father's voice was the loudest of all. More like the father he had known before, especially on Saturday nights after the Royal George had turned out.

Mason of the *Courier* ushered them into the tiny room which had been added to the house just before the war. It was littered with fire-fighting gear and work clothes, and some old ledgers, as if it had not yet made up its mind what it was supposed to be.

'Now, you work with an officer all the time, right? And you've been at it for some while, I believe. With another officer originally?' He was making notes in shorthand. 'He died, is that right?'

Downie gripped the dish towel and was twisting it in his hands. 'Yes. He was very brave. He was awarded the George Cross, the highest . . .'

Mason held up his pencil. 'You get pretty close to somebody in those circumstances, I'd say?'

'Yes.'

Mason smiled. 'And what about *Mister* Lincoln here? You can tell me – how does *he* rate?'

Downie looked away. 'That's not for me to say, sir.' He faltered. 'We work well together.'

Mason nodded. 'And he saved your life.'

Downie looked at Lincoln. 'He saved my life. Yes.'

Mason scribbled a few more notes and closed his pad with a snap.

'I'll send you a copy when it comes out. Your mother has given me a photo. Should do the trick.'

Lincoln tried to relax, muscle by muscle. The *Courier* only came out once a week, and was very local in its news and views.

Mason had gone. Downie said, 'Was that all right, sir?'

Lincoln tried to laugh it off. *He saved my life.* 'You did fine.' He looked around. 'Now I do need that drink!'

What would his father say and do, in front of his friends and the people he was obviously using to his own advantage, if he knew the truth? *That I was afraid. Unable to move. Not only once, but other times. Because I tried to prove something. To match something which wasn't worth the effort.*

It seemed an eternity before the guests departed, some pausing to slap him on the shoulder, others too far gone even to speak. A few remained with his father in the front room, where more serious matters would be under discussion.

Eventually Lincoln made his way upstairs to bed. Once he stopped to adjust a blackout curtain, and saw the matching roofs of the houses on the opposite side of the street. A full moon: it was like daylight. He thought of the first mine; he had been told that if it exploded it could knock down six streets. Like this one.

He *had* had too much to drink after all.

If the sirens wailed tonight, somebody else could do all the running.

He saw the camp bed at the end of the passageway; Downie was already fast asleep, or pretending to be. Probably like me, he thought, regretting he had ever agreed to come here.

He stripped off his uniform and struggled to untangle his tie. Maybe he could think of some excuse tomorrow. Go somewhere, just to walk and talk. Find out things.

He almost fell onto the bed. The sheets were crisp and clean. They would be; his mother did everything. While he . . .

He did not know how long he had been asleep, or what had awakened him. A sound, a dream? He opened his eyes and saw a shaft of moonlight shining from the window, where it had not been before.

The house was completely still and silent. Until the next time.

He stared again at the moonlight, and realized that Downie was there, holding the curtain aside while he looked out at the night.

'Gordon?'

He saw him turn and drop the curtain, plunging the room into darkness again. Not before he had seen the moonlight reflecting on his skin like silver.

It was a dream. In a moment he would wake up and . . .

He reached out and gripped his hand, then felt the sheet being pulled down, the pressure of his body beside his.

'I'm here.' As if he was trembling. 'Mike?'

This time, it was not a dream.

Chris Foley stood on the waste-littered slipway and looked up at the raked, overhanging bows, and despite his borrowed duffle coat he could not contain a shiver. Excitement, disbelief, even doubt. It was certainly not the breeze from Falmouth Bay.

It was a fine, clear morning, after a stay overnight in a commandeered boarding house. Unable to sleep. Pacing the room. Waiting for today. Now.

The boat builder was watching him with interest. His name was Gilbert Tregear, and he was as Cornish as you could find anywhere; his family had been building boats for as long as anyone could remember. Tough, square and with skin like leather, Foley could imagine him without effort as a smuggler or a pirate, or one of Nelson's men.

Tregear said, 'Well, this is the moment. You can walk a deck, test every nut and bolt, test the joinery with your fingers, but down here you really gets the *feel* of a fine craft.' His pride was something lasting, a legacy of all those years.

Foley shaded his eyes and studied the flared bows. Despite the dangling wires and hoses, power lines and streaks of grease and oil, he could see the grace of the hull which appeared to be leaning over him, preparing to kick free of the land. *The feel of a fine craft.*

It was all true, but something he found hard to accept. What he had not believed possible after 366.

Tregear must have taken his silence for doubt. 'I'll have her in the water day after tomorrow. Two more days after that, an' she'll be yours. Not your first command, I hear?'

Foley walked slowly down the slipway. Beyond the square, business-like stern he could see the stretch of Falmouth Harbour and Carrick Roads. A few more paces and the impressive silhouette of Pendennis Castle would be visible on the headland, and St. Mawes on the opposite one. He had been here once for a holiday with his parents, long ago, before Claire was born. He had never forgotten the place, the fishing boats, the yarn-telling sailors, local people much like Tregear. Enough to excite any eight-year-old boy.

When his father had been taken ill; it had seemed to happen more often in those days. The coughing, the breathlessness, the aftermath of gas attacks in Flanders in that other war.

How Falmouth had changed. Grey or camouflaged hulls of all shapes and classes, building, being repaired, or just pausing between convoys or patrols along this coastline where smugglers had once roamed. Still did, according to a customs officer he had met.

And in the River Fal itself he had seen newly finished landing craft lying in groups, waiting for the invasion which only the armchair strategists dared to predict.

He looked up at the hull again and saw a sailor's head and shoulders vanish instantly. That had happened a lot. Quick, curious, even nervous glances. Some of the newly drafted hands, faces he would come to know like those he had left behind. The wags and the characters, the skivers and the skates. Those you could rely on, come what may. Those you might have to watch. But all volunteers for Special Service. Jack always moaned about everything. That was his strength.

He thought of the man who was to be his first lieutenant. Not some eager, partly trained subbie but a full two-ringer, a professional sailor of the Royal Naval Reserve. What the regulars had once termed *Really Not Required*. That joke had misfired a long time ago.

Lieutenant Peter Kidd was a tall, strongly built sailor who had lived by the sea until it had claimed him for its own. He had served his time in small freighters and a collier, and was five or six years older than his new commanding officer. A man who would be hard to know, Foley thought, but well worth knowing. Blunt, almost brutal in his descriptions of the work in progress, or the service of some particular rating. He had been blown up twice, and had joked about it. *The sea can't stomach a proper sailor, so it spat me out again!* And there was another officer, a 'third hand', in their small company, Sub-Lieutenant John Venables, twenty years old and very determined, and straight from a course on tactical minelaying. He looked as if butter would not melt in his mouth. He seemed in awe of his first lieutenant, but inclined to be a little sharp with the men working under him. Kidd had said casually, 'I'll soon hone him into shape!'

It was still hard to remember everything. The boat was a few feet longer than 366, and broader in the beam, the bows impressively flared to allow for the extra speed, and to retain stability in all but the worst seas.

257

Foley had met the senior motor mechanic for a few minutes, but his name had slipped his mind. A calm, intelligent-faced man with a faint accent, Welsh or somewhere close. His excitement over his new appointment was infectious. He had spoken of the four-shaft Bristol motors as if they were almost human. 'Seven thousand B.H.P., sir! Thirty-six knots, see? Like a bird, she'll be!'

He had found himself thinking of Shannon, 366's chief; would he still be brooding over his unfaithful wife? How would he react to Dick Claridge's command?

It was behind him now. It had to be.

Designed originally as a motor gunboat, his new command was well armed with machine-guns and Oerlikons. But nothing heavier: she *would* need to fly like a bird if things proved difficult.

And the mines, all twenty of them. They would still take some getting used to. 366 had laid mines several times, and swept them, too, under special and difficult circumstances. There had not been much she had not done or attempted.

He pushed the memories away and said, 'She'll do me, Mr. Tregear. I'm lucky to get her!'

He was still not sure if he meant it.

He would miss young Allison, *Tobias*, just as he had missed the bright and abrasive Harry Bryant when he had been promoted and gone off to a command of his own. And those who had trusted him even when all hell had broken loose. And those who had died.

Like the old R.N.R. skipper who had lost his little ship, but had somehow survived. When Foley had gone back to the sick quarters to collect his personal belongings he had found the other bed empty and stripped. The old skipper had apparently died of a heart attack.

Sister Titmuss had put it differently. '*Broken* heart, if you ask me. He had nothing else.'

He shut it from his mind. The past was the past, and better kept that way.

'Lieutenant-Commander Foley here?'

Foley turned, off guard. It had happened before and he had been caught unprepared, as if it was someone else. He had caught a glimpse of himself in a shop window on his way here, the new rank on the sleeves, two and a half stripes. Like an awakening.

'That's me!' He saw the boat builder hide a grin.

The workman who was clinging to one of the slipway's trestles called, 'Phone for you, sir! Mister Tregear's office!'

Tregear said, 'No peace for you, not even here!' He turned away to shout something at one of his men who was trailing a length of wire through a puddle of oil.

Foley smiled. 'Or for you, either!'

He climbed up from the slipway and felt the noise and confusion from the rest of the yard closing in on him. To think that when he had found adventure on that holiday here in Falmouth, all those years ago, his sister Claire had not even been born. Now she was in love with her Polish pilot; an *affair*, as his mother had dismissed it. Perhaps she did not remember her own war, the separation and the fear.

He picked up the telephone. On the wall opposite him someone had written a few numbers, with an added warning. *Not on Wednesdays. Her old man is off work then!*

'Lieutenant-Commander Foley?' It was a woman's voice.

'Speaking.'

She said, 'I love you.'

He covered his ear with his hand, to exclude the noise, everybody else.

'Margot! It's you, darling! Have you been waiting long?'

'Ssh. Listen, we might get cut off.' He heard her quick intake of breath. '*Again*. I had to use a lot of flannel to get through to you as it was!' She was either laughing or crying.

She said, 'My friend Toni, you know, the one who met your Number One . . .' and hesitated as if her confidence had suddenly left her.

'Tell me, Margot. Don't stop. I've missed you so much.'

She said, 'I don't know what you must think, Chris. But Toni has a friend in Cornwall. A place not far from you, a village called Philleigh. Her friend owns a cottage there.' She was fainter now, the line or her breathing, he could only guess. 'I've got a few days' leave. I could see you, be with you, if you can get away . . .'

He said, 'I'll be there, no matter what. You don't know what this means to me.'

'I'll call you, darling Chris. I think we're going to be cut off.

I wanted to tell you how much I need to be with you, and I thought . . .'

This time she was cut off.

Foley replaced the receiver very gently.

Nothing must spoil it. He opened the door, the noise crowding in again.

Not even the bloody war.

Tregear said, 'I've got some more details to show you,' and watched him curiously. A young man who had known a lot of danger. The kind you read about in the papers, or heard about on the news. One who had known suffering.

He opened his file with elaborate care. It was always the same, even after all these years. You build something, give it life, watch it sail away.

He looked at the young officer beside him. Going into heaven alone knew what. He seemed not to have a care in the whole world.

Foley grinned at him. 'Fire away, then! I'm all attention!'

He could still hear her voice.

Paymaster Lieutenant-Commander Philip Brayshaw leaned back in his chair and regarded his friend with concern. He had removed his jacket and had opened a window behind the blackout shutters to admit some cold air. There was thin frost on the puddles outside his office but the heating had gone berserk again, and the radiator pipes hummed with heat, as if they were about to explode.

He said, 'I'll shoot that damned stoker if he can't get his bloody boiler to behave!'

He watched Masters filling his pipe, saddened, but pleased that he had come to his office to share his thoughts.

Masters said, 'I've heard they're going to reduce the personnel and facilities here. Quite soon, that was the buzz.'

Brayshaw nodded. 'Supposed to be confidential, but signals so intended are usually the easiest to intercept.' He became serious again. 'And I hear that you're leaving us shortly. Not permanently, I hope?' He held up his hand before Masters could speak. 'I *know*, it's all hush-hush. I should be used to it!'

Masters tamped down the tobacco in his pipe. He had been

back to Weymouth again, to the old boarding school, and had gone right through the translated procedures for the German midget submarine until he thought he knew them by heart. The two engineers had been pleasantly surprised at his grasp of the details. They were, in fact, simple enough.

Bumper Fawcett had been onto him again, too. A temporary replacement would be coming direct from H.M.S. *Vernon*. All very secret, of course. Perhaps Fawcett had already written him off. *Were a submariner.* He should know.

He clicked his lighter and hesitated. It was still not too late. Things had moved even faster than he expected. *It was still not too late.* He turned the lighter over in his hand, and remembered her giving it to him in the restaurant. Suppose she had taken part in some secret operation? He clicked the lighter again and watched the flame. She may have been taken by the enemy. It was different for Wykes and his staff. They had the responsibility, but none of the terrible risks.

Tomorrow he would go to London. Like the last time, but with a difference.

He said, 'If I screw things up, Philip.' Their eyes met through the drifting smoke. 'That package in your safe . . .'

'Leave it with me.' No names, no promises. Why they had always got along so well. Always . . . it was only a matter of weeks, not even three months yet. The navy's way.

He thought of Chris Foley, probably envied by those who scarcely knew him. Promotion and a new command. A veteran at twenty-five. Perhaps he could share his hopes and his fears with his girl, if she had decided to join him.

They heard the clanging sounds of a shovel from the cellar. The stoker was making another attempt to control his boiler.

Brayshaw said, 'Soon, then?'

'I'll be seeing the intelligence people before Friday. After that, it's anybody's guess.'

Secrecy was everything, and yet how many people knew about the proposed operation? Starting with the 'catch' being towed into Portland, then transferred to a temporary hiding place in the old school swimming bath. More men would be needed to hoist it on a special crane through the roof of the building. Then the R.A.F.

would take over, with one of their giant lorries known as 'Queen Marys', normally used for transporting large aircraft, bombers, when there was no other way to move them. People would talk. *D'you know what we had to shift today, dear?* He forced himself to relax. It happened all the time. The planners were used to it.

And it mattered. All the work, the sacrifice and unstinting courage of the countermeasures team would count for nothing if this new and easily operated weapon could be used to destroy all hope of invasion.

He did not need reminding of his own first beast, and those which had quickly followed, when every move and breath felt like the last one on earth. As it had been for so many of the people he had known.

How much worse for the overloaded infantryman, trying to wade and struggle ashore at a place of which he had never heard. The moment they had all been waiting for, dreading, but still a part of it. And then being killed, gutted by the unseen mines, with landing craft blown to pieces within sight of victory.

It mattered, all right.

'And if it goes wrong . . .' He did not finish; he did not need to. Brayshaw knew all about him. His father had been killed at sea during the Spanish Civil War; an accident, they said. His mother had died soon afterwards. She had never really come to terms with his death.

Apart from his uncle, an ex-commander who had transferred to the Royal Indian Navy and had chosen to remain out there when the war had started, there was nobody else. He was reminded of the young torpedoman, Downie. Perhaps it was why he had felt so sorry for him. Responsible. They had something in common.

Brayshaw said, 'Who knows, David, you may be offered a seagoing command after this job.'

Masters thought of the moment when he had climbed into the cockpit of the midget submarine. Wrongly named, in any case; it remained at the same depth all the time. A strange sensation, but how different from the real thing, out in the open sea. *It was still not too late.* A seagoing command. It would be the loneliest of all time. As first lieutenant of another T-Class submarine, before he had been given *Tornado*, he had taken part in several attacks on enemy shipping, mostly off the coast of France and down into Biscay. Moments of suspense, chilling tension when the enemy's sonar had tapped along the hull like Blind Pew's stick, and wild excitement at any successful attack, a blurred glimpse of a ship in the crosswires, going down, and the sounds of metal tearing apart under the waves. A ship dying. But they had all been together; it was their strength. It was not so long ago that he had been unable to think about it, remember it. There was always *Tornado*.

Brayshaw said, 'The Old Man's moving on too, did you know?'

Masters tapped out his pipe. He did not remember smoking it. 'Another buzz.'

'Getting a barracks appointment. Chatham, I think, God help him.'

'What about you?'

He shrugged. 'Another captain will come along. He'll need someone who knows about misinterpreting signals, and where the paper clips are stowed. I'll survive.'

It was time to go. Tomorrow, London. At least it would be a different hotel, otherwise he would always have been looking. Hoping. He stood up. *He still would.*

He thrust out his hand and smiled. 'Like the song, Philip. I'll be seeing you.'

Brayshaw stood staring at the closed door, for how long he did not recall. He did not know the extent of Masters' orders; it was better that way. But Rear-Admiral Fawcett had been like a bear with a sore head since *it* had happened, and there had been Top Secret signals flying back and forth, until one from the First Sea Lord himself had killed the speculation stone dead.

He glanced at the safe and thought about the little package, and the girl who might never see it again.

Masters was quite alone, and when it came down to brass tacks, his was the only decision which would mean success or disaster, life or death.

He sighed. Once before, he had seen envy on Masters' face. But now he knew what it felt like for himself.

He picked up a shovel from a fire-prevention bucket and used it to hammer the radiator until the banging in the cellar stopped.

He murmured under his breath, 'I'll be seeing you.'

17

Second Thoughts

True to his word, Gilbert Tregear had his latest creation afloat and alongside the pier without fuss or ceremony. A new keel would be laid down before another week had passed, and work begin all over again.

Builders and mechanics became fewer, and naval uniforms took over.

Chris Foley was aboard early on this particular morning. It was not just another hull, not any more. Gear was properly stowed, guns cleaned and trained fore and aft, all lines flaked down. Even the new paint was dry and had lost its smell. The hull had suddenly become a naval vessel in her own right. Almost.

She even felt different in the water, he thought. Nearly a hundred tons of her despite her rakish appearance; he could compare the motion with 366's livelier behaviour even in harbour.

And this was the day. Once again he glanced along the length of his new command, at the men he would soon know as well as they would him. A few older hands this time, with good conduct badges to prove it; badges for 'undiscovered crime', they called them. And their collars were scrubbed pale to distinguish them from most of their small company, whose collars were still dark blue like their best uniforms, which they were all wearing today. Foley had done all the necessary signing to make the handover official, and tried to remain composed, outwardly at least, while Tregear and the officer from the contracts department had countersigned each document.

'Standing by, sir!'

Foley heard the first lieutenant acknowledge the shout.

Dougie Bass had arrived in Falmouth the previous evening. Even he had been unable to hide his surprise at the speed with which things had moved after his request for a transfer.

Must 'ave influence in 'igh places, sir! And he was here, on this special day. No longer a killick coxswain but a petty officer now, with the crown and crossed anchors on his sleeve to prove it. As an acting P.O. until his new rate was confirmed he still wore his seaman's square rig.

They had had a drink together and Bass had confided, 'Never thought I'd leave the old girl, sir. But then, when you left, I asked meself, 'ow will 'e manage without me?' As ever, he knew exactly just how far he could go.

Kidd saluted. 'Ready, sir.' His strong features were expressionless. Perhaps thinking she might have been his own command? The sea was his life. This might be his last chance.

Foley looked over his shoulder and saw a rating right up in the bows, the Jack carefully folded over his arm, the halliards ready and in place. Aft, another seaman was at the staff, a brand-new White Ensign clipped into position. Two leading hands stood to one side, their silver calls raised, moistened on their lips to prevent any last-second discord.

He saw that a crowd had gathered on the shore, as close as they dared to Tregear and the officer from the contracts department. There was also a full commander who had come from Plymouth to represent the admiral. Yard workers, who had seen it all before, some women from the canteen, three small boys who must belong to somebody. And right there by the office where he had taken her call was Margot, the only woman in uniform here today. When he had left her it had still been dark, and he had hated to let her go. *You ought to be right there, beside me.*

She had hugged him again, her body still hot against his. *I shall be.* She had pulled his hand to her breast. *In here, I shall be with you all the time.*

Foley realized that Kidd was still waiting, perhaps weighing up the one man who might change his whole life.

'*Make it so!*'

As Kidd wheeled around to call the hands to attention, Foley saw the new plate below the bridge. Every other boat he had served in had carried just a number. Nicknames perhaps, but never a proper title in the true naval tradition.

'Pipe!'

As the calls trilled in unison it seemed as if a signal had been passed to the entire boatyard. Even the gantry came to a sudden halt, a hoist of timber still swaying from its tackle. Sailors aboard a harbour launch to one of the bigger ships in the anchorage were waving their caps, their cheers drowned by the blast of a tugmaster's siren. On the rickety pier some of the workmen were also waving, and two of the older men had removed their hats and stood at attention, perhaps remembering.

Foley stared at the gleaming new ensign as it reached the truck and broke out to the cold wind. Behind him, he knew without looking, the Jack would have been hoisted at exactly the same time.

And she was sharing it with him. *I shall be with you all the time.*

'Carry on!'

The calls trilled again and then there was silence.

H.M.S. *Firebrand* was in commission. And she was his.

Another secret signal, and the towering gantry began to move once more, as the crowd broke up and men went about their work. Some remained to watch a little longer.

For they had built her, and would probably never see her again.

'Dismiss the hands, Number One.' He looked at the small masthead pendant. 'They did pretty well, I thought.'

Kidd smiled, the deep crow's-feet around his eyes very noticeable. 'Aye, sir. I think I can smell some of Nelson's Blood in the offing!' He saluted again and faced the waiting company. Larger than 366's, thirty in all. He could imagine what Bass would be asked, and how he might answer. 'Old Chris? Good as gold if you keep yer nose clean and do yer job proper!'

He turned and saw her walking towards the hastily rigged brow, small and erect, oblivious to the stares and occasional whistles.

Foley said, 'Someone I'd like you to meet, Number One.'

H.M.S. *Firebrand*'s first guest had arrived.

266

Gilbert Tregear paused by his office door. The official visitors were hanging about, waiting for the bottles to be opened, he thought grimly. Something every new commanding officer had to expect. The builder, too.

He saw the pretty Wren with the dark hair pause at the top of the brow and salute, the side party responding equally smartly. But he saw the smiles, could almost feel the warmth of it. So young; let them have a few moments on their own.

'Now, if you'd step into my office, gentlemen, I've got something rather special I'd like you to taste!'

He closed the door. It never failed. They were ready and waiting.

Until the next time.

Masters sat on the edge of the bed and waited patiently for his call to be transferred, then transferred again. The hotel which was to be his home for three nights was smaller than the previous one, on the fringe of Chelsea, and close to the river; he had caught sight of it from the taxi. He did not know London well, and felt completely out of his depth.

Eventually a bored voice took his message, and yes, he would be expected at the Admiralty tomorrow. At nine o'clock. They obviously did not believe in rushing things.

The hotel was yet another commandeered place for officers either on passage somewhere, or those who were actually employed here in London. He had seen several senior officers downstairs, some with red tabs on their jackets, others equally high-ranking from the R.A.F. It seemed he was the only guest from the Royal Navy.

Perhaps he would take a stroll. Maybe have a quiet drink somewhere, if there was such a refuge. But first . . . He picked up the telephone again. He had to check his notebook before he could tell the operator the number; it reminded him how infrequently he had called the house with its damp wallpaper.

He was surprised when Petty Officer Coker answered it himself.

'Just thought I'd check up with you, make sure it's all quiet.'

'Glad you rang, sir. I was wonderin' what I should do.'

Masters tensed immediately. Coker rarely got rattled about anything. Never, as far as he could remember.

'What is it?'

'Just after you left, sir. I called the station, but you'd already gone. The lady rang. Wanted to talk to you. Worried about something, she was. I couldn't tell 'er where you'd gone – it's supposed to be secret. And in any case . . .'

Masters said quickly, 'But she's all right?'

Coker considered it. 'Upset. Sorry she couldn't speak to you. I told 'er I'd give you the message when you got in touch.'

He was sounding calmer. The buck had been passed.

He added suddenly, 'She left a number . . . just in case.'

Masters was on his feet. She was alive. Safe. And she had called him.

'You did fine, Coker. Give me a second and I'll jot it down.'

He thought for a moment that Coker had hung up, or that they had been disconnected.

Then Coker said, 'I can do better than that, sir. I've got the address – it's the same number.'

Masters found he was nodding, trying to follow it. Coker wanted to impart something, even though it went against his code of doing things.

'Tell me. It means a lot.'

He watched the pencil as it moved across the page. He did not write the last part. It was Chelsea. A flat, perhaps not far from this hotel. She had mentioned the Thames to him, he could not recall in what context.

He heard Coker's heavy breathing and said, 'Thanks very much. I might bump into her.'

'Yes, sir.' The gentleman's gentleman again. In control.

'You know where I am if you need me. Leave a message, will you?'

He put down the telephone, Coker's last words still in his mind. *Be careful, sir.*

He looked out of the window, but could see nothing. The hotel was in a small square, no sounds, no traffic. You could die here and nobody would know.

He glanced at his case by the bed; Coker had packed that, too.

268

Then, very deliberately, he put on his raincoat and reached for his cap.

Coker had kept the address for some reason. When she and Critchley had been lovers?

He felt the lighter in his pocket. She had probably walked from her flat to that other hotel, when she had been going out with Lalonde. She might not be there. She might refuse to see him. She did not even know he was in London, let alone the reason for his being here.

Downstairs he found a young woman sitting behind the reception desk, unravelling a khaki jumper and rolling the wool into a ball ready for reknitting. Probably some uncomfortable service garment, sent home by a husband or boyfriend, but real wool, a common enough arrangement with the clothing ration so strict. She had a radio behind the desk for company, with music playing.

She eyed him with some amusement.

'Taxi, sir? Round here? At this hour? Like gold dust, they are!'

He told her the address, but she had to call the elderly porter who was polishing shoes in the adjoining office.

He was more forthcoming.

'Down towards the bridge.' He saw Masters' expression and added impatiently, '*Chelsea* Bridge. Dead opposite Battersea power station.' He grinned, and accepted half a crown without a blink. 'If it's still there, o' course!'

Masters stepped out of the hotel and turned up his collar. The air raid notice was not on display.

When he reached the river it was easier, and there were plenty of people in the streets. Almost everybody seemed to be in uniform, and he caught snatches of conversation in languages as varied as the uniforms: Free French, Polish, American, and others he did not recognize.

One taxi rattled past but it was towing an auxiliary fire pump, another part-time job. Like so many of the people to whom he had spoken, air raid wardens, firewatchers, first aid workers, and of course the Home Guard, bemedalled veterans from the Great War. And all of them would have to be back at their regular jobs or homes tomorrow. If, like the bridge, they still existed.

Masters looked up at the sky. It was clear enough, except for a few patches of cloud. But still no sirens.

A few more cars passing now: some people, doctors among them, still managed to get a petrol allowance. He looked across the river; even in the darkness he could see the towering chimneys of Battersea power station. And here was the bridge. He turned his back on the water and walked swiftly across the road.

Someone shouted, 'Wot's up with you, mate! Got a death wish?' A car surged past him, and he heard laughter. Not a doctor that time.

He saw some figures hurrying down a side street, carrying blankets and, he thought, sleeping bags. The Underground stations were said to be full every night; men, women and children, afraid for their safety, not wanting to be alone when the raids started.

He stopped and looked up, as if somebody had called his name. The old porter knew his Chelsea. This was the address.

There was a little porch, and at a guess about six expensive flats, with separate letter boxes and bell buttons. It was too dark to tell one from another. He groped for his lighter again, and halted.

It was still not too late . . .

He clicked the lighter. In the darkened porch it was like a flamethrower.

There it was, Number Seven. *De Courcy.* He closed the lighter, but not quickly enough. A slurred voice yelled, 'Put that bloody light out! Don't you know there's a war on?'

It seemed an age before her voice reached him from a heavily meshed speaker.

'Who is that? I can't come down.'

He touched the protective mesh. 'It's me, David.' There was no sound. 'David Masters. I got your message.'

'David? How can that be? I was told . . .'

He said, 'I want to see you. I know I should have warned you.' He got no further.

'It really *is* you! I – I thought for a moment . . .' A buzzer intruded noisily. 'Come up, David. Top floor, I'm afraid. You'll have to forgive me . . .'

She was silenced by the door clicking itself open.

He saw a handrail and gripped it. There was a tiny shaded lamp

270

on the first landing and he saw a stirrup pump and a bucket of water beside the nearest door. He was still holding the lighter in his hand like a talisman.

Right on cue, the rising wail of sirens followed him.

He was almost at the top of the stairs when he saw the flash of a torch playing against the wall. He was not even out of breath. All those walks from his quarters around *Vernon*, and later whenever he could find the time in Dorset, had served him well. Even though on so many occasions it was because he had been unable to sleep.

She was holding the door open, her face very pale in the reflected torchlight. The rest of her merged with the shadows, a dark cloak, and some kind of shawl over her head and shoulders.

'Come in – you must be cold. I'll get some extra heat going. It was clever of you to find this place . . . so dark everywhere.'

Upset, Coker had said. Masters waited for her to close and lock the door, and all the time she was speaking in the same disjointed sentences.

'I'm fine. Really, I was worried about you, Elaine.'

Perhaps the use of her name triggered something. She moved a small table lamp and gestured to a chair. 'Have a seat. I'll make some tea, or perhaps a drink would be better.'

He wanted to hold her, like that other time. Wait for whatever it was to settle, or leave her.

With only one light it was difficult to see the room itself. There were a few pictures, a figurine, of a ballet dancer, on top of a cabinet.

He said, 'The sirens went off just now,' and glanced at the windows. 'Trouble with the blackout?'

She moved past him and did something to an electric fire.

'No. Nothing like that.' She put her hand up to her face. 'I'm a mess. I didn't want you to see me like this.' She added almost sharply, 'Where have they put you this time?'

'It's called The Warwick.'

She brushed past him again. 'Oh, that dump. It's quite a walk, or did you find a taxi?'

He watched her, feeling the tension like something physical. 'It did me good.'

She had not heard him. 'As soon as I phoned I knew it was wrong. Unfair, to both of us, I suppose.'

'I'm very glad you did.' In a minute she would ask him to leave, make some excuse. And then what?

He said quietly, 'I didn't bring the jasmine brooch. It's tucked up in Philip Brayshaw's safe. If I'd only known . . .'

She was behind him now, and he could smell the perfume, but only faintly, as if it was some emanation of the room. He could hear her breathing, fast and unsteady. If he moved now he knew he would ruin everything.

'How could you have known?' She had her hand on his shoulder. 'My mother gave it to me. Just before we were separated, and I came over here. When I got a job with Captain Wykes' people. Eventually.' The hand moved away, and then returned to his shoulder. As if she was trying to decide something.

She reached out with her other hand and tilted the table lamp slightly.

'That is she.'

It was a photograph of a young and beautiful girl, posed in her ballet costume, not unlike the figurine on the cabinet.

He said, 'I can see where you get it from, Elaine. She's lovely.'

'That was *Swan Lake*. Before my time.'

A window pane quivered, and the familiar *crump . . . crump . . . crump* of anti-aircraft fire intruded.

She half turned. 'Not near. If we went on the roof we could see it. I keep a little garden up there. In tubs, that sort of thing . . .'

She walked to a window and adjusted the curtains. 'In the cabinet, David, do you mind? I was having a shower when you got here. I must have had a dozen since I got back. The landlord will have something to say about *that*.'

Masters bent and opened the cabinet. There was a half-empty bottle of brandy and some glasses.

She said, 'There's another bottle somewhere. Captain Wykes knows all the right people.'

He poured two glasses; one had already been used. When he turned towards her he saw that she was sitting by the photograph

272

of her mother. She took the glass from him and shook her head as he moved the light.

'*No!* Not like this!'

He sat down beside her and very carefully put his arm along the back of the sofa, not touching her, but close, so that she would know it.

She said slowly, 'My mother is dead.' She shook her head. 'Six months ago, and I've only just found out. She had been ill for a long time. I've been so worried about her . . . wanted to get her out of Guernsey somehow.' Some of the brandy slopped unheeded over her knee. 'It can be done, you know.'

It was destroying her. Masters tugged out his handkerchief and pressed it on her knee. He felt her stiffen and begin to pull away, then, abruptly, she covered his hand with her own.

'My father had been smuggling letters through to me. He always claimed that she was all right. Improving. Things like that. *Lies.*'

He took the glass from her fingers and put it on the table. He could see what she was wearing now, the old boat cloak she had worn before, and underneath, some sort of dressing gown. She had been wearing slippers when she had opened the door for him, but one of those was now missing. Her bare foot outlined against the dark carpet made her seem broken, defenceless.

He said, 'Tell me. It's why I'm here. I knew something bad had happened.'

He took her hand and lifted it to his lips. 'Tell me.'

She watched him as he lowered her hand again, then looked where he had kissed it.

'Nobody forced me to go. I wanted to. I was born there, had friends. You know.' She shook her head again. 'I shouldn't talk about it. To you, or anybody. But you know that.'

He said, 'You went over to the Channel Islands?'

'It's not that difficult. Two agents were looking after me. I was supposed to meet my father, persuade him to defect, get away. It was all arranged. What we had discussed in the past.' She looked at him with the same haunting directness. 'But I think you knew about *Commander* Critchley? He promised me, do you see?'

She looked towards the window again, and he saw a pulse leaping in her throat where the dressing gown had fallen open.

Crump . . . crump . . . crump.

She said, 'My father had already gone. France, maybe Germany. Perhaps another big contract.' She spat it out. 'With the enemy!'

She seemed to realize that his arm was behind her shoulders and said, 'One of the agents was not all that reliable. He had links with the French Resistance. With them you need to be on your guard. Always. To them my father is a traitor, a collaborator – it is all they can see, all they can think. I was lucky. I have to tell myself that.'

She rose suddenly, but held up her hand as he, too, stood. 'No. Hear me!' She picked up her glass and walked to the window, the cloak swinging round her as she turned back to stare at him. 'We met some patriots while we were there. They needed convincing. Some were women, local people, one I even thought I knew, from the past. But I said nothing. It was bad enough.' Her voice was faint, tensed in anticipation of the memory.

She took a deep breath and walked towards him. 'I think they enjoyed it.' She pulled the shawl from her head and sat beside him. 'My father was a collaborator, that was all they needed.' She ran her fingers up through her hair. 'They stripped and searched me – I don't need to describe it. Then they did this, sheared off my hair, like they do to any whore who collaborates with the enemy.'

The chestnut hair he remembered, shining in the restaurant, or in the grim bunker at Portland, had been hacked crudely away.

'I have washed it again and again. My body too . . . It will grow again. As I said, I was lucky.' She swivelled round with her back towards him. 'What do you see?'

She lowered the cloak and dressing gown from her shoulders, baring her back.

There was plaster, in strips, in the shape of a swastika.

She covered her shoulders. 'A woman did that, with a knife. Then more of our people came, and I was suddenly free. The rest is history.'

She did not protest or resist as he put his arms around her, his face pressed against her hair.

Occasionally gongs rang insistently in the street, ambulances, fire engines; he neither knew nor cared.

Once, she said, 'What time tomorrow, David?' Then, 'Can you

274

set the alarm? I have a razor you can use.' She was half asleep. Like a coma.

Another time, there was more flak, and Masters thought he heard shell splinters clattering over the roof, probably fired by guns which were miles outside of London.

She murmured, 'I can't let you go out in this.'

Perhaps it was the brandy, and what had gone before, but he doubted it. Shock, grief, fear, it would have broken most people, even the ones who were trained and hardened to their work.

He guided her to the other door, which was still ajar. There was a bedside lamp, an empty glass on the floor.

He said, 'Get some sleep. I'll doss down on the sofa, and get some tea for us in the morning.'

The bed had not been slept in, but there was lipstick on one of the pillows as if she had cried herself into forgetfulness.

She said, 'Do you still have your pipe, and the lighter I brought you?'

He smiled. 'Of course.'

She nodded, and felt her hair again. 'I'd like some water, David.' She was studying him, her eyes very like the sea in the mellow light.

He said, 'If the raids come this way, you'll have to lead me to the shelter.'

She touched his arm and said quietly, 'I want you to know. To believe. Maybe we were lovers. But never in love. It matters, *to me.*'

Masters walked into the other room, his shoes soundless on the carpet. He had seen the kitchen when he had arrived, and found his way there, pausing only to pull a curtain aside and peer out. A few pinpricks of light, a long way off, south of the river, not even any sound or tell-tale glow in the sky.

Put that bloody light out! Don't you know there's a war on? But not this time.

He filled a glass with water. Utensils were scattered everywhere. He would have to find the things for making tea before he left.

Nine o'clock at the Admiralty. *If it's still there.*

She was in bed when he returned, the sheet pulled up to her chin, watching him. No challenge this time. No defiance.

275

'Thank you. I'll have a sip later on.'

'How's your back?'

One hand emerged over the sheet and touched her hair again. 'They say they can fix the scars.' She took his hand, and then gripped it. 'Kiss me, David.'

She must have found her perfume. It was on her cheek, her throat, and as she pulled his hand down, on her bare shoulder. 'Now, David. Lie with me.'

He kicked off his shoes and unbuttoned his jacket, without realizing what he was doing.

He was beside her, the sheet and blanket gone, her body pressing his. She seized his hand and guided it over her breasts and down her body, pulling it hard against and into her.

'*Now*. I can't wait.'

There was nothing beyond these walls. Beyond his belief, beyond whatever he had imagined it might be.

He spoke her name but her mouth captured his; she arched her back, and gasped as he entered her and they were one.

When the All Clear sounded, much earlier than usual, it passed unheard and unheeded in the small quiet room near the river.

A different car was waiting for him at Dorchester, but the same blonde Wren he remembered from his last trip to London. He had been away three nights.

Somehow he had managed to reach the Admiralty on time for his meeting; he still did not know how. Like a barrier breaking down, and every inhibition gone. They had fallen into an exhausted sleep, and when the alarm clock had sounded, something he did not recall setting, they had clung to one another as if for the first time, and she had given herself to him with a fervour which had left them both breathless.

If the captain at the Admiralty had suspected anything, he had kept it to himself.

Masters was glad it was not Wykes. It was better shared with strangers.

The operation had a name, *Pioneer*. It had suddenly become real, a fact.

The captain had said, 'All the new mines have been tested

276

and stored. The Germans have no intention of continuing with experiments. They're ready.'

Masters had recalled her anguish when she had told him of her father's defection. He must have given the word. Why he had left Guernsey without knowing or caring about his daughter, and the lies he had told her over the past months.

'If you have any second thoughts?'

He had shaken his head. It had become personal.

The blonde driver asked, 'Good trip up the smoke, sir?'

What would she think if he told her?

Three nights. Learning one another, exploring, every intimacy shared.

He said, 'It was fine. Is Leading Wren Lovatt back yet?'

She hid a smile. He did not want to talk about it.

'Back tonight, sir. We were all so chuffed when we heard about her getting some leave.' Their eyes met in the driving mirror. 'So right for her – she's a real sweetie.' She frowned and jammed her feet on clutch and brake as a farm lorry backed out of a gate in front of her. *'Idiot!'*

Masters tried to relax, reflect on things he must do. First, speak with his replacement, a lieutenant-commander from *Vernon*. They had met a few times over the past months, but he would not know much about the individuals who would be under his control, temporarily or not.

He had once served under Critchley, but had requested a transfer. At the time he had wondered why.

He thought of their last night together. Lying side by side, making each moment last. And last.

She had spoken only briefly about Critchley. How he had promised to help her mother escape from Guernsey, to get proper treatment.

'He was so convincing. He never seemed too busy to help, to advise.' She had added bitterly, 'And of course, he was my father's *good friend.*'

There had been a long pause. 'That night he was supposed to come to the house, to tell me the progress he had made. But as I discovered, he was with another woman, doing what he did best!'

277

The bedside light had been left on and she had raised herself on her elbow to study him, afraid perhaps that she might forget.

'He made me ashamed, and when he rang me, I told him so. He just could not believe that I felt as I did. Like that woman in Guernsey said. A whore.'

Masters had touched her, in ways he would never have believed possible, and she had responded, matching every mood of his love.

And tomorrow he would be on his way to Plymouth; by car, the urbane captain had assured him.

The start of a new venture. Perhaps his last.

The car passed the Wrennery, and he saw the formidable Second Officer 'Tommy' Tucker glance at him without recognition. But she had arranged Margot Lovatt's leave, had even seemed pleased in some way. The family . . .

Then he saw the gates, the master-at-arms' portly figure hovering, ready to see him over the side. He was back.

Nobody would mention it. Nobody was supposed to know.

Even she had said nothing about it, although she must know or guess what was intended.

He was reminded of one of Bumper Fawcett's favourite quotations.

'The impossible we do at once. Miracles take a little longer!'

It was decided.

18

One Hand for the King

'Stop, starboard! Slow astern, port!'

Foley stood in the forepart of the bridge, one hand resting on the rail below the screen as he watched the gap of choppy water narrowing, *Firebrand*'s dark shadow reaching over the jetty, and the sudden flurry of spray from the reverse thrust of screws. They had done and achieved so much in only a few days. There had been a sense of urgency from the moment they had run up the ensign for the first time, and any remaining faults or slip-ups had been instantly pounced upon by specialists, as if they, too, were under pressure from on high.

Bass was on the wheel, legs loosely spread, eyes moving occasionally to gauge the last approach, alongside the jetty. Any casual observer would think he had been aboard all his life.

Foley felt very much the same. On the passage from Falmouth he had sensed the strangeness wearing off, so that engine beats, shipboard sounds, even men's voices, were becoming familiar, pushing any remaining reservations aside.

He saw a seaman on the foredeck, a heaving line already held easily in his hand, watching a group on the jetty, who in turn were sizing up the newcomer with professional interest.

Foley licked his lips, tasting the salt. After Falmouth this inlet seemed even smaller. Shabbier.

He looked over at the crowded moorings. He had been expecting it, prepared for it, but it was still a shock. ML366's bridge was covered with paint-smeared tarpaulins, and patches of new timber stood out in the hull like raw wounds. They were taking their time, and he wondered how Allison was coping both with the work and Claridge, his new skipper.

He leaned over and saw the bow edging towards the point of contact. Lieutenant Kidd was there, pointing now, and a man with one of the big rope fenders.

'Stop, port!'

The heaving line snaked over the guardrail and was neatly caught by one of the handling party, without anybody apparently moving. Down aft, Sub-Lieutenant Venables had been ready and waiting. Mooring lines were being hauled ashore, someone yelled a greeting, a Wren on her bicycle paused and dismounted to watch as *Firebrand* came to rest. *Like cracking an egg*, as Dougie Bass would have said.

Foley had even got used to her name, instead of a number on signals, requests and instructions.

Kidd had looked it up in his dictionary. *Firebrand, kindler of strife*, was one definition. When you considered her maximum speed and the racks, empty now, which would soon be loaded with mines, it suited her.

He wondered how the other experimental fast minelayer was progressing, and who might be her commanding officer.

Kidd joined him on the bridge, light-footed for so powerful a man.

'All secure, fore and aft, sir.' He hesitated. 'She did well, I thought.'

'So did you, Number One.'

They were getting there.

Kidd was watching a seaman who was leaning on the guardrails, a foot on the lower one.

'Got the weight, have you, Brett?' That was another thing about him; he never had to raise his voice. The offending seaman jumped clear of the rails to stand almost at attention.

Foley turned away. He was learning their names too, but more slowly. And as was normal, the ones he met and worked with more closely had become not merely faces, but individuals.

The Chief, down there now in his engine room, a motor mechanic named Morgan Price, did indeed come from Wales, and his pride and enthusiasm over his four-shaft Bristol motors had not diminished. The signalman now tidying flags in the locker was named Pottinger. A Coastal Forces veteran, he had been blown up twice, and had been one of four survivors when his M.T.B. had gone down. When Bass had asked him about it, the signalman had replied drily, 'It was getting too damn dangerous, 'Swain. That's why I volunteered for this little lot. Minelaying is a bit cushier, I reckon!'

Foley had heard them laughing about it.

He thought of Falmouth again, the day he had left Kidd in charge for an hour while he had gone with Margot to the station.

It had come upon them so suddenly. Like the excitement and disbelief of being together, always brief, never more than a few hours when they could talk and touch, sometimes afraid to think of, or believe in, the future.

He saw a leading seaman up forward by the newly hoisted Jack and recalled his name. Irvine, Tom Irvine. They had served together in those early days. The rookie sailor and the newly minted subbie.

At the station she had leaned out of the carriage window, their faces only inches apart: so many things to say, but never the right words when you most needed them. Around them there were others, in the same moments of parting. But they were quite alone.

'When you're settled, Chris, let me know. If need be I'll apply for a transfer to be near you. If it's possible.'

They had held hands, oblivious to the stares and the knowing grins, then somewhere a whistle had shrilled and doors had started to slam; a few latecomers had burst through the ticket barrier. She had a seat by the window, and her case was on the rack. In it was the black nightie one of her friends had loaned her. It had been hanging on a chair in the cottage bedroom. It had remained there.

Another whistle, and with a jerk the train had started to move. Hands, then fingertips, and then just her face and arm at the window before the train had gained speed out of the station.

He still had her cap. She had asked him to keep it.

Kidd was saying, 'I've a list of jobs I'd like to discuss, sir. I

281

get the feeling we're being rushed, so it's really a question of priorities.'

The good first lieutenant, Foley thought. Probably just what he needed.

Someone said, 'Messenger's comin' aboard, sir!'

He felt his muscles tighten. He should have anticipated it. But so soon?

A seaman, smartly dressed and in white belt and gaiters, marched across the deck from the newly rigged brow, his boots clumping noisily.

Leading Seaman Pottinger said harshly, 'Look where you're going in them big daisy-roots, mate – that's fresh planking you're stamping on!'

Foley glanced over towards his old command.

It was only another memory.

The lieutenant-commander looked up from his desk, and fixed the sub-lieutenant with a penetrating stare.

'Lincoln, isn't it? We've not met before, but you've been away on leave, right?'

Lincoln thought it sounded like an accusation. 'Some of us were overdue for it, sir.'

He had heard about Masters' temporary replacement as soon as he had returned to duty: Lieutenant-Commander Mark Crozier, another regular, straight from H.M.S. *Vernon* like Masters, but there was no other similarity. So he would keep calm, not let it get to him.

'Don't I know it.' He turned over some papers. 'Sorry I've got to lumber you with this one.' He looked up again. Pale eyes, very steady, very cold. 'Southampton, or just this side of it. A beast reported last night, but our team from Portsmouth was diverted. So there's no time to hang about. I'll check on the state of things in the meantime.' He pushed the familiar package across the desk with his other hand, the one Lincoln had heard about. Somewhere along the way Crozier had suffered an injury, a faulty detonator, somebody had said. He had lost most of his left hand and wore a glove to conceal its mechanical replacement. At any other time he would have been beached, and as a regular officer he would always have that at the back of his mind.

Crozier said, 'Is your rating on top line?'

'Yes, sir. He'll be ready.'

Crozier let his gloved hand fall to the desk and thrust it out of sight, as if ashamed of the metallic thud.

'I've seen his record, used to work with Clive Sewell. Knew *him* pretty well. Sorry he bought it. Surprised, too, that his rating volunteered to remain in the render-mines-safe section.'

'You did, sir.' He knew immediately that it was the wrong thing to say.

Crozier said coldly, 'That is not what I meant. You get to rely on someone too much and you become vulnerable.' His eyebrows lifted slightly. 'Or careless?'

The telephone rang and Lincoln tried to compose himself. Why did he always rise to it? Take it as something personal?

Crozier was saying, 'Can't help that, *I've* got work to do, unlike some apparently. Tell my driver to do it. Are you deaf, man?' He smiled suddenly. 'Fast as you can.' He slammed the phone down. 'The car will be ready in ten minutes. You can use my driver – we've wasted enough time as it is.'

Through the window Lincoln saw Downie sitting on a bench, turning his cap slowly in his hands. In his working rig, the worn satchel by his feet, still managing to look fresh and alert.

Lincoln tried not to go over it all again. It had started at the pub, his father's local. Another of those boisterous, insincere parties where everyone had drunk too much. Downie must have seen it coming; he had wanted to stay away, and had offered to repair something in the kitchen. But Lincoln had insisted. Now it was too late.

He had heard one of his father's friends having a go at Downie. *Nice-looking lad like you, and no girlfriend to play around with? But then I suppose in the navy you make your own amusement, eh?*

Lincoln could hear the laughter now, see Downie's eyes watching him. He should have known, taken more care. Because of his anger, or the constant need to prove something. Like a voice repeating. *He should have known.*

It had been the last night of his leave. And there had been an air raid. Sirens, gunfire, ambulances clanging through the street.

Exactly like the nightmare. The shouting, the bared teeth. His father leaning over the bed, his voice like a scream. Too much to drink . . . they had both fallen asleep in the same bed.

He had seen his father's fury and sweating outrage turn to shock, then fear when he had seized him and slammed his body against the bedroom wall. Even that seemed like part of the nightmare. Hitting him again and again, while Downie tried to pull him off.

I would have killed him otherwise.

They had travelled down to Dorset in the same train, but in separate carriages. That was yesterday.

The whole street must have known about it. Even his mother had been screaming at him, shielding her battered and bleeding husband, the man who had always treated her like a servant, and sometimes worse.

They had spoken only once. Downie had said, 'Sorry about what happened. It was because of me.'

Lincoln had gripped his arm, angry, confused, determined. 'Still want to keep us together?'

Downie had nodded. Nothing else.

Crozier said, 'Still here, then?'

Lincoln left the office, closing the door as loudly as he dared.

It might all come out anyway. His father would say nothing; he put his own hopes and ambition before everything else. But somebody would. He saw Downie get to his feet and jam on his cap.

They regarded each other, officer and assistant. Part of the team.

'Southampton. All set?'

Downie nodded slowly. 'It's good to be back,' he glanced round, 'sir.'

Lincoln heard a car start up and saw the gates being opened.

Good to be back. When they might both be dead before another day had passed. He had proved nothing. He had solved nothing. But he was ready, perhaps for the first time in his twenty-one years.

Leading Wren Margot Lovatt got out of the car and opened the

284

boot. She was about to take Lincoln's untidy bag when Downie shook his head and stowed it with his own.

She saw him smile, and felt the warmth of recognition, the memory of David Masters leading this youth from the field, the air still thick with smoke and the stench of blazing fuel. A burned-out plane and its dead crew, and the lieutenant who had held the George Cross. Downie's officer. His friend.

In her two and a half years in the W.R.N.S. she had seen and learned a lot. A far cry from her quiet upbringing in Petersfield. The doctor's daughter . . .

Perhaps women were quicker to recognize such things.

She leaned over to fasten the boot and felt the pendant move against her skin. Always a reminder, as if she needed one.

She looked at the typed destination, about fifty miles away. It should be quiet enough, through part of the New Forest. Like peacetime, if you could forget the checkpoints and the barrage balloons.

She said, 'We should be there about lunchtime, sir. I know the road pretty well.'

Lincoln climbed into the back of the car. Downie, after a slight hesitation, got in beside her.

The gates slid past and they were out on the road.

She thought of that one visit to *Firebrand*. Chris had told her, 'You're a part of this. She's not a rival.'

She remembered her father's voice on the telephone when she had called to tell him she and Chris were getting engaged, whatever that meant in wartime, and that she wanted to bring him home, whenever that was possible. Her father had surprised her, more than she would have believed.

'By all means. I was telling your mother the other day. It's time we cleaned out Graham's old room. I'll get onto Lucy right away. Mister Warren is a good hand at decorating.'

He had been genuinely pleased, happier than she could remember. Maybe they had finally accepted what was past.

She and Chris were in love. It seemed to shine far brighter than the uncertainties. And . . . she confronted it . . . the danger.

She had told her closest friend some of it. 'You see, Toni, I've never done it before.'

Toni had regarded her fondly, but with a certain amusement. 'Twenty-one *and* a virgin? That really is something to brag about!'

She wondered if he had put Toni's drawing somewhere safe from prying eyes. He would keep it with her cap, he had told her.

After that first time, when he had gone back to *Firebrand* to prepare for the takeover, she had lain alone in the bed and touched herself, where he had touched her, and remembered every precious sensation.

She was afraid, and she thought he was, too, although he was careful to hide it from her.

He was used to danger; he needed to be. They must hang onto every second together.

She saw the young officer's eyes in the driving mirror and thought of Masters, the bond which had formed between them when everything had been against it.

Masters was away somewhere, and the two-and-a-half ringer, Crozier, had taken his place. Not for long, she hoped. Unforthcoming and impatient. She wondered what he had been like before.

Downie was watching her gloved hands on the wheel. He had not learned to drive, although his father had owned a little van for the business. If there had been more time . . . He turned as they passed two large dogs jumping and snapping at a stick held by a grinning farm labourer. Now they were going to another job, and he wondered how Lincoln was taking it. If anything came out about the trouble . . . He frowned. *When* it came out, what would happen? *To me. To Mike?*

He saw the girl's shoe press the brake pedal; it was probably the same hill where she had pranged the other car. She was very pretty. Her boyfriend was the lieutenant, now promoted, he had heard, who had been in command of the motor launch when they had found the dead airman; she had been there, waiting, when they had got back. And after Clive had been killed she had stroked his face, stopped him from breaking down completely.

Maybe he should request a transfer, before anything worse happened. Back to general service, or to another branch entirely.

He lowered his left arm and squeezed it between his seat and the door. He kept his eyes fixed on the road, the car bonnet

286

swaying from side to side between the ragged hedges and past the occasional cottage. Then he felt his hand gripped tightly, only for a few seconds. But it was enough.

If there was any future, it was already decided.

Captain James Wykes took off his cap and shook it over the stove, the droplets of rain hissing back at him.

'It's all moving a little too quickly for my liking.' He watched Masters unfasten his waterproof tunic and stretch the muscles of his back. 'How did it go today?'

Masters recalled the moment when the perspex dome had been fastened down by the selected artificers who had followed his every move and request. It did not take long to get the feel of the midget submarine. Everything within reach, like a toy. A deadly toy.

'It went well, sir.' He sensed the other man's uneasiness. It was rare for Wykes, he thought. But it was too late. Either it was on, or it would have to be cancelled.

He had gone over it a hundred times. The midget would be carried on a special trestle on the casing of a conventional submarine, complete with the container which held the mines, not an easy job for any submarine commander. The boat which had been chosen was *Trojan*. Another twist of fate: she was the same class as his own command.

Wykes said, 'It's yet to be confirmed, but all our information points to Monday. That gives us five days. The Germans have kept the area well sealed, as you can imagine. All the mines will be loaded into one ship, which will transport them to St. Malo.' He snapped his nicotine-stained fingers. 'Piece of cake to them. In St. Malo they will be offloaded into big naval lighters, like those they used in the Med. After that, we've lost them. The next time we meet will be in deadly earnest.'

Masters saw the chart in his mind, surprised how easily it had all come back to him, after the desk and the 'incidents' he had visited in one role or another.

Time was the enemy. The midget submarine was too slow to make a safe approach under its own power. *Trojan* would have to get them as close as possible before being launched. Even then

287

there could be problems. As one artificer had commented, 'After all, sir, it hasn't been done before!'

Masters had seen their faces, and could guess what most of them were thinking. Another death-or-glory type. Somebody with nothing to lose.

He could even smile about it. They were wrong on both counts.

A seaman brought some mugs of tea, and when he departed Wykes produced a flask and topped up each one with brandy. 'Keep the ruddy cold out!'

It *was* cold, and the wind across Plymouth and Devonport Dockyard promised snow. Nobody really knew what it would be like once the midget was cast adrift and left to her limited resources, and the man at the helm.

Masters had thought about it when he had unfastened the wrist compass, the same one he had seen lying by the corpse of the previous pilot.

Wykes was sipping the hot tea. 'We shall know by this time tomorrow.' He half smiled. '*I* shall know, and I will tell you myself. You know the drill. Any letters you want to leave, I can deal with.'

It was still early, but already growing dark outside the building. When the dockyard workers went home another team would move the midget into one of the basins, and on board the waiting submarine. There must be no breach of security at this critical stage.

Wykes said, 'She told me you'd been to see her, by the way.'

'I don't see that anyone could object to that, after all she's been through.'

'I'd have done the same. She's a fine woman, a brave one too. Things often jump the rails on these missions. There's always the risk of betrayal, or some misguided interference. She could have been killed, I know that, and all because a handful of "patriots" were ready to condemn her, simply because she was her father's daughter!' He was getting angry. 'It was pure luck that some of our people were there and quick to act.'

'She told you about the scars on her back?'

'I saw them. Her hair, too. We shall have to accept that in any occupied country most people just want to be left alone, to survive,

288

until by some miracle the enemy is not there any more. Maybe it would have been like that here, if . . .' He took out the cigarette case. 'But *if* is often the margin, eh?'

'I'd like to call her when things start moving, sir. I tried a few times before I was driven down here.'

Wykes watched the smoke floating over the stove. 'I know. I thought it best to prevent it.' He shrugged. 'In my place, God help you, you'd have done the same. But we'll see. R.H.I.P.'

Somewhere a door slammed, and Masters heard a car splashing across the yard. So typical, he thought. Timed to the minute.

Wykes replaced his cap and said, 'I must be off. I'll be in London until *Pioneer* is completed.'

'I don't envy you, sir.' *Completed.* One way or the other.

Wykes glanced around. 'C-in-C Plymouth is in charge as of now. His staff will fill you in on conditions, and timing.' He thrust out his hand. 'Good luck. And remember, one hand for the King, eh?'

Masters watched him leave. He had first heard that sentiment as long ago as Dartmouth, when he had been a cadet. 'One hand for the King,' an old instructor had told him, 'but keep the other one for yourself!'

A lieutenant coughed politely, the same one who had hardly been out of Masters' sight since his arrival in Plymouth.

'I can show you to your quarters, sir.' Again, that curious glance.

Cell, more likely. 'Thanks. Lead the way.'

He would write a letter. In the same breath, he knew he would not. It would help neither of them if he were killed or captured.

But she would know.

Operation *Pioneer* had begun.

H.M.S/M. *Trojan* left Devonport Dockyard under cover of darkness, guided almost as far as Plymouth Sound itself by a powerful harbour launch. Only a small, hooded blue sternlight led the submarine through crowded moorings and past heavier, anchored warships. It was bitterly cold, the conning tower and casing treacherous for the remaining watchkeepers on deck.

Once in open water all the usual checks were carried out, especially the trim of the boat, to allow for the midget's extra load abaft the conning tower. For Masters it was a strangely unsettling experience. He had never been a passenger in a submarine before, except when he had been under training, and even then he had been given enough to do. But in *Trojan* he soon found time on his hands. Too much time.

He had met *Trojan*'s commanding officer two or three times; he could not recall exactly when or where. It was like that in submarines. The same rank as himself, an experienced skipper who had seen plenty of action in home waters and in the Mediterranean. He would not need to be reminded of this latest responsibility. He must keep to a time factor, and avoid every kind of shipping, which was hard enough in these waters. If enemy contact was made it would be up to him, his skill and determination, to give them the slip. One depth charge, even a near miss, would finish everything. There would be nothing left.

Perhaps he had expected it to be easier, to be accepted, to fit in. *Trojan* was, after all, a twin of his last boat. He had noticed when they were at diving stations that the navigating officer had wedged his enamel mug under the ready-use chart rack, exactly as he had done during his short time in *Tornado*. When he glanced around he sometimes imagined different faces, heard other voices.

They had made him welcome enough, and had cheerfully found room for the four artificers who would have the final word on the midget's readiness.

They surfaced at night, but no cancellations or new orders were received on the W/T. They had the sea to themselves.

Masters spent most of his time studying the chart and the drawings which Wykes' staff had carefully marked, with notes about known local hazards. *Trojan*'s commander had joined him several times, and had checked the calculations which were already prepared for the midget's solitary passage. On the chart the course appeared more roundabout than necessary, considering that speed was essential, but allowances had to be made for tide and current to obtain the best result with minimum delay.

Trojan's commander had remarked, 'Five knots is no pace-maker, David, but in those waters it's much safer!'

Masters sat on a locker with his back to the control room's

bulkhead, where he was least in the way. Where he could see and feel everything, as he had done before. Until that day.

In those waters, the commander had said. Masters leaned forward and felt the waterproof tunic drag across his shoulders. Where had the time gone? They were in *those waters* now.

The soft, purring vibration of the electric motors, the tension, and the smell. People said that metal did not have a smell. How could it? They had never served in submarines. It had a smell, and a taste all of its own.

He watched the faces. The hydroplane operators, hands moving occasionally on their wheels, studying the tell-tale dials, holding the trim. The navigating officer at his table, feet wide apart, staring at his notes and licking the point of a pencil. And the coxswain, somehow always the centre of things, eyes never still. Compass, depth gauge, revolution counter. Like a submarine's heartbeat.

All exactly the same, he thought. Even the firing controls, the 'fruit machine', as it was called, which translated what the submarine commander's eye saw in the crosswires into action. The bearing and range of the target. The estimated speed and course, even when the target was zigzagging. It was all fed into the machine.

Trojan, like the other boats of her class, mounted eleven torpedo tubes, with reloads for good measure.

Her skipper would be thinking of that, too. If he sighted the most tempting target in the world he would have to let it slip through his crosswires. Until his passenger, his liability, had gone, he and not the enemy was a target.

Masters turned to glance at the control room clock but checked himself. If he had overlooked something it was too late now. Or soon would be.

The commander walked away from the periscope well and stooped to speak to him. Without his cap he looked somehow younger. More vulnerable. Did he have a girl back in England? How would she be taking it?

'Won't be long, David. I'm going up to have a look-see.' He looked over at the navigator and added, 'Pilot thinks we're in the most suitable place.' They grinned conspiratorially at one another.

Diving or surfacing, the two most dangerous moments for any submarine. And yet there was no outward show of anxiety or hesitancy. It was not even like a well-practised drill, more as if they were simply doing what was quite natural to them. And yet, even in a well-used boat like *Trojan* there had to be someone doing it for the first time. Perhaps hating the unwanted passenger with his lethal cargo. Lookouts had appeared near the vertical ladder to the conning tower and the bridge. Each wore dark glasses, so that after the control room lighting, dimmed though it was, they would be instantly ready. Swaying very slightly to the motion, they looked like a group of blind men waiting to be guided somewhere.

'Sorry we didn't get much time to yarn, David.' He sounded very calm, but his eyes were on the gauges. 'When you get out of it, we shall be listening for your signal.' He touched his shoulder. 'Here we go, then.'

He could have been discussing a quiet drive in the countryside.

Masters felt his body tense, as if he was standing there by the well.

The hydrophone operator reported, 'All quiet, sir!'

The commander looked at the sealed watertight door. A company of about sixty, plus the four artificers. Masters saw one of the lookouts reach out and grip the arm of the man beside him. Friends, or simply two people thrown together by the war? Sealed in a steel coffin if the worst happened. Every door clipped shut. Final.

The first lieutenant was ready, his slide rule in one hand, always aware of the need for a perfect trim, so that water could be pumped from tank to tank, his responsibility at times like this.

Masters looked at the depth gauge. Ninety feet. As deep as it was safe to run in these waters, unless it was an emergency. A last chance.

The commander stood by the well, outwardly relaxed, his eyes on the curved deckhead with its wires and pipes, as if he could somehow see through and beyond the hull itself.

'Thirty feet, Number One.'

The response was immediate. The subdued trembling of air forcing water from the ballast tanks. Not an emergency, but firmly controlled.

Masters imagined the submarine rising towards the surface, the

292

hydroplanes keeping the process stealthy, like the hands of a swimmer heading for the surface.

Like a great shark, a shadow. The officers and ratings merely incidental.

Something clicked loudly and the coxswain shot the offending equipment a hard stare, a rebuke, as if it were something human.

'Periscope depth, sir!'

The commander made a quick gesture and bent over as the periscope hissed smoothly from its well, then snapped down both grips and pressed his forehead to the pad and waited for the lens to clear as it broke surface.

Another gesture, and the periscope rose a little more, the commander moving slowly around the well, his feet brushing against the coaming with practised familiarity.

It would be dark on the surface, or nearly so. But there was always a last-minute risk. Masters saw the commander snap the grip handles into place and straighten his back.

'Down periscope!' He stepped clear as it hissed down into its well.

A torpedoman was holding out a stained old duffle coat and he slipped his arms into it, his expression completely absorbed, his eyes on the coxswain's back. 'Stand by to surface, Number One!' The quick gesture once more. 'Open the lower lid!'

He strode to the ladder, but paused to glance at the control room. His world. His eyes passed over Masters without seeing him, then he gripped the ladder and began to climb.

Masters found that he was holding his breath, as if he was there, doing it.

Each man had to be packed exactly into the tower so that no space or time was wasted. The lookouts and gun's crew. But first the skipper, with only the bridge hatch, still clipped, between him and the sea.

Even now he would be considering, preparing for unforeseen hazards. Surface vessels, engines stopped, perhaps warned of their presence at this pencilled cross on the Pilot's grubby chart. Or an aircraft, unseen in the periscope, diving out of nowhere to straddle and rake the dark shadow.

'Surface!'

Masters heard the air booming into the tanks, saw the hydroplane operators swinging their wheels, holding her down until the last moment, when she would break surface, the sea parting across her dark flanks, and he could imagine that first bitter taste of salt water as the hatch was flung open.

The ladder was empty, and there was cold air blowing across the control room. A figure loomed through the dimmed orange glow and touched his arm.

'Ready, sir?'

It was now.

19

A Hell of a Risk

David Masters pressed his back into the pilot's seat and made himself carry out another check of instruments, course, and approximate speed. He was geared for it, had gone over it so many times during the preparations for *Pioneer* that he had considered himself ready for everything. After the passage from Plymouth, the routine going on around him, diving and surfacing, he had tried to face each possibility, item by item.

And then the actual moment of surfacing, the sudden rush to make the midget ready for launching: it had all been over in minutes. Hands helping him up and into the torpedo-shaped hull, quick words of advice, even best wishes from another vague figure, and it was done. The perspex dome was fitted over him, bolted down and made airtight. Someone had patted the dome, and he had seen a hand giving a thumbs-up. Then he had been alone.

Trojan had dived, slowly and carefully, but even so there had been a few moments of anxiety when the supporting trestles had remained, clinging and thudding against the hull and, more to the point, against the steel cylindrical container beneath it.

Perhaps *Trojan*'s commander had waited on his bridge until the very last second. After that he would be thinking only of his responsibility to his boat and his men.

Half an hour ago. Masters could recall each part of it, without fear and without panic. Something he had dreaded when the midget submarine had responded to its own motor and rudder, and he had turned the bow with its crude iron fore-sight towards the east.

The motion was unsteady, far more than his practice trips in the dockyard basin, and with the sea washing past him only a foot or so below his cockpit it was a test for any man. Complete and utter isolation, like nothing he had known before. He had stood watches at sea on an open bridge in several submarines, with nobody but the lookouts for company, and only his own instinct to tell him when to call the commanding officer, or to order an emergency dive. But always there had been a sense of belonging, others to turn to if things went badly wrong.

He swallowed hard as the hull dipped over again, thankful that he had never suffered from seasickness. He watched the small instrument panel, the controls which connected him with the torpedo-shaped container beneath him. Four mines, with their precise but delicate timers, almost exact copies of the German weapons which this midget had been designed to deliver when the time came. The boffins had done well to respond so quickly to the Admiralty's unexpected demand.

Four mines, not as big as those normally carried by surface vessels or submarines, but, as the bespectacled Beamish had explained, 'Enough to flatten a street.' Or, in this case, a ship loaded with an even smaller, deadlier version. He could picture the bay where the ship was anchored as if he had been there before. Depths, the lie of the headland, and the reported whereabouts of coastal artillery.

He peered at his watch. An hour to go, if he was on the right course, if he did not get completely lost. Then what?

He reached for the oilskin pouch by his left foot. A flask and some chocolate, the sailor's favourite 'nutty'. He eased the steering and checked his compass. Again . . . At any other time he would have wanted to laugh. The hot tea and the chocolate were wonderful. If he laughed, he knew it might not be easy to stop.

He ducked sharply as something pale seemed to burst over his head. But it was a gull, floating, perhaps sleeping, when this strange creature had driven it up and away, its angry screams lost beyond the thick perspex.

He sealed the flask. Keep it for later. He steadied his thoughts again, a physical effort this time. Suppose there was no later?

Where was she now? What was she doing, in the flat near

Chelsea Bridge, opposite the power station? *If it's still there.*
With the photograph of her mother who, like herself, had been
betrayed. Poised in her costume. *Swan Lake*, she had told him.
Why didn't they make the bell buttons easier to see in the dark?
You needed a lighter to . . . Masters shook himself and stared at
the compass. A close thing. He felt his breathing coming under
control again as he adjusted the air flow. His mind had started to
drift, hallucinate.

Like the corpse laid out with the midget submarine on display at
Portland. The wallet with the photo of his other life, and his girl.

He loosened his collar and took several deep breaths. *A close
thing.* He tried to relax, to ignore the monotonous humming of
the motor. It was easy to imagine the other pilot becoming dazed,
barely conscious, the midget taking over, turning in a complete
circle perhaps, using up the batteries, losing its way.

Elaine might never know. Wykes would see to that. A matter
of security. He wondered if she had seen Philip Brayshaw about
her brooch. Her mother's last gift.

He shifted in the seat, and felt the hard nudge of the pistol
against his hip. To defend himself? Or to end it all if things went
wrong? Nobody had explained.

He leaned back and stared at the sky; there were stars, but no
moon. They were moving from side to side as the hull pushed
through small waves.

He stiffened with disbelief as a sharp blade of light swung across
the sky, and down, it seemed, across the water. He could even see
hand and fingerprints on the perspex, the water dappled across the
torpedo back-sight directly in front of him. The dome would stand
out like a giant dish cover. At any second . . .

The light went out. A routine test, maybe. They did it often
enough along the coast of Dorset.

He gripped the steering control and squeezed it until the pain
calmed him. He must clear his mind of everything else. Kick all
the doubts and fears aside. Above all, *believe what you just saw.*

Like the description and the sketches he had memorized. Caught
for a mere few seconds in the swinging searchlight beam was the
headland.

He peered at his watch, expecting it to be shaking. It was not.

One and a half hours. To the minute. No matter what else happened . . . he spoke her name aloud. 'We made it!'

After all the usual delays and diversions the car was eventually directed to an auxiliary fire station on the edge of Southampton.

Lincoln climbed out and stared at the sky. There was still a lot of smoke, like low cloud, and the familiar smell of charred wood hanging in the air.

They had passed several fire engines and trucks full of A.R.P. personnel, the mopping-up process. The aftermath of two swift air attacks during the night.

He looked at the Wren and said, 'That was a good piece of driving. You were right about our arrival. It *is* lunchtime!'

Downie stood on the pavement, staring along the street. Most of it bore signs of damage from previous raids; some of the houses were empty and beyond repair. Southampton was and always had been a prime target for the Luftwaffe.

He said, 'Here's somebody, sir.'

It was a police sergeant, carrying a steel helmet in one hand and a mug of something in the other.

'Mr. Lincoln, sir? You're expected.' He beamed at the Wren. 'We *are* honoured today!'

A door opened and another naval officer stepped into the hazy sunlight. Lincoln recognized him from somewhere, one of the Portsmouth team who had been diverted for some reason. His overalls were filthy; even his cap had not escaped.

He held out his hand. 'You made it then, good show! I'm Roach, Tom Roach. Just enjoying something hot and strong!'

He was grinning, his features devoid of strain. Light-headed; Lincoln had seen it in others after a successful encounter with a beast. He had even known it himself, but only at a distance, something elusive. The fear had always remained.

Roach glanced at Downie. 'This your chap? Mine's out the back, spewing his heart up! Tough as a lion, but he always throws up when it's over and done with. Me, I prefer a tot of something!'

He seemed to get a grip on himself.

'The sergeant here will take you to your job. I had a quick dekko before I was called away. A Type Charlie from what I could see in the bloody blackout.'

Lincoln asked, 'Why were you diverted?' He clenched his fists. It was starting.

'Oh, the other one was near a railway. There was an ammunition train due to move, and there was a raid on anyway. Not much choice, really.' He laughed, a little wildly. 'Inconsiderate lot!'

Margot Lovatt stood by the car, one hand on the open door. It was painful to watch. One so elated he could scarcely stop himself from laughing. The other tense, staring at him as if he hated what he saw.

The sergeant said, 'I'll show you, sir. The place is roped off, but it's pretty deserted at the best of times. They've taken a battering over the years.' He looked at the girl. 'You can stay in the fire station, miss.' He tried to smile. 'Powder your nose an' have a cup of tea, if you like.'

The door opened again and a fireman peered at them. His eyes settled on Lincoln.

'Call for you, sir. A Commander Crozier.' He winked at the sergeant. 'Had a bit of trouble getting through – shame, ain't it?'

Lincoln entered the office and picked up the telephone.

Crozier sounded as if he was speaking from the end of a tunnel, and there was an intermittent murmur on the line. The air raid, he thought.

'So you got there. Had a look at the thing yet?' He did not wait for an answer. 'Is Lieutenant Roach there?'

So he was a lieutenant? Under all that dirt he could have been anything.

'Yes, sir. I'll get him.'

'*No.* Listen. When you've finished, let me know. Then report back here to me.'

Lincoln pressed his free hand against his forehead. *Not another one. Not so soon.*

Crozier's voice was suddenly louder. 'I've had an officer of the Judge Advocate's department on the phone. You'll have to see him. There's been some sort of complaint or allegation, didn't make much sense to me.' A pause. 'Are you still there?'

Lincoln cleared his throat. 'Sorry, sir. I think I know what it is. When I was on leave . . .' He got no further.

'Well, just get on with it. Everything seems to be happening today.'

Lincoln put down the telephone.

The Judge Advocate's department. An allegation. He tried to remember all the faces on that night. His father, spitting with fury, beside himself. His 'friends'. Only one face stood out, the man named Mason of the *South London Courier*. A comparatively small, weekly paper. All it needed.

He left the office and passed another fireman sitting at a switchboard. A radio was playing music, a woman's voice. Vera Lynn.

Lincoln heard and saw none of it.

Downie picked up his satchel. 'Ready, sir?'

Lincoln said flatly, 'Do we walk?'

The sergeant shook his head. 'Use my car. I'd not want to see your fine vehicle all messed up by the rubble!'

Margot said, 'I'll wait here, sir,' and hesitated. 'As long as it takes.'

Afterwards she wondered why she had said it. But she remembered the sudden exchange of glances, the tall subbie and the fresh-faced seaman. It made her feel like an intruder, and a witness.

She looked at the lieutenant, Roach. Maybe they were all like that before and after an 'incident'. But she knew they were not.

It was not far to the location but, as always, it seemed to take for ever, the police car lurching over scattered bricks and slates, past houses with empty windows, torn curtains blowing out in the wind like banners, a milk cart overturned, broken glass everywhere. Some houses were past victims, boarded up, bedrooms open to the sky, even the wallpaper still visible. A Union Jack had been painted above one front door, and *Welcome Home* written underneath.

Lincoln sat beside the sergeant, trying to hold himself together. He could feel Downie's hand on the back of his seat, hear his breathing. It would ruin both of them. Humiliation and disgrace. He felt his lip quiver. It would be worst of all for Downie, after all he had gone through. All he had lost.

The sergeant said quietly, 'There they are.' As if he was afraid of disturbing something.

Another policeman and an air raid warden stepped out of a ruined doorway.

'Number Thirty, sir.' The policeman looked tired out, but relieved. They always did. It was somebody else's job now.

The sergeant said, 'On the left side, sir.' He did not get out of the car. 'Mrs. Patterson's place. Near miss last month, poor old girl.'

Lincoln checked his pockets, then deliberately stepped over the tape which had been pulled across the street. A sign which said UNEXPLODED BOMB lay on the ground. Which raid, he wondered? It looked as if there had been several.

'Come on.' He heard Downie fall into step with him, his feet loud on the littered pavement.

Lincoln paused and looked along the empty street. Some wickets had been chalked on a wall, where children had played cricket in happier times. A shop with all the front blasted out had a sign painted beside it, *Open As Usual*. Some wag had added the word *More*. It was not very different from the street where he had lived for most of his remembered life.

'This is it, sir.' Downie was waiting by an open door. The hallway had been stripped, the plaster gone from the ceiling. But it was still a house. A home.

The mine had ploughed through the back of the building and come to rest in what must have been the living room, where Mrs. Patterson had probably sat in the evenings, trying to lead a normal life. There were smashed slates everywhere; the parachute must have caught on the broken timbers remaining after the previous raid. Lincoln stared up at the fragment of sky he could see beyond the leaning shape of the mine. Roach was right. A Type Charlie.

Dust was falling; it was snow. Tiny flakes, when moments ago the sky had been clear.

He said abruptly, 'Go and find a place to take cover. Run out the line. You know what to do.'

'I'd like to stay.' Downie opened his satchel. 'It looks easier than the last one. Why don't we . . .'

Lincoln knelt and touched the mine for the first time. It would be simpler and safer to detonate it right here, from a safe distance. There was not much left to preserve. People should not be expected to endure such conditions.

He thought of Crozier, and of Masters, what he would say and think when he got back from whatever he was doing. *Get on with it.* But it mattered. Of course it mattered.

He brushed the dust and plaster from the fuse cap.

Go by the book. Just like the classroom. Take your time. You're not going anywhere.

Downie was beside him, tools ready, one hand resting on the cold metal, near his.

Lincoln said, 'After this, I think you'd better get a transfer.' He heard his intake of breath, an unspoken protest, but he persisted, 'I'm no good at this. At *anything*, can't you see that? When I got my Mention, it was for nothing – it was the dog that saved you, not me! I couldn't move. I was going to tell you, I wanted to, but things seemed to carry me along. And then . . .'

Downie said quietly, 'I knew. I didn't lose my memory. I only pretended. It was better that way.'

'All the time, you *knew*, and let me go on playing the hero?'

Downie said, 'Let's keep together,' and smiled. 'Mike?'

They both looked up as an aircraft roared over the street, that familiar whistle of the Spitfire. What Lincoln had once wanted to fly. To show his father. To prove something.

The sound died away but the vibration remained a little longer.

Enough to make the mine slide a few inches into the bank of fallen bricks. Lincoln cried out as the full weight of it ground over his foot, crushing it inside his boot, pinning him there. The agony was overwhelming.

He saw Downie staring at him, then turning as they both heard the soft, almost gentle whirr of the mechanism.

Then and only then did Lincoln manage to scream. '*Run, Gordon! Run!*'

In fact it was not much louder than the fuse.

Downie knelt beside him and clung to his arm. He might have murmured something.

Then there was nothing.

*   *   *

302

David Masters jerked his body back and forth in the cramped seat and rubbed his eyes roughly with his knuckles. It was unnerving. Despite every precaution he had felt himself becoming drowsy again, head lolling against the perspex dome, mind drifting. It played every kind of trick; even the sound of the electric motor was lulling if you allowed it.

He adjusted the air supply and peered out into the darkness. Fewer stars now; perhaps just as well.

He checked the time and went over the final approach, piece by piece.

There was a boom of buoyed nets across the narrowest part of the entrance to the bay. The Germans were taking no chances; perhaps they had the X-Craft in mind after the successful attack on the mighty *Tirpitz*.

But it would not work here. Even at high water one of those little four-man submarines would be hard put to squeeze under a fully loaded freighter to lay the explosive charges. At the change of tide, it could even be crushed under the target and go sky-high with it.

The intelligence report had described the boom, and the elderly passenger boat which was used to open and close it. After this, they would probably not need the bay again.

High water was just before dawn, when the freighter was expected to quit the bay and pass over the mines.

Masters could picture them in their special torpedo-shaped container, directly under him. When they were set off by the freighter he would be well away, provided the batteries and the air did not run out. Waiting at the rendezvous for *Trojan* to appear.

The midget was fitted with a small homing signal, rather like the ones carried in dinghies for finding airmen down in the drink. Like the one Lincoln had discovered in the wreck of the *Latchmere*. He frowned. Something still troubled him about that . . . He rubbed his face. He was drifting again, at a time when he needed to be fully alert.

And the young seaman, Downie. He could still hear his cry of despair. *He was my friend.*

Then suddenly he heard it, felt it. The *thrum-thrum-thrum* of a heavy marine engine. He stared abeam and twisted round to look over the quarter. Not an E-Boat, fewer revolutions, but what was it doing here? Then he saw the darker shape of the vessel, on the port bow, making no wash, but from the bearing he knew it was heading for the boom. But how could that be?

He saw the blink of a signal lamp, a recognition of some sort to the shore battery, or another unseen position around the headland.

As if to settle the matter the boat's sides lit up, dangerously bright against the black water, leaving nothing in doubt.

Before the light cut out, Masters saw the painted replica of the red and white pilot's flag.

He was fully awake now. Like a slap in the face and worse. All that work and planning crammed into this operation and they had missed the one glaring flaw. Nobody had thought there would be a special pilot, coming here, just to make certain everything went smoothly.

He could see it as if it had already happened. The pilot would be on board the freighter when she passed through the boom. The pilot cutter would go ahead to a planned rendezvous so that he could be taken off without delay once the freighter was clear.

He forced himself to confront it. The pilot cutter would spark off the mines before the freighter was anywhere near them. A good captain and pilot would still have time to stop or run the ship ashore. Either way, the plan would be wrecked.

He looked at the compass and altered course very slightly. It gave him time to consider what he must do. There was no other way. And there was no one he could ask.

He would have to steer across the entrance immediately after the cutter had gone, and drop the mines at the last moment.

There would be no rendezvous with *Trojan*; she would have long gone. No skipper would risk his command on the surface in daylight, off an enemy coast. He would be abandoned. To go ashore and give himself up? To try and find somebody who might hide him until he could contact one of Wykes' agents?

He thought of Elaine's description of her own experience: the Germans were not likely to be in the mood for leniency. An example would have to be made, if only to save the neck of the German officer responsible for the security arrangements.

There was no other way. *Accept it.* No wonder they had issued him with a pistol. The final alternative.

He steadied the hull on a new course to cross to the shelter of the headland.

For a moment longer he imagined he had dozed off, or slipped into a semi-conscious daze.

Then he heard it. The same powerful diesel. He rubbed his face to restore his senses. How long had it taken? What was happening?

He saw the momentary crest of broken wash, and felt the sea push the midget on its beam like a toy. The unmoving shadow he had identified as the old boat used to open and close the boom was as before. The pilot cutter was heading away, the boom was shut again. He had not even seen it.

Slowly at first, and then quite calmly, he accepted the facts.

The pilot had remained aboard the freighter. He was probably going all the way to St. Malo. Or thought he was.

Masters readjusted his seat and tested the air. He had stopped counting how many times.

The delay so far had cost him the rendezvous with *Trojan.*

He felt his face crack into a smile. 'Good luck to them!'

The way was clear. He would move into position, as planned, and start the attack. After that?

Bumper Fawcett would be on his toes, in touch with Wykes or one of his contacts at the Admiralty. He steadied the steering, and deliberately flicked down the four small switches on the panel. All red. Bumper would hear all about it. *Miracles take a little longer.*

Aloud he said, 'Here we go, then!'

He peered at the slow-moving shadow of the headland. Closer, closer.

And she will hear about it, too.

Afterwards.

'Course, North-fifty-East, sir.' Bass watched the dim compass light flicker, but knew from experience that it was eye-strain. How many hours had they been out at sea? He pushed it to the back of his mind as he heard Sub-Lieutenant Venables say, '*Sixteen*, sir!'

305

Bass could picture the released mine falling astern, responding to its sinker, to be ready for the next Jerry who came this way. Venables had a stop-watch in his hand. He was like that, he thought. He could not really take to him. Even the other subbie had been all right once he got the hang of things. He wiped his mouth, tasting the salt and the high-octane.

He saw Foley moving to the port side of the bridge. Pitch-dark, but no hesitation now. They were all getting used to *Firebrand*, and Bass no longer felt so guilty about his transfer.

Foley raised his binoculars and looked astern. Four more mines to go. At the briefing before sailing he had heard all about the need for more minelaying in French coastal waters. Combined R.A.F. and American bombing raids of railways and marshalling yards were playing hell with German supply lines, and their coastal sea-routes were becoming vital.

He heard the first lieutenant giving orders to the working party down aft, Kidd still not raising his voice.

He imagined he heard a splash, and Venables said, '*Seventeen*, sir!'

Foley glanced at the sky. It was cloudy again, and there was snow frozen on the bridge screen, like sandpaper on the handrails.

Even with all this going on around him, she was never far away. She would have to watch her driving if it was like this where she was . . .

And Masters; he wondered what he was doing. It had been fairly obvious in the briefing that he was somehow involved with the secret operation *Pioneer*. Maybe this minelaying was connected with it in some way.

The motion was heavier now; getting rid of the mines had something to do with it, but *Firebrand* was off the Cherbourg peninsula, 366's old stamping ground, and feeling the strength of the Atlantic coming up the Approaches.

'*Eighteen*, sir!'

Foley looked at his watch. It would be light by the time they sighted Dorset again, but a flotilla of motor gunboats would be waiting to escort them for the last stretch.

They had already made contact when still within sight of the coast, and one of the M.G.B.s had made a signal. *'Give it to them, Chris!'*

When he had trained his glasses on the gunboat's bridge he had seen her skipper grinning at him. It was Harry Bryant, his old first lieutenant. Not an M.T.B. after all, but still one of the Glory Boys.

He rubbed his gloves together. 'We'll have some ki after this, 'Swain.'

Bass grinned. 'Too right, sir!' He jerked his head as another mine went over the stern. 'One to go!'

The signalman turned from the voicepipes. 'Signal, sir! W/T says it's Priority!'

'Twenty, sir!'

Foley said, 'Go down and get it, Sub.'

Kidd clambered into the bridge. 'Something up, sir?'

'W/T, Priority. Strange for them to break silence.'

Venables returned and said, 'To all units, sir. *Pioneer terminated.*'

Kidd remarked, 'We're none the wiser. Must have blown it.' Casually said, but Foley knew him better now. His way of concealing his feelings. His own bitter experiences.

'Shall I lay off a course for base, sir?'

Foley walked to the rear of the bridge and saw some of the hands clamping down the empty launching gear. A good bunch. He was lucky.

Bass called, 'Ki, sir?'

Let's get the hell out of here before the krauts wake up to us.

He thought of Portland. The secret. *The catch of the season.*

There had been rumours. There always were. But there was something else.

He realized that Bass had asked him something, but his mind refused to let go. The staring face of the dying German in the little submarine, on that ill-fated operation with the coastal minelayers. Masters would know. Masters *had* known.

He thought of the girl with the chestnut hair, and Masters' help in getting leave for Margot, so that they . . .

He swung round. 'What time's high water, Number One?'

Kidd frowned. 'Where, sir?'

307

Bass exclaimed, 'Gawd, there's a big raid somewhere!'

Through the uncertain flurries of snow, Foley saw the clouds light up with an inner glow, red and orange like a furnace door flung open. Then came the explosion, loud and heavy enough to make the hull quiver, like one of their own mines.

'That was no raid, 'Swain.' He looked back at Kidd. *'There!'*

Kidd looked over the screen as it lifted and plunged against the dark water.

'I served as an apprentice in one of the old railway steamers. Used to run back and forth to the Channel Islands. That's where it happened, whatever *it* was.'

It all came together like forgotten fragments. Masters, and the captured midget submarine. The lovely girl who worked with the Intelligence people. She was a Channel Islander; someone must have mentioned it.

'That was *Pioneer*. It wasn't terminated after all.' He was speaking to Kidd and all the others, and to his ship, his new command. 'There's somebody out there right now, trying to get home. That signal was to all units. But there's only us.'

Kidd looked at the sky. The glow had vanished, as if it had never been.

'It's a hell of a risk, sir.'

'For me, you mean? I'll carry the can, right?'

Kidd nodded gravely. 'Right. Somebody will be on the phone to Admiral Dönitz right now. The whole place will be like a hornets' nest.'

'He had time to get clear. Otherwise it wouldn't have happened.'

Like that other time. Another voice. Not a warning, but a plea.

Kidd said suddenly, 'Let's take a look, sir. I'll lay off the course.'

Foley walked to the voicepipes. 'Chief? We're going to search for somebody.' He could imagine Price's face now; the memory of Shannon was already fading. 'So when I call down, give me all you've got, right?'

Morgan Price sounded very calm. 'The whole lot, sir.' With pride. Like Pottinger, the leading hand who had choked off the

308

messenger for trampling over the new decking in hobnailed boots, in *his* ship.

Another signal, as he had expected. *Return to base.*

Another hour went past, the sky got lighter, the sea stayed empty. Hostile.

Kidd said, 'We tried, sir. But for your own sake . . .'

They might never meet up with their escort. Tony Brock would not be pleased, and neither would anyone else.

'Bring her round, Number One. Ring down half-speed. I'm only sorry that—'

'W/T, sir!' It was Venables, his reserve suddenly gone. 'Faint signal!'

Kidd said, 'Might be a downed flier, sir. But if you think it's worth risking?'

'I do. So let's move it!' Sharper than he had intended. 'Sorry, Number One. I'm getting past it.'

Surprisingly, Kidd grinned. 'I've got a six-year start on you!'

Half an hour later they found him, the tiny rubber dinghy almost awash, Masters sprawled across it, one arm dangling in the icy water.

Foley stood in the forepart of the bridge, his glasses trained on the drifting dinghy.

'Dead slow.' He tried to hold the glasses steady against the heavier motion as *Firebrand* eased down. 'Scrambling net, starboard side. Two good men.'

He heard Kidd say, 'I'll go myself.'

Foley lowered the glasses and wiped them. The snow was getting heavier. But it *was* Masters, and he had not moved. Probably dead, after all he must have gone through.

How did I know it was him? It had to be.

'Stop engines!'

He strode to the side and leaned over the screen, saw Kidd and a seaman hanging down on the scrambling net, the sea swooping over their legs as the hull swayed in the current.

Pottinger was at the guardrails and suddenly turned to peer up at the bridge. He was grinning. Laughing.

Bass breathed out slowly, 'He *made* it, God damn it!'

When Foley looked again the dinghy had been hauled aboard.

A trophy, or an excuse, should they need one when they got back.

Masters had snow in his hair, and his lips were blue with cold, but he managed to climb into the bridge, clinging to Kidd's arm until he was seated in one corner, with a blanket wrapped around his shoulders.

He said, 'You came back for me.' Then, 'I'm glad it was you.'

It was a moment Bass knew he would always remember.

Old Chris'll get you home, you'll see!

As he turned *Firebrand* around he could not recall if he had spoken aloud.

Firebrand picked up speed.

Going home.